Praise for Edward Wright

'Complex, fast paced and well plotted, with an exciting denouement'
Guardian

'A fast-paced stand-out thriller from Wright' *Financial Times*

'Entertaining contemporary mystery . . . Wright is a gifted storyteller, with a relaxed style which makes his narrative flow and brings his characters vividly to life' *Sunday Telegraph*

'*Damnation Falls* is a gripping portrait of a small American town, haunted by old scandals' *Sunday Times*

'A very superior whodunit, rich in period detail and aching with the kind of nostalgia produced by that unique movie fusion of trash and true feeling. The research is thorough and well-digested. But the book's real triumph is one of sensibility. Deeply satisfying stuff; exciting, intelligent and tender where it most matters'
Literary Review

'The kind of art that stirs up old memories and pierces the soul'
Chicago Tribune

'A clever plot, pinpoint characterisation and just enough tension to keep you hooked' *Big Issue*

'Absorbing . . . storytelling turf tilled by William Faulkner and Flannery O'Connor and Thomas Wolfe. In this redemptive fable, though, you can go home again, if you're willing to pay the price'
Wall Street Journal

Edward Wright grew up in Arkansas and was a naval officer and a newspaperman before discovering the greater satisfaction of writing fiction. Although transplanted to California, he remains partial to barbecue and bluegrass music. He also has an affinity with film noir. Among his regrets are never having met Will Shakespeare, Robert E. Lee or Hank Williams. He and his wife Cathy live in the Los Angeles area but get away whenever possible to the lakes and trails of the eastern Sierra Nevada. Edward was awarded the coveted CWA Ellis Peters Memorial Dagger for his novel *Red Sky Lament* in 2006. Visit his website at www.edwardwrightbooks.com

By Edward Wright

Clea's Moon
The Silver Face
Red Sky Lament
Damnation Falls
From Blood

FROM BLOOD

Edward Wright

This book is for Ann,
who played the hand she was dealt.

An Orion paperback

First published in Great Britain in 2010
by Orion
This paperback edition published in 2011
by Orion Books Ltd,
Orion House, 5 Upper St Martin's Lane,
London WC2H 9EA

An Hachette UK company

1 3 5 7 9 10 8 6 4 2

A CIP catalogue record for this book is available from the British Library.

ISBN 978-0-7528-8408-0

Typeset by Deltatype Ltd, Birkenhead, Merseyside

Printed and bound in Great Britain by Clays Ltd, St Ives plc

The Orion Publishing Group's policy is to use papers that are natural, renewable and recyclable products and made from wood grown in sustainable forests. The logging and manufacturing processes are expected to conform to the environmental regulations of the country of origin.

www.orionbooks.co.uk

Acknowledgements

Part of the pleasure of writing this book has been the chance to immerse myself – through reading, conversation, and that slippery thing called memory – in one of America's most tumultuous periods. I found valuable background material in Dan Berger's history of the Weather Underground, *Outlaws of America*, and in the memoirs of two of the group's former members, Bill Ayers and Cathy Wilkerson. I'm indebted to my editor, Sara O'Keeffe, for her strong insights and high standards; my agent, Jane Conway-Gordon, for her never-ending encouragement; and my wife, Cathy, for being there, as always, from first faltering step to journey's end.

Booksellers Bobby McCue, Linda Brown and Mike Bursaw, and editor George Easter, have shown me more kindness than I had any right to expect. Alan Kessler, M.D., has guided me through the tricky landscape of medical trauma, and Ron Mardigian has been generous with his expert advice.

Digging into the past has also reminded me of the importance of long-lasting relationships. I'm lucky to have been friends with Lucille Enix, Mary Ann Maskery and Diane Spatz Smith since my newspaper days in Chicago and Los Angeles. Paul Longinotti and Louise Miller Row have stuck with me ever since Hot Springs High School, making them the steadiest and most patient of friends.

PROLOGUE – 1968

In the darkest part of the night, there is a special quiet to the grassy and tree-shrouded areas of a large university campus.

With no sign at its entrance, the building stands on the edge of the sprawling grounds, half obscured by greenery. Three stories tall, it has an anonymous institutional red-brick look, and those who ask its function are sometimes told that it houses administrative offices of the university, which it once did. That well-rehearsed fiction has concealed its actual role for two years.

Tonight the building's rooms and hallways are silent, emptied of their usual complement of analysts, linguists, and retired military officers. The only lighted room is the reception area on the first floor, where Danny Kerner, the night watchman and a graduate student in philosophy, is on duty. Danny sits, feet up on his desk, paging through an essay by Nietzsche.

He has long hair, like most of the male students at LaValle, but he prides himself on not fitting others' preconceptions. As an undergraduate, while his friends were partying or demonstrating for the liberal cause *du jour*, he was working nights to pay his tuition. Now, at twenty-three and just starting a family, he relies on the extra income from this job to get him through graduate school while avoiding more handouts from his wife's parents. He tries not to show too much curiosity about what goes on during the daytime in this somewhat mysterious location. Still, the secrecy demanded of the building's staff – he was required to sign a pledge not to disclose anything he saw there – has intrigued him.

He turns the page and reads the next passage: *At bottom, every human being knows that he is in this world just once. Many die too late, and a few die too early ... Die at the right time – thus teaches Zarathustra.*

Somber material, but Danny reads it with equanimity. He's feeling almost serene, the result of a decision he reached only hours ago, before he left the apartment to begin his night shift. In the coming days he will apply to divinity school, the first step in training for the ministry. For weeks he has wrestled with the question, and Peggy has wrestled with it too.

'I know I can teach philosophy,' he told her in one moment of doubt. 'I don't know that I've got it in me to—'

'Stop right there,' she interrupted, her voice intense. 'You don't know yourself as well as I do. You're a good person, a brilliant student, and you'd make a wonderful minister.' She held up the baby and jiggled her gently in front of him. 'Tell Daddy he'll look very sexy in a clerical collar.'

Refilling his cup with barely warm coffee from a flask, he pauses in his reading and recalls one night when his curiosity about the building was boosted an extra notch. On his rounds, he found an unlocked door – a rarity in a place where every door was normally double-locked. He entered to make sure there were no intruders and found himself in a medium-size room with locked filing cabinets ranging alongside all the walls, a large table in the center, and detailed topographic maps pinned up on cork boards. One map, he noted, bore the title *Dien Bien Province.* Another, showing what looked like a city and the surrounding countryside, was labeled *Ha Noi.*

He backed out of the room quickly, double-locking the door with his set of keys.

Ha Noi, he thought. *Hanoi. Vietnam.*

I don't know what they do here, but it sounds closer to the military than the university. Some kind of research place, maybe, squirreled away here in a quiet corner of LaValle. Some of the campus firebrands, he reflected, would love to know about this place. They'd probably burn it to the ground.

Danny had strong feelings about his government's involvement in that small Southeast Asian country, where 30,000 Americans and untold numbers of Vietnamese had died, with no sign of a let-up. Students whispered rumors of undercover connections between the Pentagon and certain universities – Michigan State was one of those mentioned – but LaValle's name had never cropped up. If the

Pentagon was running or funding a secret Vietnam War think tank on this university's campus, he thought, someone should know about it.

He told Peggy about his discovery. Her response was immediate. Holding the baby in her arms, she cried out, 'Don't, Danny. Please don't. You'll get fired, and maybe worse. You need this job. We need the money.'

Feeling torn between family and conscience, he kept quiet.

Having made his hourly rounds tonight, Danny returns to his station and leans down to inspect the small, carefully wrapped bundle he has placed under the desk to shade it from his reading light. 'All quiet,' he mutters. He sips at his coffee; it's now cold. The clock on the wall reads a quarter past two: another forty-five minutes until his next inspection trip. He retrieves his book but is distracted by thoughts of Peggy. Two days ago, a full-blown case of the flu put her into the campus infirmary. She'd resisted going because of the baby, but Danny had assured her that Tina would be fine.

A muffled, ambiguous noise from somewhere makes him look up. *What was that?* In the blackness outside the window, a late November wind has kicked up, and tree branches are scraping against the bricks of the outer wall. He settles back down.

Were he not so drowsy, he would know that the sound came from elsewhere – the rear of the building, where three black-clad figures wearing ski masks have worked their way up an old and rusted fire escape to the second floor and forced open a window. Now, carrying flashlights, burglar tools, and a heavy canvas bag, they prowl the corridor until they come to a large office in the heart of the building. Jimmying the lock with minimal noise, they open the door. Two of the figures peel off as sentinels, the third enters the office and begins to work.

Twenty minutes pass.

At his station, Danny drains the last of his cup and checks his watch. In a little over five hours, he'll be able to visit Peggy. *Can't take Tina, though. Don't want to expose her to Mommy's flu.* He wonders if Peggy's fever allowed her any sleep tonight.

Picking up the Nietzsche, he looks for the quote from Zarathustra but is reluctant to resume reading. He's simply too happy – with thoughts of Peggy and Tina, with his recent life-changing decision – to read about death, no matter how abstract the argument.

Tina-Marina, he says silently, using his favorite nickname for her, *you may be the only one getting a good night's sleep. You don't know how lucky—*

It is his last thought.

A deafening blast tears through the quiet night, audible at the farthest reaches of the campus and even in the town itself. As the building's guts are torn apart, a white fireball blooms in its center, a thing of beauty, rendering the area around it as bright as day for a few seconds. Bricks and mortar fly like shrapnel, shredding the trees. The fireball fades to the color of molten lava, and the upper two floors, almost in slow motion, collapse onto the ground level. The night watchman's station, like everything else on the first floor, is crushed beneath tons of rubble.

The doomsday noise gradually dies away. Minutes pass, and flames begin to lick at the wreckage.

Police, firefighters, and campus security swarm over the site. One of the bombers, apparently injured in the explosion, is found nearby. Eventually the fire is extinguished, and the digging begins. At first light, Danny Kerner's mangled body is removed from the debris. At the same time, claims of responsibility are being telephoned to news organizations.

This is the Red Fist, the female caller declares. We strike at the heart of the war machine.

But the horror is not finished. A young woman appears at the disaster scene. She has just bolted from the campus infirmary and is still racked with fever. Her words are laced with hysteria, and it takes a while for rescue workers to understand.

'I was sick,' she sobs. 'I couldn't take care of her. He didn't want to bring her here with him, but … Oh, God.'

The police commander on the scene is summoned. He huddles with the young woman, then steps back, his face frozen by her words. He summons the senior firefighter, who listens intently, then begins bellowing orders to his men. They swarm over the still-smoldering site, hacking and digging at the charred remnants of what will soon become known to the world as the Crowe Institute.

An hour goes by. Finally one fireman, his voice cracked with strain, yells that he has found something. He lifts a tiny bundle, wrapped in a singed blanket, from the wreckage, his face twisted in grief.

Reporters and camera crews press in, but police hold them back. 'No pictures of this!' the fire captain screams. 'I'll break the first camera …'

Peggy Kerner sinks to her knees, wailing, and all the others stand silent as the soot-streaked fireman carries what remains of her baby to the ambulance.

In all the attacks, the riots, and the bombings that plagued America in the tumultuous 1960s and '70s, the Crowe Institute bombing of 1968 had a special notoriety. It stirred up calls for vengeance, transformed the thinking of the radical left, and sent one militant to prison and others deeper underground. Over the years, most of them either were captured or resurfaced and surrendered.

All but two …

From *The Big Underground*
by Thomas Hollis (Decker House, 2002)

One

Shannon Fairchild was a mess.

The face staring back at her from the borrowed pocket mirror bore a shiner that radiated in jolly reds and blues from her left eye over to her hairline and down to her cheekbone. The left half of her mouth was bruised and swollen, both upper and lower lips, and she could still taste blood whenever she swiped the inside of her mouth with her tongue, which – given that she had little else to do while sitting and waiting for her case to be called – she did fairly often.

Separated from her purse, she made an effort to tame her hair by running her fingers through it, but that only caused it to give off the odor of cigarette smoke and other bar smells.

Shannon wore last night's outfit – cotton pants, short-sleeve blouse, and scuffed lightweight sneakers. Imprints of dirt from the floor pocked her knees, hips, and rear.

Worst of all, her shirt front had two crusty dark gold stains. She had vomited not long after they deposited her in the cell the night before. Drunk as she was, she was still aware that throwing up on yourself was not good hygiene. So, planting her feet carefully, she leaned well over the toilet bowl – while trying not to look within its unspeakable depths – and let fly. Except for the two random droplets, her aim was mostly good.

'Lookin' for Ralph,' she'd heard one of the other women in the cell observe. Shannon hadn't understood until the woman repeated the name louder, this time in a reasonable approximation of the sound of food coming up.

Now, sitting in the San Malo Municipal Court with the light from the windows hurting her eyes, Shannon let her mind stray back to an old English lit class and tried to find the appropriate literary term for *Ralph*. She finally decided it came close to fitting the definition of onomatopoeia. But not quite. She spat on a shred of paper towel and began to rub at the stains, but her efforts only awakened another old odor, so she gave up.

She started to pass the mirror back to its owner, a female bailiff who was a sympathetic sort, but was interrupted by a voice.

'Borrow that, hon?' It was Rhonda, sitting two chairs down from her, stretching out a big hand. They sat in chairs lined up against the courtroom wall, watched over by the bailiff, two of a half-dozen miscreants waiting for justice.

'Why not?' Shannon passed her the mirror, although she could think of several reasons why not, beginning with the fact that Rhonda had inflicted those very bruises she'd just been studying. But she felt too sick and wasted to find room for enmity. Especially since she and Rhonda, when not fighting, were usually friends. It was complicated.

Rhonda gave her oversize, homely features a going-over in the mirror and, apparently satisfied, passed it back to the bailiff with a thank-you smile. She had definitely gotten the better end of things last night. It had started when Shannon dragged her backward off her barstool and connected with a roundhouse slap, but after that it was all Rhonda. The older woman had about ten years' experience on Shannon, along with twenty pounds, and she didn't fight girly-style but with her fists, the way her old man, Bullo, had taught her. By the time Bullo and the bartender joined forces to break them up, she was giving Shannon a good pounding. Once halted, the whole incident might have evaporated like the smoke from Bullo's cigar, were it not for the two off-duty policemen drinking at the table under the Budweiser sign.

So why did I start it? Shannon asked herself. The answer came quickly: *Because every now and then I drink too much, and because I get crazy stupid when I do.*

She heard the court clerk call her name and got up.

'Good luck, hon,' Rhonda said.

'You too.'

'Oh, I'll hafta do some time. This weren't my first.' Rhonda said it with a chuckle, glancing over at the bench where Bullo sat, his tattoos and biker regalia mostly covered with a jacket. He thrust his big chin upward in an encouraging gesture.

As Shannon stepped to the front of the courtroom, the public defender materialized at her side. He was young and earnest-looking, and they had spoken briefly an hour earlier.

The judge, who resembled an ex-football player who had gotten a good look at the underbelly of humankind and had not blinked, studied Shannon for a few seconds and then buried himself in some papers. After a minute, he looked up again.

'You understand your guilty plea?' he asked her.

'Yes, your honor.'

'This is a nice town. We don't like fighting in public here.'

'No, your honor.' Regardless of her flaws in other departments, Shannon knew courtroom etiquette.

'I see this is your first such offense, but you have a DUI on your record,' he went on.

'Yes, sir.'

'And a license suspension.'

'Yes, sir.'

'I'm guessing you might have a problem with alcohol.'

When the PD's hand brushed her arm, she realized an answer was called for.

'I, uh …'

'What?'

'Sir, I don't think I'm an alcoholic.' She swallowed. Her head began to throb again. 'Your honor.'

'Maybe you are and maybe you aren't,' the judge said, looking grim, 'but I have a feeling you're an accident waiting to happen.'

'Uh—'

He interrupted her, turning to the public defender. 'Anything to say on your client's behalf?'

'Yes, your honor. Miss Fairchild runs her own business. She's a graduate of UC San Malo, where her parents teach—'

Shannon's courtroom decorum slipped. 'I thought you weren't going to mention them.'

The PD showed his inexperience by looking flustered. The judge leaned forward.

'Your attorney is saying good things about you. I don't think it's a good idea to interrupt him.'

She pursed her sore lips as the public defender went on.

'Uh, and she is working toward her Ph.D. She's also concerned about her mental health and has regularly seen a psychotherapist for the past year.'

'A Ph.D. in what?' the judge asked her.

'History.'

'When do you expect to finish?'

'I don't know, your honor.' *How about never? Because I haven't been to a class in four years, and the idea of writing a dissertation fills me with … what's that word? Angst.*

'What's your business?'

'I clean houses.'

'Uh-huh. I've met your parents. They're good people.' He glanced down at the papers in front of him. 'Do you see a therapist for any particular reason?'

She swallowed again. Her mouth tasted like old dishwater. 'Just a few problems I'm trying to work out.'

'Good luck with that, but don't let me see you here again.' The judge closed her file with a snap. 'Seven days in jail, suspended, and a year's probation.'

She thanked the PD and made her way unsteadily down the aisle. She had almost reached the exit before she spotted Beth sitting in one of the back rows. Her sister rose and came over.

'How are you?' The look on Beth's face, a mixture of concern and disgust, was so exaggerated it was almost comical. Beth tended to fly her flags out front. She was direct, outspoken, and caring. She was also the Good Sister.

Shannon had not seen her for weeks – since Thanksgiving, to be exact – and when it had come time to make her single phone call from jail the night before, she had been somewhat surprised when her fingers, slowed by alcohol, fumbled their way through Beth's number. On reflection, of course, it made sense. She didn't have a lawyer. Her sometime boyfriend was out of town. And she couldn't stand the idea of hearing her mother and father's sad voices over the phone when they learned of her latest scrape.

Thus, Beth, wife of Richard, mother of Champ and Skipper – or Scamp and Chipper, as Shannon sometimes called them. Beth the soccer mom, the manager, the fixer. Although three years younger, she sometimes struck Shannon as miles more mature and maternal. Beth would know how to break the news to their parents. The only price Shannon would have to pay was Beth's disapproval. But she was used to that.

In Shannon's sometimes cruel childhood shorthand, Beth was 'Barbie,' a creature of dolls and well-brushed golden hair and good marks for obedience. Shannon saw herself in more heroic terms: the no-nonsense, task-oriented sister, the athlete, the daredevil. Somewhere around age ten, she had given herself a nickname too. But that name was secret.

'I'm okay,' she told her sister as they exited the courthouse. 'Feeling stupid, though, you know?' She looked around for an escape route, started thinking up an excuse to leave.

'Did I hear right? You won't go to jail?'

'Won't go to jail. Just have to be a good girl from now on.'

Beth saw no humor in that. She produced a cell phone and began dialing. 'Mom and Dad—'

'You told them, huh?'

'I did. They knew you wouldn't want them to show up. But they made me promise that you'd call them as soon as you got out of court. So …' She handed over the phone.

'Shan? Honey? Are you all right?' Her mother's usual unruffled academic voice was replaced by a tone of concern.

'Hi, Mom. I'm just fine.' Shannon heard the rustle of papers. 'You in your office?'

'Yes. Do you need to go to the hospital or anything?'

'Oh, God, no. It was just a … a dumb thing. I'm embarrassed. Can we not talk about it?' Beth was watching her closely, and Shannon felt the overwhelming urge to get away, out of the bright sun, to find a private place. 'I should get going.'

'Wait. You sure you're all right?'

'I'm sure.'

'You can prove it by coming over for dinner this Saturday,' she said in an insistent tone, one not characteristic of her.

'Mom …'

'Come on. Meatloaf.'

'All right, if it's meatloaf. Tell Dad I'm okay so he doesn't have to call too.'

She clicked the phone shut and handed it to Beth, who gave her a hard look. 'They tell me they haven't seen you since Thanksgiving. I don't mind coming here and helping you clean up your mess, but they deserve a little more attention from you.'

'I'm going to see them this weekend.'

'They care about you, and for some reason they don't want to say hard things to you, so I guess I'm elected.' Beth was very much in soccer-mom mode now. 'You're too old for this,' she went on, stepping in closer and lowering her voice as people passed them on the steps. She wrinkled her nose as she got the full effect of Shannon's lapse in hygiene. 'Hanging out with trashy friends, getting messed up in bars …'

'Then why don't you fix me up with a nice guy? Somebody like Richard?' Shannon didn't even have to apply the sarcasm; it was implicit. Beth knew how Shannon felt about her husband: Richard the IRS agent, the tax man, the guy with the soul of a pocket calculator.

Beth ignored the jab. 'Mom and Dad love you, and you should spend more time with them. I love you too, but I'm running out of patience.'

Shannon felt a retort forming, something suitably sarcastic, something about how hard it must be to grow up the perfect daughter, having to put up with the fallible one. But she didn't utter it. She knew Beth was right.

Leaving her sister, she had barely taken ten steps on the sidewalk when she saw the old Volvo parked up ahead, and she groaned out loud. As she approached it, there he was, corduroy elbow out the window, wearing a look of mixed worry and embarrassment.

'Hello, Daughter.'

'Oh, Dad.' She shook her head. 'I didn't want you here.'

'I know,' he said with forced joviality. 'I wasn't going to butt in, just thought I'd check with Beth to find out what happened. But then

I saw you headed this way …' He made a face as he saw her bruises. 'Bet that hurts, huh?'

'I guess.' Her tongue went exploring again. No more blood, at least. 'But you should see the other guy.'

He laughed at that, which released some of the tension between them – some, but not all. He couldn't erase the look of concern from his face. Was it the embarrassment of hearing that his thirty-four-year-old daughter had rolled around a bar-room floor taking punches from a motorcycle mama named Rhonda? No, she thought. Shannon's checkered history, dating back to her early teens, had no doubt prepared them for such behavior. Besides, her parents were not innocents; they were smart cookies. It would take more than this to shock them.

He looked at her with a half-smile, not speaking. As the seconds ticked away, she felt the tension level ratchet up again and grew angry with herself for placing such a high value on his opinion of her. *If you wouldn't expect so much of me*, she said to him silently, *I wouldn't let you down so hard.*

Finally he spoke. 'We worry about you.'

'I know you do. Would you stop, please?'

'Can't do it. It's in my contract. See, right here.' He held up a palm and traced across it with a forefinger. 'Section Three, Subparagraph Six. Subject: Daughters. You worry about them. When they're little, you worry about them getting hurt. When they're growing up, you worry about them hooking up with the wrong boys. And when they're grown, well …'

'Yeah?'

'And when they're grown, you worry about all the new ways they can get hurt.'

Seeing her jaw tighten into a stubborn line, he came up with a grin. 'All right, then. I guess bruises can heal.' He began telling her a funny story about one of his poli-sci classes. She was disarmed by his wryness and by the fact that, throughout the conversation, he hadn't actually accused her of anything. Her father could never judge her as harshly as she judged herself. She asked herself why she had not made more of an effort to see her parents and couldn't quite come up with an answer.

'Did your mom invite you over Saturday?'

'Uh-huh. I'll try, Dad.'

He caught her hesitancy. 'We have, uh, a reason. Something we've been meaning to talk to you about. This'll be a good time for it. So put us on your calendar, all right?'

Bruises and courtroom appearances notwithstanding, there was still work to be done, and noon found Shannon at Mrs Kranz's house, a comfy-elegant place located up one of San Malo's pretty and pricey canyons, for the weekly visit by the Clean Machine, Shannon's house-cleaning business. Mrs Kranz was out shopping and visiting friends, and with Shannon's assistant cleaning another client's place, Shannon enjoyed the chance to work in solitude. Unpacking her supplies and donning earphones, she spent the next four hours going through the house, dusting, vacuuming, mopping, scrubbing. She worked to the pastoral sounds of Beethoven's Sixth, and before long she felt herself slipping into what she sometimes called the Zen of cleaning – far from the Municipal Court, from the soreness of her face, from the sordidness of the night before.

She changed sheets and did the dishes, with Django Reinhardt and Stephane Grappelli now providing the bounce and inspiration. Moving on to the toughest job, the main bathroom, she stripped down to her underwear, tied up her hair with an elastic band, and attacked the room with rags, mop, sponge, and foaming cleanser.

Passing the fogged-up mirror, she indulged in what had become a goofy ritual. One hand on hip, the other behind her head, cheesecake style, she arched her back and formed her lips in a Marilyn pout. As usual, it didn't work. Not enough curves. But she was satisfied with most of what she saw. Ever since tomboyhood, she'd had long legs, slightly broad shoulders and an economical midsection. Looking critically – the only way she looked at herself – she noted a slight roll of flesh over the waistband of her panties. *Back to the jogging*, she said silently.

She shifted into a Schwarzenegger pose, standing sideways to the mirror and straining to produce a biceps. Damn. Where was the biceps? She broke into a helpless grin, then immediately cursed as it made her face hurt again.

Into the shower, worst job in the bathroom, she worked at the scum-caked walls, headphones on, music player strapped to her upper arm, jogger-style. Suddenly remembering where she was, she cued up Handel's 'Water Music' and hummed along.

Here, at least, she could feel in control of things. In control and almost happy. The Clean Machine.

'My goodness.' Elva Santiago looked wide-eyed as Shannon settled herself onto one end of the sofa in her therapist's office and slipped off her dark glasses. 'What happened to you?'

Three days had gone by, and the bruises had darkened into a yellowish-green – not as scary as the fresh rainbow of colors, but more gloomy, even a little sickening. *Green is not a color that sits well on the face*, Shannon had said to herself as she did a mirror check that morning.

She told Elva the story, trying to keep it light. It was dumb, she said. Silly. Just one of those things. We're really friends—

'But what started it?'

'Oh, God. We were just … sitting there at the bar, you know? Talking. The bartender got us into a kind of trivia game, seeing if we could list all the towns along the coast with Spanish names. San Diego, La Jolla—'

'I know about the Spanish names,' Elva interrupted gently.

'Right. And Rhonda, who had had several beers, said a lot of them were named after Spanish saints. And I said this town was different because it was named after a guy who was born in Wales. She said I was full of shit, because the Spanish had settled California, not the Welsh. I said I could prove it the next time I came in. And she said I was showing off 'cause I was a college girl. She said it two or three times. *College girl.* And I just … hit her.'

'You hit her?'

'Yeah.' Shannon burrowed down slightly in the pillowy sofa. 'Slapped her. A pretty good one, too. But after that—'

'Shannon, when was the last time you hit anyone?'

'I don't know. When I was … junior high, maybe. Wait. I hit Sue Galloway in the tenth grade.'

'Shannon …' The therapist leaned forward, hands clasped on her desk. She appeared to be on the verge of saying something parental, something like, *You can't hit people.* Instead she said, 'Do you have any idea why you did it? Really, I mean?'

'Uh-huh. Because when she called me a college girl, she made it sound like I was acting superior. Like I was too good to be in that bar, where some of my best friends are. It was a way of saying I didn't belong.'

'Well, let me tell you something.' Elva's voice was quiet, but her manner was firm. Shannon had often noted that the therapist, without being heavily judgmental, refused to let her get away with phoniness or self-deception. She could feel another dose of that coming.

'You *are* too good to be in that bar.'

Shannon shook her head stubbornly. Once again she felt the discomfort of revealing her secrets and vulnerabilities to a younger woman. Elva was somewhere in her mid-twenties, and Shannon often found herself wishing the therapist were a more motherly type – although with her stout build, chunky artisan jewelry and the oversize muu-muus she liked to wear, Elva did give off a kind of young earth-mother vibe.

She readied a reply, but Elva held up a hand.

'It's true. You're a college graduate. You could hold your own with people like yourself, but you go there because you feel comfortable.'

'Among the under-achievers, you mean?'

'I didn't say that. I don't want to minimize the value of friendship. But let's put it this way: no one challenges you there.'

'I should find a bar where I'm challenged?'

'No, I think you should find challenges elsewhere. You know, this is connected to things we've talked about.'

'Uh-oh. Here we go again.'

'I think you decided a long time ago – for reasons we haven't gotten at yet – that you were unloved, or not loved as much as your sister was. This is surprising, because from what you've told me about your parents, it sounds as if they love you a lot. But you've spent years trying to show them how little you resemble them by avoiding a career—'

'I have a career.'

'I know, and I don't want to minimize that either. You have your own business. But you could be a Ph.D. today, maybe teaching college. You decided to drop out, for reasons that aren't totally clear to me.'

'Or to me either.'

'You even find various ways to mess up here and there. You're lucky, by the way, that you didn't have to go to jail.'

'I know it.'

'But the messing up – the drinking, the fighting, the boyfriend who could be trouble—'

'Could we not talk about TeeJay today?'

'All right, we'll save him for another time. I just wonder if the messing up, the rejection of the Ph.D., isn't meant to be a message to your parents, a message that says, "Look how unlike you I am."'

Shannon had heard that theory, and the fact that it made sense troubled her. 'Maybe.'

'Did you talk to your parents about the thing at the bar?'

'Uh-huh. A little. I'm having dinner with them tomorrow night.'

'Have you had the nightmare lately?'

'No.' It was true. At least six months had gone by. *Wouldn't it be wonderful*, she thought, *if that particular hobgoblin had just faded away, like an old bruise?*

'Even though you've avoided talking with them about your dream, this may be a good time to raise it. Just describe it, explain how it's bothered you, and see if they suggest any possible reason for it. After all, they've known you a lot longer than I have.'

'Why don't you—'

'I know you'd like me to try some kind of interpretation, but as I've said, it's always better if the patient comes up with the answers herself. Then you and I can discuss it.'

'But you have an idea, don't you?'

The therapist went silent for a while, her pretty, chubby face taken over by an unnaturally somber look.

'Talk to them,' she said.

Shannon lived in a scruffily picturesque beach town just down the coast from San Malo. The charming city where she had grown up and now worked her job and saw her therapist – and made occasional court appearances – was in a real estate bracket well beyond her means. San Malo had always been a pleasant place to live, but in recent years its rich canyon homes with their red-tile roofs and Mission-revival architecture had begun to attract money and celebrity from LA, with Hollywood names buying up some of the grandest homes. It had become so inviting that most of the people who worked within its limits, those who swept its streets and picked up its trash and cooked its meals and cleaned its homes, could not afford to live there. So they lived in towns like Ben's Beach.

Despite the name, Ben's Beach had no beach to speak of, just a mile or so of main drag fronting the highway that ran by the ocean on its way north to San Malo. Shannon's neighborhood was one of bumpy asphalt streets, no sidewalks, and often shabby one-story houses, many with front porches almost obscured by vines and shrubbery. Her place, built during the Second World War to house an army family, had the hastily built look common to the period. But with its wind chimes and rattan furniture on the porch and a veritable forest of greenery grown up around it, the house had achieved a quirky kind of permanence.

Her street, a quarter-mile from the ocean, sometimes caught the scent of salt air. It held a mixture of over-age hippie families, twenty-something dropouts, and yuppies seeking to gentrify the area. Shannon knew most of her neighbors, along with their dogs, cats, and children. She liked it there.

She arrived home still a little tense from her time with the therapist, a common occurrence. So she changed into sweats, arranged herself on a floor cushion in the small living room, put on her sound-canceling headphones, and meditated for twenty minutes. Then she tossed a salad, grilled some fish, mixed a rum and Coke, and had her dinner at the kitchen table.

Afterward she settled into one of her squeaky rattan chairs on the porch as the darkness came down, the curtain of greenery almost blocking the lights from the street. A breeze stirred the wind chimes, a gift from her mother when Shannon was in graduate school. 'From my hippie days,' Mora told her. 'You want history? These old chimes have seen a lot.'

For the past three days, she had submerged herself in work, coming home tired each night. It was an effective way to put off thinking. But her forty-five minutes with Elva that afternoon had stirred the water just enough to bring things to the surface.

First thought: *Bad girl.*

The image Shannon presented to the world was what an old boyfriend once characterized as *Back of me hand to ye*: tough; capable; funny, sometimes sarcastic; impervious to harm. 'The thing is,' he had told her, 'you care a lot more than you let on.'

Now that she'd had some time to put the bar fight in perspective, she felt ashamed and embarrassed by it. *What were you thinking? You don't go around hitting people. Where did you get this hair-trigger behavior? So Rhonda called you a college girl. So what?*

She rubbed cautiously at her mouth and cheekbone. Most of the hurt had faded. All that was left was the shame. 'So I'll apologize to her,' she said softly.

Almost as troubling was the thought of what her mother and father must be thinking. The prospect of dinner with them made her uneasy. Despite what Elva had said about Shannon trying to act out her differences with her parents, she had never knowingly wanted to hurt them.

Speaking of Elva, why this renewed interest in her nightmare? The therapist seemed to have an idea about it but was reluctant to express it first. Soon Shannon was putting together a short list of explanations for the dream. Let's see: Too much drinking? Always easy to blame alcohol. Incipient paranoia could also fit. A brain tumor, maybe. How about abduction by little green men?

One more rum and Coke, twenty minutes' browsing through a book from her night table. And so to bed.

The phone woke her up. When she was able to focus her eyes, the bedside clock said it was almost midnight.

The voice was Beth's, but unlike any Beth she had ever heard. The words came out in frantic gasps, tinged with hysteria. Long seconds went by, a full minute, before Shannon was able to realize what Beth was telling her, the sickening awfulness of it.

As she sat on the edge of the bed, the phone jammed to her ear so tightly it hurt, she heard other sounds in the background – voices, shouts, the crackle of a radio, the whoop of a siren suddenly cut off. By then, Beth's words had melted into sobs, but Shannon had heard enough.

She knew that something important in her life had changed. What she couldn't know yet was that everything had changed.

Two

She saw it from a long way off.

When still more than a block away, she could see the area around her parents' house illuminated with a pulsing glow that bathed houses and trees in an ominous light, alternating between blue and a bloody red. As she drew nearer, she saw that it came from the lights atop fire trucks and police cars. The street shone with puddles of water, and their surfaces also pulsed with the colors.

The curbs were jammed with cars, so she double-parked a few houses away, then walked, her legs unsteady. In a hurry and half awake, she had pulled on sneakers without socks and donned a parka over a pullover and cotton sweatpants. Her legs were already cold.

She reached a barricade manned by police. Neighbors in various levels of dress and undress stood around. The familiar front yard was an alien place now, a muddle of equipment, crisscrossed hoses, small lakes of water, and yellow-slickered firefighters. Somewhere a generator hummed loudly. A work light harshly illuminated the area.

The house was gone. In its place was a jumble of blackened wood still being soaked by two big hoses. The streams of water churned up greasy clouds of dark, stinking smoke.

Amid all the activity there was no sign of Beth. Shannon started to duck under the barricade, but a uniformed policeman stopped her, and not politely.

'That's—' She stopped as her voice caught in a croak, then took a deep breath. 'That's my parents' house.'

The cop took in her frazzled hair and wild-eyed look, then went over to one of the firefighters and spoke to him. The man came to her.

'Yes, ma'am?' He had a thick neck and a neatly trimmed mustache, and the name on his helmet was Walden. The *ma'am* sounded irony-free. 'Do you live here?'

'No. It's my parents' house. Ray and Mora Fairchild. My sister called me from here, told me they'd been …' Another breath. She felt as if she'd run a mile, and she leaned on the barricade for support. 'Where are they?'

'I talked to your sister,' Walden said. 'They were taken to Good Samaritan, and I think she went with them.'

'What happened? She told me that my father—' She stopped, unable to finish the sentence, unable to repeat Beth's words. *If I don't say them out loud*, she thought, *maybe they won't be true.*

'I'm sorry. You'll have to ask at the hospital.'

'But what happened here?' She heard the mounting shrillness in her voice but couldn't keep it down.

'We don't know yet. But the police are looking into it, and our arson people, too.' He surveyed the scene over his shoulder. 'I have to get back. I'm sorry about your parents.'

Police? Arson? Her mind barely had room for any of it. Trying to avoid the hoses, she stumbled back to her car. Amid all the half-focused thinking as she had dressed tonight, she had still remembered to stuff her cell phone into a pocket of the parka. Sliding behind the wheel, she dialed Beth's number and found her at the hospital. Her sister had regained control, but just barely.

'Beth, what—'

'Just come, Shan. Right away.'

She spotted her sister in a waiting room down the hall from the hospital's emergency room. Beth, who also looked as if she'd dressed in ten seconds flat, jumped to her feet and hugged Shannon – grabbed her, more accurately, as if she were drowning and Shannon were a life preserver. As they hugged, Shannon tried to frame the question but couldn't, because she dreaded the answer. She could only wait.

Finally Beth released her. 'Daddy … he's gone,' she said. Her eyes were inflamed but dry. She sank back onto the sofa, where Shannon joined her.

As the words sank in, Shannon felt sick, dizzy. She'd feared as much since Beth's first call and the hysterical words, *I think Daddy's dead.* For the past hour, she'd tried to block them out, but now they took over.

It was true. Dead. In a fire.

She felt numb and empty. When a parent dies, the grown-up child is supposed to have time to plan, to adjust, maybe even to grieve a little in advance. Not like this. A gray mist swam through her head, right to left, and she felt very near to fainting. But women don't faint any more, she told herself. She leaned forward on the sofa, head between her knees, breathing deeply, her face grim. Women don't faint.

'There's more.' Beth's voice was shaky. 'They think somebody killed him.'

'What?' Shannon straightened up. 'Oh, no. No.' *That must be a mistake,* she thought distractedly. *How could anyone possibly want to kill him?*

Beth nodded. 'There was a policeman at the fire, and then I saw him here. He's talking to the doctors—'

'What about Mom?'

'She's hurt bad.' The last word dissolved in a kind of ghastly hiccup, and then the tears returned, full flow. During their childhood, Beth had always been the one to cry, the one easily hurt during Shannon's rowdy games. A cry-baby, she'd called her, and their parents would come to her rescue and chide Shannon for being so rough with her. Tonight, however, she saw her younger sister differently. Beth was soft in some ways, tough in others. She was not ashamed to cry, which was a kind of toughness in itself.

As Shannon waited for the sobbing to cease, waited to find out about her mother, two men entered the room, one of them in medical greens. Shannon guessed that the other was the policeman Beth had mentioned. He was medium height and square-cut, with short, graying hair and little extra flesh on him. She put his age at somewhere in his fifties. He looked tired and somewhat wary, as bearers of bad tidings often do.

Shannon was introduced to the doctor, named Simons, who was the hospital's on-call surgeon, and the detective, whose name was Orlando. The doctor spoke first. The two women stood, as if to mark the solemnity of the moment.

'I'm very sorry about your father,' he said to Shannon. 'As I told your sister, he was dead when he arrived at the hospital.'

'And Mom?' Shannon asked.

'Your mother has serious injuries,' the doctor said. 'She's being treated for burns and for a bullet wound in the chest.'

Beth's sharp intake of breath told Shannon her sister hadn't known about that.

'I've just taken out the bullet, and she's being moved into intensive care. The burns are painful but not life-threatening. The bullet, though ...' He cleared his throat. 'It penetrated a lung, and there's been a lot of bleeding. We've managed to stop it for now.'

Shannon and Beth traded glances of helplessness and near despair.

The doctor gave them a quick smile that did little to encourage them. 'We'll know more in a few hours. There's no need for you to stay. If you like, you can leave your number at the nurses' station, then check back with us around nine a.m.' He nodded to the detective. 'Now I have to get back.'

When he was gone, Shannon started to question the detective, but Beth broke in. 'I have to go,' she said, wiping her eyes. 'Richard and the boys. I know they're frantic, and now I have to tell them.' She gave Shannon a last, distracted hug, then pulled out her cell phone and dialed a number. As Beth left the room and walked down the hall, her voice filtered back. 'Honey?' It was full of tears again.

Shannon turned to the cop. 'What can you tell me?'

Instead of answering, he studied her face. *The bruises*, she thought.

'You the one that was in a fight down at that place in Ben's Beach the other night?' he asked mildly. 'The Nook?'

'Yeah. So?'

'Nothing. Just thought I recognized you from one time when I was there a while back. I stopped in with a friend, and you were at the bar with a guy in a T-shirt.'

'So you're good with faces,' Shannon said. 'And T-shirts. In your job, you need to be. Will you please tell me what happened to my parents?'

'I will. You can help me, too, if you'll tell me whether you know anybody who'd want to hurt them.'

'Oh, we're bargaining?' She fought to keep her anger down. *Relax*, she told herself. *Both of us want to find out who did this.*

'No. I'll tell you what happened and hope you can help me.' He paused, looking thoughtful. 'For starters, I don't think it was random. Somebody wanted very much to hurt them. And did.'

He glanced at his watch. 'I've been off duty for a while, and I hate to talk in hospitals,' he said. 'You want to get out of here?'

She was aware of the stale smell of her own breath. 'I could use a drink.'

His face lost some of its sympathetic look. She knew what he thought of her. 'After all this, don't you think most people would?' she asked, almost belligerently.

'I suppose. But I don't drink, and you probably shouldn't right now. If you don't mind, we'll go someplace else.'

She did mind but was not up for a fight, especially with a policeman. She looked around, as if searching for something. 'Before we go, I want to see my dad. Can you help?'

His look turned dark. 'I saw him,' he said. 'With respect, I'm not sure that's a good idea.'

'I'm not leaving here until I say goodbye to him.'

He nodded. 'Then let's go find that doctor.'

Five minutes later they stood over a gurney in a quiet hallway as Simons unzipped the top of a body bag. Shannon kept her gaze on the floor until she was ready to look, but even before she raised her eyes, her nostrils were struck with the odor of seared flesh. Her eyes closed, then opened, then swiveled to what was left of her father's face.

She made a sound deep in her throat and leaned hard on the edge of the gurney to keep from falling. Then the doctor closed the bag over her father, and she turned away, eyes fixed now on the wall, and began taking deep breaths. *All right*, she thought, *it's real. He's gone. And I'll see that ruined face for ever. But I had to look. I owed him that, didn't I? How can you say goodbye without a last look?*

Tears would come later, she knew. For now she felt only the shock of loss. That, and a small, building sense of rage, which started in her hands, in the fists she made, clenching and unclenching over and over.

Three

They found an all-night convenience store, where they got jumbo coffees, and then Orlando took them up Arroyo Grande, the city's broadest canyon, and into the hills. He drove a generic unmarked police car, and it had an air freshener dangling from the rear-view mirror, one of those things shaped like an evergreen tree with an odor that does not come from nature. He noticed her jiggling it.

'Last two guys who had this car smoked a lot,' he said. 'I smoke myself, but I don't like the smell of butts. I thought I'd air it out a little. Call me a neat freak.'

'I clean houses for a living,' she said, idly watching darkened homes go by, their size and richness increasing the higher up the canyon they drove. Her mind was neither on the homes nor on the conversation. 'I know a few things about neat. You got nothing on me.'

When he reached the big turnout by the old mission, he pulled over. San Malo and its bay lay below them, the city winking here and there with tiny lights in a secret code, the bay immense and dark except for an occasional lighted oil-drilling platform, perched almost on the horizon like a scattered enemy fleet deciding when to invade.

'We used to park up here in high school,' she said as Orlando first lowered his window and then lit a cigarette. 'Mission San Make-Out, we called it.' A blink of memory: First time a boy ever felt her up, it happened in the front seat of his daddy's Olds Cutlass in this very spot. He was a devout Catholic, she remembered, and the nearness of Mission San Malo just beyond the adobe wall lent the act a forbidden quality that made it all the more delectable to both of them.

'This feels a little like a date.' She glanced at him, aware that she was talking nonsense but not caring. Anything to block out the hospital, the sounds, the smells. Her head felt lighter than air, the way it did when alcohol took hold of it. 'You have a thing for younger women, perchance?'

He shook his head. 'I've got a daughter your age. She's had some problems. Maybe you remind me a little of her.'

'Because I've got problems?'

'Don't take offense. I heard about the thing in the bar, and I saw you with your sister at the hospital. She's wiped out with grief, and she'll go home to her family and somehow work it out. You, I'm not sure how you'll work it out. You've got the grief, all right, but something else too. Rage, maybe.'

His words nailed her so precisely, they almost made her dizzy. She said with a strange formality, 'Would you excuse me for a minute?' She got out, closed the door, and walked a few steps to lean on the fender, looking out at the winking dark but not seeing it.

Somebody shot my father and my mother, she thought. *Assailant unknown, as the cops would say. Father dead, mother hanging on.*

She was suddenly very near to being an orphan, and she wasn't ready.

Just as bad, she had no place to put the anger. The emotion that curdled inside her made her stomach ache, then spread downward to weaken her knees, upward to shorten her breath.

So much anger, she thought. *Enough to almost make a poor girl faint. No way to let it out.*

'You okay?' the detective called out to her.

She slid back into her seat and closed the door. 'Just needed a little air.'

A business card lay on the dashboard in front of her. 'My number,' he said offhandedly. 'In case you need it.'

She scanned it, noting that his first name was Thomas, then pocketed it. She reached for her coffee and took a sip. It was still very hot.

He inspected her closely. 'It took guts, what you did back there.'

It took a second for her to understand he was talking about the hospital. 'He was my father. He couldn't help how he looked dead.'

'I'd have to agree with that. So you want to know—'

'Wait.' She held up a hand, ran the other through her hair. 'Before I hear the details, can I have one of those?' She pointed to his cigarette.

'Sure.' He shook one out for her and lit it. 'If you promise to knock the ashes outside.'

'So where's your arsenal?' she asked him, lowering her window.

'Why do you want to know?'

'Policemen fascinate me. They have the power to kill.'

He nodded slowly, giving her a steady look. He seemed willing to wait until she was ready to hear about her parents. 'They do,' he said, 'along with the paperwork and the investigation that always follow. Let's not forget the bad dreams. And, for some of them, the crack-up.'

'You speak from experience?'

'I've never killed anybody.'

'Ever shot anyone?'

'Once. I didn't enjoy it.'

'All right, maybe we like to generalize about you guys.' Another sip of coffee. 'So where's your arsenal?'

He laughed, just a quick exhalation of breath. 'Here.' He patted the left side of his waist. 'And in the trunk. Satisfied?'

'Uh-huh. Us reformed academics, we're always full of questions. Don't mind us.'

'You were at the university? Where your parents— '

'I did graduate work in history. I only act like white trash part of the time.' She sucked on the cigarette once, then again, and exhaled vigorously. 'I don't usually smoke.' She took a big swallow of her coffee and made a face as it burned its way down.

Orlando was saying something.

'Hmm?'

'Now?' he asked.

After a moment's hesitation, she nodded.

'All right. Someone – probably more than one person – went into your parents' house tonight, attacked them, and set fire to the place—'

'A fireman told me there was going to be an arson investigation,' she broke in. 'But he didn't say they know for sure.'

'My guess is they do,' he said, 'and they'll say so soon. The whole place stinks of kerosene. Doesn't take a genius to know somebody torched that place.'

'What about my parents?'

'Your father was shot in the head, your mother in the chest. They meant to ... Are you all right?'

'Huh?' Shannon realized she had closed her eyes tight – an involuntary reaction dating back to childhood, when she had screwed her eyes tightly shut to ward off unpleasant sights or sounds. It sometimes worked for a child, but hardly ever for an adult. *Bullets*, she thought. *Tearing into my father's head, my mother's chest.* She opened her eyes and said, 'Yes. Go on.'

'Whoever did it apparently meant to kill both of them, but they may have been in a hurry at the end, what with setting the fire and getting out of there, and didn't quite finish it with your mother. She's a schoolteacher, right?'

Shannon nodded. 'Both of them, at UC San Malo. They're in – they were in the Political Science department.' She noticed something in his expression. 'Why?'

'Oh, I was just thinking. Your mother was found on the front lawn. Somehow she made it out of a burning house with serious burns, a bullet inside her, and her hands tied behind her back. Sounds almost superhuman to me – hardly schoolteacher behavior, unless I just don't know my schoolteachers.'

She was silent. It didn't fit her own image of her mother either. Then, noticing Orlando's grim expression, she asked, 'Is there more?'

'Yes. Are you sure you want to hear it?'

'No. But tell me.'

He took a last heavy drag and flipped his cigarette out the window. 'Sometime during the takeover of the house, probably before anybody was shot, two of your mother's fingers were cut off,' he said quietly in a cloud of smoke, 'and three of your father's.'

'What? No.' Her stomach tightened.

He looked at her impassively, then nodded.

'But what does that mean? Why—'

'I think they were trying to get your parents to tell them something. Maybe where they kept their money.'

She heard the breath whistle out of her, heard herself almost whisper, 'They didn't have any fucking money.' She felt lightheaded. 'So people really do that. Cut off fingers.'

'I'm afraid so. The bad ones. Now, I'd appreciate it if you'd try to help me. Can you think of anybody—'

'No,' she broke in. 'And this isn't a flip answer. I know of absolutely no one who'd want to hurt my parents. You can talk to all their friends, everyone at the university, and I'm sure they'll tell you the same thing. These are ...' She paused as she realized she was still falling into the present tense. But she went on forcefully, 'These are good people.'

He nodded and was about to speak when her cell phone rang. She pulled it out of her pocket and answered.

'This is Dr Simons,' the voice said, in a tone more urgent than she remembered. 'Your mother is conscious. She wants to talk to you.'

'Have you called my sister?'

'I will. But listen, she only wants to talk to you, and she's very insistent.' He suddenly sounded impatient. 'You'd better hurry.'

While Shannon was absorbing that, he added, 'I'm saying I don't think you have much time.'

Mora Fairchild was almost lost in the bed amid a jumble of tubes and monitors, her face partly hidden with bandages and an oxygen mask. The smell in the enclosure was sharp and penetrating, the smell of pain.

Shannon stepped up to the bedside, leaving Orlando and the doctor outside the curtain. Her mother's left hand was encased in a big mitt of white gauze. Shannon found the right one, careful not to disturb the tube stuck in it, and held it gently.

Mora's eyes, foggy with painkiller, strayed over to her daughter and focused on her, then widened. Her mouth formed a weak half-smile, and a little gasp came out. Shannon knew she was hurting.

'Mom?'

'Shan.' It was little more than a drowsy murmur. Shannon leaned over, gently pulled the oxygen mask downward a few inches so she could hear her. The ravaged face was not the one she knew.

'Mom, I'm here. I love you.' Her throat swelled with emotion, choking her words into whispers. Shannon could almost physically feel her slipping away.

A few shallow breaths, then: 'They killed Ray. Bastards. I saw it.'

'I know.'

'We didn't … tell them anything. I was so proud of him.'

'Oh, Mom.' Half-formed thoughts jostled for space in her head. *What did she mean? What could she have told anyone? What secrets could she have been guarding, even at the cost of her husband's life?* It made no sense.

'Shan.'

'Yes?'

'You have to …' Her eyes closed, and her face twisted in pain. Shannon wanted to say, *Please don't. Just rest.* But her mother's hand tightened on hers.

'Listen. Don't tell po—' Her breath caught, but she pushed the word out. 'Police.' A new intensity in her voice. 'You have to find them and …' She slowed down, each word an effort now. 'Warn. Them.'

This was followed by a ragged exhalation of breath. *She's losing her air,* Shannon thought wildly. *If the air goes, she'll die.* She heard the words, *Don't leave,* and realized she had spoken them.

She moved to replace the oxygen mask, but her mother shook her head, took another determined breath and sighed. 'God, he's so full of hate. We should have guessed …'

Eyes on Shannon now, burning right in. Was that a smile or a grimace? Her next words came out all in a faint, husky rush.

'We're giving back the treasure.'

'Mom? What treasure? Warn who?' *She's hallucinating,* Shannon thought.

A long silence. Her mother's eyes were fixed on the ceiling now, and the grip of her hand loosened a little. 'You're …'

Shannon leaned in close, tears coming to her eyes. *What? I'm what? Warn who?*

The eyes closed, and the grip loosened completely. But her mother's chest continued its almost imperceptible rise and fall.

Shannon stood there for a full minute, waiting for anything. Nothing came. There would be no further message, at least not for now.

'Don't go,' she whispered. 'I mean it. I need you. Do you hear me?'

She replaced the mask and kissed her mother on the forehead. The doctor entered, and she left. Fighting to control her voice, she spoke to Orlando.

'*They. Them.* She said *them.* There was definitely more than one.'

As she spotted Beth coming through the doors at the end of the hall, she heard Simons's voice speaking urgently to the nurse. Immediately afterward came a high-pitched electronic note, loud and pitiless, the atonal music of death.

Something fractured within her, a dam breaking. She turned away from the detective and strode blindly down the hall, sobbing loudly, thinking, *I'm the cry-baby now.*

Four

Home, close to first light, her head full of cotton batting. A sad, whispered call from Beth; a short, necessary talk about funeral arrangements. Hanging up, she took a sleeping pill and lay on the couch, still dressed, waiting for it to take effect. It did not. Another, then, which did about as much good as an aspirin. Her thoughts were alive with sights, sounds, scents – a smoldering house, her mother's quivering voice, the smell of burned flesh. So she began dousing the pills with Scotch, and eventually she began the long drop toward the place where she could lose the memories, at least for a few hours.

Mom. Dad.

And *them.*

Her fists clenched and unclenched one last time, and she fell into sleep.

She awoke in the early afternoon, groggy but full of nervous energy, telling herself that, with her parents suddenly and horribly dead, she should be doing something. Detective Orlando had given her his cell-phone number – she wondered if he did this for all victims' kin – and she called it.

After again expressing condolences in his deliberate way, he got to business. 'There's no question now about arson. But that's the least of the charges facing these characters, whoever they are. We're still looking for a motive. When we make the arrests, maybe that part'll become clear. By the way, I appreciate your passing on the word from your mom that there was more than one attacker. You left so fast after that, I didn't get a chance to ask if she'd told you anything else.'

He fell silent, waiting. Shannon thought quickly. *The rest is just a riddle*, she thought. *I can always mention it later, say I'd forgotten it for a while.*

'No, she didn't.'

'All right, then. I'll be in touch.'

As the day progressed, she talked to Beth twice, and by the end of the second conversation they had reached an implicit understanding that Beth was going to handle most of the arrangements. Fine with Shannon. Occasional sisterly rivalries aside, she could not deny that Beth was better at this sort of thing.

Unable to bear the confines of the house any longer, she put on her sweats and drove her six-year-old Jeep Cherokee up the coast until she reached the freeway exit that led to the San Malo harbor. She often jogged around her own neighborhood, but the harbor was her favorite running place. Over the years, Shannon had found that when she ran, a kind of alchemy occurred. She was able to transform emotional baggage into physical activity and sweat it away. As Elva Santiago once told her: If it works for you, it's cheaper than therapy. Although Shannon had never mentioned this to her, it was also an effective hangover remedy.

She ran easily at first, past motels and restaurants on her right and, to the left, a multicolored array of sailboats in the marina. She passed other runners and strollers, recognizing some of them, wondering if she was the only one who was running from death on that fine day.

As always, she ran to music. Today it was Ravel's 'Bolero', for the inexorable rhythm. When that orgasmic piece had ended, she fiddled with her player and switched to the most serious running music in her arsenal, the first movement of Shostakovich's 'Leningrad' symphony.

Her lifelong love of music had begun sometime around age eleven or twelve, when she suddenly became aware of its power to soothe, agitate, transform. Her parents had nothing to do with her new interest. As her mother put it, 'Honey, I can barely carry a tune. Your daddy can't carry one in a bucket.'

She ran to the sound of drums. The music was strong, warlike. She needed it. Every time the image of her father's charred face or the sound of her mother's faltering voice threatened to intrude, she pushed it down and ran harder. Her eyes glistened, but she blinked away the tears and kept going.

Even amid the music she could hear snatches of her mother's final words. First was the word *them.* Two or more people had come into her parents' home and taken their lives. Deliberately, sadistically, questioning them all the while.

You have to warn them. Surely not the murderers? Then who? And what about *Don't tell police*? Why the need for secrecy? Almost without thinking, Shannon had told Orlando that more than one attacker was involved. She couldn't imagine her mother meant that to be kept from the police.

Then what? The warning? The words *We're giving back the treasure* sounded almost hallucinatory, but the rest did not, especially: *He was so full of hate.* Of course he was, whoever he was. But who in the world was she supposed to warn? And of what? It was enough to make her ebbing headache return.

The martial drumbeat took her all the way around the curve of the bay until she ended up, panting and sweating, at a small park where mothers walked with infants in strollers and teenagers sat holding hands. It was one of the best views of the city. Gazing inland, she beheld one of California's prettiest communities, looking both sleepy and rich at the same time, an array of white stucco and red tile, palm trees and winter camellias, tumbling from the foothills down to the bay.

Halfway up she could make out the open space around the old mission, a place that had once been rich and magical to her. As a child. Shannon had stepped inside the sanctuary and been struck by its beauty. Then she thought of last night, when she sat just outside the mission's walls and heard Detective Orlando describe the most sickening details of her parents' deaths. The place would forever be spoiled for her.

She collapsed on a park bench and sat there looking out to sea until her breath quieted and her heartbeat calmed. Throat dust-dry, she drained most of the water from the bottle she carried. After a few minutes, she was joined by an old guy in a voluminous canvas coat. The park was also a favorite of retirees, she recalled, and sometimes the down and out.

'You remind me of my daughter.'

Her eyebrows went up. She could be curt with men who gave her unwanted attention, but this one looked harmless. So she answered him with the faintest of smiles.

'She's a banker, in Denver.' He was tall and fleshy, with pale skin and auburn-gray hair cut so short it did not match the rest of his looks. His forehead was a mass of old freckles, and an untended mustache covered his thick upper lip. But he was not otherwise unshaven, and he wore decent shoes, so she decided he was probably respectable.

'Really.'

'Uh-huh.' He was staring out at the water now, arms spread wide over the back of the bench, relaxing in the winter sun. 'She's knee-deep in snow right now. I tell her I've found Heaven, right here on the Pacific coast, and she should join me. They need bankers out here, don't they?'

'You bet.'

'But she's got the life she wants, so why should she listen to her old man? Children have to find their own way.'

'I suppose.' She looked at her watch: Time to start the long jog back.

'You have children?'

She shook her head.

'Parents?'

She hesitated. Too soon, that question. It was too soon. Why did he have to ask . . . ?

'Cleave to them.'

'Sorry?' She turned to face him, looking him up and down. His eyes were the palest blue. He looked utterly sincere, but somehow remote, like a teacher addressing a class.

'It's in the Bible. Every child should cleave to her parents and give them unconditional love. Even if she hasn't seen them for a long time; especially then. Like my daughter.' A pause, and his voice became more faint. 'Like you.'

'What?' She stood suddenly, giving him a hard look. He appeared to be strongly built under all the flesh, and he returned her gaze with no expression save a slight crinkling of his brows, as if he were turning a problem over in his mind.

She decided now that he was crazy, just another of the demented old park bench denizens she sometimes encountered on her jogging.

'Enjoyed talking to you,' she said as she turned her back to him and slid her earphones into place.

Turning her back was a mistake. An instant later she felt a strong hand grasp her upper arm. She felt the calluses, and the muscles beneath.

'What the hell?' She tried to twist out of the grip but could only turn halfway. He leaned in close to her, and she expected the over-ripe smell of the unwashed. But it was only the scent of a light aftershave.

She looked around at the vista of toddlers and nannies and young lovers. No one was looking at her. The flesh of her upper arm was pinched and twisted, and she was ready to yell in pain, to shatter the peaceful scene, summon help. The only thing that held her back was lingering sympathy for the old man. Mental illness must be a terrible—

'Don't you ever wonder about them?' The words came softly, almost pleadingly.

'Sir, back off.' She kept her voice as controlled as possible. 'I mean it.'

Only sissies scream, she told herself. *I can handle him.* She always jogged with a small canister of pepper spray in her pocket, but she needed her right hand to get at it, and that hand was already beginning to tingle with approaching numbness. Mental snapshots of a self-defense class from years ago blinked behind her eyes as she shaped her left hand into a tight fist, the knuckle of her middle finger protruding. Where should she aim? One of his eyes? The thought made her wince. Could she do it? She took a deep, noisy breath, and …

His grip loosened. He dropped his gaze, returned to the bench, and took his seat, where he leaned back in his old position and looked out to sea again.

She began running. *Just crazy*. She could have dreamed the whole thing, she thought, except for the dwindling hurt in her arm. On the way back around the harbor, she ran slowly to the sound of Chet Baker's trumpet and João Gilberto's soothing samba voice. By the time she reached her starting point, most of the ugly encounter was tamped down. She struggled for a while with his last question, but eventually decided she could safely forget it too, because it made absolutely no sense.

Five

A familiar gleaming red F-150 pickup sat at the curb in front of her house. As she pulled into the driveway, TeeJay came down the front porch steps.

'You're back,' she said. She got out, and he quickly reached for her. As usual, he smelled vaguely of grease and engine oil and things automotive. To her it was almost as pleasant as something good on the stove.

'Shan? What the hell?' He hugged her hard, seeming unable to frame the real questions.

'How did you hear?' She lifted her head off his shoulder and tried to smile at him. They were almost the same height.

'It was in the Frisco paper this morning. As soon as I saw it, I headed back.'

'I thought nobody but old World War Two sailors still said Frisco.'

'I had an uncle who used to call it that.' He looked uncomfortable, shifting his weight from one foot to the other. He wore his usual jeans and nylon jacket, and she felt sympathy for him, the way a grieving widow might empathize with the mourners' discomfort at her husband's funeral. 'You feel like telling me?' he asked.

'Sure.' She closed the car door. 'Come on inside.'

They opened beers and sat on the porch for a while, where he asked about her bruises and she told him, wanting to get it out of the way, treating the story like the sad joke it had become. The air quickly turned cool, so they moved inside. She sat quietly for a moment, gathering all the strands, then began talking slowly and deliberately, starting with the phone call from Beth on that haunted night. She was able not to cry as she told it, being past tears now, and he listened intently, asking an occasional question.

At one point, talking about her mother's death, she stopped, feeling the sadness come upon her again.

'Let's us take a break,' TeeJay said. 'You hungry?'

They went out to her favorite garlic roast chicken place and brought dinner home. She set everything up at the kitchen table, and they ate. She was ravenous, surprised to find that everything – the chicken, the salad, the additional beers – tasted wonderful. Sorrow is strong, she thought, but not strong enough to elbow aside one of the basic human needs. She felt a nudge of guilt but pushed it away. She knew what her mother and father would be telling her right now: *Eat.*

Afterward they arranged themselves on the motley pile of oversize cushions that decorated her sofa, chairs, and living-room floor, where she finished the story. When she reached her mother's last words, she once again decided quickly to keep the warning secret. If the police shouldn't hear it, she thought, then no one else should either, at least for now.

'More than one,' TeeJay muttered. 'A gang thing, maybe. I didn't know they even had gangs in that town.'

'They don't. San Malo is the California Riviera. Gangbangers and house cleaners and auto parts salesmen can't afford to live there.'

'And she couldn't describe any of 'em?'

'No. Maybe she could have. But she didn't have time to tell me.'

He lay back on his cushion, eyes on the ceiling. 'I'm just so sorry, Shan.'

He looked almost delicate lying there, with his slight frame and fine-boned features. But she knew that was deceptive. TeeJay wasn't a big man, but he was wiry – 'stringy,' as he put it. He moved almost with a dancer's grace, and she had felt the strength in his hands.

She had noticed him the moment he first walked into The Nook about two months ago, and he clearly noticed her. Before long he was buying her a rum and Coke, and she was admiring the sinuous dragon that wound around his right biceps, its forked tongue reaching out to taste the skin at the point where upper arm met deltoid muscle.

TeeJay was unassuming, with the speech and demeanor of the garage mechanic he had been not long before. But his jeans and black T-shirt were clean, as were his hands and nails. Now, he told her, he worked for an auto parts distributor as a kind of salesman and trouble-shooter whose job took him up and down the coast.

He seemed comfortable in a bar, ordering a drink, getting to know people. Shannon had been sitting with Rhonda and Bullo, and a few minutes after the introductions TeeJay was playing liar's poker with Bullo, then ducking outside for a few minutes to admire Bullo's Harley Davidson Road King. When they returned, Bullo delivered his casual imprimatur: 'This old boy knows bikes.'

Shannon was coming off a year-long thing with a Ph.D. candidate in English lit who wore a fedora and knew a lot about wine. He was handsome, in a bearded, Irish poet kind of way, and brilliant, and he helped with the dishes. They were good together, if a slightly odd match. She sometimes regarded him as an experiment, to see once again if she could fit neatly into the kind of life her parents were living. Since the quest for her own Ph.D. was dead in the water, she should have known the experiment was doomed.

He wanted her to finish her degree and go off somewhere with him to live the life of two happy academics. He couldn't understand how she could be happy cleaning houses. It became an issue. Then one day he mentioned the disparity between the spotlessness of her clients' homes and the disorder of her own place. 'It's almost as if you want to neaten up other people's lives but not your own,' he said.

That did it. She ended the relationship by belittling his choice of dissertation topic. Spenser, for God's sake. *The Faerie Queene.* He moved out, taking his books and his Tom Lehrer albums.

So when dark-eyed, long-haired TeeJay Goss walked into The Nook in his biker boots, a trucker-style wallet chain dangling from his belt, Shannon was ready. She had never really dipped into the blue-collar pool, and it seemed inviting. There was a whiff of something different about him. Not danger, exactly. Adventure, maybe. She'd have to see.

And it went well. They had gone on road trips up to the Bay Area and the Sierra Nevada, camping out sometimes. Neither was very inquisitive about the other, but she learned a few things about him. His name was short for Tommy Joe. He had grown up in Mississippi, was orphaned young, and had lived with relatives. Because of remarks he dropped here and there, she thought he might have been in trouble with the police at one time. He was not very well educated, a fact sometimes reflected in his speech, but he liked to read, which quickly endeared him to her. She sometimes slipped him books she thought he might like.

She discovered his other tattoos, none as large or as dramatic as the forked-tongue dragon. And she showed him hers. Although she liked to think of herself as a transgressive type, she had not given in to the growing practice among younger women of hiding tattoos in the most intimate places. Hers, both modestly sized, could be seen, or partly glimpsed, whenever she went out for a warm-weather run. Just above her left ankle were a pair of swept-back wings copied from a painting of the god Mercury she had found in an art book. To her they represented both the speed of running and the freedom of mind and heart she wished for herself but had never quite found.

And at the base of her neck in back was a yin-yang symbol in crimson and black. She had chosen it simply because she liked it. Later, on reflection, she saw it as representing both the warring sides of her own personality and the balance of the well-ordered life. When the Irish poet had made a mild joke about the symbol, she had told him in a flash of defensiveness that people chose tattoos to represent not necessarily what they had but what they desired.

TeeJay clearly liked her but was sometimes puzzled by her. She had more brains and more education than most women he'd known. Her library fascinated him. He joked occasionally about two of her seemingly contradictory qualities – her fondness for strong drink and her concern with physical fitness, expressed in jogging, yoga, and what was, between lapses, a generally healthy diet.

Sexually, he was experienced, probably more than she, but short on technique. She didn't see that as an insurmountable obstacle.

Two things about him especially suited her. Like her, he was undemanding. And because of his job, he was not always available. They got together whenever they felt like it, once a week or so.

Now, with the darkness outside complete and the stereo turned low, the country voice of Iris DeMent singing about a dying town, she finished the story and stretched, yawning.

'I'm thinkin',' he said, 'it might be a good idea if I stayed over tonight. If you'd like for me to.' He pulled a shiny condom wrapper from his pocket. 'I come prepared.'

'I'm thinkin' the exact same thing,' she said in an approximation of his drawl.

'Don't talk Southern if'n you don't know how.'

'I reckon I'll just have to learn, then, won't I?'

They moved into the bedroom, where she undressed him and made love to him with an aggressive urgency that surprised her. She felt like a dry desert traveler who suddenly came upon a spring and could not drink enough. *In the midst of death*, she thought, *we make love.*

'Speaking of basic human needs,' she murmured in the middle of it all.

'Hmm?'

'*Shhh.*' Afterward they lay in her bed, sharing one last beer. Then, setting the bottle down, she took his hand and said, 'Would you do something?'

'Sure. What?'

'This.' She guided his hand. 'And this. And—' She exhaled almost explosively. 'This.'

He nodded once, smiling faintly, and took over.

She just had time to think: *This old boy learns quick.* Then all thought dissolved into pleasure.

It came for her that night.

Like an old lover. Or enemy. Like one who knows her better than herself, like a former friend who knows when she's at her weakest, it came back.

The nightmare.

It began, as always, with cold, the kind that penetrated deep, that made her bones feel frozen and brittle; that made her shiver without ceasing, the kind of shivering that is indistinguishable from fear.

Then the lights. Bright, soaring, sweeping, sometimes stationary, mostly moving by too fast to identify. Gay and festive, but to her just frightening, because she didn't know what they represented, or where she was.

Then the crying. A symphony of crying, from low sobs to breathless moans to full-out wails. Constant, helpless, and heart-rending.

The cries, of course, were hers.

Finally, the face.

A man, the light behind him, making his hair into a kind of halo and the rest of him into a dark and threatening blob. He's speaking to her, but she can't hear the words for her own sobs. Looming, he leans down, blotting out all light, reaching for her.

Her cries become screams. She can't stop them. They go on and on until she chokes on them, until she can't breathe …

She awoke in the middle of the night, gasping. Lurching out of bed, she made her way into the living room, where she wrapped a blanket around her and sat, shivering, on the couch.

'You okay?' TeeJay asked from the doorway.

'I had a bad dream.'

'What about?'

'Oh, I've had it before. It's hard to describe. I get cold. And there are bright lights. And a man.'

'What does he do?'

'Nothing, really. He just leans over me. And that's where I always wake up.'

She laughed in a dismissive way. 'I know it doesn't sound very scary. It's just that … I haven't had it for a long time. And now it's come back.'

He sat down and put his arm around her. TeeJay didn't always know the right words to say, but she didn't mind. Usually his arm around her was enough. Tonight, however, was different.

The room was lit faintly by the front porch light, and, turning her head, she could just make out the ugly scar that started at his Adam's apple and traced an indirect route up to his left ear. It was the reminder of a close call with the blade of a plow at age twelve, when he had been living on a farm with a foster family and got into a tussle with a friend. The thought of all that blood on the skinny youngster's neck, the terror he must have felt, made her shudder.

They sat that way for a long time until her shivering stopped.

'I just remembered,' she said in a wispy voice. 'My mom and dad. They had something to tell me. I was going over for dinner, and they were going to tell me something.'

'Any idea what?'

'No. But my dad made it sound important. Now I'll never know.'

'Maybe they wanted to tell you what a damn good daughter you've been.'

She just shook her head wearily. *Why bother to dispute that?* she thought. If she'd been a good daughter, she wouldn't feel so full of guilt.

'You want to go back to—' he began, but she interrupted him, saying something in a voice so soft he missed it.

'What?'

'I said I want to kill them.'

'I know.'

'No, you don't. I want to … I'm probably not capable of it. But I want to burn them up. Or something worse.'

'Well,' he said in a casual, throwaway voice. 'Well, then, anything I can do, you just say the word.'

Six

The Faculty Club was full and noisy, warmed by more than a hundred bodies. The cremations had taken place quietly the day before. This was a memorial gathering for Raymond and Mora Fairchild, two of UC San Malo's best-loved teachers.

Although she had grown up around and attended the university, Shannon had never seen this room before. It was a mock-Gothic retreat with deep carpeting, paneled walls, and stained-glass bay windows, where the faculty held teas, awards, and ceremonial dinners and entertained the occasional rich alum or visiting government official. Despite her knee-jerk cynicism, the place impressed her. Well-dressed people stood about sipping wine and eating from a well-stocked table of finger food.

She stood by a plaque-lined wall wearing an unaccustomed black dress and high heels and holding a glass of wine. It was her third. Her feet were beginning to ache. Although not an expert at makeup, she had done a reasonably good job of covering up the remnants of her bruises. TeeJay, his long hair tied in a ragged ponytail, wore a denim sport jacket he had dug out of the back of his closet. One by one, those in the crowd gravitated to her spot to express sympathies. A lot of them she knew. Some had taught her, some had studied alongside her. One of the well-wishers was her old Ph.D. candidate boyfriend. He kissed her cheek and held her hand, and it was good to see him. He gave TeeJay a firm handshake and a mildly questioning look and moved on.

Beth and Richard stood nearby, with Scamp and Chipper, their blond surfer-boy cowlicks tamed by comb and water, looking uncomfortable in their miniature suits. Beth spoke animatedly with two of her old professors. She had majored in art history, and i junior year her husband-hunting radar had detected a handsome business major named Richard Kinsey. Now, it was fair to say, she was happy and fulfilled. It was also fair to say, Shannon reflected, that she was a good wife and mother and had no doubt made her parents proud.

Ralph Giddings, the university president, stepped up to a microphone-rigged lectern under the largest window and spoke eloquently for a few minutes about the university's loss.

Shannon barely knew Giddings, and she only half-focused on his words. Standing there amid the gentlemen's-club atmosphere, she again felt the shape of the world that had once held an attraction for her, the world she might have joined. If she had tackled that dissertation, she could have been faculty today. Assistant, maybe even Associate Professor Fairchild, holding classrooms rapt with her concise take on the fall of the Roman Republic or the swing between liberalism and nationalism in the French Revolution. Her favorite students would drop by her office in the late afternoons, and they'd talk about life and academia. Some of the young guys would quietly lust after her, because she'd be a babe, no doubt about it, well into middle age.

What had happened? To this day, she didn't know for sure. Only that as soon as she realized she was within spitting range of a Ph.D., she became frightened. Of what? Not of the dissertation. She knew she could nail it.

Then what? Well, of replicating her parents' lives, for one thing, of dutifully following the trail they'd blazed. And what was wrong with that? Was it so freaking important to be different, not to be like them? She'd never been able to answer that.

She returned to the present as a much more familiar figure stepped up to the lectern.

'This community has lost a piece of its soul,' Peter Bridger began ... 'Ray and Mora were scholars, teachers, friends to all of us.'

... still a few years shy of sixty, Bridger had the complete ... stooped posture, the ill-fitting suit, the baldness ... fringe around his ears. He had guided her ... Italian humanism and the conflict ... the Greek city-state and had consulted with her on her dissertation. Shannon felt a rush of remembered affection at the sight of him.

'I'm lucky to have known them longer than most of you,' Bridger went on, 'from their college days at Ann Arbor, when the three of us were young, questioning, and full of the fire of youth. I believe it was nineteen sixty-eight when I met them – my junior year. I was more the scholarly drudge even then, but those two …' He paused and smiled broadly. 'Those two wanted to drink the cup of life down to the dregs. They loved learning, but their passion was for all of life, for justice, and it sometimes took them into the streets, where some of the best of our youth carried the fight.'

'What's he talking about?' TeeJay whispered.

'I'm not sure.'

Bridger spoke for a while about their teaching careers, then finished by saying, 'Our love and sympathies are with their daughters, Shannon and Elizabeth, both of them alumnae, and their grandsons. We celebrate the lives of Raymond and Mora Fairchild.' He raised his glass, and the crowd followed the gesture.

He stepped away from the lectern, and the conversation level rose again. Deserting TeeJay for a minute, Shannon made her way to the area behind the lectern, where a montage of photos had been set up. She saw her parents through the stages of their lives and careers, going back to their college graduation pictures. One picture was a family snapshot taken in front of the house when she was about fifteen and Beth about twelve. She studied the photo, noting how tiny Beth seemed and how compact her smiling parents looked next to their already gawky teenage daughter.

'We miss you.'

'Hmm?' She turned around to find Bridger smiling at her, his shiny head tilted at the odd, birdlike angle she remembered. She kissed him on the cheek.

'We miss you,' he said again. 'We talk about you in the department every now and then. We say you're one of those who got away, and we wish you'd come back and finish that Ph.D. Never too late, you know. As I recall, you and I had picked out a dissertation topic …' He paused, and she knew he was searching his memory for the title.

She prompted him. '"The Sisters of Madame DeFarge: Th

of Women in the French Revolution,"' she said wryly. 'But that's all behind me now.'

'I'm sorry to hear that. What are you doing with yourself, Shannon?'

'I have a house-cleaning business.'

'Uh-huh.' His smile was non-judgmental. 'Well, I'll wager you're the best house cleaner in the state of California.' He touched her arm lightly. 'But we need scholars and teachers even more.'

He seemed about to add something, but then glanced to his left. 'I think this young lady wants to talk to you, so I'll give you up.' He pressed her hand and left.

'Are you Shannon?' The woman was a thin, slightly breathless blonde wearing flat-heeled shoes and an unbuttoned sweater over a plain dress. Her angular face was somewhere between pretty and plain. 'I'm Lonnie Brown. I'm doing graduate work in poli sci here, and I studied under your mother. She was my favorite. I miss her terribly.'

'Thank you.'

'It was an awful thing. I cried the day I heard.' The woman was about Shannon's age – one of these thirty-something graduate students, Shannon thought, the kind who never want to leave the groves of academe.

'I just want you to know how much I was affected by her death and how special she was.' Her eyes seemed unusually bright – the eyes, Shannon thought, of someone with strong interests, strong passions.

'It's nice of you to say that.' Shannon looked around for TeeJay. Time to leave.

'Do you think we might get together for coffee some time? Talking with you would almost be like staying in contact with her. You know?'

Shannon turned her full attention to the woman. Her posture was a little tense, and her smile seemed a permanent fixture. Even if she was harmless, the last thing Shannon wanted to do was reminisce [illegible] her mother with an over-eager stranger.

[illegible] There's just too much going on right now. I hope you [illegible]

[illegible]red, but only for a second. 'I do,' she said. [illegible]nd left.

[illegible]ialized at her side.

'Oh, nobody. One of my mother's students. She wanted to get together, and I told her I didn't have time.'

'Little old for a student, isn't she? I'll get together with her.'

'Bet you would.'

'Look at this.' He pointed to one of the photos in the display behind her. It showed a young Ray and Mora, roughly dressed and marching with others at the head of a ragged formation on a city street. Ray held a flag aloft by its staff, and Mora thrust a fist into the air. Their faces were alive with energy, and they looked both brave and frightened.

'What are they up to?' TeeJay asked.

'Beats me,' Shannon said, leaning in for a better look. 'Some kind of a demonstration, I guess.'

'So they were the demonstrating type back then.'

'I guess. They hardly ever talked about it.' Shannon took his arm and turned to leave, but stopped for one last glance back at the photo. Something about it disturbed and excited her. It must have been the look on her parents' faces, a look she had never seen them wear.

As they began to make their way through the thinning crowd, she glanced toward the doorway at the far end of the long room. A man was going out, a big man, slightly stooped, with thinning hair and an oversize coat. Sighting him, she felt the sense-memory of a painful grip on her arm.

She pushed her way through and around people, trying to get to the door. When she reached it twenty seconds later, she stood at the top of the steps and looked out over the campus, scannin ach figure she saw on the walkways.

TeeJay caught up with her. 'What?' he asked, s g a little exasperated.

'I thought I saw someone.' Troubled looked left to right but spotted no one familiar. 'No shaking her head. 'Couldn't have been.'

Seven

On the surface, Shannon's life settled into something resembling its old rhythm. She went back to her cleaning business, where she and Priss, the young woman who assisted her, had to quicken their pace to make up for Shannon's recent lapses. The Clean Machine cut a swath through the upscale neighborhoods of San Malo, leaving behind buffed floors, sparkling tile, and the scent of pine, lemon, and ammonia.

After printing one vaguely worded story about the murders, the city's newspaper returned to the usual local issues – rising real estate prices, Tinseltown celebs making the San Malo party circuit, the latest charity wingding. Even though Shannon was relieved that she didn't have to see the awful memory rehashed in print, still she was surprised. Granted, the local paper was a rag, a vanity publication run by one of the town's land barons who used it mainly to promote his business interests and his friends' social lives. But still … The crime was an extraordinary one, the victims beloved citizens. She would have thought their lives and deaths would have been worth more ink.

She r[illegible]ated to The Nook, promising Garrett the bartender she'd be good, [illegible] once again allowed to take her place with the regulars. Everyone had heard about the murders. Garrett slid her a rum and Co[illegible] asked, saying, 'On the house.'

Rhonda came over [illegible] her two days in the county lockup and emerged to hea[illegible] 'Oh, hon,' she said, giving Shannon's shoulder a muscul[illegible] thing to happen. What a thing.' It was hardly eloqu[illegible] felt.

On another day, she sat in her accu[illegible] [illegible]tiago's office for a long forty-five minutes, talking [illegible] sudden deaths in her life as Elva murmured h[illegible]

'I know you're supposed to grieve,' Shannon told her. 'I'm not sure I've ever gotten around to that. Real grief, I mean. This doesn't feel like it.'

'Everyone grieves differently,' Elva replied. The therapist, as usual, was wearing a flowing, ethnic-looking robe, and her office smelled heavily of something Shannon associated with wind-chime souvenir shops.

'I've just realized that I'm no longer somebody's child,' Shannon said. 'So I'm really a grown-up now. About time, huh?'

She made a joke of it because she wasn't ready to tell Elva just how deep her feelings ran. All through her life, through good family relations and bad, her parents had been Shannon's twin anchors. Sometimes disapproving, sometimes saddened by her choices, but always loving, always encouraging. Now she was adrift in strong current, and she was only beginning to feel the existential chill that went along with that realization.

Elva, who had spoken little during the meeting, touched Shannon's shoulder as she left. 'I think you should come in for an extra session this week,' she said. 'How about Friday at two?' She looked as if there was something unexpressed on her mind.

TeeJay took off on another of his out-of-town jobs, this one down in San Diego County, return date undetermined. Shannon called Detective Orlando every day, and for a while he encouraged her with talk about men he had questioned, most of them young Latinos with prison records or questionable documentation. But none of it panned out, and after a while she stopped calling. As unbelievable it might have seemed a few days earlier, she was beginning to make room for the possibility that the savagery that took her parents' lives might never be completely explained.

Beth called to talk about things that needed doing.

'We should clean out their offices at the university,' she said. 'I've talked to the administration and they're expecting us, but no hurry. I'll take Mom's if you take Dad's.'

'Okay.'

They discussed what to do with the family property. After years of feeling on … family, Shannon knew she was now being asked to reenter what was left of it, to carry her share of responsibility. She felt unprepared.

The charred remnants of the house, they decided, would have to be bulldozed and the lot eventually put up for sale. Then there was the question of the garage and its contents.

'I thought everything burned,' Shannon said.

'No. The boys and I drove by just yesterday. There was that walkway alongside the house, remember? The fire just kind of scorched the side of the garage. I imagine it's still full of stuff – you know what pack rats Mom and Dad were. Maybe we should have a yard sale.'

'Fine with me.'

'We need to see if there's anything valuable we want to keep. Would you mind?'

'Look, I don't—'

'Richard's working extra hard these days, and I think Skipper is coming down with a cold. Could you just go over and look around? Let us know what's there.' A plaintive wail from one of the boys in the background. 'Got to go. Thanks, Shan.'

'Great,' she said, hanging up. She stood in her kitchen for a moment, trying to decide whether to go right away or wait a day, when she heard a knock at the front door.

Opening it but leaving the screen locked, she saw a young man, neatly dressed. 'Good afternoon,' he said. 'I'm Special Agent Tim Dodd, with the Federal Bureau of Investigation. Are you Shannon Fair...ild?' She nodded. 'May I speak with you for a moment?' He slid a ca... through the gap in the doorway, and she looked it over. Next to an ... [em]bossed seal of the Department of Justice, the card confirmed his id... stood a... Behind him, down where her entry path met the sidewalk, ...an, older and heavier.

'Do you have some ... badge? Don't FBI agents carry badges?'

'I sure do.' He produced a wa... gold bad... open, and pressed it against the screen. Photo ID,

'Just like in the movies,' she said, unloc... looked in order.

'Yes, ma'am.' He had a nice smile, and ... crush on in... of a track star named Owen she had had a jumper. Tim Dodd probably could have gotten in with just the card, she thought.

The agent beckoned to the other man, who trudged up the path to the porch, and they came inside. 'This is Harold Birdsong. He's retired from the Bureau, and he consults with us.'

'Sit anywhere,' she said, indicating the jumble of sofa, chairs, and cushions. Shannon was not the sort to apologize for a messy room.

'You like to read,' Birdsong said, eyeing the floor-to-ceiling bookshelves that took up most of the wall space in the living room. 'And listen to music,' he added, pointing to her stereo rig, which included an old-style phonograph, and her stacks of CDs, audiotapes, and vinyl. His voice was a lazy mumble as befit his rumpled appearance, a stark contrast to his companion's youth and energy.

The comments didn't seem to require an answer, so she took her seat. Since they were in no hurry to get to the point, she began. 'You're the first FBI people I've ever met,' she said. 'What's it about?'

'Your mother and father,' Dodd replied. He sat military-straight, perched on the edge of her sofa.

'Yeah?'

'Our sympathies over the loss of your parents. We've been in contact with the San Malo Police Department. Detective …' He consulted a pocket notebook. 'Orlando. He's been helpful. We've spoken with some of the faculty at the university.'

'What about? Wait a minute.' She shook her head, confused, then looked again at the card she still held, noting this time the address in fine print at the bottom.

'You drove all the way up here from LA to look into two murders?'

'Yes, ma'am.'

'Why is the FBI interested?'

'We think there may be a connection between the murders of your parents and a federal case we've been working on.'

'Which would be?' She heard the first hint of impatience in her voice.

'I wish I could give you the details, but I can't. At least not at this point. I'd just like to ask you some questions, if you don't mind. Your answers could help us. If we're wrong, we won't bother you again.'

She stared at him, then over at Birdsong. The retired agent, who looked like an older and much jowlier version of Detective Orlando, seemed content to listen. He had unwisely chosen her basket chair to sit in and was sunk so deep she wondered if he might have trouble extricating himself. He looked back at her from under heavy eyelids, showing nothing.

'I don't like being mysterious,' Dodd continued. 'If this connection we're wondering about turns into anything, then at some point we can be more open with you.' He spread his palms wide. 'All right?'

'Is this about who killed them?'

He shot Birdsong the briefest glance, then said, 'Yes.'

'Then ask anything.'

He paged back and forth in his little notebook. 'Did your parents talk to you much about their college days?'

'Not much. I know they went to the University of Michigan, and they both did graduate work here at UC San Malo.'

'Do you know if they were active politically?'

'I think they were. Just the other day I saw a picture of them taken at some kind of march or demonstration. And I remember my mom saying they both showed up at the Democratic Convention in Chicago in … ' She searched her memory for the date.

'Nineteen sixty-eight?'

'That's right.'

'Do you know if they belonged to SDS – Students for a Democratic Society?'

She nodded. 'I think they mentioned that to me once.'

'And what did they do in Chicago?'

'I have no idea. Marched, I suppose. They were against the Vietnam War, like most people their age. I've seen some movies about Chicago. So they probably marched, chanted, maybe sang some peace songs. Is this important?'

'Do you know if they were involved in any fights with the police there?'

She hesitated, less pleased with the direction their conversation was taking. 'In the movies I saw, it was the police who picked the fights. But if I had to guess, I'd say no. My parents were pretty peaceable, both of them.'

Another page in the notebook. 'Do you remember anything about your parents' friends while you were growing up? Especially friends who may have been from out of town?'

She sat back, crossed her legs, and looked up at the ceiling, thinking. Hazy figures moved in her memory, but she couldn't put faces to them. 'When I was little. Every now and then. I don't really remember … Wait: One was my uncle Don. My father's brother.'

'That would be Don Fairchild?'

'I suppose. He came for a long visit when I was around eight. But he died a few years later, so I didn't get to know him well.'

'Do you happen to know where he lived?'

'New York, I think.'

'Do you remember any others?'

'Nope. I mean no names, and barely faces. Just some grown-ups who showed up a few times. I'd be playing some game on the floor. They'd sit and talk and then leave.' She shrugged. 'I suppose that's not much help.'

Another page. 'Do you remember if your parents ever talked about going to Cuba with a group of students?'

She gave Dodd a long look. 'Cuba?'

'Yes, ma'am. As part of a—'

'You mean were they Communists?'

'I'm not sure that every student who went to Cuba was a Communist.'

'Is this about who killed them or about whether they were good Americans?'

'Miss Fairchild—'

'Oh, hell.' She stood up. 'Maybe you're trying to find out who killed them. But I don't like the sound of this. If you don't mind, I think I'll just work with the local police.'

'They don't have the tools we have,' Dodd said, rising from the sofa.

'They don't have the agenda you have either. Excuse me, will you? I've got things to do.'

Dodd went out the door. Birdsong, after a protracted struggle, emerged from the basket chair a little breathlessly. As he passed her on the way to the door, he said quietly, 'You've got every right.'

'Hmm?'

'If I'd just lost my parents, I wouldn't feel like answering anyone's questions either.' He tried to smooth out his lapels, a losing battle. 'The Bureau has procedures it needs to follow. They go by the book. I'm not on the regular payroll any more, so I've got a little more freedom. Less red tape, you know?'

'What are you consulting with them about?'

'An old case.' He patted most of his pockets and came up with a card. It bore just his name and a phone number. 'That's my cell. You can reach me any time.'

His face, she thought, was not unkind. He looked like a man who had known some sadness.

'Why should I want to reach you?'

'Because we really do want to find out who killed your parents. And when the federal government's on your side, you've got a powerful ally.'

'Like I said—'

'You'll work with your own police force. That's fine. I may check in with you from time to time. I hope you'll keep my card, just in case. Never know if you might need it.' He offered a pudgy hand, then was gone.

Eight

Shannon had once enjoyed the smell of burned wood. But as she stood in her old front yard, regarded the blackened jumble of the house where she had grown up, and inhaled the stench still rising from the ground, she knew that from now on it would represent for her the smell of death.

She turned toward the garage. The door was closed, but she noted that the hasp that had held the lock at the base of the door was broken, and a strip of yellow police tape had apparently been torn away and now lay crumpled on the concrete driveway. The police may have broken the lock, she surmised, but if they had removed the tape, why hadn't they taken it away?

The door went up with a jerky protest, then lodged itself overhead. She stepped inside. It was semi-dark there and, as she had feared, the electric light no longer worked, but she had brought a flashlight. She shone it around.

Everything was in disarray.

Beth was right about their parents being pack rats, but this was more than that. Things that had once been stacked in boxes on both sides of the garage had been pulled off their shelves and dumped onto the floor. Shining the light carefully, Shannon picked her way among the debris, occasionally bending over to examine something. Books, old clothes, hubcaps, sleeping bags, bottled water, an oscillating fan, rolls of paper towels. A framed oil painting of a landscape that she remembered vaguely from years ago. A radio with a crack in its plastic shell.

After ten minutes she knew there was nothing valuable there. Just a lifetime's accumulation of things. Seeing them strewn on the floor made her first sad, and then angry. Who would trash the place like this? Surely not the police. Could the people who killed them have done this first, looking for something? Then she remembered the discarded police tape and the broken lock and wondered: *Could they have come back later, to do a more thorough search? And if so, for what?*

The light fell on a cardboard box that had lost only part of its contents, and she recognized some familiar articles. Toys and mementos from her early years, and Beth's too. A soccer ball, now flattened, that she had kicked endlessly around the backyard; a doll Beth had loved, most of its hair now missing; a few picture books. A memory tugged at her, and she dug through the small stack of books, looking for one in particular. She almost missed it, because it had lost its front and back covers and some inside pages too. But there it was. She lifted it out and flipped through it, awkwardly holding the flashlight wedged between chin and shoulder.

A little girl, about the age Shannon had been when she first opened these pages, passes her time dejectedly in an orphanage in Elizabethan England until her true father, a pirate king, returns from a long voyage and, as promised, carries her away. Her new life is one long adventure, sailing the Spanish Main, sparing English ships while they raid the enemies of Good Queen Elizabeth. At first she is confined to simple tasks aboard ship – cooking, cleaning, and wielding a deft needle to repair torn trousers and doublets. But soon she's allowed to trade needle for cutlass, and she proves as brave as any man aboard ship. The final pages were missing, but Shannon vividly remembered the ending: The girl saves her father's life, she is hailed as his new first mate, and they sail off together in search of gold and adventure.

The only thing she couldn't quite remember was the title. *The Pirate Girl*? No, but something like that. The book was a touchstone for her, a sign that girls could have adventures just like boys, and she threw herself into the fantasy. In those years, the back yard was her quarterdeck and the sweet gum tree her mainmast.

Drifting, her mind took her back to a spring day when the back yard rang to the imaginary sounds of cannon fire and the ring of pirate steel. Wielding her plywood sword, Shannon bounded up a rope ladder to the lowest limb of the sweet gum tree and, employing the choicest of pirate oaths, dared Beth to follow. Beth, who was seven, did her best but slipped and fell to the ground on her back. Unpiratical wailing ensued.

Shannon feared punishment, and her mother came down the back steps with a grim set to her mouth. But after calming Beth's tears, she simply took Shannon aside and said, 'I don't mind you being a pirate. I'd be one too, if I were your age. But every pirate captain needs a first mate, and first mates have to be carefully trained. Look how much Beth wants to follow you. If you show her how to climb that ladder – and all the other things she needs to do – you'll have a great first mate. See what I mean?'

She did. Their games thereafter were not always without incident, but Shannon remembered her mother's words. Funny, she'd never realized how much Beth wanted to follow her …

She looked around the dimly lit jumble of belongings, all that was left of her parents' physical world. She felt immensely sad. And underpinning her sadness was a toxic layer of guilt. *I couldn't wait to separate myself from them*, she thought. *To move on, to be free. All because of this feeling that I was odd, different, that I could never measure up*. But her sessions with Elva had begun to teach her that those feelings came from within and did not reflect reality. Her parents had loved her and tried to stand by her, even when she had made it hard for them to do so. Somewhere along the way, she should have had the grace to thank them.

'Too late for that,' she muttered.

'Too late for what?'

Startled, she dropped the book and turned. A silhouette stood in the garage doorway outlined against the brightness.

'Ohhh.' A sympathetic sound. 'I feel like I'm interrupting. You must be going through your family's things. It's a sad job, isn't it?'

The figure advanced and turned into the young woman from the memorial: Lonnie something. Lonnie Brown. She wore jeans and work boots and a denim shirt, tail out.

'Wow. Dark in here.' She looked around. 'Can I help?'

'No, thanks.'

Lonnie's sleeves were partly rolled up, and Shannon glimpsed old bruises on the underside of one forearm. As before, the woman gave off an odd vibe – a kind of high-strung, over-friendly pushiness – and once again Shannon felt uneasy.

Lonnie looked around, made a whistling sound. 'Whoa, you've really got a mess here. I honestly wouldn't mind helping you—'

'I said no thanks,' Shannon repeated, dropping any pretense at politeness. 'This is not a good time.'

'Oh, I think it's a perfectly good time.' Lonnie took a step closer, still smiling.

'What?' Shannon fought the urge to back away. She began to feel a touch of menace from the other woman, like a sour smell.

'Trouble with you is, when somebody reaches out a helping hand, you slap it away. I'd call that unfriendly.' The smile was still there, but devoid of any good will. The eyes above the smile brightened merrily.

Shannon assessed the situation. She had several pounds on Lonnie, along with a couple of inches of reach. She had never been afraid of another woman. Still, she knew that in violent situations, physical advantage could sometimes be canceled out by another quality. For want of a more specific term, one could call it pure meanness. She sensed that it was something Lonnie possessed, and she tried to prepare herself for trouble.

She moved slightly to her left and back, placing a sizable pile of junk between the two of them. As she did so, Lonnie made a countermove that gave her a new avenue through the clutter.

The woman was stalking her. Fear began to take hold, like a small voice speaking to her, and she despised herself for hearing it. She made one last attempt at boldness. 'Get the fuck out of my garage.'

'What's the matter? Afraid?'

'Not of you.'

'Fibber.' Lonnie's head made a wagging motion. 'Big fat fibber.' Then, in a singsong, schoolyard voice, *'Shan-non is a-frai-aid.'*

She pulled the edge of her shirt back just enough to expose the hilt of a knife in a scabbard. 'Y'see, I came prepared. But I don't think I'll need it.' A maniacal grin. 'I can handle you without it.'

Feeling fear blossom, like something hot in her stomach, Shannon looked around for something to throw. The only thing at hand was a moldy sleeping bag at her feet. Stooping, she grasped it by its strap and flung it at the intruder – who simply batted it away and came for her.

The woman caught her in the midsection with a bony shoulder and drove her painfully into a metal shelf. Then, raising her head quickly – and Shannon this time saw the wild, open eyes and what almost looked like bared teeth – came up with the heel of her hand under Shannon's chin, cracking her teeth together and wrenching her head back.

Shannon flailed wildly with her fists, but it was not enough. Still blinded by the blow to her chin, she felt the other woman spin her around by the shoulders, then grasp her right wrist with both hands, swing it down and then sharply up between her shoulder blades.

Shannon yelled once but felt her breath cut off by the rush of pain that gripped her shoulder. Lonnie wrapped her left arm around Shannon's neck, using her forearm as a bar against her neck, cutting off more wind. She jammed her captive up against the shelves.

'*Ow*. God.' The words came out involuntarily. Shannon couldn't remember this kind of pain.

'*Ow* is right.' Lonnie sounded almost giddy with delight. 'I could dislocate your shoulder real easy. And I will. In, uh, let's say ten seconds. If you don't tell me where they are.'

'What? Who? I don't know—' The hand went up an inch. '*Ahhh!*'

'Wrong answer, bitch. Girly-girl.' The woman's mouth was at her ear now, whispering. For all her thinness, she was surprisingly, frightfully strong. Shannon felt fear cover her like a blanket, like a damp fog. She knew the woman could do what she said she could do, and the prospect of that kind of yet-undiscovered pain sickened her.

'Who?' Shannon's voice was a whisper too. They could be two girlfriends, sharing muted secrets in a dark garage. 'Just tell me, please. Who do you want?'

'Nadja and Ernesto. I'm going to start counting now. One, two—'

'Oh, God. Listen. I don't know those people. How can I—'

'Three, four ...' She was counting in a little girl's voice, and she pressed herself up tight against the length of Shannon's body. 'Five, six ...'

Shannon heard a futile moan gathering in her throat. She gritted her teeth, wondering how she could stand it. She couldn't.

'Seven, eight …' The hand crept up another half-inch, and Shannon made a keening sound through her nose. She closed her eyes, and deliriously imagined wild animals gathering around her …

Wait. It was a real animal. A dog. Barking his fool head off. Then a voice.

'Everything okay in there?'

Shannon was able to turn her head one painful inch to her left, far enough to make out two more silhouettes in the doorway. A man with a dog on a leash. A big and vicious-sounding dog.

'I said everything okay in there?' The man's voice was insistent. He had seen something from the sidewalk. But how much?

'I'm scared of dogs,' Lonnie called out in a theatrically hysterical tone. 'Take him away.'

'What are you doing to her?' The man took a step closer.

'Oh, fuck.' This was said in a final whisper to Shannon. 'You're just so lucky. Next time you'll tell me, won't you, girly?' Lonnie released her grip, turned on her heel, sprinted past man and dog, and was gone.

'Quiet, Zeus,' the man commanded, and the dog, a bristling German shepherd, fell silent.

Shannon collapsed on the littered floor, taking deep breaths, her right arm throbbing and useless. She felt awash in anger and humiliation.

The man approached her. 'What happened? Are you all right?' He pulled out a cell phone. 'Should I call nine-one-one?'

She let a breath out noisily. A sign reading *Don't tell police* flashed before her eyes but was pushed away by the pain in her shoulder and the accompanying thoughts of sweet, sweet vengeance.

'Nine-one-one would be really nice.'

Nine

The two uniformed officers, neither as old as Shannon, were polite, but she could almost hear the calculations being run in their heads. *Two females. They know each other. Sounds like a little hair-pulling between neighbors.*

This one's got a minor record and is on probation. But the dog walker says it looked like the other one was the attacker, so …

'Ma'am, you should let us take you to the hospital first, get somebody to look at that shoulder.'

'Nope.' She spoke through clenched teeth, shaking her head, feeling particularly stubborn. She knew she was being irrational, refusing medical help after having the police called, but rationality was not her strong suit at the moment.

It took half an hour to work her way up through the bureaucracy, but eventually she found herself seated next to Detective Orlando's cluttered desk at the San Malo Police Headquarters, giving him a play-by-play.

'She asked me about two people. She said I knew where they were, and she'd break my shoulder if I didn't tell her.' Cradling her right arm in her lap, Shannon felt a chill as she put the experience into words. Lonnie was right: *You're just so lucky.*

'What two people?'

'Ernesto and somebody – I don't remember the other name.'

'Can you try to remember?'

'I've tried. I was a little preoccupied at the time, and I wasn't processing information the way people normally do.'

'Right.'

'On the way over here, I was thinking. Ernesto sounds Hispanic. You've been looking at Latinos, haven't you? For the murders.'

'Among others.'

'Well, maybe Lonnie's connected in some way, and maybe she's looking for the killers too.'

'Why would she think you know—'

'Where they are? Beats me.'

He looked dubious. 'I won't rule anything out. But let's stick to what's important right now, like finding this Lonnie.' He checked a phone number under the glass on his desk, dialed it, and was on the phone for a few minutes. As he spoke, she took her first leisurely look at him in the light of day. His tanned and trim look contrasted with his graying hair, which was cut almost military-style. He looked like a man who worked hard to stay fit and presentable, a man who would not go gentle into late middle age.

She let her eyes roam, idly comparing the detectives' cubicles to the 'cop shops' she'd seen on TV. She decided that this room was quieter. Men and a few women sat doing paperwork or talking on telephones, and except for the sight of a holstered handgun here and there, these people might have been insurance adjusters.

'That was the registrar at UCSM,' Orlando said as he hung up. 'There's no Lonnie Brown registered in any of the schools. No female Browns with any first name that could be a variation of Lonnie.'

'She's not a student,' Shannon said slowly. 'I guess I should have caught on faster. She lied to me about studying under my mother.'

Another thought caused her face to go slack.

'You remember something?' he asked.

'No, not exactly. Just thinking. If she's capable of this— '

'Could she have been part of the murders?'

Shannon nodded, swallowing, beginning to feel vaguely sick. *This woman who whispered in my ear, who called me girly-girl. Was she one of those who cut off my mother's and father's fingers and then killed them?*

'The FBI came to see me,' she said. 'About my parents. Do you know why they're involved?'

'Yeah. We can talk about that in a minute.' He reached in a drawer and pulled out a form. 'This Lonnie, though. Give me a description of her, and include every little thing you can remember.'

'All right.'

That took five minutes. Orlando typed the information onto a form. 'We'll put the word out,' he said. 'Murderer or not, she sounds dangerous. If she's in the city, we'll find her.'

'What do I do in the meantime?'

'We'll have a patrol stop by your house on a regular basis.'

'That's it?'

'That's all we have the manpower for.'

'What about my sister's house?'

'Hmm?'

'They should check on my sister's place, too. We don't know that I'm the only one this crazy woman's after. And my sister has children.'

He hesitated only a moment. 'Fine. There are things you can do, too. Be careful. Check your windows and doors. Try not to go anyplace alone, especially after dark. Carry a phone with you. All common-sense stuff.'

She wasn't convinced. 'Should I get a gun?'

'We don't advise people to do that, especially if they don't know firearms,' he said. 'And, as you probably know, there's a waiting period to buy a weapon. But if it makes you feel safer, by all means.'

'You know something? I think it would.' She uncrossed and re-crossed her legs, wincing as the weight of her arm dragged at her shoulder. 'The bigger and louder the better. Now what about the FBI?'

'Right.' She saw a new expression on his face and at first could not read it. But as he began to speak, she knew it for what it was: discomfort.

'I'm afraid they weren't very forthcoming,' Orlando said. 'It's some old federal case, and they seemed not totally sure about your parents' connection. But they were sure enough to want to take over the case.'

He paused, and she realized that his eyes no longer met hers – they went idly around the room, spending a few seconds on a far bulletin board, a passing cop, her knees by his desk.

'What does that mean?'

'They've claimed jurisdiction,' he went on, pulling a ballpoint pen out of his shirt pocket and rolling it between thumb and fingers. 'We've given it to them. You've got federal agents looking for whoever killed your parents. I think that's good news for you.'

'Well . . .'

'One more thing.' A smile appeared to hurt his face. 'Those things I told you the other night, the details about the crime scene. The cut fingers. That was premature. It was based on a couple of quick conversations I had at the hospital. I jumped to a conclusion, something I usually try not to do. I apologize if I misled you. You shouldn't repeat those things to anyone.'

'What?' She began to squirm in her chair. Something felt wrong. 'I want you to handle this, not some FBI guys from LA.'

'I'm sorry. It's out of our hands.'

She forced herself to sit still. Her face felt hot with anger.

'Is this . . .?' She swallowed hard. 'Is this the reason the newspaper paid almost no attention to it? Is somebody trying to keep this quiet?'

'No.' Still his eyes looked away. Despite all this, she found herself liking him. *A decent cop*, she thought. *A terrible liar.*

Another painful smile. 'I have to get back to work.'

She was already out of her chair. 'Bet you do.'

Ten

The cup of hot tea was a tip-off.

In the year that Shannon had been coming to the clinic, Elva Santiago had never offered her anything to drink. Their sessions had been conducted strictly by the numbers, therapist and client, until today. When Elva offered her the tea, Shannon had a feeling this was going to be no ordinary meeting.

Elva took a good ten minutes to lay it out. She started by nibbling around the edges, but by the time she had finished, there was no doubt about the shape of her theory. There it sat, like an elephant in the room, huge and ponderous and impossible to ignore.

'Abused?' Shannon's face registered her shock. 'You mean in a sexual way.'

'I doubt that we'll ever know for sure,' Elva said. Her round face was slightly flushed, a sign that this had not been easy for her either. 'Unless some adult who had knowledge came forward. Otherwise, it's just a theory. But when you think about it, it explains a lot. Your nightmare, of course. The fear it brings out in you every time you experience it, even now as an adult. The dark figure of a man leaning over you – that's a classic image in childhood sexual abuse.'

'Well, maybe, but—'

'And the feeling of being an outsider, someone who didn't belong in your own family. You've told me you had this feeling as long as you can remember.'

Shannon gripped the fabric of the sofa on both sides of her knees. This didn't sound right. It couldn't be right.

'Your reluctance to follow your father and mother into teaching, even after all the work you did toward a degree. The anger you've expressed, both as a child and as an adult. The way you acted out against your parents, as if to distance yourself from them. It's really pretty common, Shannon. We sometimes see it in kids who are adopted, and we see it in kids who've been molested. You're not adopted.'

'I haven't been molested either. Don't you think I would know?'

'I'm not sure you would. It's the sort of thing a little girl would repress, would push down so deep it would eventually be forgotten.'

'I push it down, and then later I pull it out? Why would I do that?'

Elva put on a patient look. 'I've been doing some reading in the literature. There are two kinds of memory – what some people call autobiographical memory, the normal kind, where people can recall events and put them into words. And then there's another kind, an earlier kind, where a very young child might be imprinted with a strong experience – a trauma, for example – but not have the capacity to evaluate it or even the words to describe it. Such a memory might be buried for years, and when it resurfaces, it's not as a narrative but more as something the way a child would experience it. Sounds, maybe. Or intense physical feelings. Pain. Cold. Fright.'

Shannon sat with arms crossed, wearing a stubborn look. 'Let's say something happened. We don't know it was sexual abuse. But something happened. Why would it wait until age nine or ten to resurface? That's when I started having the nightmare.'

'I just don't know. Maybe something triggered it. We could try going back to that age and ask if—'

'My father couldn't have done anything like that.' Shannon interrupted her, shaking her head over and over.

'We don't know it was your father. Research shows that in many cases the abuse comes from a family friend.'

'This is bullshit.'

'I'm sorry, but I had to bring this up. It's only a theory, and I've tried to be careful about raising it with you. What I've suggested could explain several things, but it's only an idea. You need to ask yourself if it has any relevance to you.'

Shannon's gaze swept the small room, as if she were looking for someone to whom she could appeal. A higher court. A second opinion. Her eyes swept over the books on the shelves, the titles dealing with hypnotherapy and regression theories and chakras. Once again she noted that Elva's framed master's degree in marriage and family therapy came from an institution Shannon didn't know. San Malo was a hive of high-priced therapists, and the main reason Shannon had picked Elva was that she was young, just starting out, and affordable.

'You get what you pay for,' Shannon muttered.

'I'm sorry?'

'Nothing.' She stood up. 'I need time to think about this.'

A minute later she stood outside clinic, breathing deeply. It was another typical sparkling day, one of the city's winter trademarks, and the unpleasant thoughts triggered by her talk with Elva receded in the bright sunshine.

Her gaze roamed idly around the clinic's mock-Spanish exterior. The city officials of San Malo had decided decades ago that much of their city's charm came from its Mediterranean-style architecture. From that day, any new construction had to adhere to a particular look – white stucco, wood beams, red tile roofs. Visitors thought it looked charming. A few residents, Shannon among them, thought it looked cookie-cutter-style, a place almost too perfect, like something put together just for tourists.

What this town needs, she once told TeeJay, is one of those modern Bilbao-type things, a building that looks like it exploded and is going to rain shrapnel down on everybody.

Now, after Elva's words, the shrapnel imagery had new meaning for her. She felt wounded. The idea of her father molesting her when she was small, the idea of her parents being so criminally careless as to let another adult do that to her – it was unthinkable. A final, unnecessary attack on the names of two good people no longer around to defend themselves.

What if it did explain her isolation, her odd-girl-out feeling since childhood? There could be other explanations. Whatever the answer, this cut-rate therapist had not found it.

And what a terrible sense of timing, to spring this on her just a few days after her parents were murdered. Shannon knew Elva had had this theory cooking for a while and seemed reluctant to talk about it until now. Maybe, she thought, her father's death had given her a kind of opening. If the father turned out to be the villain in this drama, the therapist may have reasoned, it would be easier to bring it up after his death.

No. Shannon shook her head. She couldn't find room in her head for the idea.

'So long, Elva,' she said aloud as she walked to the Jeep – not forgetting to sweep her eye across the landscape, on the lookout for a thin blonde woman with a fixed smile. Settling in behind the wheel with the car doors locked, she suddenly wanted very much to hear TeeJay's voice. She pulled out her phone and dialed his number but got only a recorded female voice saying archly that Mr Goss was unavailable, so please leave a message. She had heard the voice before and guessed that it was an old girlfriend, something that didn't bother her. Nor, she knew, should she expect to reach TeeJay whenever she wanted. He carried a cell phone mainly for business, he told her, and usually left it turned off. Mr Goss was often unavailable, she reminded herself. It was part of his rough-hewn charm.

'It's Shannon,' she said simply. 'Call me.'

She punched in another number and asked a question of Garrett at The Nook. Armed with another number, she dialed it. She spoke for a moment, then heard Bullo yell to Rhonda in the background:

'It's Shannon,' he bellowed. 'She's lookin' for a piece.'

Eleven

Bullo's real name was Ronald Wilson, but someone with that name was not meant to wear biker leathers and straddle a Harley. He earned his nickname sometime back in his twenties, when, riding with a merry band of outlaws who called themselves Road Kill, he got juiced on muscatel and spun out into a field where a bull was watching over his cud-chewing harem. The bull approached, and Ronald, almost too drunk to aim, managed to land a fist on the bull's snout. The animal snorted indignantly and sauntered away. Thus, Bullo.

The name was a comfortable fit, for Bullo had a taurine neck and shoulders that thickened along with the rest of him as he cruised into middle age. Among the regulars at The Nook, he was known as Rhonda's old man, a decent enough character but a bad drunk, and a guy who – although his dope-dealing and gun-selling days were mostly behind him – had a certain familiarity with weapons.

Bullo and Rhonda, it turned out, lived in a trailer park a few miles up the coast from San Malo. It was easy to spot from the highway, a collection of trailers on concrete pads surrounded by motorcycles and pickup trucks. A cozy nest of bikers and truckers.

She joined the two of them at a picnic-style table beside their mobile home, where they sat in the shade of a tree with a pitcher of iced tea and a pack of smokes. The blue-green Pacific lay glossy and spread-out across the highway, its sounds drowned out by the whish and roar of passing traffic.

'This is nice,' she said, pointing toward the ocean.

Bullo nodded as Rhonda passed her a tall glass. 'So what do you need, exactly?'

'I was hoping you could tell me.'

'Is there somebody after you, hon?' Rhonda asked as she filled the glass. 'Is this anything to do with your folks?'

'Maybe.' Shannon felt uncomfortable. It was not her style to put herself in another's hands. She didn't particularly like Bullo and sometimes suspected that he was not kind to Rhonda. But she had little choice. She was a novice with guns, and he was an expert.

'What kind of a person?' Bullo asked.

'Does it matter?'

'Well,' Bullo said, stone-faced, 'if it was, say, a ninja warrior or maybe a professional assassin ...'

'All right. Let's say nobody's after me, but I'd just like to have some protection. Against ... you know, burglars and things.'

'Uh-huh. When you was in court, the judge said somethin' about a DUI. Anybody get hurt?'

'Why?'

'If it was a felony-type, you'd have a hard time gettin' a gun. Through the regular channels, I mean.'

'It was a misdemeanor. I flunked the breath test.'

'Good enough. You ever fire a gun?'

'No.'

'Oh, boy. We got our work cut out for us. But this'll be fun. We'll go to the firin' range, pop us some caps, try out a few pieces, and find the right one for you.'

'I'm not sure what that means, but let's go.'

'And you'll be payin'.'

'For the gun? Sure.'

'For the bullets, too, and the range time. Shootin' guns costs money.'

Two hours later they emerged from Duke's Firing Range and Gun Shop. Shannon's right hand was cramped, her injured shoulder ached anew, and her hearing was distorted, even after using the Mickey Mouse-style ear protection. She, Bullo and Rhonda all smelled of burned gunpowder. But she was strangely happy and relaxed.

She now knew what 'popping caps' meant. She had fired a .22 and a .38 revolver and a .45 semiautomatic. Bullo had shown her two shooting stances, both of them two-handed, and she had gradually settled into the right-foot-forward stance that felt most comfortable to her. ('The FBI uses that other one,' he told her, 'but I don't think much of it.') Her aim was wild, although under his tutelage it improved somewhat.

After all the gunplay, they stood at the sales display counter in the front, and amid much discussion of pros and cons, she settled on a .38 revolver with a two-inch barrel. She liked its compactness and had even lobbied for a lighter-weight .22. But Bullo was adamant. 'You won't stop your Aunt Minnie with a .22,' he said, as Rhonda gravely nodded assent.

She filled out the forms and supplied her fingerprints to the clerk and was told she would have to wait ten days for the background check to go through.

'Damn,' she said during the ride back. 'What do I do in the meantime?'

'I think I can help,' Bullo replied.

At their trailer, he went inside for a few minutes, then emerged. 'Here.' He handed her a heavy parcel wrapped in a rag. 'Long-barrel .38 and a box of shells,' he said. 'It's actually Rhonda's.'

'Thank you.' She was touched.

'It's a rental,' he said. 'Five bucks a day sound fair? You can settle with us later.'

'Watch after yourself, hon,' Rhonda said.

'I will.' Shannon pulled onto the highway and started back to San Malo. The inside of the Jeep was beginning to take on her scorched smell, a rough but not unpleasant scent.

At one point during her training, she and Bullo had taken a break to switch guns while Rhonda happily fired off a 9-millimeter Beretta in the stall next door, giving off little squeals of pleasure every time she tagged one of the inner rings.

'Takes *cojones* to aim a gun at somebody and pull the trigger,' Bullo had said, his meaty fingers inserting shells into the magazine of the .45. 'You think you can do it?'

'I don't know, even if we take the *cojones* out of the equation. Have you, uh . . . ?' She had tried to phrase the question casually but failed. 'Have you ever shot anybody?'

'Nope. Never.'

'Really?'

He'd nodded. 'Never had to. I threw down on a dude once, guy who disrespected me. Held a gun to his head. He actually peed his pants. But he didn't give me enough reason to do that. It was overkill, you know? Just swingin'-dick behavior.'

'So you don't think you'd—'

'Oh, if I thought somebody was comin' for me or Rhonda, I'd do what was necessary. That's what guns are for: To do the necessary.'

He'd given her a lopsided grin that did nothing to soften his features. 'I can tell you're never gonna be a sharpshooter, but that don't matter much. If somebody comes at you, your best chance, just fill the air with flyin' lead, and then run as fast as those long legs'll carry you. That oughta work.'

As she drove, she glanced occasionally at the vaguely sinister-looking cloth-wrapped package on the passenger seat. She drove with her left hand to give her throbbing shoulder a rest.

If the time came, would she be able to do the necessary? No telling. But now at least she possessed something that made her feel a little less exposed.

Look me up again sometime, Lonnie – or whatever your name is. Girly-girl.

Twelve

Back at her house, she had just closed the front door behind her and dropped her bag and the heavy parcel onto a nearby chair when she heard a faint sound. It came from the back of the house, and it sounded like a small but definite click, like the latch of a door. Or the cocking of a gun.

Her throat tightened. She opened her mouth wide and took two deep breaths as silently as she could, then stepped over to the chair and unwound the cloth from around the .38. Fumbling with the box of shells, she extracted one, released the cylinder, inserted the shell, then slapped the cylinder back into place, hoping the metallic noise would carry through the house. She couldn't tell if the bullet was under the firing pin, but it would have to do.

She stood uncertainly, breathing shallowly, listening hard. No noises. She moved through the small living room into the kitchen, where she had a view of the back door. It was closed. Stepping over to it, she grasped the knob and opened the door. It was unlocked.

Someone had been in the house and had left by the back door as she came in the front.

She locked the door, then checked the entire house. No one was there.

But there were signs. Clothes rearranged in the drawers. Bottles out of place in the medicine cabinet. Spots free of dust on the shelves where books had been moved aside.

Someone had been looking for something. But who? And for what?

Her heartbeat finally began to slow. Sitting down heavily on her living-room sofa, she picked up the phone and called the police, who showed up quickly – she was already on their radar – and took her report. When they had left, she looked up the numbers of a locksmith and her regular handyman. The locksmith was available immediately to change the locks and add heavy-duty deadbolts to her doors, but when she asked the handyman to upgrade the security of her windows, he began pleading a busy schedule until she broke in, her voice at a high pitch, talking of break-ins and emergencies and the need for immediate action lest she become the victim of a terrible crime.

'Okay,' he said. 'I get over there today.'

Although she was in no emotional shape for it, she had a job scheduled that afternoon. Leaving the handyman and locksmith a key behind a plant on the porch, she drove to the Flemings' place on Pomegranate Way. Mr Fleming, a screenwriter, and Mrs Fleming, a former actress whom Shannon had seen a few times on TV reruns, were about to return from a six-week Mediterranean cruise, and they wanted their house looking 'camera ready,' as he put it.

Once again, she had the house to herself, but it was hard to bring her old energy to the job. When she unpacked her two big canvas bags, there atop the cleaning gear sat Rhonda's handgun, now fully loaded, to remind her of all that had happened since the last time she had visited this house. She turned on her player and cued up some early Dylan but barely heard the music for the noise in her head. It was mostly dialogue, about poppin' caps and swingin' dicks and fillin' the air with lead – and also thoughts about a shadowy presence in her own house going through her things, violating her sense of place.

When she left several hours later, the house was clean, but her head was still cluttered.

She headed to the campus and, for the first time in years, prowled through the warren of faculty offices where her mother and father had worked. The administrator gave her the key to her father's office, and she unlocked the door. On the outer wall next to it was a small brass frame holding a card that said *Raymond Fairchild, Ph.D.*, followed by the words *Political Science*, and under that his office hours. The next occupant, she reflected, would need only to slide in a new card.

It was a typical scholar's office, maybe a little neater than some. Books lined the walls, and almost all the floor space not already occupied by his desk was taken up by two chairs for students. The department head had already gone through Ray's files, removing any that could be useful for student record-keeping. Shannon would go through the rest.

The office staff had provided her with several cartons to pack things in. She checked the desk drawers but found only the usual office supplies and left them there for others to deal with. Looking around at the countless books that lined the shelves, she silently thanked the department head for deciding to offer them to the university library, except for any the family might want.

She scanned the shelves and quickly spotted something familiar – Winston Churchill's four-volume *A History of the English-Speaking Peoples*. Her father had mentioned it as one of his proud possessions, signed by the author. She picked up Volume I, opened it, and found Churchill's signature, dated 1959. Next to that was a yellow stick-on note with her father's slanted scrawl: *Inscribe for S's birthday*. Her father, who had quietly urged her to return to the study of history, had meant to give the set to her. Lifting the four volumes off the shelf, careful not to damage their brittle dust jackets, she placed them in one of the cartons.

Another shelf was devoted to radical politics, focusing mostly on the 1960s and '70s. She had heard of some of the authors – Régis Debray, Frantz Fanon, Eldridge Cleaver, and of course Che Guevara – but had not read them. Ray Fairchild, against some opposition, had developed a course on the most recent wave of American radicalism and the writings that had inspired it. Some of his colleagues had argued that it was too early for such study, but he had forged ahead, and before long it was one of the school's most popular courses, touching off heated debates in almost every class. Shannon, an undergraduate at the time, had been tempted to sign up, but she didn't want to draw attention as Daddy's girl.

A memory nudged at her, the photo of Ray and Mora marching militantly down an unknown street. Apparently Professor Fairchild's interest in the subject went beyond the purely academic.

She pulled the dozen or so volumes down from the shelf and packed them too.

Next came her father's framed diplomas and a few family photos. One last look around. What was that up on the top shelf? She reached for it.

'Well, I'll be damned.' It was her childhood picture book about the little pirate girl, but a different copy, this one complete and pristine. And there on the garishly bright cover was the title she'd mislaid in her memory – *The Corsair's Daughter.* How could she have forgotten it? Especially when it had been the secret name that Shannon had given herself, romping around the yard, barking orders to Beth, terrorizing any of the neighborhood kids who dared try to take part in her fantasy.

What was her father doing with this? Leafing through it, she quickly found an inscription on the title page. *To Ray and Mora, valiant friends in a stormy and cutthroat world. With gratitude deeper than I can express ... Dee North.* The author had signed the book for Shannon's parents, then added a postscript: *The other copy's for the pirate girl.*

She dropped the book into the box along with Churchill and the framed photos.

It all took her less than an hour. As she headed down the hall with her single heavy carton, she was stopped by the office manager.

'Did you want to clean out your father's locker too?' the man asked.

'What locker?'

'Sorry. I thought you knew about it. He had one of the faculty lockers in the basement. I can open it for you now, if you like.'

She felt tired from a day spent house-cleaning and packing, and she knew her impatience showed on her face. 'Sure.'

After stashing the box in the Jeep, she followed the manager down a flight of stairs to the basement. Much of the space was taken up with heating equipment and air ducts, but one end was lined with a double row of lockers.

The manager located the locker, searched through a ring of keys, unlocked the metal door, and stepped back. 'I'll leave you to it.'

She swung the door open. The overhead lighting was dim but adequate to show her that all the locker held was two large legal-size plastic box files, each with a lid.

She hefted the top box out and, careful not to strain her back or her sore shoulder, placed it on the floor and removed the lid. Inside was an array of what looked like files – papers, clippings and photos.

After a minute's examination, she squatted down on her heels to get more comfortable. She went through the boxes as quickly as she could, opening a file, extracting a piece of paper or two, scanning it, replacing it, and moving on.

After five minutes, she felt strangely out of breath and sat down on the cold floor. She didn't yet know the meaning of the files, but she knew the general shape of them. And although she had not a shred of proof, she felt the first tingle of an idea that somewhere in these files was a hint, a notion, a clue as to why her parents had died.

Like the little pirate girl – what was her name? Arabella, that was it. Like Arabella, she felt on the brink of a journey. She didn't know her destination, but she knew she was going.

Thirteen

She sat at her kitchen table, a second cup of black coffee at hand. The kitchen was a lived-in room, where she cooked and ate and sometimes worked. With its linoleum floor, FDR-era wallpaper, and sturdy, thrift-shop oak table, it usually felt like a refuge.

Tonight, though, was different. The curtains, normally open, were closed, since recent events had given her the feeling that the world held threats and some of them could be aimed at her. The house was quiet, with none of her beloved music playing. Aside from the low whir of a car going by on the street, the only sound was the occasional rustle of paper.

At least her home felt marginally safer. When she had returned from the campus, she found the locks changed and new keys left, as agreed, under the mat outside the back door. Inside, she did a walk-through and found that the handyman had done a reasonably good job with the window latches. Her home security, if not perfected, had at least been upgraded.

The contents of the two boxes lay spread out in front of her. She had spent the last two hours going through them and had just scratched the surface.

She knew about history – had been, in fact, a historian in training before she stopped trying – and she had seen immediately what the boxes held. This was history of a different, more personal, kind.

What she found in the files was the intersection of a particular period of America's recent history with human lives. The lives of her parents, to be sure, but of others as well.

The photos grabbed her attention first. They were almost all of young people, marching, demonstrating, holding sit-ins, massed for meetings in giant halls. Here and there were close-ups, snapshots of various faces. Some looked familiar, probably because of her fondness for TV documentaries, but their names were harder to retrieve.

Three photos included her parents. One showed them sitting on the floor side by side, jammed into what looked like an office with a small mob of others, apparently part of a sit-in. Another photo was a duplicate of the one she had seen at the memorial, with her mother and father marching at the head of a large formation. Three other young people were at their side, two men and a woman, also dressed in military-style fatigues.

The third photo stopped her. In it, the same five people, wearing the same clothes as in the march, leaned against a brick wall, obviously exhausted. One of the young men held a cloth to Mora's face, which was bloodied. Ray and the other two, including a tall, striking young woman, watched them. At the far right of the photo, a fire hydrant spewed water, and a knot of figures, eyes streaming, knelt to wash tear gas off their faces.

What hurt you, Mom? she wondered. *Did you fall? Or did somebody hit you?*

The bulk of the material in the files consisted of clippings, mostly of newspaper and magazine articles. As she got into them, she was finally able to attach names to some of those familiar faces: Abbie Hoffman, the frizzy-haired jester of the Yippie movement, wearing love beads and talking into a reporter's microphone; Tom Hayden, the somber-faced leader of Students for a Democratic Society, speaking at a rally; and Bobby Seale, a Black Panther chieftain wearing an angry scowl, fist in the air.

Most of the clippings were from the 1960s and '70s. There was much on SDS, which began as a liberal student organization, struggled to become more activist as America's involvement in Vietnam grew, and finally collapsed in 1969 under pressure from more radical groups to 'bring the war home.' Two of those groups dominated. One was Weatherman, later called the Weather Underground. The other was known as the Red Fist.

The groups' members went underground in the late '60s and early '70s and, as gestures against the Vietnam War, began bombing various government targets. Even the Pentagon was hit.

As Shannon leafed through the articles, some incidents jumped out at her. One was the 1970 explosion – apparently an accident during the making of a bomb – that blew apart a Greenwich Village townhouse and killed three members of Weatherman. The other, two years earlier, was the bombing of the Crowe Institute, a government-affiliated research facility on the campus of LaValle University, in which a night watchman and his infant daughter were killed.

Shannon drained her now cold coffee cup. She debated refilling it but decided not to. Any more coffee and she'd never get to sleep. It was well past midnight, and she was tired, but still her brain hummed with activity, connections, threads of narrative.

The Crowe bombing, she read, occurred after the Red Fist decided to drop out of society and wage its war from secret locations. The townhouse explosion gave birth to the Weather Underground. Both groups had brilliant, charismatic leaders – Bernardine Dohrn and Bill Ayers of the Weather Underground, Diana Burke and John Paul West of the Red Fist. All four were hunted by the FBI.

Shannon turned the page and took in a quick breath. There, side by side, were wanted posters for Burke and West. She fumbled her way through a separate pile of papers to find the photos showing her parents at the march and its aftermath. Her eyes were drawn to two of the remaining three figures, the tall, dark-haired young woman and the sturdily built man at her side.

Diana Burke. And John Paul West.

A sound in the street made her jump. It was the quiet squeak of brakes as a car slowed, then stopped. Holding her breath as she listened, she could hear the engine idling.

She got up quickly and made her way to the living room, where she carefully parted the drapes.

'Well, hallelujah,' she said under her breath. It was an SMPD patrol car. As she watched, a uniformed officer got out and approached the house, playing a flashlight over the door, windows, and porch.

She opened the curtains wide and gave him a goofy grin and an exaggerated wave. He waved back and returned to his car.

'Thank you, Mr Detective Orlando.' Her scrapes with the police – minor by most yardsticks – had not endeared her to them. But at this moment, the sight of a blue uniform, stopping by to check on her well-being, warmed her heart.

She sat back down at the table, trying to refocus on what had jolted her just moments earlier. Once again she stared at the grainy black-and-white images from the wanted posters. Diana Burke and John Paul West.

Her mother and father had marched with, and possibly been friends with, two of America's most notorious radicals, people wanted for the murders of a student and his baby. She reached for one of the photos and held it up, staring at the blood on her mother's face. Had her parents done more than just march?

The phone rang, startling her anew. She went to the living room to pick it up.

'Hey, Shan?'

'TeeJay! Where are you?'

'I'm, uh, still down in Dago.' After a second, she got it: San Diego. Where did he find these nicknames? 'I just picked up your message. Hope I'm not callin' too late.'

'No, no. I'm up.'

'You sounded … I don't know, worked up. How you doin'?'

She hesitated. When she called him, she had felt overwhelmed by events, especially the attack by that crazy loon who went by the name of Lonnie. Now she felt marginally more in control of her life. And she was determined not to be the whiny, dependent girlfriend.

'I'm okay, I guess. Just wanted to hear your voice.'

'That's good. Any word from the po-lice?' True to his roots, TeeJay hit the word's first syllable harder than the second.

'Not much. But get this: The FBI is involved in this thing, for some reason.'

'No kiddin'.'

'Two of them came over yesterday. They asked some general questions about my mom and dad. I don't think I was much help. Later I found out they've taken over the investigation. Just came in and pushed the local cops out of the way.'

'How come, d'you suppose?'

She started to reply but paused.

'Shan?'

'Just a second.' She let the phone drop to her side and thought for a few seconds, weighing the pros and cons of telling him everything she knew. Then she reflected that she knew very little. Orlando had retracted his account of the murders, and she was just beginning to put together the fascinating story of her parents' renegade friends. She decided there was nothing wrong with being extra careful.

She raised the phone in time to hear him say, 'You still there?'

'Sorry, I had to check something in the kitchen. I don't know what's going on with the police or the FBI. All I know is, I'm beginning to get the feeling that nobody'll ever be caught for this.'

'Huh. Well, damn.'

'So when are you coming back, roving boy?'

'Well, that's the thing. My manager, he wants me to head up to San Berdoo next. We've got one of our main warehouses there, and they're havin' some trouble with inventory, and he thinks I'm just the guy to straighten 'em out.'

'Really? So ...'

'So it could run into weeks, maybe months.' He let out an exasperated whistle of air. 'I was lookin' forward to seein' you, but ...' He let the thought trail off. It occurred to her that he didn't sound all that sorry. An idea elbowed its way into her mind, and before she had time to examine it, she expressed it.

'Tommy Joe, are you dumping me?'

'What? Hell, no. Soon as I can bust loose from this thing, I'll be back down and look you up. We'll go out. Okay?'

'Okay, then. Sure 'nuff,' she said in a sarcastic approximation of his drawl.

'Talk to you later.' He hung up.

It's your fault, she told herself. *You go looking for Mr No Strings Attached, and look what you wind up with.*

She went back to the brightly lit kitchen. The papers and pictures littering the table called out to her, but she felt too tired. Tomorrow.

She went to bed. In her sleep, she found herself on a street, striding along with a band of marchers. The scene was chaotic, with chanting and flag-waving and a sense of impending disaster. Somewhere up ahead, she knew, were the police.

Marching alongside her was Diana Burke, who took no notice of her. Shannon felt the urgent need to reach out, grab her sleeve, and shout out an important question.

But what was it?

Fourteen

In the morning she joined Priss to help her finish an especially tough job, a house put on the market after the death of its longtime owner, an elderly bachelor. The house had 'good bones,' as Priss put it, but it had not been cleaned especially well in decades. The Clean Machine had been hired by the real estate broker to make it glisten, and Priss had put in two days there already.

She and Priss worked well together. The young woman had broad, open features and a chunky build, with a sprightly sense of humor and a good work ethic. Like her boss, she seemed content cleaning houses. Shannon sensed something sad in her background – a romance gone sour, maybe – but Priss volunteered nothing, and Shannon knew better than to pry.

Each worked with headphones on. When passing in the hall or working a room together, they had perfected a system of hand signals as complex as those of an NFL referee. Priss, she knew, was partial to '70s rock. Sometimes, when Shannon turned her volume down, she could hear her companion vocalizing along with Stevie Nicks on 'Landslide' or the Eagles on 'Already Gone' or, louder yet, doing one of Bob Seger's stadium-rattling anthems. After four hours, the old place had taken on a glow, and they packed up.

Back at the house, her stomach spoke to her urgently, and she whipped together a big, filling lunch. The papers atop the kitchen table left her no room, so she ate standing up at the counter. She ate for nourishment, not for pleasure, and as soon as her dishes hit the soapy water in the sink, she took her seat at the table and returned to the past.

First, though, she spent a few minutes puzzling over an anomaly, the one item that did not seem to belong with all the other contents of the boxes. Nestled within a separate manila file folder were two stiff pieces of legal-size photocopy paper stapled together. The one on top was her birth certificate. She'd seen the document before, and this copy confirmed what she already knew about her beginnings. She'd been born, her parents told her, during a vacation down in Puerto Vallarta, Mexico. Her mother had often repeated the story.

It was hilarious, she would say. *Not at the time, you understand. It was scary then. We thought we'd allowed enough time, but you … well, you must have been very impatient to be born, because you came early. And so we found a nice clinic with a wonderful English-speaking doctor who looked a little like Ricardo Montalban. And you arrived, squawling and hungry and just … just beautiful.*

Was I, Mommy?

Yes, Shan. Yes, you were. My beautiful black-haired girl.

And then Beth came, and she was blonde.

That's right. But you were the first.

The document bore an official Mexican government seal at the top, and the entries had apparently been handwritten, in barely legible lettering, by someone at the clinic. All the particulars seemed to be there: her parents' names and last US residence – Ann Arbor, Michigan – and Shannon's full name, including her middle name, Patrice, which she disliked and never used.

She glanced at the page underneath it and noted that its printed words ('Attending physician,' etc.) were all in English rather than Spanish. It was a different document. Her father must have stashed copies of Shannon's and Beth's birth certificates in this place for safekeeping.

But what were they doing in this mass of tangled and violent history? She couldn't come up with an answer, so she set the folder aside and went back to the rest of it.

She found more on Burke and West, who for a couple of years had been two of America's most prominent outlaws. Media darlings, reputed to be linked sexually as well as politically, targets of the FBI, objects of hatred and contempt by those on the right. Both were raised in privilege, both joined SDS during their years at Columbia University but soon moved to the radical fringe to fight both racism and the Vietnam War.

In an interview with an alternative weekly paper in Boston, West called the war 'racist from top to bottom,' saying privileged whites were sending black soldiers to Vietnam to fight Asians.

In the same interview, Burke declared that the women of the radical left were 'too busy to make coffee and babies' and were fighting alongside the men. 'When we face off against the pigs, we say, "Chicks up front!" If the cops have it in them to hit a woman, we'll hit back. We're not afraid. Power to the people!'

Photos accompanying the article showed West raising a fist in the air and Burke leaning meditatively against a doorframe, her long black hair hiding half her face. There was something naggingly familiar about that face, Shannon thought, and not just because it had invaded her dream last night. But why?

More clippings, more history. One of the bombers had been found injured near the Crowe Institute blast scene, and he had implicated West and Burke as the masterminds. West's fingerprints had been found on one of the tools used to jimmy a lock on an outside door. At other times, both he and Burke claimed responsibility for a series of bombings against government targets, so linking both of them to the fiery deaths at the institute was simple.

Gradually, the bombings tapered off. By the time the war in that small Asian country ended in 1975, they had stopped. Years went by. One by one, the radicals who had gone deep underground either surfaced, willing now to try their luck in the courts, or were apprehended. Even the leaders of the Weather Underground, Dohrn and Ayers, surrendered in 1980, having had two children during their years on the run.

By the mid-1980s, Shannon read, almost all the major fugitive radicals had surfaced. Some had served their sentences and were back in society. Others, charged with the most serious crimes, were still in prison. Some, it appeared, would die there.

Only two names remained on the list of fugitives: West and Burke. They were accused of crimes as horrific as any committed by the radical left. If found, they could be put away for life. The FBI had chased their scent for decades and never found them.

'Not a day goes by that I don't think of them,' the lead FBI agent of the case was quoted in an article in 1994. 'I ask myself where they are, what they're doing, what they may look like today. A lot of time has gone by, but there's no statute of limitations on murder and terrorism, and we never really stop looking. I want them to know that.'

The agent's name was Harold Birdsong.

She let out a long breath. 'All right,' she whispered. Finally, something was beginning to make sense. So that was what the big, shambling ex-agent was doing following the young one around. Retired or not, he was still on the trail of two of the country's most wanted. His quest had brought him here to San Malo in the aftermath of the murders of Ray and Mora Fairchild – two people who once had known Burke and West.

Had they also known where the two fugitives were hiding? It seemed almost certain, Shannon thought, recalling her mother's words: *We didn't tell them anything.*

One task in particular pressed in on her, something she knew she had to do. Setting up her laptop on the kitchen table, she fired up the Internet connection. She searched her parents' names and got several hits, all of them related to teaching. She tried various combinations, pairing the names up with Burke and West and then with the terms *radical, bomb, arrest.* Nothing.

Best she could determine, her parents had never been arrested, had never been mentioned in connection with radical activity of any kind, at least not in the mainstream media.

She closed the laptop. Her parents may have associated with radicals, may have marched with them, may even have gotten involved in dust-ups with the police. But that was the extent of it. At some point they had left all that behind, and they lived the rest of their lives as law-abiding citizens. Shannon, who ranked cynicism and rebellion high among her favored qualities, was surprised at the depth of her relief at discovering this.

But could she be sure? What was it the Secretary of Defense had said just the other day upon being quizzed about the missing weapons of mass destruction in the rubble of Iraq? Absence of evidence is not evidence of absence.

She was looking for evidence that her parents had not joined forces with baby-killers. How to find it?

Back at the kitchen table, she poured a glass of wine and, as she began to think about dinner, arranged the papers into various stacks of related material. A stack of photos. A stack of general background on radical politics. A stack on Chicago, 1968. The townhouse. The Crowe Institute. Burke and West.

A single page slid out from between the pages of another article, something she had missed. It was an article from *Newsweek*, published two weeks after the Crowe Institute bombing, during the furor over the search for the leaders of the Red Fist:

> *Like their counterparts in the Weather Underground, Red Fist leaders have adopted* noms de guerre. *Burke calls herself Nadja, after a Red Army sniper who, during the siege of Stalingrad, killed dozens of encircling Germans until they pinpointed her location and blew her up in a hail of artillery. West calls himself Ernesto, after the given name of Cuban revolutionary demigod Che Guevara.*

Fingering the page, she stared at it, feeling a tiny flutter in her stomach. Nadja and Ernesto. Now she remembered the names of those sought by her tormentor Lonnie, who had been prepared to hurt Shannon hideously to learn their whereabouts. And possibly had committed two grisly murders for the same reason.

In an instant, Shannon was back at her mother's bedside in the hospital, inhaling the awful odors of pain and dying, hearing her mother's voice.

We didn't tell them anything. I was so proud of him.

'Oh, Mom.' Shannon realized she was speaking aloud.

Don't tell police.

You have to find them and warn them.

Now she knew who her mother meant, and why it was so important the police not be told.

Shannon was being asked to warn Burke and West that someone was after them, someone even more dangerous than the FBI.

Her parents, for reasons unknown, had protected two revolutionaries, bombers, terrorists, murderers. Now they wanted Shannon to do the same. It seemed an impossible task.

She recalled the fat, gauzy bandage that covered her mother's hand in the hospital bed, covered the hideousness underneath. At the tip of the bandage was a dime-size stain, dark red and crusted. *Damn you, Orlando. You told me the truth the first time, didn't you? And a lie the second.*

You're the pirate girl, she told her mother silently. The adventurer. I can't even imagine how brave, how tough you are.

Warn them.

How in the world could she do this?

No, she told herself. The question was: How could she *not*?

'I will, Mom,' she said to the memory. 'I don't know how, but I will.'

Fifteen

Dinner killed her hunger and was instantly forgotten. She went to the phone.

'Beth …'

'Shan? What is it?'

'Just thinking. You remember any of Mom and Dad's friends? I don't mean the ones on the faculty, or neighbors. I mean people from out of town. Visitors. You remember anybody coming to the house when we were little?'

'Ah, let me think.' Fussing sounds in the background, followed by the clatter of small feet. Scamp and Chipper. Beth was one of those women sometimes referred to as a natural mother. Although Shannon often quietly admired her sister's maternal qualities, they always seemed as alien to her as a natural flair for math. One sister born with them, the other not.

'Vaguely,' Beth said finally. 'Uncle … Don, was it? God, that was years ago. The late Uncle Don. And just a few others, but no names or faces, so they could have been anybody.'

'Same with me,' Shannon said. 'Just fuzzy memories. Along with Uncle Don, I think I remember another one, some guy who played with me in the yard. How's that for being specific?'

'You were older, so you should have a better recall …'

'I know. Just thought I'd ask. Everybody okay? How is Chip … uh, Skipper's cold?'

'Low-grade,' Beth said solemnly. 'It's not enough to keep him out of mischief. Did you get a chance to take a look in the garage?'

'I did.' *Did I ever.* 'There's nothing valuable in there, so a garage sale sounds fine to me. Listen … Have you noticed any police cars in your neighborhood lately?'

'Yeah.' A tone of surprise. 'Why?'

'It's nothing to worry about. That detective, Orlando, said he'd send someone around every now and then to check up on us. Just a precaution, he said. And, uh … until they answer all the questions about Mom and Dad, he said we should be careful. Lock your doors, don't let the boys run around the neighborhood. You know.'

'Okay.' Beth seemed about to phrase a question, but Shannon wasn't finished.

'There's a woman,' she said, speaking quickly. 'Blonde, skinny, calls herself Lonnie Brown. She turned up at the memorial, told me she'd studied under Mom. But she didn't.'

'She … didn't?'

'No. She's a fraud. The police know about her. Thing is, if she shows up at your place, don't let her in, all right?'

Beth was silent. Shannon could feel her tension, her unasked questions, and knew she'd failed in her effort to keep her sister from worrying.

'All right, I promise you I won't let her in,' Beth said finally, her voice strained. 'But why?' The boys' chattering went on in the background, and Shannon knew that Beth's concerns went far beyond her own safety. Still, she didn't want to cause her to panic.

'She's cracked, that's all. I suppose there's a chance she might be dangerous. If you see her, call the cops right away. And make sure Richard knows about her. I'd rather you were too careful than not careful enough.'

As she spoke, she marveled at her own words. Beth had always been the careful one, the sensible one. And now here was Shannon lecturing her on caution.

She gave Beth the police detective's phone number. 'Everybody be careful,' she said one last time. 'This won't last forever.'

Beth mumbled a distracted goodbye, and Shannon knew her sister was already thinking of her family. *I hope I scared her just enough*, she thought.

She looked up another number and dialed it.

'Shannon! It's good to hear your voice.' Peter Bridger sounded genuinely pleased.

'I hope I'm not—'

‘No, no. I eat my dinner early these days.’ *Since your wife died*, Shannon could have added. ‘And there are no papers to grade at the moment. How are you?’

‘Good. I’ll try not to keep you long. I just wanted to ask you a few things about Mom and Dad.’

‘Ask away. Wait a minute. Are you busy tonight?’

‘Uh, no.’

‘Where are you living?’ When she told him, he said, ‘Why don’t you come over? I’m, oh, fifteen minutes away, and I’d enjoy seeing you. I just opened a nice cabernet.’

Less than twenty minutes later they were arranged in garden chairs around a rough-hewn table in his backyard. The air was seasonably cool, so she kept her thick sweater on. He wore a jacket and muffler. He had lit a candle on the table, and they sat in its fluttery, moonlike glow.

Shannon felt relaxed for the first time in days. Bridger had always been easy for her to talk to, and she found herself falling back into the comfortable rhythms of their old conversations. They talked for a while of books and scholarship, and she tried to rise to meet the challenge of his wide-ranging intellect.

Then the subject of Ray and Mora arose, and her sadness returned.

‘I know you’re still grieving,’ he said. ‘I am too, and I wasn’t nearly as close to them as you were.’

‘I don’t know if that’s true.’ No need to pretend with him, she told herself. ‘I wasn’t as close to them as I should have been. I just …’ She shrugged.

‘What?’

‘I always felt as if I should be fighting them, not loving them. Growing up, I sensed that they were worried to death about me, although I couldn’t figure out why. They never expressed it. But I could tell. They always seemed to be watching me, waiting for me to make some awful mistake – crash the car, get arrested, get pregnant.’

‘Shannon, every parent—’

‘No, not really. Because I watched Beth grow up behind me, and they had none of those worries with her. They just seemed to assume that she’d turn out all right. And she did. With me, it was the opposite assumption, and you know what? I think I fucked up just to show them they were right about me. Sorry for the language.'

He smiled. In one of his lectures on Elizabethan England, Bridger told his class that English was so rich a tongue, one could curse for hours without resorting to the half-dozen or so 'lazy gutterisms,' as he called them.

'You're not being fair to yourself,' he said. 'As I recall, you had a pretty normal growing-up.'

'There were things you didn't hear,' she muttered.

'Oh?'

'I ran with one of those "bad crowds".' She made quotations marks in the air. 'Junior year in high school, my boyfriend – he was in his twenties – dealt drugs around the UCSM campus. I had a couple of run-ins with the police. Drug arrests. They went into my juvenile record, which is sealed, and my folks were able to keep them out of the paper.'

'I didn't—'

'Senior year, I had an abortion.'

'Oh, Shannon.'

'I was the proverbial mess. By the time I started college and got you for my adviser – thank you, by the way, for putting up with me – I was sick of being the poster child for bad behavior and was trying to start over. Getting deep into books was something I loved, and that carried me through all those years.'

'Until you stopped.' He leaned over to top off her glass. In the candlelight the red liquid seemed to hold a dark, flickering fire.

'Yeah. Well, that's another story. I'm just saying that while I was growing up, I acted like a rebel because, in some odd way, I felt it was expected of me.'

'I'm trying to understand.'

'Me too, even today. I was just getting back into some kind of balance with Mom and Dad when they were killed. I even saw a therapist for a while, and one of the questions that came up was why I acted so crazy with them.'

In the pale candlelight he looked sad. 'I wish I could help. You said you wanted to ask me something about them.'

'Uh-huh. I've been going through some of their things, books and papers, and ... Remember when you talked at the memorial about their college days and how they were very political? You said their beliefs took them into the streets.'

He nodded, his hairless head almost glowing in the soft light. 'I remember.'

'Can you be more specific? It's important.'

'Ah, let me think. I knew they went to Chicago in sixty-eight to demonstrate at the convention. On our campus, that made them celebrities. They walked the walk, as students like to say.'

'And did they stay that way?'

'Well, they mellowed, as we all do. But I think they hung on to their principles. Last year, at the candlelight vigil on campus right after the invasion of Iraq? I saw them there, and we laughed over the fact that very few other faculty showed up. I'd say your mother and father remained politically involved all their lives. When you were a child, your house was always a good place to go for a lively discussion of how our country was being run.'

'I've come across something that suggests they were friends with Diana Burke and John Paul West. Do you know who they were?'

'Yes,' he said, drawing the word out slowly. 'The radicals. They're famous.'

'They bombed a building and killed some people way back when. And they've never been caught. That picture of Mom and Dad marching? Burke and West are right alongside them.'

'Interesting. I guess I didn't recognize them.'

'I have another picture taken after the march. Burke and West are there too, and Mom's face is bloody.'

His nod was almost imperceptible this time. 'When they came back from Chicago, her head was bandaged. She said a policeman hit her with his nightstick.'

'God.' Over the last few days, a new mother had taken shape in Shannon's mind; and a new father too.

She pressed on with her questions. 'While they were here, do you know if they had any visitors from the old days? Anyone who might have been political?'

He thought, then shook his head. 'I'm afraid not. What's this really about, Shannon?'

'Dr Bridger, I hope you'll forgive me if I don't tell you everything right now. Let's just say I'm looking into their past. Please don't mention any of this to anyone.'

'Even the police?'

'Especially the police.'

'All right. You're appealing to the conspirator in me, and I suppose there's just enough of that young man left.'

She drained her glass of wine, felt the liquid warm her all the way down. She felt suddenly nervous. 'One last thing I have to ask: Back then, when they were, as you say, dedicated ... Could they have been capable of doing anything really violent?'

'As in setting off bombs?'

'Or anything like that. Could they have?'

He waited a long time before answering. 'Shannon, I'd like to say no. These were good and gentle people, but the time we're talking about was a terrible and confused time. Our leaders were being assassinated, students were being shot down on campus, and we were in a wrongheaded, tragic war. Some of the most brilliant and well-intentioned people among us decided to answer the violence of the war with more violence. I wasn't one of them, and I don't think your parents were either.'

She sensed he was holding something back. 'But?'

'But they were deeply passionate about their beliefs, and I couldn't see far enough into their hearts to know everything about them.

'The answer is, I simply don't know what they might have done.'

She got up and laid a light kiss on his smooth head. 'Goodnight.'

Back home, with nothing on TV, she poured a short wine nightcap, put some Ladysmith Black Mambazo on the stereo, and began finding space for the books she'd brought from her father's office. The shelves in the living room and bedroom were filled many times over, with books jammed horizontally atop the vertical ones, and a couple of piles on the floor demanding places of their own. But the bookshelf in the hallway had a few spaces left.

As she rearranged the old books and loaded the new ones onto the shelves, she saw that one of them, *The Diary of Che Guevara*, held a bookmark, and she opened the book to it. There was nothing unusual about the spot – no marginal notations, not even a chapter break.

The bookmark, she noted, was actually a postcard. The picture side showed a colorful mob scene, a mass of tie-dyed, face-painted humanity dancing, playing instruments, chasing balloons. *Greetings From San Francisco: A Happening in Golden Gate Park* read the caption. Someone had inked an arrow pointing to an indistinguishable dot far back in the crowd and labeled it ME.

She turned it over. Postmarked September 1975, it was addressed to her parents. The scrawled message read:

Summer of love long past & it's gotten ugly here. Lots of burned-out people, including yours truly. But there's work to be done, the one thing I'm good at. Found a place just a few doors from the Dead. The war's finally over (yay!), but was it worth the price? Peace & Love to you & little Shannon ... Henry

Henry. Why was that name so familiar? She carried the card into the bedroom, where she dropped it on the bedside table and got undressed. After her trip through the past, she felt covered in history, as with a fine dust, so she ran a shower and got in. As the soapsuds rinsed away, she turned up the hot water and leaned against the tiled wall. Her head was full of junk. She breathed deeply, inhaling the steamy air, and little by little she felt the clutter begin to loosen.

Henry. A face slowly appeared out of the steam, then more of him. A fancy jacket – buckskin? – with fringe, a kind of cowboy hat. A smell of something. Incense? Dope? Then his voice, full of fun. Joking with her. But sadness in the background: What was that? Beth, crying. Because Henry wouldn't play with her. Only with Shannon.

A shadow darkened her thoughts. Could Henry be the figure in her nightmare, the phantom, the one leaning over her? Could Elva have been right? She couldn't know; the images were too vague.

More memories of herself and this strange, childlike adult involved in rollicking games. He seemed to want to please her, and she could hear her parents' voices in the background. *Henry, you don't have to spend so much time with her. Sure I do. We're playing pirate. Leave us alone.* And on they would go, traipsing around the backyard, with Beth wailing for attention.

Her eyes, squeezed shut in her effort to remember, flew open.

Gasping, she leaned over to turn off the hissing spray. She knew his name. The rest of it. Concentrate. Just before Henry left, they spent time sitting on the front steps. He had Shannon's colored chalk, and he was drawing exotic images on the sidewalk – elephants, sailing ships, unicorns. And at the end, he signed his name with a flourish.

Then he was gone. The drawings, and his name, remained there for days until it rained.

Henry ... She saw it, as in an old snapshot: Henry Goines.

There was more. She knew it. Almost tearing the shower curtain as she parted it violently, she strode dripping out into the kitchen and turned on the light. Hastily drying her hands, she began pawing through the piles of paper until she found the photos. Oh, Lord, there he was. The one with the skinny limbs, the elongated, slightly sad face. Henry was the fifth figure marching alongside Ray, Mora, and the celebrity outlaws. He was the one tending to Mora's wound.

She slammed the pictures onto the table, almost giddy with what she'd found, and the slap of her hand on wood sounded like sudden knowledge, like certainty.

Back under the covers and finally dry, she exhaled deeply and turned over onto her side, trying to sleep. Be quiet, she said to her mind. You can be quiet now. She willed herself to relax, starting with fingers and toes and working up to the deepest part of her.

Henry Goines, she said to him in her mind as she felt sleep approach. *Ray and Mora knew where John Paul and Diana were hiding. They died rather than tell.*

Do you know where they are too?

I need to find you.

Sixteen

She was up at sunrise, her mind on a low boil. She jogged around the neighborhood, the houses ghostly in the wispy fog off the Pacific. Back at the house, once her heart and breathing had slowed, she put out coffee and a bowl of cereal, settled in at her computer, and went to work.

Henry Goines. Last seen in the place TeeJay called Frisco, after the Summer of Love had clouded over. She did a white pages search under Henry's name and turned up nothing in San Francisco. Expanding her search to the Bay Area, she turned up an H. Goines in Mill Valley but, upon calling the number, she found herself talking to a Harriett.

Running a general Internet search on Henry's name, she ran across him in a few contemporary accounts of the marches and demonstrations of the 1960s. Not a leader, but not part of the faceless mass either.

An excerpt from a book about the period referred to him as a second-year medical student at the University of Tennessee who 'carried a bag of gauze and alcohol and salve, ready to treat wounds from billy clubs or copious weeping from tear gas.'

He treated Mom, Shannon thought. *Bandaged her. Thank you, Henry.*

She wondered if he had finished med school. But the tone of his postcard, the reference to those who were burned out, suggested otherwise. And yet, he had said, *there's work to be done, the one thing I'm good at.* What kind of work could a former med student do? Especially one who must have been familiar with the weaknesses and the temptations that burned out the young?

She thought hard, then typed in *San Francisco clinics.* Lots more hits. After reading through some of the entries, she added the words *drug treatment* and, after more reading, the words *free clinic.* The articles that turned up told her of a small cultural phenomenon in which many casualties of the drug scene since the '60s, most of them young, had been treated at free clinics in San Francisco by a band of dedicated doctors and their helpers.

One of the clinics was described as 'a block away from the graceful old Victorian once occupied by the members of the Grateful Dead.'

Right. Henry's card had said, *Found a place just a few doors from the Dead.* And another piece fell into place.

Henry had once lived in the neighborhood, part of the Haight-Ashbury district made famous by the Summer of Love in 1967 and notorious during the drug-fueled excesses of the '70s. Would he have worked at the clinics? If so, was he still there? She collected a list of clinics' phone numbers and began dialing.

Almost an hour later she took a break, quietly elated. No Henry, but she had spoken to people – receptionists, volunteers, a couple of doctors – who knew him. He had worked at two of the clinics, then moved on. Fortifying herself with a bottle of apple juice, she went back at it.

Two more calls, and pay dirt. A Betty Boop-voiced receptionist at the Mind and Body Free Clinic in the Lower Haight told her Henry helped out there on most week nights.

'Do you have an address and a phone number for him?' Shannon asked, wanting to reach through the line and hug her.

'Just a number.'

Shannon wrote it down and said, 'I'm really grateful.'

'Have a beautiful day,' the receptionist chirped.

An instant later she was dialing it. The phone rang for a long time before a man answered.

'Henry? Henry Goines?'

'Nope. Leave a message?'

'Uh …' After a brief hesitation, she gave her name and left two numbers, home and cell. 'Please tell him it's important.'

Hanging up, she felt almost giddy. *Easy*, she told herself. *You haven't talked to him yet. You don't even know that he can help. One step at a time.*

Too nervous to wait, she drove to the bank. She had no idea what the next few days might bring, but she wanted to be prepared, so she drew out $1,000 in cash, which made a noticeable dent in her savings, then gassed up the Jeep.

She was on her porch, about to open the front door, when she heard the house phone ringing.

'Hello?' It came out breathlessly, so she repeated it.

'Shannon? Is that you, little girl?'

'Henry?'

'Well, I'll be … Wasn't really sure I'd ever talk to you again.' She had forgotten his voice, but hearing him now brought it back to her. A soft, tenor drawl, somewhat nasal. Not exactly like TeeJay's accent, but more like it than not. 'Your folks give you my number?' A pause, and she could almost hear him calculating, realizing fully now the strangeness of hearing from her, knowing that it must mean something. 'Is anything—'

'Henry, they're dead. Both of them. Mom and Dad. Somebody broke into the house and killed them.'

She heard him gasp, take a breath, then say quietly, 'Oh, Lord,' immediately followed by, 'Who did it?'

'I don't know. I've been trying to find you because …' How to say it? 'My mother, just before she died, asked me to find somebody. Two people you know. Or used to know.' Her words sounded vague to her. She began to wonder if this was a huge mistake. Could she trust him? She wanted to blurt everything out, but forced herself to slow down. 'One is called Nadja. The other—'

'No!' Henry's voice came loudly over the phone. It was not a strong voice, and she could hear the effort behind it. 'Don't say any more. No phones. If you want to talk to me, we've gotta see each other. Okay?'

'I guess.' Henry was a good three hundred miles up the coast, and just navigating through his densely populated city could take an hour or more. 'Maybe we could meet halfway,' she said hopefully.

'I'm sorry, girl. I'd meet you, but I don't drive any more. Lost my license. You'll have to come on up here.'

Stop quibbling, she told herself. *You've found him. Now go to him.*

'All right. Give me your address and an idea of where it is. Henry?'

'Yeah?'

'I'm leaving right now. Be ready.'

Seventeen

She packed a change of clothes in an overnight bag, then reflected for a moment, pulled out a larger bag, and packed more. Fifteen minutes after hanging up the phone, she was outside under the carport, throwing the bag into the backseat.

'Taking a trip?'

She turned. Harold Birdsong stood on the sidewalk, as rumpled as before.

Think fast. 'Yeah,' she said, working on sounding casual. 'An old college friend, up in San Luis Obispo. She's invited me to stay with her for a few days.'

'San Luis Obispo,' he said, walking over. 'That's not far, is it?'

'Naw.' She drawled it the way TeeJay might. 'Less than a hundred miles. Easy trip.' She looked around for Dodd, the younger agent, but did not see him. 'You need me for something?'

'Mm? Oh, no. Just thought I'd stop by.' He shuffled his feet a tiny bit. 'Well, that's not quite true. Actually, I came to talk to you. Should've said so right away. I've been retired so long, I've lost the gift of gab.'

'I'm kind of in a hurry.' The sight of the shambling Birdsong, with his unmade-bed look, took her back to the conversation with both men and the sour note on which it ended. She did not want a replay.

'I'll try not to keep you long. I heard you were attacked the other day. Are you all right?'

Of course. He would have heard something about it from Orlando. But how much? She decided to play it down and say nothing about the names Nadja and Ernesto. If Birdsong had a clue, let him bring it up.

'Yeah. I was going through things in my parents' garage, and some crazy woman jumped me. I told the cops about her, and they said they'd look for her. I'm fine now.'

'Glad to hear. I think I have some good news about her.'

Shannon was instantly intrigued. 'Really? Tell me.'

'I'll be glad to, but let me take things in order.' He looked vaguely uncomfortable. 'We got off to a bad start the other day, didn't we?'

'If you mean the kind of questions the other guy was asking about my mom and dad, yeah.'

'I'd like to get past that, if we can.'

'Maybe.' She leaned back against the Jeep, not the least bit relaxed. 'If you answer some of my questions.'

'I'll try.'

She ticked them off on her fingers. 'First, why did you take this case away from our own police?'

'The FBI asked for jurisdiction, and San Malo granted it. This is part of what I came to talk to you about. If you'll let me do my spiel, I think it'll all become clear.'

She looked doubtful. 'Second, the night my parents died, that detective named Orlando told me things that were done to them – awful things, before they were killed. Then, just the other day, he told me the FBI had stepped in and I should forget what he told me. The newspaper here barely ran a story on it. I get the feeling that somebody's already trying to rewrite history, and that somebody is the FBI.'

His fleshy face seemed to add an extra fold of concern. 'I'm not going to lie to you. Terrible things were done to them, and once we got a feeling for who might be behind it, a decision was made to keep some of the details quiet. We don't want certain people to know everything we know. If it's treated like a local murder, a one-day news event, they might relax just a little, and we might get closer to them.'

'I'm still hearing riddles.'

'Well, I'm ready to start talking. All I need is your attention for a few minutes.'

She chewed on her lower lip. Henry Goines was waiting for her, and she needed to hit the road. But she also wanted to hear what Birdsong had to say.

'So where's the good-looking one?'

He laughed, a kind of fat man's wheeze. She liked the sound of it. 'He got called back to LA for a couple of days, leaving me here to do what damage I can. We're not really attached at the hip, but I'm glad if I can help the Bureau with any of their current cases, and working with him gives me an extra kind of legitimacy.' The more he spoke, the easier she found it to decipher his mumble.

'Are you a private detective now?'

'No. Retired, just like I said. All I do is consult with the Bureau occasionally. It's a nice supplement to the old pension.'

'Good for you. Well, I'm listening.'

He pulled a large folded sheet of paper out of an inside jacket pocket and handed it to her. She unfolded it and found an FBI wanted poster dated February 1968. Bearing the headline *National Firearms Act*, it showed photos – one profile, one full face – of three people. The first two were the pictures she had already seen of Diana Burke and John Paul West. The third was a man named Quentin Latta.

She adopted a look of mild curiosity. 'Uh-huh?'

'It's about the one on the bottom,' Birdsong said, leaning over and pointing to the photos of Quentin Latta.

Shannon looked more closely, both at the photos and the accompanying text, which said that Latta and the other two were wanted on federal weapons charges. She saw a young man with a broad face, a pale complexion, and hair that was long in the back and already thinning out on top. He wore mutton-chop sideburns and a bushy mustache.

She handing back the flyer, and he pocketed it. 'What about him?'

'About a year after this thing was circulated, these three bombed a building. They called themselves the Red Fist, and they were setting off a bunch of bombs against government targets. Burke and West were the leaders, he was the explosives expert. But this one went bad. Two people were killed. Latta didn't get away fast enough, caught some shrapnel in his leg and was picked up right at the scene. Thing is, since they left him behind, he turned on them and sang like the fat lady at the opera. Told us about the organization, the leadership, their plans, everything. Got himself a smart leftie lawyer who made a deal – twenty years for all the information, no shot at parole. Thing is, Quentin was such a bad boy, he kept trying to kill people in the joint, and they kept adding on the years. Eventually the total came to thirty-five. A stiff sentence, but still better than life. If he'd faced state instead of federal charges, he could've gotten the chair. Two people dead? You ask me, he got himself a deal.'

'So?'

'So I've been looking for Burke and West forever. Of all the terrorists who thought blowing up buildings was a way to stop the Vietnam War, they're the only ones left. The only ones who're still underground. I may be retired, but I still want them.'

A look crossed Shannon's face, and Birdsong nodded. 'You've done the math, haven't you?'

'Thirty-five years, you said.'

'Uh-huh. He got out two months ago. Here's what I came to tell you. I think Quentin Latta is looking for Burke and West too, and I think he tortured and killed your parents in an attempt to find out where they are. He may even have found out—'

'Not from them,' Shannon said quickly, remembering her mother's words: *We didn't tell them anything.*

'How do you know?'

'I just do.'

He held her eyes for an extra few seconds, then went on. 'All right. Maybe he didn't. I'm counting on that. If he knows where they are, he's already closing in on them. If not, there's a chance he could still be around. He could even be planning to come see you or your sister, to find out if you know anything.'

Her look of alarm stopped him. 'I don't want to scare the hell out of you. I know the San Malo PD is keeping an eye on you and your sister. Besides, Quentin wouldn't see you as the enemy, just a potential source of information.'

'Well, that really puts my mind at ease.'

'All I'm saying is you might see him. If you do, please let us know. Here's a more recent picture, taken in prison.'

This photo was larger and showed the man in prison garb with a number across his chest. He was heavier and clean-shaven, including his entire head. He looked much more menacing.

The younger Quentin Latta resembled no one she knew, but this one … She stared at the photo. Allowing for differences such as hair and mustache, this one looked something like the ageing man on the bench in the harbor, the man who spoke in riddles and grabbed her so hard it hurt.

'So he's looking for these two: Burke and West.'

'I'd bet everything I have on it.' He shot her a sideways look. 'Have you heard of them? Before today, I mean.'

'Oh, here and there,' she said lightly. 'I guess they're famous. But before I make you any promises, I think you owe me more of the story. You must have a better idea of why he's after them.'

He let a few seconds go by before nodding. 'This isn't for everybody to hear, but I trust you. You've had a huge loss, and you deserve to know a few things. All I ask is that you keep this to yourself.' He glanced toward her front door, as if hoping for an invitation to step inside, but she ignored the look. So he arranged himself against her SUV, leaning back on it, a couple of feet away from her, and lowered his voice.

'I kept in touch with Quentin over the years, just to make sure he didn't have any more stray pieces of information kicking around inside his head. I saw him go through some changes. His wife left him and took their daughter someplace where he couldn't find them. That was hard on him. There was something else, though. He had always read a lot on politics and revolution, and in the beginning he was as dedicated a leftist as you'd find anywhere. Where a lot of his kind would describe themselves as Leninists or Trotskyites or even Maoists, Quentin called himself a Stalinist. Pretty scary when you think about it. He believed in what you might call a dictatorship of terror.'

'You mentioned changes.'

'That's what I was getting to. There were very few lefties in the joint, and Quentin began hanging out with the neo-Nazis, white power types, the new generation of the KKK. Eventually he bought all of it. Strange as it sounds, he went from the far left to the far right, easy as you please. But two things inside him never changed: hatred for all kinds of government; and the need for vengeance against Burke and West, the ones who left him behind.'

Shannon let disgust play over her face. 'I don't care how well you know him or what his politics are, my parents are still dead. He sounds like a sick piece of shit. If you knew when he was getting out, how come you couldn't just watch him?'

'That's a fair question. We tracked him for a while and then lost him. All those years inside, swapping ideas with career criminals, have made him a whole lot craftier.'

'I can't help wondering: How could he find these two, Burke and what's his name—'

'West.'

'—when you couldn't?'

Instead of rising to the insult, Birdsong smiled. He seemed to be enjoying all this, the trip back into the past, the look into a dark character's mind. Maybe just the chance to explain what he'd been doing with his life.

'They couldn't have stayed hidden all these years without help. Back in the day, the fugitives had a big support network behind them. It worked so effectively because most of the network was above ground – average people, mostly law-abiding except for those few minutes a day when they'd make a phone call, or transfer some money, or open their door to somebody on the run. Most of the network has moved on, of course. They've married and had children and gotten straight jobs and taken out insurance policies. Some of them probably even vote Republican today. But I think there are a few still out there, helping their old friends. And Quentin would know who they are. That's an advantage he has over us.'

'You think my mother and father were part of it, don't you?'

'I do now, although that's not something we knew for sure before they died. If we had known, maybe we could have protected them. I'm sorry for that.'

He exhaled loudly. 'One of the two people who died in that bombing was a baby girl. Someday Quentin Latta will burn in Hell for killing her. But before he does, he's got two names to cross off his list. Knowing him, I wouldn't want to be them.'

'And you? What do you plan to do?'

'Find him first and stop him. Remember, they're mine, not his.' He reflected on what he'd just said. 'Of course, the rest of the FBI wants him pretty bad too.'

She stared at the ground for several seconds.

'What is it?'

'I'm not sure, but I think I may have seen him.' She described her encounter at the harbor, the man's strangeness, his grip on her arm, his comment about her parents as if they were still alive.

Birdsong looked somber. 'A mustache, huh? And hair. Still, that could be him. Some of what he said sounds like gibberish, and he may have been just running a game on you, sizing you up. Could be he was hanging around for a while, checking on the rest of your family. That would suggest he didn't learn enough from your parents, and maybe he thinks you might know something.' He paused, and Shannon could almost hear his next question: *Do you know anything?*

Instead, he simply said, 'That means you should be very careful. If you ever see him again, run.'

'I'll be glad to.'

He pushed himself heavily off the Jeep. 'I should let you go—'

'Wait. What about this Lonnie?'

'Oh, sure.' He stuck his hands in his pockets, making his pants sag and his belly protrude. 'Someone fitting her description was picked up in a little town in Arizona just a few hours ago trying to pass a bad check, and word got to us. Everything's moving like molasses, but they've promised to send photos and fingerprints. If it's her, we have a file on her. She's one of Quentin's groupies.'

'His what?'

'Pen pals. The kind of women who write to dangerous men in prison, looking for romance or a thrill. You'd be amazed. Sometimes they send them money, sometimes they wind up marrying them.'

She had heard about such women. 'They sound like fools.'

'I agree. Some are worse than that, though. This Lonnie – that's her real name, by the way: Lonnie Brown. She's been in and out of mental treatment programs for years. She sees Quentin as a lost soul needing to be saved. Anyway, she picked up pieces of his own obsession over the years and was probably trying to do him some kind of crazy favor when she came after you. But if she's been picked up, you don't have to worry about her any more.'

'Just Quentin Latta himself,' she said, and when he shifted his gaze to the ground, she knew she was right.

Eighteen

She made it to San Francisco in a little over three hours, with one brief pit stop for gas, coffee, and a couple of granola bars. Traffic slowed somewhat as she hit the peninsula, then the urban hills came into view and memories took over. She had been there several times, beginning with family trips when she and Beth were children. Shannon had grown up in a place known for its elegant ease and Mediterranean flavor, but the look of this jam-packed coastal city never failed to capture her. Baghdad by the Bay, the local newspaper bard had labeled it before the real Baghdad intruded on America's consciousness and the name lost its Arabian Nights magic. City of fog-wrapped vistas and massive tourism, the gay and the straight, the Gold Rush and old racism, home of the Beats, the hippies, and the yuppies, the unwashed sharing sidewalk space with the unbearably trendy. Views of bay and bridges with price tags to match. *You name it*, she thought, *you can probably find it here*.

As she feared, it took a while to make her way to Henry's address. It lay in the Lower Haight, the flat, down-market cousin of the fabled hilly Haight-Ashbury neighborhood. If the Upper Haight held most of the patchouli-scented memories of the '60s, the Lower Haight was poorer, more of an ethnic mixture, with fewer places for tourists to spend their money.

She found Henry's block, framed by a dry cleaner's at one corner and a deli-liquor store at the other. Prowling side streets for a parking spot ate up precious time, but finally she was at the entrance to a skinny, anonymous four-story apartment building with some of the upper windows covered in blankets in lieu of curtains. She ran her finger down the tenants' list until she came to his number. The name tag was missing. She rang. No answer. Again, several times. Nothing.

Shannon was tired and desperate, not yet ready to lose it but getting close. She hit every button on the panel twice. Amid the cacophony of static and voices emitted by the speaker, one welcome sound: Someone buzzed her in.

She mounted three flights of wooden stairs, running her hand up an iron railing, hearing doors open and voices question as she went but never slackening her pace. On three, she located Henry's apartment near the back and knocked. Again, no answer.

'Henry, it's Shannon. Open up.'

Long seconds went by, then fumbling sounds, the click of locks, and the door opened a few inches, stopped by a chain. In the opening, a lined and weathered face almost obscured by hair.

'Henry, is that you? Let me in.'

He threw off the chain and, putting a finger to his lips, opened the door just wide enough to allow her to enter. She walked down a short passageway to a small living area with a kitchenette off to the right. The shades were drawn, lights lit, giving the place the feel of twilight.

She turned to look at him. It was Henry all right, but the years had used him up. He wore a denim shirt and jeans that looked too big at the waist. Although her faint memories of him were of a skinny man, now he appeared to be down to gristle. His hands were clawlike, and his graying brown hair was shoulder-length and oily.

By contrast, the look he gave her was almost beatific. Henry smiled hugely and reached for her hand.

'Oh, Shannon girl, it is you. I can see you.' He spoke in a near-whisper. 'When you were little, before you started to grow, you were almost chubby. Look at you now, all grown. You're a beautiful young lady.' His eyes darted around as he spoke, alighting mostly on her. They looked wasted but kind.

'Thank you, Henry. It's nice to see you … uh, again.'

'Ray and Mora would—' Something caught in his throat and he stopped, shaking his head, eyes downcast. Then he put a finger to his lips again. 'We better not make too much noise.'

He tried to smile again, but the smile crumbled, to be replaced by something that almost made her step back. It was fear, spread plainly across his face. And she knew she had infected him with it, just by calling him.

'Henry ...?'

He rubbed at one of his eyes. 'Right after I talked to you, I went down the street to get a six-pack and some smokes. Clyde, the guy at the store, is an old friend. He told me somebody came in lookin' for me this mornin', askin' if I lived around here. We got a kind of an arrangement. Clyde knows not to say anything about me, and he didn't. But the guy was askin'.'

'And that worries you?'

'Shannon.' Just talking seemed to make him short of breath. He gestured broadly. 'I been in this place for over five years. In all that time, nobody's asked for me.'

She understood. 'Was it Quentin Latta?'

The name jarred him. 'You know a lot already, don't you? No, I don't think it was. The guy was younger, dark-haired.' His eyes darted around. She had seldom seen anyone's nerves frayed so thin.

She thought of Tim Dodd. 'Could he have been with the FBI?'

'I don't know. You got a car?'

'Yeah.'

'Maybe we could drive a little, just get out of this neighborhood until I figure out what to do.'

'Wait.' She put up a hand. He was rattling on, and she could feel things getting out of control already. 'I'm not sure that's a good idea. If someone's looking for you—'

'Hmm. Yeah.' He scratched at his nose. 'I cain't stand just sittin' in here, waitin' ...' He exhaled loudly, then nodded vigorously. 'I know. We'll go up to the roof. It's private. We can talk.' He picked up an old corduroy jacket with a fleece collar, the corduroy shiny with wear. 'C'mon.'

He led her up a flight of stairs to an unmarked door, then up another short flight to a metal door that opened onto the roof. It was arranged in a kind of shabby garden, with dirt-filled wooden boxes of puny plants and flowers and a small potted tree. Plastic lounge chairs dotted the area.

The view, though, was something else. All around them, under a gray lid of winter sky, were the rooftops of San Francisco, a motley and quirky assortment of buildings with a few tiny balconies and occasional makeshift refuges like this one. The hills rose in waves and receded into valleys, and the city's cars hummed like bees. Somewhere to the north the Golden Gate Bridge was obscured by haze, but the silhouettes of downtown were visible to the northeast, including the Transamerica Pyramid and, beyond it, Coit Tower atop Telegraph Hill.

'You cold?' He indicated a chair for her.

'I'm fine. Henry, you know why I'm here.'

'Just a minute.' He walked to the edge of the roof and looked down for a moment, then returned. 'Yesterday I noticed a van I've never seen around here. Gray. It's still there today, just parked in a different place.'

Some of his nerves were beginning to rub off on her, but she couldn't afford to be distracted. 'Henry,' she repeated insistently, 'you know why I'm here.'

He sat down a few feet away and nodded, clasping his hands together, leaning forward in his chair. 'I don't know what to say, except how sorry I am. They were the best people.'

'You hadn't heard?'

'No. I don't pay much attention to news. Tell me everything you can.'

The story took her ten minutes to lay out for him. All through it, he stared at her long and hard. His rampant case of nerves seemed to have subsided somewhat. He coughed occasionally, and his eyes were clouded over with what looked like ill health. Once again she reflected on her decision to put all her trust in him. But she had no choice.

'Just before she died, my mother gave me a message for Nadja and Ernesto,' she said, nearing the end. 'That's why I tracked you down. I need you to put me in touch.'

'I'll give it to 'em,' he said quickly. 'What is it?'

She shook her head. 'She told me to find them first.'

This was her ploy, carefully planned. The main thrust of the message, of course, was implicit: *Someone is after you.* Her mother's other words, about the man full of hate – Quentin Latta, apparently – and a cryptic reference to a treasure, could be significant, but they seemed to pale next to the urgency of warning Burke and West about the man who was tracking them down. If she simply told Henry the gist of her mother's words, he would send her home now and take on the role of messenger himself. She believed that her mother's first command, *Find them*, was as important as her second.

Henry sank back in his chair, looking stubborn. 'You don't know they'll even talk to you. These are people—'

'I know who they are and how long they've been hiding. My mother wouldn't have asked me to do this if she didn't think I could. I promised her. You need to help me make good on this, Henry. Put me in touch with them.'

A look of anger passed over his face, then went away. 'I been watchin' out for 'em for a long time,' he said. 'They trust me. There aren't too many people left they can trust.'

'I know.'

'You got a phone?'

'Uh-huh. Don't you?'

'The phone company cut me off a year ago. I don't use it that much anyway. I get messages through the apartment manager, and there's a pay phone here in the building. But I need yours now.'

She pulled it out of her shoulder bag and handed it to him. Henry walked across the roof, dialing a number as he went, then began talking. He talked for what seemed like a long time. At times he became agitated, pacing back and forth. Once he squatted down, holding his head in his free hand as he spoke.

Finally he returned and gave her the phone. 'I'll take you,' he said. 'But you'll have to do like I say. You drive, I give directions. No guarantees about what'll happen once we get there. I'll tell you one thing, though: This isn't going to work out the way you thought.'

'I don't like the sound of that.'

'Too bad. You're gettin' a privilege nobody else ever gets.'

'Because of my parents?'

He looked at her for a long time without answering. 'Oh, girl,' he said finally, and she could swear there was suddenly affection in his look.

The look vanished. 'C'mon,' he said briskly. 'I need to pack a bag. We got a long drive. Does your car play cassettes?'

'Uh, yeah. Where are we going?'

'Montana. And that's the last question I'm answerin' until we get our tails in the car.'

'*Montana?*'

Bag packed, Henry led her down the stairs to the ground floor and then, to avoid the van parked in front of his building, out a rear entrance that led to an alley. From there he took her along a damp gap between buildings, so narrow she had to turn sideways, to a rusty gate, then out onto the sidewalk. They were a block from the Jeep.

When they were almost there, she heard footsteps. With thoughts of the gray van, she turned around and saw two men overtaking them. One was big, with a mop of curly blond hair, the other thin and furtive, with a ferret's face and a red nose. Both too scruffy, she decided, to be FBI, but that left a lot of room for trouble.

As the men caught up with them, the thin one muttered, 'Weed?'

Henry took her elbow and urged her along.

'Wanna buy some weed? Crank?'

Shannon felt relief. Just your friendly neighborhood dope dealers, she thought.

'No thanks, boys,' Henry said loudly.

'What's in the bag?'

'Huh?'

The men quickened their pace and passed them, then blocked their way.

'Gimme the bag.'

Before she could react, the thin one grabbed her bag by the shoulder strap and pulled. She resisted, but he heaved hard, swinging her around and slamming her into a car. She stumbled and almost fell. 'Fucker!' she yelled.

'Oh, she got a mouth.' As if by signal, both men pulled out knives. Curly's was a dingy kitchen knife; the ferret's a little penknife. The ferret raised his and hooked it behind her shoulder strap, ready to sever it.

'Okay, you want the bag?' she said, hearing the tremor in her voice. His hand stayed where it was. She could feel the blade of the little knife against her chest. 'How about everything in it?'

A dumb grin from the ferret. He hadn't noticed that her right hand was deep inside the bag. Now she withdrew it, raising the grip of Rhonda's long-barrel .38 until they both could see it. Her palm closed on it tightly, and the carved wooden grip warmed to her touch. The gun was half out of the bag now, barrel still buried, but her finger was visible inside the trigger guard.

The ferret backed away; Curly, too. In a moment, both men were walking quickly down the block.

They reached the Jeep, she unlocked the doors, and soon Henry's army surplus duffel bag joined hers on the backseat as they settled into the front.

'Whoa!' Henry was jubilant. 'Girl, you're a desperado.'

'No, I'm not. But that felt so great. That thing in my hand, and the look in their eyes. I can't tell you.' She giggled, feeling giddy. 'It felt like …'

'Like what?'

'I know this sounds crazy, but it felt like the first time I ever touched a boy's dick. It jumped in my hand, and I felt …' She shook her head, out of words.

'Powerful,' Henry said, grinning broadly.

'That's it.'

'You're a desperado, all right. And you don't even know it yet.'

Nineteen

By two in the afternoon they were on Interstate 80 headed northwest, leaving San Francisco and the Pacific in the rear-view. *Montana*, she thought. It seemed a long way off.

'Where exactly in Montana?'

'You don't need to know yet,' Henry said calmly. He studied a sheet of paper with handwritten notes, occasionally muttering what sounded like numbers. Freeways, probably.

'Any idea how long it'll take us?'

'Huh-uh. Never made the trip before. We'll know when we get there.'

'Great.'

From time to time he turned around and looked behind them, holding the position for several seconds. After the second or third time, she asked, 'See anything?'

'Nope. And that's fine with me.'

She drove as fast as she dared, just focusing on the road. No point worrying about what she couldn't control.

After an hour Henry was visibly more relaxed. He lit a cigarette without asking, and she cracked his window using her controls. 'One o' my last two vices,' he said, sucking in the smoke and coughing lightly.

'The other being?'

'Alcohol. Beer, mostly. I'm no alcoholic. I'd know if I was. But I like a drink every now and then.'

'You sound like me.'

'I knew it. We're soul brothers.'

'That's right out of the sixties, isn't it?'

'Well, girl, a lot of me is still stuck there.'

She decided to be direct. 'For a guy who drinks and smokes, you don't look too healthy to me.'

'I'm a lot healthier than I used to be.'

'Really.'

'Uh-huh. When I moved to the City – that's what we call it there – I was burned out on politics, marchin', all that. I wanted me some peace and love. There were a few thousand young 'uns just like me who wanted the same thing. We found it in music and drugs, mostly. I had some medical trainin', and I thought I'd help out at some o' the clinics. Other folks were tryin' to stop the war, I was just tryin' to heal people. But the work, it brought me too close to drugs, and I got hooked for twelve years. It ruined my teeth, my stomach. Eventually I managed to kick it, with help from friends and some good doctors. But I've had shaky health ever since. I'm just lucky I can still work. I help out at one o' the clinics. I think I've saved a few lives over the years, and I believe I've saved my own, too.'

'I'm glad for you.' She wanted to see if she could get him to talk about Burke and West. 'What got you burned out on politics?'

'People started dyin',' he said simply. 'I didn't sign up for that. I realized that the world I moved in was divided right down the middle, between the ones who thought settin' off bombs could stop the war and those who thought every life was precious. For a while I was with the bombers; I thought that as long as we hit just property, we could make our point. But then it all went wrong ...'

'The Crowe Institute?'

'Hmm. Right.' He turned to look at her. 'You've done some diggin'. The Crowe Institute. That turned me around and sobered me up. I couldn't stay mixed up in anything that killed people, so I walked away.'

'But the others kept bombing, didn't they? Burke and West and the others?'

'Yeah,' he said, exhaling the word slowly. 'They were extra careful after that, and they never took another life. They told me the institute was a horrible mistake; that they never meant for that to happen. They said it was Quentin's fault, not theirs. At that point I didn't know whether to believe 'em or not, but it didn't really matter.

They went deeper underground, and I popped right back out into the world.'

'But you never lost touch with them, and you even helped them from time to time, didn't you? Why?'

Henry's hands gestured, sculpting the air, searching for words. "'Cause of all the people I ever knew, they're the most unforgettable. 'Cause they opened my eyes, showed me what injustice looked like, told me we could fight it. 'Cause when I left 'em, they understood and forgave me. I wouldn't take back the time I spent with 'em. They're not perfect. They're just the kind of people who live life deeper than the rest of us. Bein' around Diana and John Paul made everything sharper, made me feel high, but without drugs. Even though I don't believe everything they believe any more, I'd still give my life for 'em.'

The intensity of his words stunned her. She'd never known anyone like the people he described. Hearing him, she understood how cult members might feel about their guru. That kind of magnetic leadership could accomplish much good or – she thought of the baby buried in the rubble of the Crowe Institute – the very opposite.

The rest of the day felt as blurred as the passing landscape. After more than seven hours of driving, much of it across the high desert of northern Nevada, they spent the night in a motel in a town called Wells. Tired as she was, Shannon made time for one task before turning out the light. She called Priss and told her she was being forced to take some time off for family business. Priss's sister, a college dropout with a spotty job history, had been looking for something to do, Shannon knew. Why not ask her to fill in temporarily?

Priss agreed reluctantly. 'I don't think cleaning houses is one of her career goals.'

'It wasn't one of mine either,' Shannon said. 'Tell her it's good, clean, honest work. Emphasize clean. And tell her the money's not bad.'

The next morning, in brisk weather and under a heavy overcast sky, she and Henry stocked up on sandwiches, crossed into Idaho, and were soon passing through a landscape of lava beds resembling the moon's surface. Henry began pulling cassettes out of his pocket and popping them into the player. Much of it was from the '60s, what Shannon thought of as angry rock, music with a political message.

Her rear had begun aching miles ago. 'Why did you lose your license?' she asked him.

'Too many DUIs, years ago.'

'I can relate to that. But you're clean now.'

'Uh-huh.'

'Are you a good driver?'

'Used to be. Shoot, I drove a VW bus cross-country all the way from Chicago to, uh …'

'To where?'

'I forget. It was a long time ago.'

She pulled onto the shoulder. 'I think you should slide over here and drive for a while. Don't hit anything, okay? I want to relax.'

After that they swapped over every hour or so. By the afternoon they could see the Rocky Mountains up ahead. As they gained altitude their surroundings took on more grandeur. A high-country pass ushered them into Montana, and by the eight-hour mark they had reached the city of Butte, situated in a bowl a mile above sea level and ringed by the Rockies. The mountaintops were white, the air was frigid.

With Henry at the wheel, Shannon was preparing to ask him once again how much farther they had to go when he slowed and took an exit ramp.

'What's up?'

'I need to stretch my legs.' He pointed to a rest area in a grove of trees, with two picnic tables. 'We can eat too.'

'Come on. This'll slow us down. And it's cold.'

'Here, take my jacket. Stop'll do us good. Ten minutes. I'll bring the food.'

Grumbling, she walked over to the nearest table and sat. It was late afternoon, and the light was just beginning to fade. Thick patches of dirty snow lay on the ground. Shannon had not seen the sun in two days. The Rockies loomed behind them, one barrier crossed. How many were left?

She heard Henry's footsteps and turned as he slid onto the bench seat across from her.

But it wasn't Henry. It was a bearded man in a parka with a floppy hood. He arranged himself in his seat, hands clasped on the table, eyes on her.

She gripped the edge of the table and swung her legs violently out from underneath, painfully banging one knee in the process. She looked around wildly. Where was Henry? There, still at the SUV, with the door open. Her heart thudded in her chest. The gun was … in the Jeep. Bracing her hands on the bench, every muscle tensed, she prepared to spring up.

'Hello, Shannon.'

Wide-eyed, she turned her eyes back to him. Who the hell? *Don't panic*, she told herself. She opened her mouth, but nothing came out.

'I appreciate your coming all this way.'

Then she knew. She couldn't quite recognize him, there weren't enough clues to go by. The hood, a full beard. He could be almost anyone.

But he wasn't.

Twenty

'Well.' She let out a ragged breath. 'Yes.' She heard new footsteps, and this time it was Henry who sat beside her.

'That was pretty goddam cute,' she said mildly, without turning her head.

'Had to do it this way,' he said. 'Less you knew the better.'

John Paul West grinned faintly at her. 'Anyway, you came,' he said. 'You have a message for me?'

She nodded.

'From Ray and Mora?'

'From Mora. By the time she talked to me, my dad was dead.'

He nodded, and his eyes seemed to soften. To Henry he said, 'How is she?'

'She's good. I think she's got what it takes.'

'I'm very glad to hear that. All right, then.' He got to his feet. 'Let's go. Henry, would you mind following us? Shannon can ride with me.'

'Wait a minute. Where are we going?'

'To my place.'

'What about … Diana?'

'In time.'

He drove a dust-caked Chevy Blazer. It had been parked at the rest stop, but Shannon had barely noticed it. *So much for my powers of observation*, she thought.

She studied him as he drove. Even with the hood thrown back on his shoulders, it was hard to tell for sure. He was heavier than the young revolutionary he once had been. His hair, like the beard, was starting to gray, as was the hair on the back of his strong-looking hands.

As he pulled onto the freeway headed east, he said, 'Tell me about Ray and Mora.'

When she hesitated, he added, 'We were good friends, the best. But I haven't seen them in years. Tell me whatever comes to mind about your family: you, your sister; the kind of life you had with them.'

And so, recognizing the incongruity of sharing personal things with this stranger, she began talking about growing up in the house on Dale Drive. About her childhood games, the complex relationship with Beth, the warmth of her parents' home. He proved a good and nonjudgmental listener, with an occasional question that filled in a detail or sent her off in a fresh direction. Almost without realizing it, she found herself edging into darker areas – her feelings as an outsider, her inability to fully absorb and return her parents' love. Her problems as a teenager. Her nightmare.

The darkest story she saved for last, intending to skim over the surface and be done with her revelations. But he asked for all of it, and so she hesitantly returned to that day in the late winter of 1987 …

She came unsteadily out the door of the clinic, giddy from the anesthesia but also hurting and feeling nauseous.

Looking around, she spotted Wade, her dope-dealing boyfriend, sitting in his sleek white 300ZX. Her hand groped in her pocket to find what was left of the money he'd given her for the abortion. She owed him change.

He leaned over to open the passenger-side door. As she started for it, she heard the quick squeal of brakes, and there was the Volvo, Dad at the wheel, Mom beside him, faces hard as stone. The Volvo blocked the sports car's exit, and her parents got out. Mora came to her, took her by the arms, studied her face wordlessly. Shannon broke down, and Mora's arms enveloped her.

Over Mora's shoulder, she saw her father pull Wade out of the bucket seat and back him against the car. Shannon expected violence, but Ray simply leaned into the young man's face and spoke intently. Wade, fearing blows, raised his hands, but Ray slapped them away and leaned in farther. His face bore a look Shannon had never seen.

In a minute it was over. Wade, looking in her direction, shrugged his shoulders, got in his car, and drove away.

They took Shannon home and put her to bed, telling Beth her questions would have to wait. Mora went to the kitchen while Ray sat near the bed, occasionally leaning over to take her hand. Neither spoke for a long while. As more of the anesthetic wore off, Shannon's brain churned with guilt. She felt dirty and lost. Finally, eyes closed, she muttered, 'I really fucked up, didn't I?'

'Yes,' Ray said.

'What's going to happen?'

'Nothing. You're going to go on being our daughter. The daughter we love more than we can even express to you.'

Mora came in bearing a tray. 'Soup?'

Shannon's eyes misted over. 'Yes,' she said. 'Soup.'

When she finished her story, John Paul went a long time without speaking. 'Don't let me sound glib,' he said finally, 'but if this is any help, I think I understand. All of it.'

'I'm not sure you do.' *How could you?* she thought. He was a stranger to her; empathic, maybe, but still a stranger.

He let that go. After three hours of driving, they pulled into Billings. It was the biggest place she had encountered in the state, but it retained some of the look of the frontier. Darkness had fallen when he drove through part of the downtown and into an area of renovated buildings that had an Old West flavor. A few more blocks, and he came to an early 1900s wood-frame house with a small front yard, wedged between two commercial buildings. He pulled into a side driveway and watched in the rear-view until Henry had pulled in behind him. 'Home,' he said, getting out and starting up the front steps. 'Come on in.'

The front was a small office suite, the back a comfortable living room, with worn Western-style furniture. 'Two bedrooms upstairs,' he said, turning on lights.

Shannon spotted law books in the main office. 'You're a lawyer?'

'I have a law degree,' he said carefully. 'I was about to start law school back when the world began to fall apart and I found better ways to occupy my time. Later, after I dropped out of sight and the anti-war movement lost its steam, I finally got to law school, but under a different name.'

'How could you do that?'

Henry guffawed. John Paul gave her a patient look. 'We didn't always do everything right,' he said. 'But after years of practice, one thing we got down was identities. Especially birth certificates, Social Security cards and driver's licenses – although I have to say some of today's licenses are a lot harder to duplicate. There were two document experts in the network, one in New York, one in Chicago. It was the way we managed to stay hidden. Over the years I've had many jobs, dozens of addresses, and used twenty or thirty names.' He gestured for them to come back to the living room, which was next to a small kitchen. 'Get you something to drink?'

They all had beers and settled into comfortable chairs. 'I don't practice law,' he told them. 'That would raise my visibility too much. I do legal research for small law firms that need help. I never go into court, and I never do anything that would get my picture in the paper. I try to work on cases where I can do some good. Just last month I helped a disabled worker get a big settlement from one of Montana's largest mining companies.'

He stopped, and Shannon realized she was staring. 'What?' he asked.

'Sorry. It's just sinking in. Who you are, I mean, and how long you've managed to do this.'

The two men merely looked at her calmly. 'I mean, here I am, knocking back a beer with a big-time fugitive. Shouldn't we have the shades drawn or something?'

'We really don't need to,' John Paul said with a small grin. He took a long pull at his bottle. 'I know what you mean, though. It has to do with the way people think about going underground. They think it means disappearing. You don't disappear, of course. You find a way to live that doesn't call attention to yourself. Mao Tse-tung used the metaphor of fish swimming in the ocean. The guerrilla army is the school of fish, and the ocean is the peasant population. You just submerge yourself in the ocean and swim along with everyone.

'In the process, you find small ways to lower your profile. You alter your appearance, you take an anonymous job. You grow eyes in the back of your head. After a while, it all becomes second nature.'

He was giving her a glimpse of a world her parents had known, at least from a distance, and she was fascinated. It made her feel somehow closer to them. 'The ocean. Is Henry part of it?'

'You bet he is. Without him I doubt that Diana and I could have made it. And all the others, too. The ones who helped hide us, especially at the beginning. The ones who drove us from one state to another, looking for a place to go to ground.' He sighed. 'A lot of them have dropped by the wayside. Your parents, bless them, were not the last, but they were two of the best. Now they're gone. But Henry keeps going. He's a soldier.'

He studied her, as if trying to judge how much more information she could handle. But he glanced at his watch, and his expression changed. 'I'm sorry. I should have offered you something to eat. And you'll stay here tonight. But just tonight. You'll have to leave tomorrow.'

'I'm honestly not hungry.' She leaned forward, suddenly tense. 'Do you want to hear my message?'

'Yes, I do.'

She felt the silence in the room as both men focused all their attention on her. Speaking slowly and carefully, she repeated her mother's dying words, every one. *They killed Ray. Bastards. I saw it. We didn't tell them anything. I was so proud of him. Don't tell police. You have to find them and warn them. God, he's so full of hate. We should have guessed.*

John Paul nodded soberly as she spoke. He showed no surprise until she came to the words: *We're giving back the treasure.* Then he smiled a little, his eyes glistening.

'Thank you, Shannon. I'll never be able to thank them. Just you. It was brave of you to do this.'

'It's Quentin Latta, isn't it? He's after you.'

'Yes.'

'You already knew, didn't you?'

'I've heard. Henry's not the only one I'm in touch with. Word gets around.'

'Then you didn't really need to hear from me?'

'Oh, yes, I did.' His voice was emphatic. 'Your mother meant for you to find me, and that's what you did.'

'Do you know what that means about the treasure?'

'I think so.'

'What?'

He glanced at Henry. 'It's private.' He got up. 'Now, let's get you settled in upstairs. I'll sleep on the couch down here.'

'Wait.' Her mind raced with too many questions. 'Where's Diana?'

'In the morning,' he said quietly.

'Damn it, I came a long way.' Her impatience, coupled with her mounting exhaustion, made her voice crack. 'I want to know now.'

The two men exchanged wary looks. For the first time John Paul looked unhappy with her.

'All right,' he said finally. 'It's simple, really. Diana and I are no longer together.'

'Where is she?'

'I don't know.'

'Wonderful.' She sent Henry an accusing look. 'Is this what you meant? That things weren't going to work out the way I thought?'

He nodded uncomfortably.

She turned back to John Paul. 'You know I'm supposed to find both of you.'

'I understand that's what you promised Mora.'

'Well?'

'We separated years ago, before I moved here.'

'You're divorced?'

'We were never married. Technically, I mean. We both thought marriage was a middle-class convention, unfair to women, and that each of us should be free to walk away any time we chose.'

'So you walked away.'

'Actually, she did. Let me make something clear. I love Diana. I think I always will. And I'd like to think she still feels the same way about me.'

'Then why—'

'It was politics that split us up.' He made a vague, helpless gesture, and frustration showed plainly on his face. 'Politics has always been the strongest force in our lives. For years we thought the same, struggled for the same things: ending racism in this country, ending that barbaric war in Vietnam. We would have given our lives for those causes.

'But little by little, as the war wound down and we realized that we were never going to be able to radicalize the entire country over that issue, I wanted to move away from militancy. I just wanted to work for simple fairness, trying to get an equal deal for everyone. I saw that my legal work could give me a new focus. You might say I became de-radicalized.' He shook his head slowly. 'Diana didn't understand. We both wanted to fight the system, but she was dedicated to using the old tools.'

'You mean—'

This time it was Henry who spoke up. 'Violence.'

'Bombs? That sort of thing?'

John Paul nodded, clearly not enjoying the conversation.

'I don't get it. The war's over. That war, I mean. Now we've got a new one going in Iraq, but nobody's bombing the Pentagon because of it.'

John Paul took a breath and started to reply, but Henry broke in again. 'These days, the far left doesn't have many things to get violent about, but the environment is one of 'em. Diana's got a new cause.'

Shannon's mouth hung open. 'The environment,' she said softly. 'You mean the people who fight logging, that kind of thing?'

'Among other things,' John Paul said. 'But it goes way beyond trees. There's a new breed of environmentalists who are as militant – dangerous, even – as any of us in the old anti-war movement. They believe in direct action, and their targets are logging companies, oil companies, dam-builders. But public utilities, too, like electric companies who lay power lines through the wilderness. Anybody who doesn't fit the right definition of green could get hit. The activists spike trees, and loggers sometimes get injured as a result. They blow up power lines, gas lines, oil pipelines.'

His face took on a pained expression. 'In my gut, I'm opposed to anything big, whether business or government, and I generally sympathize with the radical environmentalists. I'd like to see less logging, less invasion of wild places. But the fringe groups sometimes edge over into terrorism, and they sometimes hurt individuals. I'm not on their side.'

'And Diana is?'

'Apparently so. I don't know exactly where she is. She's even deeper underground now than I am. Diana has cut her ties with everyone I know, including Henry and your parents. But word filters out, and the word is that she's one of the leaders of a group called Free Earth.'

'I think I've heard of them,' Shannon said.

'Free Earth is at the far left of the environmental movement. They make most of the other groups look moderate. They have people above ground who sometimes speak for them. But the leadership is nameless and faceless, and their security is absolutely airtight. They're putting all the tricks we learned in the sixties back to use. If you believe the rumors, there's a hard core of a few dozen who go out and wreak havoc. Just recently, they burned down a ski lodge that was being built by a conglomerate called the Swann Group on the edge of a protected wilderness area. And this hard core is backed up by hundreds—'

'Just like your old underground,' Shannon said.

'Right. People who donate money, who give them shelter when they need it, that kind of thing. But it's the hard core who are the faceless ones. I'm told that some of the old members of our movement – knocking around for years, looking for a cause as important as stopping the Vietnam War – have joined up with them. Word is, the one at the very top of their pyramid is a woman, and some people believe it's Diana. But who knows? That could just be the kind of disinformation that helps them keep their secrets.'

'It must take money to do what she's doing. Not just stay hidden, but—'

'To stay active. Right. Diana has some money. When her mother died, she left her a pretty good chunk of the family estate, and the lawyers were able to get it to her quietly. I had some of my own family's money too. It made it possible for us to stay underground without being poor. In fact, we were pretty well-off revolutionaries, which some people might consider a contradiction in terms. To be fair, though, we plowed a lot of it back into the movement. Now, I assume she's sunk at least some of hers into the environmental movement.'

'This group, Free Earth – where are they?'

'They operate here in the West, mostly. They have an office in Portland, Oregon, but it's strictly for public relations. In practice, they're just about everywhere.'

'That really narrows it down.'

'I hope you're not going to look for her. These are dangerous people. They use explosives. Diana's never taken a human life, and I know she never would, but she's still dedicated to violence, and so are the people around her.' When Shannon didn't respond, he pressed on. 'If her sources are as good as mine, chances are she's heard about your parents. She would know about Quentin, and she'd be careful.'

'You don't know for sure.'

'I think you ought to tell her,' Henry said.

'Keep quiet, Henry.'

'Tell me what?'

John Paul looked fiercely at Henry. 'God dammit.' He rose slowly and went to the kitchen, where he got three more beers and brought them out. He didn't look at either of them, but he was clearly deep in thought.

'All right. Here it is,' he said finally as he took his seat. 'Diana and I ran the Red Fist, but I was more the theorist. She was the real leader, the tactician. Quentin wanted to take over, and he knew she was the one he would have to replace, not me. He saw her as his rival. He hated her.

'That night at the Crowe Institute, we planned to bomb the building, but we found out at the last minute that it was occupied, and we realized that Quentin had known all along that the night watchman would be there. He thought it was time to "leave some blood on the floor," as he put it. We tried to stop him, to call off the operation, but it was too late; the bomb was set. Diana and I ran, and as we went out the back, we heard Quentin yelling to her: "You're no revolutionary." He said he'd find her and kill her. Then the bomb went off.'

'And Quentin got picked up,' Shannon said.

'Right. And we denounced him, tried to separate ourselves from the killing, but nobody was convinced. One of our people had already started phoning the media, claiming responsibility in the name of the Red Fist, and the FBI found my fingerprints at the scene.'

He slumped in his chair. 'Quentin doesn't want me. Diana's his target.'

'What are you going to do about it?'

His frustration showed. 'I've done what I can. Several weeks ago, when I first heard Quentin was out, I contacted Free Earth at their Portland office, where they denied knowing anyone named Diana. I tried to get in touch with everyone from the old movement. My best chance, I thought, was two people who had been especially close to her. One of them, Katherine, either is no longer in touch with her or won't admit that she is. The other, Linc, has disappeared. There's a good chance he's with her.'

'It doesn't sound like you've done enough,' Shannon said defiantly. 'If she's in danger ...' She stopped, then plowed ahead. 'Ray and Mora would have found her.'

'Maybe.' John Paul gave her a tolerant look. 'You don't know her. If she doesn't want to be found, believe me, she'll stay hidden.'

The room was absolutely quiet. Shannon's body was worn out from the trip, but her mind would not be quiet. She stared at John Paul, still slightly amazed that she was in his presence. Another question tugged at her. 'From what you said about the changes you went through, you sound as if you could work within the system like anyone else,' she said. 'But you stay underground.'

'Oh, I could work very happily within the system, but I can't come home. I don't want to spend the rest of my life in prison. You know, that bombing back in nineteen sixty-eight was not me, because it murdered people. And yet it was me, because I helped set it up, knowing that bombs always carry risks. The law would hold me responsible, and I accept my responsibility. Not a day goes by that I don't think of Daniel Kerner and his baby daughter, who died in that building. Or of Margaret, who was Tina's mother and who, I'm sure, still mourns them both.'

His words hung heavy in the air, like an epitaph to a time long past.

Twenty-One

Her bed was comfortable. The air felt thin to her sea-level lungs, and at that high altitude, she should have slept the sleep of the exhausted. But her mind was inhabited by John Paul's stories. It was well past midnight when she finally dropped off.

She opened her eyes to see the faintest pre-dawn light beginning to bring out the shapes in her room. Noises filtered up from downstairs, and she knew their host would keep to his promise to get them on the road early.

She showered and dressed and came downstairs to find a pot of coffee on the stove and a platter of fresh fruit and sweet rolls on the kitchen table. John Paul was apparently at work, his office door closed. She poured a cup of coffee, then went upstairs to check on Henry. He lay still, deeply asleep, mouth open, one scrawny hand clutching his blanket. She hadn't the heart to awaken him yet.

Back downstairs, the office door was still closed. She went out to the Jeep, opened the rear hatch, and lifted out one of the two box files she had taken from her father's locker. When planning her drive to San Francisco, she had had two reasons for taking them with her. First, if Quentin Latta were to break in and find them, he would know that she was acquainted with her parents' past and might surmise that she had become a threat. And second, having the files with her might trigger some useful questions for Henry.

But now she had come to an information source much more vital than Henry. And her time for questioning John Paul was running out.

She carried the box inside and laid it on the coffee table in the living room, then sank onto the sofa with her coffee. Lifting off the lid, she debated where to start. West, Burke, or Latta? What were her most pressing questions?

She heard faltering footsteps on the stairs and a tired 'Mornin'' from Henry as he went to the kitchen, then the rattle of a coffee cup.

The first file she pulled out was the one containing the two birth certificates, hers and Beth's. She started to put it aside but, on instinct, opened it. She pulled the two documents apart at the staple and looked over the one underneath.

It was not Beth's birth certificate. It was her own.

This made no sense. Shannon shook her head and tried to refocus on what she was reading. According to what she held in her hand, she had been born at Cook County Hospital, Chicago, Illinois. Scanning the other typewritten entries on the page, a few things jibed with what she already knew – her date of birth, for example.

Other things were oddly, sickeningly wrong.

Her parents were listed as William and Helen Norris of Chicago, and she as Shannon Patrice Norris.

She held the two documents up side by side, studying each in turn. Although both appeared authentic, that was impossible. One was right, the other wrong. One was genuine, the other phony.

They had document experts, she reminded herself, recalling last night's conversation. *One in Chicago.*

All right then, she thought grimly. *I'll just have to find out which—*

'How long have you known?'

She turned her head to see Henry standing behind her, seeing what she saw, looking unutterably sad.

'Known what?' Her stomach was beginning to clench. She dreaded his answer.

'Have you talked to him about it?' He indicated the closed office door.

'Why would I?' And then it struck her, and for a moment she could not breathe. She remembered her mother struggling to breathe as she lay on that bed, buried in medical clutter, and she felt the same desperation.

She looked up at Henry, and his face told her that he had let slip something momentous. 'Tell me,' she said in a whisper.

He shook his head, taking a small, fearful step backward.

No, she thought. *No, that's not right. Couldn't be right.* The thought was so large, so heavy, there was no room for it in her brain. It required too much thought, too much recalculation. It would be like re-imagining history, she thought wildly. *All my history.*

I'd have to go back to the very beginning and start over.

She got up so quickly she bumped the table, splashing coffee out of the cup. She went to the office door and knocked twice.

'Come on in.'

John Paul West sat at his desk with his back to her, his right hand on a computer mouse. Her chest felt tight; the words wouldn't come out. Looking around the room, as if for inspiration, her eyes fell on a bookshelf. Amid the law books and other titles, she saw an oversize and brightly colored volume. Walking over, she pulled it down.

The Corsair's Daughter.

He swiveled around in his chair. She raised her eyes to find him looking at her and at the book she held, his expression, like Henry's, full of sadness.

'Are you my father?'

For ten seconds the silence in the room was absolute. He leaned forward, elbows on knees, never taking his eyes from her. Finally he spoke.

'Yes.'

Something loosened inside her, like the easing of a gateway to let water through a dam. She didn't feel joy, or even satisfaction; it was more like relief. Not relief at finding a father. That knowledge, she knew, was still incomplete. There were layers to it, and the final knowledge could carry pain with it.

Instead, the feeling was akin to a voice that said, *Of course. Of course he's your father. It explains things. It explains* you.

'Why did you . . .?'

'Give you up?' His chair creaked as he stood, looking awkward, speaking across the six feet that separated them. 'We had to. We tried for six months, but then we knew it wasn't possible. A baby girl. It was two years after the Crowe Institute, and every cop and FBI agent in America was looking for us. We were on the run. We honestly tried to make it work, but after six months we knew it couldn't. It was dangerous for all of us, and, looking ahead, we could see no life for you underground. So we looked for the finest people we knew, people who wanted a child and who would give you the best possible life.'

'Ray and Mora Fairchild.' It was the first time she had ever spoken their names without the knowledge that they were her true parents.

'Yes. Ray and Mora. They did it for us, but they genuinely wanted you, because they had been trying to have a baby since they were married. When she got pregnant, Diana visited them in Mexico, where they were spending a year before graduate school, and that's when Mora first broached the idea of adoption. She was the first to really understand what lay ahead for us. Diana was reluctant. She truly wanted to keep you. But after you were born, we both understood that you needed a better home. We gave you up only with the greatest reluctance. But we never questioned the rightness of the decision.'

He gestured toward the doorway. 'Would you like to sit out there, have some breakfast?'

'No, let's finish this.' Her voice was hard.

He sighed. 'We kept in touch with them over the years, as much as our situation would allow, to learn about you. Diana wanted to see you, but it was too dangerous. We sent you one of our books—'

'One of your books? You wrote it?'

'Uh-huh. When the war ended, we were a little adrift. We got the idea of writing books for kids, books that might make them feel that they could accomplish something. The author's name is a play on Diana's first name and my last. One of our old friends from the movement worked for a children's press, so it wasn't hard to get them published. Anyway, we were very happy to learn that you liked the book.'

'Oh, I did. It was the perfect book for a little girl. You know my favorite part?' Her sarcasm rose like bile. 'It was where he comes back for her.'

She tossed the book aside. It struck the wall and dislodged a framed picture, which fell to the floor, its glass shattering.

He winced at the sound, but her eyes continued to bore in on him. She felt swept by loss – first her parents, taken so hideously from her, and now the loss of Diana and John Paul, the ones to whom she had first belonged, the ones who had given her away. Given her away so they could keep running. As the knowledge took shape, she felt the first stirrings of hate for the two of them.

'I couldn't come for you,' he said almost under his breath. 'I wanted to – we both did – but I couldn't. I did manage one visit to your home, though, and I found it hard to take my eyes off you all the time I—'

A sudden realization. 'You were Uncle Don.'

'That's right. I was Uncle Don, who had to die later, to explain why the family never heard from him again.'

She rubbed her forehead, intent on a thought just taking shape. 'Mom,' she said almost dreamily. 'Her last words. They were so confusing. Just before she died, I tried to ask her who I was supposed to warn, and she said, *You're* … and couldn't finish the thought. I thought she was telling me something about myself. But it's so simple now. She was using a different word that sounded just the same. She was trying to say the words: *Your parents*.'

He nodded gravely.

Her voice turned brittle. 'My real parents – the ones who did the work of raising me – were tortured and killed so their two old friends, the celebrity fugitives, could stay safe. If you ask me, you don't deserve the name *father*.'

He mouthed the words *I know*, but nothing came out.

She heard noises in the kitchen. 'How much does Henry know?'

'All of it. As I said, Henry's a soldier. I've always trusted him. Diana did, too, until she went off to find her new life.'

He studied her, trying to read her expression. 'I can't blame you if you hate me, and I know you won't believe this. But we never stopped loving you. Being separated from your child doesn't mean you stop loving her.'

'*Being separated*,' she said mockingly. 'That sounds so passive. Why don't you just say you dropped me off on somebody's doorstep?'

He looked totally vulnerable, and she was glad she had wounded him. 'Is there anything I can—' he began.

'You've done plenty,' she said, turning abruptly toward the doorway. 'Just give us directions out of town. And we'll leave now.'

She went to the door, stopped, and turned back to face him.

'You know what pisses me off? You two mad bombers get careless, get pregnant and have a kid, then decide that she'd be a drag to you, so you palm her off on somebody else – and everybody just falls in line. "Sure we'll take the little bundle of joy. You just go ahead with your romantic life on the lam, with your mugshots on the cover of *Time* magazine, and we'll do the hard work you don't have time for. Anything else we can do for you?"

'You get to walk away from everything, don't you? You bomb a building and walk away. You have me and walk away.'

Then she strode out into the living room. 'Come on, Henry. I've delivered my message. Let's hit the road.'

Twenty-Two

Snow began falling within an hour after they left Billings. Shannon drove with fierce concentration, her brow furrowed as if she were working on a particularly thorny problem. For the first few hours she shook off Henry's attempts at conversation, and the only sounds were the engine drone and the wet slapping of the wipers. When he took his turn behind the wheel, she sat trance-like, looking out at the white and gray landscape speeding by.

South of Butte, with a river valley to their left and high forest land to their right, Henry tried again. He cleared his throat loudly and started off, 'What you heard back there. I know that's a lot to, uh—'

'He said you knew all about me.'

'That's right.' He seemed relieved at the chance to talk about it finally. 'I couldn't tell you 'cause—'

'I get it, Henry, okay? It was a big fucking secret. Lives hanging in the balance, that kind of stuff. They asked you to keep the secret, and you did. It was Diana's secret, and John Paul's, and then it became yours and, oh yeah, let's not forget Ray and Mora, it was their secret, too. Everybody knew except little Shannon. So we'll just let her grow up weird, thinking she's strange, not knowing why. And all the time, here's the reason she was so messed up: She didn't really belong in that family.'

'You did too, girl. Ray and Mora loved you.'

'Sure they did. I can see that now. They did their very best with the little transplant from—' She stopped. 'I'm from Chicago, right? That's very funny. I thought I'd never been to Chicago, and damned if I wasn't born there.'

'Yeah, you were, all right. The Mexican thing … that was just because Ray and Mora were spendin' a year down there. So none of their friends here in the States would wonder why they'd never seen her pregnant.'

'They really thought of everything, didn't they? Even the story about Puerto Vallarta and the handsome Mexican doctor. It was all a lie my mother told me. I kind of liked it, though, you know? A nice lie to tell a little girl.'

'Mora did what she had to do.'

'I know. I don't blame her. But what is it about this name of mine? *Norris?*'

'That was the name Diana and John Paul were using back then. They used it for a long time, but then things got hot for them, and they had to drop it and pick up another one.'

Just like they dropped me. She was ready with the crack, but Henry was not the object of her anger, and she didn't want to hurt him.

'Important thing is, you're Shannon Fairchild. No need to wonder who you are, girl. You're Shannon Fairchild, and don't you forget it.'

'Right. But it would have been great if Ray and Mora – the ones I used to call Mom and Dad – had told me at least some of it. Leaving out the super-secret, lives-at-stake part. But just enough to let me know that whenever I felt like an outsider, at least there was a good solid reason.'

'You really think you'da been happier knowin' you were adopted?' His voice took on a new assurance, suggesting that he'd grappled with this question before.

Her silence lasted a long time. She chewed at a hangnail. Finally she burst out: 'I don't know, okay? But I can tell you this: I'm thirty-four years old, living a life that's not particularly great, and all of a sudden I find out a bunch of people have been keeping something from me. You might call it the most important thing about me: Who I am.'

Henry didn't respond, but out of the corner of her eye she saw him nodding.

After a while, she looked his way again, and her tone softened. 'You're a good soldier, Henry. You're loyal, and that makes you better than they are.'

He shook his head. 'No. They're not like you and me. They've picked the hardest kind of life, just because of what they believe.

That makes 'em very tough and very special. And that's the reason people do things for 'em.'

'Yeah, well, I guess I just don't get how special they are.'

That wasn't entirely true, she admitted to herself. From everything she had read and heard about that pair, the word *charisma* clung to them like glue. But as soon as she considered the way they had treated her, it was easy to lose her sense of awe. In abandoning her, they had been all too human.

'Special?' Henry said with a chuckle. 'I could tell you stories. One time in Chicago, f'rinstance. We're marchin' out o' Grant Park, tryin' to get to the Convention Center, and we come up to a police barrier. A solid wall, I kid you not, all of 'em big, beefy characters with clubs and shields, just waitin' for us to try somethin'. They tell us to turn around, and I swear some of us are ready to. But John Paul just yells out, "Come on!" and charges 'em all by himself, swingin' his fists, cussin' 'em. They knock him down and start workin' him over with their clubs. Some of us try to grab him and pull him back, but the cops close ranks around him. It's gettin' ugly.'

'God,' Shannon muttered. 'What—'

'Coulda killed him,' Henry went on. 'But a second later Diana starts screamin' at us, "What are you, pussies? They're just a bunch of pigs in uniform." And she piles right into the line, and this time we're all behind her. It's a mob scene, but we're just able to get John Paul by the legs and haul him out. We make what we call a strategic retreat. Everybody's bruised and beat up, but nobody worse than those two.'

He shook his head, smiling at the memory. 'How could you not follow two people like that?'

'Maybe.' She found that kind of risk-taking hard to imagine. The sixties, she reflected, truly had been a different time. 'Were Ray and Mora ... ?'

'Right in the middle of it, girl. You woulda been proud of 'em.'

I suppose I would have. The thought took her by surprise.

Henry's look turned serious. 'All that stuff you learned from John Paul. You're not gonna, uh ... ?'

She made a derisive sound. 'Oh, don't worry. I won't rat on them. They can go on living this way as long as they want. They can be

America's most wanted all the way to the old folks' home, for all I care. If Quentin Latta doesn't catch up to them first.'

He appeared relieved. 'You wanna stock up on some food?' he asked, gesturing toward a rest stop up ahead.

'Sure.' He pulled off, and a few minutes later they were back on the road, Shannon driving, with roast beef sandwiches and jumbo soft drinks. Soon they were back in Idaho, passing through cities they had seen just the day before – Idaho Falls, Pocatello, Twin Falls. Henry had his directions out, and they negotiated a freeway interchange, swapping one number for another.

As they ate their sandwiches, Shannon reflected more on the revelation she'd been given back in Billings. *I've found my birth father*, she told herself as calmly as she could. *And I'm still trying to decide what to think about it.*

John Paul West, without question, had now taken on major importance to her. As a consequence, would Ray Fairchild fade into the background?

No, she thought. *I won't let that happen. For all the rough times I had growing up, he was my dad. He chose me for a daughter, and he played the role of father better than anyone could. I'd swap John Paul West in a second if it would bring back my father.*

More questions nagged at her. She glanced at Henry, who was making short work of his sandwich.

'Did they honestly think I'd never find out?'

'Never.' He maneuvered his sandwich to catch a slice of beef that threatened to desert its bun. 'It was better if you didn't. You'd be happier. Diana and John Paul wanted you to have a good life, the kind they couldn't give you.'

'But I did find out.' Her tone was bitter. 'And now here I am, up to my neck—'

'Understand one thing,' Henry interrupted, chewing furiously to get his food down and finish his thought. 'Ray and Mora bein' killed had nothin' to do with you. Quentin woulda come after them whether they'd adopted you or not. You know that, don't you?'

She was silent for a while, asking herself if she did, in fact, know that, but she was unable to come up with an answer. 'You think Quentin knows who I am?'

'Smart as he is, I figure he has to know. But as long as he thinks you're in the dark, he's got no reason to hurt you.'

'Then I'll have to keep him thinking I'm in the dark, won't I?'

Henry finished off his sandwich and wiped his hands on a paper napkin. His next question came out softer. 'What about Diana?'

'I don't know. I don't know, Henry, all right? I'm not feeling very charitable toward her right now. And even if I were, how the hell would I find her if John Paul himself can't?'

He seemed about to answer.

'What?'

'Nothin'. I guess you're right. How could you find her if nobody else could?'

Her memory threw up the image of Quentin Latta from the wanted flyer Birdsong had shown her. *He could be closing in on Diana right now,* she thought, *and there's not a damn thing anybody can do about it. Birdsong says he'll stop him if he can. But I'd bet almost every other cop in the country would applaud if somebody killed her off. File closed.*

That seemed to exhaust the possibilities for conversation. After a while, when Henry asked if she'd mind some music, she said no. But nothing from the '60s, she said, and popped in Mendelssohn's *A Midsummer Night's Dream.*

Henry sighed. About halfway through the first movement, he said grudgingly, 'That's kinda pretty.'

Fitfully, the snow followed them out of the Rockies. Around four, they reached the outskirts of Wells, the northern Nevada town where they had overnighted on the trip east. Some daylight was left, but Shannon was tired and irritable. 'You want to stop here again tonight?'

'Fine by me.' Henry found the same motel and pulled into the lot, aiming toward the office, but then abruptly jerked the wheel over and scooted into the nearest parking space. 'Shit.'

'What?'

'You see that?' He pointed behind them. 'In front of the office? It's that gray van.'

'Oh, come on . . .' She turned to look. 'It's a gray van, but let's not get carried away.'

'No.' His posture was tense. 'It's got California plates. I can see that from here.'

'We're in Nevada, Henry. It's right next door to California.' She was losing patience with him.

'I need to look.' He was suddenly out of the Jeep. Turning to watch, she saw him weave in and out of parked cars, maneuvering until he was slightly ahead of the van. He raised himself from behind the front end of a car, stared for several seconds, then ducked down and made his way back to Shannon.

'Well?'

'Nobody in the driver's seat. They're prob'ly in the office. And the office window's fogged up, so I can't see inside. But there's a guy in the passenger seat.'

'Uh-huh. So?'

'Big, heavy-set; wearin' a coat and a cap with ear-flaps, so I couldn't see much of him. But …'

'Yeah?'

'I thought he looked a little familiar.'

She waited. When he said nothing, she prodded him.

'Could it have been Quentin?'

The look on his face was enough. Once again she felt the numbing grip on her upper arm, heard the soft, meandering voice. Fear tugged at her.

She kicked her door open. 'Come around to this side, Henry. I'm driving.'

Twenty-Three

Shannon found the freeway interchange, where they picked up the westbound 80, and drove as fast as the snow would allow. Several thoughts nagged at her, and she tried to express them to Henry.

If it was Quentin back there, why would he pick that very motel? If the choice of motel was not random, that suggested that Quentin and his companion were on their trail. How on earth could the two have known that they stopped there?

Henry spoke up. 'Only one way: your credit card. You used it there, right?'

'Uh, yeah.' But it would take someone with police connections to track the use of a credit card, and Quentin was no cop.

'Could be he's traveling with one,' Henry suggested.

'Maybe.' Shannon was dubious. On the other hand, Henry's friend at the liquor store had said a young man was asking about him. Tim Dodd, the FBI agent? She tried to conjure up a mental image of Dodd and Quentin Latta as traveling companions and rejected it. The idea was just too far-fetched. Quentin's driver, whoever he was, had almost certainly joined him in the carnage that left Ray and Mora dead, and the FBI was trying to track them down.

'We got one advantage,' Henry said. 'The most they could know is we stopped there. They don't know how far we went. And they don't know where we are now.'

'That doesn't bring me a lot of comfort,' she answered, trying to control the nervousness in her voice. 'Tell you what: Let's hope they're headed northeast, and we'll just go the other way.'

She drove with absolute concentration, intent only on putting distance between herself and the others. Swapping off behind the wheel, eating on the road, and growing more and more tired but fearful of slowing down, they made it to San Francisco just after midnight.

She accompanied him up to his apartment, her carry-all bag clutched at her side. He unlocked the door, took a look around inside, and pronounced it all clear, but still she looked doubtful.

'I don't like this,' she said. 'You're not safe here—'

'Been thinkin' the same thing,' he said. 'Tell you what. I got a friend down on Two. Name's Myron. He's retired from the post office. We help each other out. I could just lock up this place and stay with him for a while. We'd have to wake him up, but ...'

'I don't know,' she said. 'Myron, huh? Introduce me.'

Henry led her down to the second floor, knocked several times on a door, and moments later she was sitting in the living room of Myron Berger, a sleepy, bald little sparrow of a man with delicate, expressive hands who could have been seventy or eighty but was nonetheless full of energy and goodwill. He and Henry were clearly friends, and Myron said he would be happy to let Henry use his old Murphy bed, the kind that folded down from the wall. He didn't ask why. 'My sister uses it whenever she comes,' he said. 'She sleeps all right on it, and she's very particular.'

'That'll be fine, Myron,' Henry assured him.

'You want some coffee?' Myron asked them. 'Juice?' He was almost natty in pajamas, a burgundy bathrobe and leather slippers.

'Not for me, thanks,' she said. 'I've got to go.' Shaking Myron's hand, she said, 'I appreciate your doing this favor for Henry.'

'Oh, shoot. Henry and I go way back. We've lived in this building forever. I was carrying mail when he showed up here, just a young kid, wearing paisley and smoking anything you could light.' He looked at Henry fondly. 'I've always had lots of straight friends. Henry the longest, though.'

Outside Myron's door, she gave Henry a rib-cracking hug. 'Thank you,' she said. 'I have to say it's been a mixed experience. But at least I got to see you again. You're one of the good guys.'

'Stay in touch?' he said almost wistfully.

'With your phone, it'll be easy now.' She had made a hasty stop in Reno, at a big discount store just off the freeway, bought Henry a cell phone with prepaid minutes, and programed her number into it.

Eyelids drooping with exhaustion, she pulled into a truck stop on her way south and slept fitfully for an hour. That gave her just enough energy to drive the rest of the way to San Malo. It was still dark when she reached her house. The next thing she knew, she was under her bedcovers, still dressed, dropping into a deep sleep.

But even asleep, her mind boiled, and she found herself once again marching in that ragged formation of young people trying to stop a war. Amid the shouts and chants, Shannon saw Diana Burke and John Paul West beside her, fists in the air, eyes focused on something only they could see.

This time Shannon knew the questions she needed to ask both of them, and they came tumbling out breathlessly, one after the other.

But neither looked her way. Up ahead, a blue line of police blocked the street. Shannon's concerns would have to wait. It was time to bring the war home, and people were going to get hurt.

She slept until noon and awoke surprisingly rested. After an easy run around the neighborhood, she showered and had breakfast. It was only then that she noticed the message light on her phone was blinking.

The call was from Tim Dodd, the young FBI agent. He'd been recalled to LA, he said, but would return to San Malo in a week or so and hoped to speak to her again. He apologized for leaving her with a bad impression. He sounded sincere. She wondered if she had written him off too soon. For one thing, he was cute. For another, it would be nice to find someone in law enforcement she could trust. An instant later she rejected that thought. *Don't tell police, stupid.*

Next on her agenda was sustenance. A sweep of the kitchen turned up armloads of over-the-hill perishables. She drove to the market and replenished them. When she returned, the message light on the phone was blinking again.

It was TeeJay.

'Hey,' he began in his familiar drawl. 'Tried your cell phone, too. I'm still stuck out here in San Berdoo. Borin' as hell, but I found two good bars. Been thinkin' about you. Can you gimme a call?'

She wasted no time punching in his number and was startled when he quickly answered.

'Hello, wandering boy.'

'Hello, yourself.'

'So you've been thinking about me.'

'Yep. I know it's crazy, but every girl I meet in this town's as dumb as a bag o' rocks. I never thought I'd miss a smart woman so much.'

'Well, I'm just flattered beyond words.' Hearing his voice was like a tonic. After the craziness of the past few days, it was good to be exposed to his simple, country-boy charm. 'Don't you miss anything else about me?'

'Yes, ma'am, I believe I do. Maybe I can explain it to you sometime.'

'When are you coming this way?'

'Maybe soon. You been up to anything?'

She hesitated. *Have I been up to anything? Where do I begin?*

'Actually I have, but I won't bore you with it, because it's family business.'

'About your folks? I'm sorry. You've had enough of that, haven't you?'

'It's not that, exactly. Just other things. I've been out of town for a while. It's … complicated; stuff that goes back years.'

For just a moment, she was tempted to tell him all of it. With his own family history of loss and abandonment, he would understand. Also, TeeJay had a quiet competence and toughness that could serve as a resource for her. There might be a day when she needed such qualities.

But no, she thought. It would be unfair to dump any of this on another person.

'Sorry,' she said finally. 'I just feel like I've been handed a job I don't want, and I'm mad at the world.'

'What—'

'And that's the last I'm going to say about it, because I'm starting to hear self-pity, and I hate to sound like that.'

'All right, then,' he said with a touch of his customary wry humor. 'No self-pity in this here bar. Uh, listen … I'm gonna try to get away from my job for a while. Okay if I come see you?'

'Is it okay? You get yourself over here anytime you like. The welcome mat's out.'

Hanging up, she felt almost ridiculously pleased. He still liked her. She still felt attracted to him. Nothing about this match-up felt long-term, but that didn't matter. Seeing him would be like a small respite from the challenges life had thrown at her ever since that night when she had awakened to the helpless, frightened sound of Beth's voice. It was less than a week ago, she reminded herself. But it felt like the dim past, a time when she still thought of Beth as her sister.

Twenty-Four

The F-150, covered with road dust, rolled up with a faint squeal of brakes while she was having breakfast the following morning. She went out to meet him, and he threw an arm around her shoulder as they went up her front steps.

'You hungry?' she asked him as they entered.

'Uh-huh,' he said, steering her toward the bedroom. 'For some food, too. But that can wait.'

They were together, off and on, for the next several days. They jogged around the harbor and went for a long walk that threaded its way up among some of the grand estates in the hills overlooking the city and the bay. Sometimes he stayed over, sometimes not. She had been by his place, a rented house even smaller than hers about a mile away in another corner of Ben's Beach, and tried to invite herself over. But he gently fended her off, saying it was a bachelor's hangout and a wreck. From what little she had seen of it, he spoke the truth.

Through it all she marveled at their easy congeniality. Neither demanded a thing of the other. The sex was good and uncomplicated. Their conversations were relaxed. When it came time for him to leave, she let him go. Even his leaving felt right.

This is going much too well, she thought. *But I'm not complaining.*

One night, he brought over a couple of bottles of wine, and they had spaghetti marinara, using Mora's recipe, and a tossed salad. TeeJay switched to beer early on, and Shannon plunged deeper into the wine than she had intended. Before long, dinner was over, she was two-thirds of the way through the second bottle, and the two of them lay sprawled on her living-room cushions.

He gave her a long look. 'Somethin's on your mind,' he said. 'It was there on the phone, and it's there now. You know, people say I'm a pretty good listener.'

At that moment, with the wine kicking in, she felt burdened with an almost intolerable weight of sadness, and TeeJay sounded as if he were offering to help her carry it. Realizing that she had been waiting for just such an invitation, she began to talk.

It took her forty-five minutes to tell the whole story. The only things she omitted were the locations, real or speculative, of Diana and John Paul. Even in her relaxed state, she knew that no one should hold that information. TeeJay was transfixed by her account, asking only an occasional quiet question. When she had finished, he sat shaking his head over and over.

Finally he spoke. 'So she's still hidin' out, and nobody knows where she is.'

'Nobody. Not even John Paul.'

'And you haven't told the police anything?'

'No. Not the police, not the FBI.'

'I'm with you on that. Wouldn't trust any of 'em.'

She tried to focus on him, but the wine made it difficult. 'I've got to ask you: Have you ever been in trouble with the cops?'

A wry grin. 'It shows, huh? I stole a car once when I was sixteen, and I spent six months in juvie.'

'Was it tough?'

'Oh, yeah. I learned a thing or two. I learned I wasn't the toughest kid in the barracks. Not nearly.'

'I'm sorry.'

'It's okay. I learned I wasn't the puniest either.' He came over and lay down next to her, not touching, crossing his arms under his head. 'You need help with this?'

'No. I mean … I don't know. Thanks for offering, though.'

'What are you gonna do about this Diana woman?'

'There's nothing I can do,' she said, sleepiness in her voice. 'Not a damn thing.'

Later, as he lay asleep beside her, she silently revisited his words: *You need help with this?*

She had said no, and she was reasonably sure she meant it. She didn't want to expose TeeJay to danger. But the dark brought a new perspective, as it often did. Of course she needed help, a special kind, someone canny, capable, and discreet. The choices available, though, were limited by many factors. The need for secrecy, for example, ruled out the police. She wondered if TeeJay had what she needed. As soon as the question arose, an answer of sorts replayed itself in her memory.

A few weeks after she had met him, they had driven up the coast for a long weekend in the Bay Area. On the afternoon of the second day, they went up into the hills above Oakland and enjoyed the view of San Francisco. Later, driving around Oakland, they stopped at a bar near the waterfront. As they sat drinking and watching a Giants game on the TV above the bar, a man sitting two stools away reached over for a bowl of peanuts and spilled most of them in TeeJay's lap. TeeJay muttered something in an irritated tone, and the man picked up on it.

'Say something?'

'Nope,' TeeJay answered mildly, brushing at his lap. 'Just cleanin' up after you.'

Shannon stole a look at the man, who was sitting with a couple of friends. He was big, almost NFL-size, and his smaller friends wore anticipatory grins, as if they'd watched this scenario many times.

'I mean, if you're all *bothered* by it, I can come over and clean you up myself,' the man said, rocking his beer bottle gently back and forth in a large fist. 'I can even clean up your girlfriend's lap too. Free of charge.'

Shannon saw a change come over TeeJay's face, and she knew his sense of machismo was about to get him seriously hurt. She grabbed his wiry arm and hung on. 'No,' she whispered fiercely. '*No. I mean it. Let's leave now. Please.*'

Seconds went by, and then she saw his face relax. 'No harm done,' he said in a loud voice without turning to the other man, and he patted Shannon's hand and hoisted his beer.

Relieved, she marveled at his steel-jacketed self-control. Seconds later they were talking and laughing again as if nothing had happened.

Sometime after that Mr NFL slid off his stool and headed for a neon sign that read *Men's*. TeeJay slapped some money on the bar, leaned over and said quietly to her, 'Go out and start the car. I'll be right along. Hurry, now.' As she left, she saw him strolling easily toward the men's room.

Two uneasy minutes passed as she sat behind the wheel. When he reappeared, he was carrying a bundle under his arm, thickly wrapped in paper towels, and when he got in, she saw that he wasn't wearing his usual biker boots.

'TeeJay …'

'Drive. Gonna be people comin' outta that place pretty soon.'

She drove, all the way to their motel, where he excused himself and went into the bathroom. She heard the sound of running water for several minutes, then he emerged, once again wearing his boots. They looked damp.

'You going to tell me what happened back there?'

'Nope.' He was examining his fingernails. 'Let's go get us some dinner, huh?'

And that was it. Except … After he went to sleep that night, she went into the bathroom and looked around. A single ruby drop, unmistakably blood, shone next to the cold-water tap, a spot he'd missed. In the wastebasket she found a mass of wadded paper towels, all soaked with water. The ones on top were reasonably clean. The layer underneath was pink. The ones at the bottom were stained a sickening dark red.

She crept back into bed and could tell that she'd awakened him. 'You cleaned your boots, didn't you?'

'Uh-huh.'

'You going to tell me now?'

'Sure, if you want. I went in, popped him with my elbow. He went down. And I stomped him.'

'You …?'

'Stomped him. I sure didn't feel like breakin' a couple of knuckles on him.'

As she lay there trying to think of something to say, his hand grazed her thigh. It felt like a small electric shock. She tried to erase the image of blood from her mind, then realized that she did not want to. As she grabbed his hand and swung his weight atop her, she let the image wash over her, a strange and powerful new aphrodisiac.

Now, lying in her own bed, the memory of that night in San Francisco faded, and she rolled over, ready for sleep. The last thing to take up space in her mind was the question, *You need help with this?*

Yes, I need help with this, she said to herself, *but I won't ask him. My wandering boy is tough, no question, but not tough enough to take on the likes of Quentin Latta.*

Twenty-Five

The next morning his cell phone rang and, as usual, he didn't answer it. Later he checked for messages and told her the job needed his attention again. 'I'll see you in about a week,' he said. 'We can talk about this thing of yours. I might have an idea.'

'Don't wander too far,' she said.

In the afternoon she went through her mail and paid bills, then sat in the most comfortable chair on her porch and browsed through a history of the Gilded Age she had long meant to read. It was well researched and written, but it felt dry as dust.

The experience of the last few days had touched her deeply, because it affected her life and the person she was. But it had also affected her feel for history. She now felt a link to some of the most turbulent years of modern America, and the knowledge had re-awakened the historian in her. She was a part of those years, and she felt a hunger to know more about the time when she was born, when her country fought and lost a useless war, when tens of thousands of Americans and millions of Southeast Asians died. When revolution was in the air breathed by Diana Burke and John Paul West and others. The revolution never really materialized, but lives were lost in the imagining of it.

Lives were still being lost today, people close to her. And possibly more to come. Almost certainly more to come.

She had played a small role in the beginning of all this, she thought, and she was still part of it. What role would she play now?

She fixed dinner and ate without paying attention. Afterward she curled up on her sofa, bolstered by pillows all around, put on headphones and listened to the first movement of Prokofiev's Fifth, the music swollen with yearning, reaching for something unattainable.

Throughout the piece, she reached for something, too – understanding. In recent days she had made a life-changing discovery about herself, her very nature. Was she meant to learn from it, or to do more? To act on it?

She felt as if she stood at a place in the woods where many paths converged. Her choices were almost without number. The old Shannon might have done nothing. But she did not feel like the old Shannon.

Restless, she got up and put on her sweats. A light run would help her sleep. She put Rhonda's .38 in her pocket, but the handle stuck out, and the weight, she knew, would throw her off her stride. Instead, she pocketed her usual small canister of pepper spray and headed out.

In the night chill off the ocean, she ran along the shabby main drag of Ben's Beach, then threaded back through parts of her neighborhood. The streetlights threw out only patchy light, but she knew every irregular, potholed step of the way. After twenty minutes she was pleasantly winded and ready for bed.

Mounting her front steps, she noticed that the porch was dark, the light out. This struck her as odd, since she remembered replacing the bulb only a few weeks earlier. She began to fiddle with it, but it dropped suddenly out of its socket and fell to the floor, shattering with a soft pop. 'Shit,' she muttered.

'They told me you cuss a lot.'

She froze mid-breath. The voice had come from the corner of the porch, where a chair and small table sat. Her eyes darted to the spot but saw only a shadowy void.

Her right hand crept toward the pocket holding the pepper spray.

'Don't reach for it, whatever it is,' the voice said with a lazy authority. 'I'll have to come over there and take it away from you, and somebody might get hurt.'

Run. She turned, her heel crunching on broken glass, and lunged toward the steps, but he was faster, exploding out of his dark corner, grabbing her by the sweatshirt's hood draped on her shoulder, and lifting her off her feet. Propelled backward, she slammed into her front door and crumpled to the planks of the porch.

Breathless, her ribs sore, she crouched by the door as he resumed his seat.

'If I'd come here to hurt you, you'd be hurt by now.'

'I am hurt.'

'Not that much. I'd like you to take that chair over there. And watch the broken glass.'

She got up carefully, went to the chair on the other side of the porch, and sat down about ten feet from him. She squinted to get a look but could make out only a shape.

'I won't keep you long,' the voice said. It was deep, almost gravelly, with an accent she couldn't place. It was not the voice of a young man. Quentin? No. Quentin's voice had been lighter, more treble.

But it could be someone working for him, she told herself, and the fear that she had often experienced in recent days – the fear that she despised herself for feeling – crept back inside her.

'You've been doing some traveling, meeting up with people, learning things.'

How could he know? The thought that her travels were no secret only added to her fear.

'I'm here to ask you what you plan to do next.'

'Who the hell are you?' she demanded with more conviction than she felt. 'And why the hell should I tell you anything?'

'They told me you had guts,' he said. 'That's good, as long as you're not stupid, too. Are you?'

She was suddenly angry at this interrogation. 'Fuck you.'

'Right,' he said with a brisk laugh. 'I guess that answers my question.'

'Fuck you again.' As she realized that he had not come there to hurt her, her indignation grew. 'I think it's time you told me who you are.'

'A guy who's been watching you. Like some other people, I'm interested in you and what you do.'

'Very mysterious.'

'I know you've been with John Paul West, and he told you things. Things I already know.'

'What?'

'There are people who know who you are …'

'And who am I?'

'You're the daughter of John Paul and Diana.'

To hear this stranger, this voice, utter those words so casually almost took her breath away. And the thought that others knew, had long known … The thought was unsettling to her.

'Like I said, there are people who know who you are, who want you to be safe, and who need to know what you're about to do.'

'Look, even I don't know what I'm about to do.'

'Then you should decide. There's a kind of a war being fought out there. Diana's in the middle of it. If you go looking for her, it could complicate things for her. It could get dangerous for you.'

She took a deep breath. 'One thing I do know: Whatever this is, it's not my war. And right now I'm not planning to go looking for anyone.'

'Well …' She heard him get up from his chair. 'That would be the first smart thing you've said tonight.' He stood by the chair, still in the dark. 'If you'll go inside now, I'll leave. I was in your house, but not for long. I didn't take anything. And your doors and windows are all locked.'

What good does that do, she wondered, *if the likes of you can get past them?*

As she opened the door and stepped inside, she heard him descend the steps and say, 'You don't need to call the police, do you?'

She closed the door, double-locked it, and stood with her back to it. *What I need is a drink. Make that two.*

Twenty-Six

On her second glass of wine, she suddenly thought of Henry and dialed the number of the phone she had bought him. He answered on the first ring. After determining that he was all right, she told him, quickly and without drama, about her visitor.

'He knew about me. He said others know, too, and they want me to be safe. But they don't want me to go after Diana. Who the hell is he?'

'I don't know, girl, but he's probably part of the network. Sounds to me like he gave you some good advice.'

'The whole fucking network has known about me?'

'No. Just some of 'em. There've been rumors about you for years. Every time I heard one, I'd try to knock it down. But people talk.'

'Yeah? Well, not to me they didn't.'

He was silent for a moment. Then: 'Can I tell you a story?'

'Sure.'

'I drove you,' he said quietly.

'Huh?'

'I drove you to 'em. You remember on the trip when we were talkin' about my drivin', and I said I once drove a VW bus a long way from Chicago?'

'Yeah?'

'Well, I drove it all the way to California. And you were in the back.'

'I was . . .'

'All bundled up in the back. You were six months old, and you cried most of the way.' Sadness colored his voice. 'I felt so sorry for you, but there wasn't much I could do, you understand. I just had to get you there. I tried my best to feed you, and—' A weak laugh. 'I learned how to change diapers.'

'You drove me.' An image began to surface, but she couldn't quite make it out.

'It took me three days. You cried most of the time, whenever you weren't asleep. I think it was 'cause you were scared. We'd pass through towns at night, and I guess the lights looked scary to you.'

'Lights.' The image sharpened. Lights overhead. 'Was it cold?'

'Hmm?'

'When you were driving me. Was it cold?'

'Oh, girl, was it ever. It was December, and the heater didn't work. I had the windows rolled up, but we had to drive through snow part of the time, and it was—'

'Cold.' And there it was. Her nightmare, unscrolling now in her mind. Lights, movement, freezing cold. Fear. Loss.

'And a man leaned over me,' she said, almost to herself. 'The light was behind him. I couldn't see his face. And I screamed.'

'Oh, you really did.' The sadness in his voice deepened. 'But it was the end of our trip, girl. And the man was just picking you up, to hold you. It was Ray. He was happy to see you. Mora too.'

'I was so scared.' Almost a whisper. 'I actually remember it.'

'You didn't know it, but you were home.'

'Home.'

He let out a long breath. She could hear faint music. 'Myron's watchin' TV,' he said. 'I'll go keep him company.' He paused. 'You okay?'

'Yeah. Thank you for telling me, Henry. Goodnight.'

She sat by the phone for a while, breathing deeply, feeling an almost immeasurable sense of relief.

My nightmare, she thought. *I get it.* A tiny kid handed off to a stranger, driven hundreds, thousands of miles in the cold. Feeling terrified, knowing only that she was lost. Not knowing that at the end of her journey waited a loving couple who wanted her.

But I know that now, she told herself. *And I bet I never have that fucking dream again.*

She started to get up but was stopped by a question. Why did the nightmare first appear around age nine or ten? She recalled her last visit to Elva Santiago's office, when the therapist had talked about it.

Poor, well-meaning, misguided Elva. She had gotten some of it right – how an intense experience could implant itself in a young mind, too young for words, and replay itself as physical and emotional memories. She had just come to the wrong conclusion.

It was not about abuse. It was about coming home.

But why would the dream appear—

And then she had it. She was eight or nine when the man calling himself Uncle Don came to their house. She had last seen him as an infant, and her memory of him would have been wispy as smoke. But a shred of it remained. She saw him, and the sight of him touched off the pain of that journey years earlier, the loss and the fear. And the cold.

I guess I could have done without the visit, she said silently to John Paul West.

Twenty-Seven

The next morning she went over to Beth's house to sign some papers related to selling the family home. They sat on stools at the kitchen counter, and Beth poured iced tea from a frosty pitcher. The kitchen looked out onto her spacious backyard through big sliding doors, and they could see the boys kicking a soccer ball around. Shannon marveled at their endless energy, like that of puppies.

'Are they safe out there?' she asked.

'Sure.' Beth stirred her tea with a tall spoon. 'We've got a six-foot wall around the yard. Richard's very security-conscious, even though in this neighborhood you don't really expect …'

Eyes on the boys, only half her mind was on Beth's words. Skipper went after the ball, passing momentarily out of sight. Long seconds passed, and when he returned, a woman walked with him, her hand on his shoulder.

'I didn't know you had a nanny,' Shannon said.

'We don't.' Beth stood at the refrigerator, loudly dumping ice cubes into the pitcher.

'A neighbor?' As she watched, the woman knelt down, talking intently to Skipper. She wore pants, a nondescript jacket, and a baseball cap. Her face was mostly turned away, but the stringy, dirty-blonde hair was unmistakable.

Shannon pushed herself off the stool, her mind suddenly in overdrive. She had left Rhonda's gun in the car, naturally.

'What are you—' Beth turned and looked out through the glass. At the sight of the woman, she gasped, a ragged, noisy sound.

'Does Richard have a gun?' Shannon asked, trying to keep the mounting fear out of her voice.

'What? Yes. Oh, God.' Beth started for the back door.

'No!' Shannon yelled, grabbing her arm, words spilling out. 'Go get the gun, Beth. Go get the gun.'

Breathing quickly, Beth turned to comply. Shannon looked around wildly.

A weapon. Anything.

At the far end of the sunken living room, she saw it. In seconds she had crossed the room to the fireplace, grabbed the cast-iron poker and returned to the kitchen. She threw the sliding door back with a crash that cracked the plate glass, covered the patio in two steps and leaped off the back steps onto the yard.

At the sound of the door Lonnie stood. 'It's you,' she said delightedly. One hand swept her jacket aside, the other pulled a long blade out of a scabbard. 'Back for more?'

Shannon advanced steadily, the poker held high.

'I'm gonna have to cut you this time, girly-girl.' Her eyes were so wide she looked almost bug-eyed.

'Last time was just practice. This time is for keeps.' Crouched slightly, she held the blade low, cutting edge up. 'How 'bout I slit you from your cunt to your—'

Shannon charged, swinging the poker from side to side. The first swing caught Lonnie high up on the left arm, a glancing blow. She let out a *whoof* and retreated slightly, blade still in position. Every time Shannon swung and advanced, Lonnie retreated, making little jabs with the blade, looking for an opening.

The iron was heavy, the effort was making Shannon breathe hard, and her swings began to slow. She could hear the boys crying with fear. *Where the hell is Beth and the gun?*

Another swing, and Lonnie jabbed. Shannon heard and felt the rip of fabric as the tip tore through her sweater just over her ribs. Her arms felt like lead, and she heard her own gasps.

'Almost got you that time,' Lonnie said cheerily. Glancing down at her shoulder, she saw a bloodstain. 'Bitch. You made me bleed.' She moved in closer. 'For that, I'm gonna have to cut you slow.'

Shannon had enough strength left for one more try. Aiming for the head, she gave a mighty swing of the poker. But Lonnie ducked, and Shannon, thrown off balance, fell to one knee.

'Start with the face, I think,' Lonnie muttered, moving in closer.

An explosive bang from the patio, and wood chips flew from a nearby picnic table. Beth stood atop the patio steps, a pistol in one shaky hand, preparing for another shot.

'Lady, be careful with that!' Lonnie held up a warning hand. 'You want to hit your boys?'

'Beth, shoot her!' Shannon screamed.

But a split second later, Lonnie dashed to the ivy-covered back wall, grabbed the vines and, with surprising strength and agility, vaulted over the top and into the alley beyond. A moment later they heard an engine roar to life and tires throw gravel.

Detective Thomas Orlando pulled into the driveway only two minutes after the uniforms had responded to Shannon's 911 call.

'It was her?' he asked, unlimbering his notebook.

'Lonnie. This time it went way beyond arm-twisting. She meant to kill me. But I was just incidental. I think she came here to take one of Beth's boys. Probably to put pressure on me, for whatever sicko reason she has.'

He nodded. Although mistrust had clouded the air between them at their last meeting, he was clearly ready to believe her now.

'Damn.' Shannon shook her head over and over.

'What?'

'I should have warned Beth. I told her Lonnie was a fraud, but I didn't tell her what happened in the garage, how she came after me. I didn't want to scare Beth.'

'Don't blame yourself. You had no way of knowing she'd come after this family. Sounds like you did your best to protect them today. Tell me exactly what happened.'

She did. When she described Lonnie's athletic getaway, he asked, 'How much time between her going over the wall and the engine starting up?'

She thought for a moment. 'Hardly any. A second, maybe.'

'So she had somebody waiting for her.'

For an instant Shannon thought of her evening visitor, the one she had begun to think of as Front Porch Man. But she dismissed the image immediately. Whatever he represented, it was not the kind of threat posed by Lonnie. Someone else had been behind the wall, waiting to drive her away. Quentin?

They went into the living room, where Beth sat hugging both her children as she told her story to a female officer with as much composure as she could muster, while her husband – who had beaten the police to his house – sat stone-faced.

'So much for your protection,' Richard said to the detective. His eyes went to Shannon, and his look was hostile. 'This lunatic comes after Beth and the boys, and something tells me you know more about it than any of us.'

'Richard, don't,' Beth whispered. 'She saved the boys. She could have been killed.'

He turned to the detective. 'Well, we're obviously not safe, police protection or not,' he said. 'What now?'

'Listen,' Shannon broke in. 'You're right, Richard. As long as she's running around, you're not safe here. Why not just leave town for a while?'

'There's my work, for one thing,' he muttered.

'Take a vacation. Call it a family emergency. Go to your cabin at Big Bear, and stay until they catch her.'

Everyone sat silent as her words sank in. Beth turned to her husband. 'Please,' she said. 'Let's do that. Let's just get away from this craziness.'

Head down, he nodded. 'All right, then; the cabin.'

Back in the kitchen, she and Orlando sat at the butcher-block table and talked in low tones. 'I hear from Harold Birdsong every now and then,' the detective said. 'He's actually better about keeping in touch than the regular agent, Dodd. He tells me the two of you had a talk last week. Anything I need to know?'

She hesitated. 'Are we being straight with each other now? Because the last time we talked, I'm not sure I got the whole truth and nothing but the truth from you.'

His jaw muscles flexed, and she caught an intimidating air of tough cop from him. 'We're being straight,' he said finally. 'I work within certain restrictions, but I do the best I can.'

'How about now? Are you restricted?'

He shook his head. 'I believe an attempted murder and kidnapping took place here today. Until I'm told otherwise, that's my responsibility.'

'Good.' She found it easier to like him. 'Birdsong told me he was after a man named—'

'Quentin Latta,' he finished.

'Right. He thinks Latta killed my parents, and that it's connected to an old political feud that dates back to the sixties. This Lonnie woman … he thinks she's someone with a twisted crush on him, who's trying to help him.'

He nodded as she spoke. 'The FBI eventually let us in on some of that. Latta's very definitely a federal case, but we've got a local alert out on him. The woman, too, ever since she first came after you. I'm taking both of them very seriously.'

'I may be able to help you with Quentin.' She told him about her encounter at the harbor with the man who grabbed her and mystified her with his cryptic words. 'He looks a little different from his prison photo, though.'

'I didn't hear about that,' he said in a sour tone. 'Would you describe him to me?'

She did, while he took notes. When she had finished, she asked, 'Anything you can tell me about him?'

'Why?'

'Because he killed my parents, and I'm entitled. And because I just did you a favor.'

He allowed himself a small grin. 'I've turned up a few things on my own,' he said. 'For one thing, he went through some amazing changes in prison. He started out on the violent fringe of the far left, and he ended up in a romance with the far right. In the joint, he fell in with some real sweethearts: skinheads, white supremacists, American Nazis – among the worst and most dangerous guys behind bars. He eventually wound up with a small but very mean bunch called the Aryan Tribe. He was known as a shot-caller, the one who puts out hits on the gang's enemies. During his time in prison, several blacks and Hispanics were killed by members of the Tribe.'

He looked thoughtful. 'But it's a complicated picture. I'm also hearing that near the end of his hitch he found Jesus.'

She laughed. 'That happens a lot in prison, doesn't it?'

He tilted his head slightly, as if to get a different perspective on her. 'You're not looking for him yourself, are you?'

'Of course not. Do you think I'm crazy?'

'No. But I think you want to find your parents' killers in the worst way. More than I do, even. Nothing wrong with feeling the way you do, unless it leads you to take chances. I hope you're not doing that.'

I was right about him, she thought. *He can read me.*

That afternoon the phone rang.

'You know what day this is?'

'Bullo?'

'It's me. You know what day this is?'

'Uh …'

'It's the day you become a registered gun owner.'

'Oh.' She brightened. 'That's right. My ten days are up.'

'What are you waitin' for? Me and Rhonda, we'll meet you at the shop.'

An hour later she was back at her kitchen table, turning the new revolver over in her hand. Guns had never interested her much before, but she had to admit this one was a thing of beauty – neat, compact, utilitarian, and deadly.

It had a blue steel finish and a carved walnut grip, and it felt dense and heavy in her palm. The short barrel, only two inches, gave the gun an all-business look, as if to say, *No sport shooting for me. I'm built for close-in work.*

The shiny bullets, clad in copper and stainless steel, had their own menacing beauty. They resembled art deco objects, tiny space capsules from an old Buck Rogers serial.

The little pirate girl had her cutlass, Shannon thought. *Look what I've got.*

Hey, don't get carried away, she told herself. *Next thing you know, you'll be goin' out with all the ole boys to fire off a few rounds, have a few beers, maybe hit on some chicks.*

Bullo had already set the mood at the gun shop. 'You know you're joinin' a great American tradition,' he said, admiring the gun. 'Why don't we pop the cherry?'

'Excuse me?'

'You know. Break it in.'

'No, thanks. I want to keep it, uh, cherry for a while.' She returned Rhonda's .38 and the box of shells, paid them the rental fee, and drove off feeling very much the proud new gun owner.

Now, having cleared away the dinner dishes, she sat at the table slowly loading the pistol, feeling the weight of each bullet as it slid, a perfect fit, into its chamber. She slapped the cylinder closed the way Bullo had taught her, and it made a satisfying metallic sound. It may have been her imagination, but she thought she could feel the extra weight of the bullets as she hefted the gun.

It even smelled good, like a fine piece of machinery. And it nestled in her bag like it belonged there.

In bed, she turned off the light, stretched out under the covers, and began to go through all the self-hypnosis steps that reliably helped her to fall asleep: slowing her breathing; relaxing each individual muscle, starting with the toes and working all the way up to ears and scalp; imagining a black hole in her center, not a scary place but a safe one, where she could pack away all her concerns, then fold herself up and sink into the deepest part of it, not to reemerge until—

Her eyes flew open. She'd heard something, but, sinking toward sleep, hadn't been able to identify it. At first all she knew was that it was not one of the normal nighttime sounds. Not wind, or birds, or traffic on the street, or the labored hum of her ageing refrigerator.

Then she heard it again. It was fainter than the earlier one, but there was no mistaking it: The sound of wood moving against wood. In this old structure, very few of the floorboards fit snugly. Some creaked loudly, some faintly. She had heard one of them creak somewhere outside the bedroom, then another one.

Someone was in the house.

Twenty-Eight

She leaned over, feeling in the dark, and opened the drawer in the bedside table as quietly as she could. Her hand groped around until it found the walnut handle, and she lifted out the .38, lightly bumping the rim of the drawer.

She aimed it vaguely into the blackness. The only light came from moonlight in the windows behind her and from a far-off streetlight that shone into the front room and made the bedroom door stand out faintly as a dark gray rectangle.

'I've . . .' The word came out a croak. Clearing her throat, she tried again. 'I've got a gun. It's pointed at you.'

No answer, no sounds. She held her breath until it hurt, then gasped a lungful.

'*I mean it.*' She sat up straighter in bed. 'If that's you, Lonnie, you're a dead woman.'

In answer, another creak, this one so loud that she knew the intruder was in the room with her. There to the right, behind the wardrobe, just this side of the doorway.

She half-aimed and squeezed. The room exploded with noise.

She had forgotten to use both hands, and the kick sent the barrel skyward. Her ears rang with the sound, and she heard a voice wailing accompaniment to it. At first she thought it was Lonnie, wounded and crying. Then she recognized the voice as her own and shut up. *Don't be a wuss. You've got the gun.*

'Whoa!' The voice came from behind the wardrobe. It was male, and not one she recognized.

She grasped the pistol in both hands, steadying it the way Bullo had taught her. The air was sharp with the smell of gunpowder. She thought she could discern his outline, or a few inches of it, behind the wardrobe door. *I can shoot through the wood if I have to*, she thought.

The voice again: 'Will you stop all the crying and the shooting? I'm a friend.'

'I don't cry. And I know my friends.'

'Yeah, well, we don't exactly know each other.' He sounded aggravated. It occurred to her that gunfire would have that effect on most people. 'Henry sent me.'

That stopped her for a second. 'He didn't tell me anything. Who the hell are you?'

'I talked to him three hours ago. He said he tried to call you and got voicemail.'

'I said who the hell are you?'

'My name's Wolfe. It won't mean anything to you.'

'You got that right.' She thought furiously. 'Okay, uh, there's a light switch right behind you. Turn it on. You do anything funny, I swear to God ...'

The dark outline shifted, she heard soft scrabbling noises, and then the overhead light came on. The brightness startled her. 'Now step out. Just one step, so I can see you.'

He did, and she took in several quick impressions. Tall, maybe mid-thirties, with well-defined features. A mop of disheveled brown-black hair, the need for a shave. Almost as thin as TeeJay, but bigger and rangier, just this side of bony. A decrepit army surplus jacket. Her first thought was that she had seen him before, but then she knew she had not. Whoever he was, his sudden presence in her room, ten feet away from her, felt heavy with menace.

He stood with hands at his sides, letting out a pent-up breath, and his expression suggested someone trying very hard to show patience, without much success.

His eyes strayed a few degrees, and she realized that she was sitting up, that the sheet had slipped down to her waist, and that she had nothing on.

No time for modesty, she thought. *Modesty is weakness.* She threw back the covers, swung her legs out and stood up facing him, forcing herself to look at him defiantly, the gun not wavering. His eyes scanned her up and down, then again, with no change in expression. *I guess he's not here to rape me.*

Reaching carefully for her terrycloth robe on the back of a chair, she worked herself into it, shifting the gun from right hand to left hand and back to right.

'Out there.' She gestured with the gun. 'Down the hall to the living room.' On her way out, she noted the splintered hole in the upper doorframe where the bullet had lodged. She was disappointed to see she'd missed her target by that much, but remembered Bullo's advice to *fill the air with flyin' lead.*

Just shooting this thing will put the fear into someone, she thought. *Including me.*

Her late-night visitor preceded her into the living room, where she switched on one of the floor lamps. 'Sit.' Her voice still sounded shaky to her, and she made a mental note to control it.

He sat in a chair next to the sofa, and she sat across from him next to the table with the phone, the gun held in her lap. She picked up the phone, checked for a message from Henry.

'Nothing,' she said accusingly.

He simply inclined his head a few degrees, as if to say, *So?*

Eyes darting between him and the keypad, she punched in Henry's number. After several rings, she heard the impersonal phone company voice asking her to leave a message.

'He always picks up when I call him,' she said. 'What's going on?'

'I don't know,' he said brusquely. 'Maybe he's asleep.'

'Henry, call me,' she told the machine in an urgent voice, then hung up and turned to the intruder.

'Prove he sent you.' She could feel the tension between them.

He gave her a sour look and put his hands on his knees, but there was nothing relaxed about the posture. The hands made tiny movements where they rested, and his whole motionless body seemed to be quietly burning energy. 'All right; you took a trip with him the other day. To Montana. You met John Paul West, and you told him what your mother said just before she died. While you were there, you learned something about yourself. It came as a—'

'That's enough.' His voice told her he wasn't Front Porch Man, but that only added to her unease. 'Too many fucking people on this planet know more about me than I do about them. Who the hell are you?'

Just then she heard loud static and an amplified voice outside the house, and a bright light began flashing in the street, piercing the curtains with a red pulse like the fire that had consumed her parents' house.

She jumped up and went to the window. A squad car sat in front of the house; a uniformed officer was coming up the path.

'Somebody heard the shot,' Wolfe said, getting up slowly and moving toward the hallway.

'Don't move.' She leveled the gun at him again, but he appeared not to notice.

'I'll just stand out here in the hall,' he said mildly. 'If you tell them about me, I'm afraid I'll have to duck out the back. If you don't, we can talk some more after they leave.'

'God dammit ...' This under her breath, because the cop was knocking loudly on the door.

Jamming the gun into a pocket of the robe, she yanked the door open. 'Hi,' she said breathlessly.

The patrol cop, a young woman, looked at her curiously, then looked beyond her into the front room. 'Sorry to bother you. We got a call about gunfire—'

'Oh gee, yeah. Somebody else heard it too, huh? It woke me up. But I couldn't tell where it came from. Down the street, I think.' She looked out toward her neighbors' places. 'I thought I heard a car drive by around the same time. You think maybe it could've just been a backfire?'

The officer took her time responding. She held a flashlight and played it around the porch. 'You're Miss Fairchild, right?'

'That's me.'

'We've been asked to keep an eye on your house.' She flicked the light over Shannon's shoulder and let it roam around the living room.

'*Right.*' Shannon pumped enthusiasm into the word. 'And I've really appreciated it, I want you guys to know. It makes me feel a whole lot safer.' *Okay, time to shut up,* she told herself.

The cop looked at her again, and Shannon knew it must all show on her face, and she was sure the burned-powder smell of the gun was even now wafting out of her pocket and into the cop's nostrils …

'Thank you, ma'am. If you hear anything else, let us know.' And she was gone.

Shannon closed the door and pulled the gun out of her pocket.

'All right,' she said, without turning around. 'Get back in here and start telling me some things.'

Wolfe took his seat. His brow was lightly furrowed, and it seemed to Shannon part of his permanent expression. It made him look thoughtful but also doubtful and untrusting.

'I'm waiting.'

'All right.' Restless hands back on his knees, as if to show he was harmless. 'I didn't come here to hurt you, just to talk to you. You can search me, if you want to. I don't mind.' He gave her a wide-eyed look, all rumpled innocence now.

'I'd like to see some ID,' she said, with as much authority as she could summon up.

He dug out a wallet and tossed it to her. She fumbled it open and, trying to keep one eye on him, read the particulars from his driver's license. It said his name was Wolfe Barrett, and he lived in a place called Pine Hollow, California.

'Fine and dandy.' She tossed the wallet back. 'You say Henry sent you. I'll believe that when I talk to him. Meantime, tell me why you snuck into my house. Why not just knock on the door?'

'Sorry. I didn't want anybody to see me. You had neighbors sitting on the porch across the street. And in back, there's a house not fifty feet away. If I'd knocked on your back door, they might have heard me and taken a look out the window. The moonlight's pretty bright tonight.' He spoke a little faster than normal, as if he had a lot of information to impart and only so much time available.

'So you're careful. Like a cat burglar would be. How the hell did you get inside, anyway?'

He looked away for a second. 'I'm pretty good with locks.'

'Like a burglar.'

'I suppose. But I'm not. I'm just here to talk to you.' He looked around, appearing almost comfortable for the first time. 'Do you have any coffee? I can make it.' When she didn't answer, he went on: 'It may take a while to explain why I'm here.' Finally he said, 'Look,

I saw you reach for the drawer in the bedside table. I didn't have to let you pull the gun.' Part of his hair had flopped over one eye, and he ran a quick hand through it.

'No kidding. Then why did you?'

'To tell the truth, I didn't know you were going to shoot the damn thing. I thought you'd just wave it around.'

She thought about all of it for a long second. Somewhere down the street she heard the static of the squad car radio.

'Okay, fine.' She got up, jammed the gun in her pocket, and turned toward the kitchen. 'Let's all just make ourselves at home.'

Fifteen minutes later – an interlude spent mostly in awkward silence while she made coffee – they sat across from each other at the kitchen table, cups at hand. She'd had time to note a few more details about him. He didn't appear to attach much importance to grooming. His hair bordered on what she would call shaggy and could use a wash, his clothes were nothing special, and his fingernails were not the cleanest. She couldn't help comparing him to TeeJay, who was about the same age and who, even though he sometimes worked with his hands, always seemed to take care of his appearance.

He was good-looking, she decided, in a long-boned, brooding, Heathcliff kind of way. Not that his looks ultimately mattered any more than his grooming. The only important thing was what had brought him here with such urgency.

She caught his eye over his coffee cup and nodded, a go-ahead signal.

'Okay, here it is,' he began. 'This is Henry's idea. He knows John Paul wouldn't want me dragged into this, and so we haven't told him. Not yet, anyway. We all know Quentin Latta's got Diana on his list. He's been sniffing around the characters from the old underground, the ones most likely to know where she is. Your folks were apparently in touch with her, and he may have learned something from them—'

'I told John Paul and I'm telling you,' she broke in, 'he didn't learn anything from them.'

One eyebrow went up. 'And how do you know that?'

'It's simple. My mother told me.'

He nodded slowly, apparently about to express doubt. 'Okay, sure,' he said finally. 'But it's a long list of people, scattered all over the country. One or two of them may still be in touch with Diana. And Quentin's not stupid. If he could find your parents, he could find the others, too.'

'All right.' She took a swig from her cup. It wasn't hot enough, but she wasn't the perfect hostess. 'What's this have to do with me?'

'Henry knows Diana's important to me. He tells me she's important to you, too, even though you don't talk that way. He asked me to look you up so we could join forces.'

'Oh, he did, huh? Join forces. That sounds very dramatic.' When he didn't respond to her sarcasm, she added, 'So you know where she is?'

He shook his head.

'Then how—'

'That part can wait. Will you help?'

'Just a minute. If she's so important to you, why'd it take Henry to get you cranked up?'

'That's simple. I didn't know what was happening. I'm not in touch with a lot of people, haven't been for a long time. I live out in a pretty remote place. He called me this morning, said he knew John Paul would be furious with him for contacting me, but he couldn't see any other way. You know Henry and how he is about his friends. He'd almost rather cut off his arm than offend John Paul. But he's been thinking about it for the last day or so, he told me, and this is the answer he came up with. "She's going to die if we don't do something," he told me. "Find Shannon. The two of you couldn't do much separately, but together you'd be strong enough …"'

His words trailed off when he realized she was staring at him, mouth open. 'What?'

She shook her head, trying to clear it. The words *Find Shannon* had reminded her of her mother's last words: *Find them and warn them.*

And now he had found her. She felt a chill. What if she had been too quick to trust him?

She put her cup down deliberately. 'There's something wrong here. You know too much.'

'I don't—'

'No.' She waved away his interruption. 'You're too young to be close to any of them, and you know too much about them. Who are you?' Below the level of the table, her hand crept toward the pocket of her robe. Panic began growing in her chest, tightening her throat.

'Who the hell are you?'

His smile was crooked and did not do much for the rest of his face. But at least it was a smile, and the first one he had shown her tonight.

'You haven't guessed?'

'I haven't . . .' It struck her then, almost like a blow in the face. The enormity of it was overwhelming, and she had to push back from the table and stand up, looking down at him, this stranger who didn't look strange to her and spoke of her with such familiarity. Her hand nestled in the pocket of her robe, and she felt the solidity of the pistol grip, but she knew she couldn't shoot him now, not ever, not if what she suspected were true.

She had gotten up so fast the blood-drain from her head made her dizzy and unstable, and she leaned forward to brace herself on the tabletop with her free hand. She had to hear him say it, and so she waited, just looking at him with the most vulnerable expression she had ever worn in all her thirty-four years. Then, in almost a whisper: 'What haven't I guessed?'

His answer came immediately. 'That I'm your brother.'

The rest of the blood drained from her head in a rush, her knees buckled, and she fell, enveloped in a fog so complete she barely felt her temple thump against the table edge. The next thing she felt was her body fold up like an accordion, and a split second later she was lying rather comfortably on her side on the linoleum floor.

Twenty-Nine

He went to her and raised her head off the floor, cradling it in one hand, and the fog quickly dissipated.

'Wow,' he said. 'You all right? I think you—'

'Oh, no.' She pushed him away with all her diminished might. 'No. I didn't faint. I *don't* faint.'

'Right.' He leaned back on his heels. 'What I meant was, you just got dizzy. Here.' He offered a hand, and after a second's hesitation, she took it. A moment later, she was seated again. He slid the coffee cup toward her, and, holding it in both trembling hands, she took a sip. She swallowed noisily and finally spoke.

'Well, *son* of a *bitch*.'

'That pretty much says it.'

She made a face over the coffee. It was time for a decision, whether or not to believe him, but she realized that she had moved past it already. For better or worse, she believed this stranger's story. It explained how he could know so much about her and why Henry would send him. *Besides*, she thought, *look at him. He looks a little like me. He has both John Paul's and Diana's features, just as I do, along with the rangy, thoroughbred build of the young Diana.*

Staring into her cup, she said quietly, 'If you call me Sis, I'll shoot you.'

'Don't worry, I won't.'

'And I'm not calling you Bro, either. Not Big Bro or Little Bro. What are you, anyway?'

'We're twins. The fraternal kind.'

She had thought she was past surprise. She looked at him again, really studying him now, the shape of his brow, the planes of his face, the curve of his lips. There really was a resemblance, not the look of identical twins but of any siblings born of the same parents. *If others looked at us side by side*, she thought, *I'll bet they could tell.*

'Twins,' she murmured. 'How long have you known about me?'

'I'll tell you everything you want to know,' he said, leaning forward, looking at her intently. 'I've got answers to every question you have. But first we've got to make a decision.'

'I know. Diana.' A long sigh. 'Look, I've been thinking about her for days. There is nothing I can do. I know now that when my mother – my adoptive mother, Mora – asked me to warn John Paul and Diana, she really wanted me to find them and connect with them. Once she and Ray were dead, she wanted me to know my real parents. The warning part was almost unnecessary. John Paul knew about Quentin Latta being on the rampage before I met him, and I'm sure Diana knows about him, too. From what I've heard about her, she's pretty good at taking care of herself.'

'Up against him, she may not be good enough.'

'Well, what am I supposed to do?' Her voice rose with the level of her exasperation. 'Even assuming we could find her, which is not exactly a slam-dunk, what can I do? Or you? We're not cops or bodyguards. You're not a cop, are you?'

'No.'

'Well, then. My boyfriend would probably be better at this than either one of us. TeeJay. He's a tough customer. Maybe you should hire him and go off on your crusade to save Diana. He'd probably enjoy the adventure.'

Wolfe seemed about to ask her a question.

'What?'

'Nothing. Maybe you can tell me a little about him. Later, though. For now—'

'I'm just thinking you might have some kind of inflated image of me, maybe something you got from Henry. I don't have any special skills. I clean houses for a living. That bullet I just put in the wall? That was the first time I've ever fired a gun in a real emergency. If you'd have been an elephant in my bedroom, I would've missed you.'

'I don't want you for special skills, marksmanship or anything like that.'

'Well, then?'

'I want you because Henry knows you, and he said you're what I need. You're what she needs. I trust him.'

'I trust him too. He's a wonderful guy, but—'

'Look, do it for Henry or do it for Diana, or for both of them. They're both worth it.'

'Yeah. You're talking about the woman who stuck me in a VW van and mailed me across the country when she decided I was going to be too much trouble to raise.'

'Did you ever think that maybe she did it for you?'

'Well, I suppose that's always the rationale parents use, isn't it? Doing what's best for the child? I don't know ... Call me crazy, but I think when you hand over a six-month-old kid to a strange family, it's going to mess with her head a little, know what I mean? It did with mine.'

'I'm sorry. Funny thing is, once I learned about you and what had happened to you, I envied you.'

'Why?'

'Because you were with folks who loved you. Because you had one of those all-American lives I could only dream about – growing up in a great town and never having to leave it, getting to graduate from the same school where you started, having the same friends for years and years, getting to go to college. I didn't have any of those things.'

'You mean the family who raised you ...?'

That seemed to amuse him. 'The family who raised me?' he said, speaking deliberately. 'They weren't very good at parenting. They had other things on their minds.'

'You said you had to move around a lot?'

'Oh, yeah; a lot. First through twelfth grade, I went to eight different schools. Never more than two years at any one place. I never really finished the twelfth, so I had to fake my high school diploma.'

'That's awful. It must have been very hard to make friends. Why all the moving around? Were your parents part of the underground?'

'You might say that.' He sat motionless, waiting for her to get it.

And then she did. 'They raised you,' she said in a near-whisper. 'Diana and John Paul.'

He nodded.

She felt the anger stir in her and knew it must show on her face.

'They kept you and sent me away. Why? Did they think I wasn't tough enough? If that's it, I don't like their reasoning. I never got a chance to show them how tough I was.'

'Slow down.' He held up his hands in a peace gesture. 'I was fifteen when I found out about you. I overheard them talking, and I put enough of it together to demand to hear the rest. And so they told me everything.

'When they learned that Diana was going to have twins, at first they planned to keep both of us, crazy as that sounds. Our parents were great at storming the barricades, but not so good at practical things. Then, after your mother – Mora, right? – volunteered to take one of us, they decided it should be you. A boy, they figured, would adapt better to life on the run. On the surface, their logic was good. Unfortunately, before long they found out that my health was shaky, and it caused them a lot of trouble.'

He showed one of his rare grins. 'Although they never said so, I sometimes wondered if they hadn't regretted their decision. Everything might have been different, you know? I'd have had the great American childhood, and you could've grown up playing hide-and-seek with the FBI.'

'Your health was bad?'

He nodded. 'That happens sometimes with twins in the womb – one twin gets its share of what it needs, the other doesn't.'

'You look fine to me.'

'I'm glad.'

'So where does "Barrett" come from?'

'It's the name they were using when I got my first driver's license.' He shrugged. 'I liked it, so I kept it.'

He shifted in his chair. 'Can we get back to what brought me here? There's a man named Quentin Latta out there somewhere, and he's tracking down Diana. If we can find her first, we might be able to stop him.'

'How?' She gave him a wide-eyed, incredulous look, underscoring the impossibility of it all. 'What can we do?'

When he didn't answer, she went on. 'You said you've got some guns. Is that what you're talking about – going after Quentin Latta with guns blazing? That sounds pretty ridiculous.'

'I'm talking about doing what we have to do. Forget about guns blazing. If we find him and sic the police on him, that'll stop him, won't it?'

She fiddled with her coffee cup. 'It might. At least I know the FBI is looking for him.'

'Will you help me?'

Their eyes locked over the table. She could see the urgency in his, and she knew he could see the doubt in hers.

'Forget about everything else,' he said. 'All the mistakes she made. She gave birth to you. Isn't that reason enough? If he kills her and you did nothing to stop it …'

Shannon thought hard. The idea that she could save Diana from someone as murderous as Quentin Latta was inconceivable to her. She simply was not up to the task. More important, though, she obviously did not feel Wolfe's passion to take on this mission. *He must love her*, she thought.

His words were powerful, but they were not enough. She got up unsteadily. 'Before we decide anything, I need to talk to Henry.' She went to the living-room phone and dialed his number again.

This time, after several rings, she got an answer.

'Hello?' A tentative voice, not Henry's.

'Myron? Is this Myron?'

'Yes.' He sounded fearful.

'Myron, it's Shannon. Where's Henry?'

'I don't know.' She heard an audible gulp. 'He's gone.'

'What do you mean?'

'He went out to the store last night and never came back. I've called the clinic, I've been to his apartment, but it's locked, and there's no answer. Henry already told me the police are … He said we don't call them. I don't know what to do. I know you asked me to keep an eye on him, but …' Near-panic choked his voice into a whisper.

Anxiety clutched at her insides. 'Myron …'

'Should I call the police?'

'No! Don't do that. Uh … Wait for me. I'm coming. I'll be there in a few hours. If Henry comes back in the meantime, call me on his phone. My cell number's already entered.'

'All right. But I'm worried.'

So am I, she thought as she hung up. Turning to Wolfe, she said, 'That was his neighbor—'

'I know Myron.'

'Henry's disappeared. We can talk about Diana later, but right now somebody needs to find him.'

'I'll go,' he said, getting up. 'I know his neighborhood and where he works. If he's anywhere around there, I'll find him.'

'*We'll* find him,' she said from the hall, where she was already pulling her bag from the closet.

Thirty

Shannon dressed and packed her bag for the second time in a week, topping it off with her recent purchase from Duke's Firing Range and Gun Shop.

'I thought you didn't want to go in with guns blazing,' Wolfe said.

'I don't. And I'm not asking for your advice either.'

Outside, the night air felt bracingly cool to her sleepy mind. The Jeep waited in the carport, but he hung back. 'We've got another option,' he said.

He led her two blocks away and down a side street, where he had parked in front of a weed-filled lot. When she saw his ride, she felt the urge to whistle. It was a pewter-gray Dodge Ram four-door truck with a heavy-duty suspension and a hulking silhouette. The finish was oddly dull, like a layer of primer before the final glossy coat.

'Horsepower?' she asked.

'Let's just say well over three hundred.'

'Take it off-road much?'

'All the time.'

'Well, if you promise to keep it on the road tonight, I'll ride with you.'

He laid her bag up front, and she spread herself out across the three-seat row in the back. Spotting a duffel bag on the floor, she started to lift it to use as a pillow but found it surprisingly heavy. 'You don't need to use that,' he said quickly.

In minutes he had the truck on the freeway headed north. Her fear for Henry was like a knot in her stomach, but the drone of the engine acted as a lullaby, helped along by the soft tones of a classical music station he dialed up. *Not the musical choice I would have expected from him*, she thought sleepily.

She saw Henry's haggard face for an instant, heard his hill-country twang, and hoped they would find him safe.

She had time for a last thought before sleep took her away: *I've got a brother.*

The three of them huddled quietly in front of the door to Henry's apartment. It was after three in the morning, and Myron, once again in his bathrobe, was distraught.

From his jacket Wolfe extracted a felt-wrapped bundle that he laid on the floor and unfolded. It consisted of six stitched pockets holding various kinds of thin tools. He knelt and quickly went to work on the lock.

He had a tool in each hand, working delicately at the keyhole, almost like a surgeon.

'Want to tell me how you got so good at—' she began.

'Hold it.' A loud click, and the lock was released. Wolfe repackaged his tools, stood up, and turned the knob. The door opened an inch.

'I apprenticed to a locksmith for a year once,' he said as he pushed open the door. The lights were on inside. For a moment, he had a view all the way into the living room.

'Myron, I think you should go back to your place and wait for us there. Please.' To Shannon, he said, 'You, uh …'

She saw the look on his face and read it for what it was. 'I'm coming in with you.'

They stepped inside, and he closed the door gently behind them.

Her nose twitched lightly. A faint smell, something that reminded her of … what? Then she had it. In high school, a friend had taken metalworking shop, and Shannon had stopped by there on the way to one of her classes. The bitter smell of metal shavings suggested something the dentist might do inside her mouth.

As they moved down the hall, she began to get a look around Wolfe's frame, and she saw the foot and leg extending out from behind a chair. Then the rest. Then the blood, all of it. A pool underneath the scrawny body, soaking the round hooked rug, turning its rainbow colors almost black. Small spatters on parts of the furniture, smears on other parts.

'Oh.' She started forward, but he blocked her way.

'Don't. You can't.'

She kept moving, and he held her firmly by the arm. 'If you step in that blood, it'll be all over for us.'

'Oh, God. Henry.'

One of his hands was visible, mutilated. A few inches away, a finger.

A crimson-soaked towel covered part of the face, but not enough to hide the round, clotted hole in the temple. Underneath a small table, she saw a crumpled bit of flesh and cartilage: a human ear.

She made a retching sound.

'Not here,' he said roughly. 'We can't help him. Come on.'

Stepping carefully, he half-dragged her down the hall to the entrance, where he used a handkerchief to set the spring lock and close the door.

Back in Myron's apartment, she was sick in the toilet for several minutes. She tried to blot from her mind the image of Henry's mutilated form but knew she would carry some of it with her forever.

She gargled noisily with tap water and dried her face. Still shaky, she took a seat next to Myron on the sofa, with Wolfe sitting nearby. Myron sat rigidly, knees together, hands clasped in his lap, eyes darting first to one, then the other.

'I suppose you found something,' he said a little too loudly.

Wolfe cleared his throat, but Shannon, although still stunned, spoke first. 'Myron …' She reached over and covered his small hands with one of hers.

'Oh, well then.' A giant sigh escaped him as he understood. 'That's why he was staying with me, wasn't it? Someone wanted to harm him.' Little sobs rose in his throat, chopping the next thought into small, sad pieces. '*He. Was. A good. Person.*'

'Yes.' She patted his hand and felt rage gather inside her. She wished she could shed tears like Myron, but rage was not a tearful emotion. She couldn't even express it – where was the target? The feeling was bottled up inside her, poisoning her.

Enough of this, she thought. *Someone is killing the good people, and we know who it is. He needs to be stopped.*

'Myron.' Wolfe leaned forward, 'Shannon and I … we're going to try to find the people who killed him. We can't explain everything, but we need your help. The important thing to remember is: We weren't here.'

Myron looked both wounded and confused. 'Why not?'

'After we leave, wait until people in the building start getting up, and then you need to call the police. Don't tell them Henry's dead. Don't even tell them he was staying with you. Just say you're worried that he doesn't answer his door. They'll take it from there. You understand?'

Myron thought for a few seconds, then nodded. 'Just say I was worried.'

'Right. Don't mention anything about us. And listen, Myron: If they ask you to go to his apartment, don't look inside. You hear? Don't look inside.'

He nodded again, and the sorrow on his face was mixed with fright.

At the door, Shannon touched him on the shoulder. 'I'm sorry, Myron. I know you were friends.'

'You've lost a friend too,' he said. Something passed over his face. He looked up at her intently, eyes shining with tears yet to fall. 'I hope you find them.'

'Me too.'

Outside the street entrance, she paused at the top of the steps. Her knees felt weak, and she sat down on the top step. 'That's what he did to my parents – he and his helpers – the sadistic piece of shit.'

Wolfe sat beside her, and the furrow between his eyebrows deepened. 'So they like to cut people up.' He shook his head over the thought and touched her arm. 'I'm sorry about Ray and Mora. But Henry … This makes it very personal for me.' He looked away. 'I'm guessing they put the towel over his mouth to keep the noise down while they …' He swallowed hard.

'Henry was as loyal as they come,' he went on. 'Still, he may have told them something. He couldn't have said much about Diana. But …'

'John Paul.' She looked stricken.

'Right.' Wolfe pulled out his phone and quickly punched in a number. After a few seconds, he muttered, 'He's not picking up. As usual.' A few seconds more, then he spoke urgently into the phone.

'Henry's gone, for good, and we don't know how much they know. I'm with Shannon. Protect yourself, and call us when you can.' He snapped the phone shut.

He looked at her questioningly, and she found the answer only beginning to take shape.

She still doubted whether she had the skills, or the strength, to do what Wolfe wanted, to find Diana and try to protect her from a frighteningly dangerous man. Besides, what would drive her to take on such a task? She felt no love for the woman. How could she? And she had all but spat in the face of the man who fathered her.

But Henry's death had sharpened her focus, and she heard her brother's voice from the night before – only hours ago, although it seemed like days. *She gave birth to you. Isn't that reason enough?*

Her birth mother was out there somewhere, and Shannon felt a powerful urge to see her face, to hear her voice. Not to love her, just to know her.

She was responding to a call, and not from logic or reason. It came from a primal place, from bone and muscle, from childhood sorrows, from lost voices in dreams.

It came, she realized, from her very blood.

With that urge came the fearful thought of time speeding up, racing away from her. Diana may be running out of time. If Shannon wanted to see her face ...

If he kills her and you did nothing to stop it ...

She stood up abruptly. 'Let's go find her before they do.'

Thirty-One

In the truck they made plans quietly. 'You said you don't know where she is,' Shannon reminded him.

'That doesn't mean I don't have any ideas.' He focused on his knuckles resting on the steering wheel, and she could almost see his mind going back, making connections, making leaps.

'There's a woman. Her name's Katherine—'

'John Paul mentioned a Katherine. He said he tried finding Diana through her.'

Wolfe nodded. 'That's her. Katherine Dimitrios. She was never one of the militants, the bomb-throwers, but she came up through the anti-war movement and met Diana when they were both with SDS. After Diana and John Paul and the others went underground, Katherine was part of the network that helped them. She knew your folks. Diana and John Paul stayed at Katherine's place in Chicago for a while in the seventies – I was little, but I can remember her. Then, years later, she visited us for two weeks while we were living on a farm in Minnesota with a bunch of hippies. That's when I really got to know her.'

A brief smile crossed his face. 'She was really something. Pretty, kind of girlish – a real contrast with Diana, who was tougher. But Katherine was also very smart and organized and, on top of all that, motherly. That's what attracted us to each other. I think she liked me a lot, and I developed a huge crush on her.'

Shannon squirmed with impatience. 'Look, if Diana has cut off contact even with John Paul, what makes you think—'

'I saw them together.'

'Who?'

'Katherine and Diana. Everybody else was out doing farm work, and the bedroom door was open a crack, and I saw them. There was no question what was going on. They were lovers. For that one time, and maybe others too, they were lovers. That explains the way Diana would look at her. And later, when we were living someplace else and we'd get a letter or sometimes one of those rare phone calls from Katherine, I could tell she was affected by it.'

'All right. They were lovers.'

'I've never lost touch with Katherine. Years later she got married, and she's happy, as far as I know. Even though we never see each other, she's always acted a little like she wouldn't have minded being my mother. I know she worried about me trying to grow up and being on the run at the same time. There wasn't much she could do, but I always felt she was pulling for me. And, of course, for Diana.'

'Does Katherine know where she is?'

'She just might. Katherine was special to her. I know she fell out with John Paul, but I think there's a chance she might still be in touch with Katherine.'

'John Paul already tried contacting her.'

'Me too. I called her just before I drove down to meet you. She lied to me about it.' He shook his head. 'It was a very polite lie, worded very nicely. I knew it was a lie, and she knew I knew.'

'So what's the next step?'

'Call her again; and this time I won't take no for an answer.' He checked his watch. 'It's still a little early in Chicago. Why don't we give her an hour?'

'Fine with me.' She leaned against the door, trying to get comfortable, and half-closed her eyes. 'It does sound as if she likes you.'

'She was there when we were born.'

Her eyes opened wide. 'Really? At the hospital?'

'Not exactly. We were born in a scruffy little apartment just off Halsted Street in Chicago. It was Katherine's place, and Diana decided to hole up there and deliver us. A midwife did the job. John Paul wasn't even there. He was out traveling somewhere.'

'Then the birth certificate ...' Her tone turned bitter. 'Nothing's real about us, is it? Nothing on paper. Everything about me is made up. You, too.'

When he didn't answer, she went on, her voice rising, 'Doesn't this bother you at all?'

He looked at her for a long time. 'Not any more,' he said finally. 'I just figure I'm free to be whoever I want to be.'

After touching down at Chicago's O'Hare International, they rented a car and emerged from the airport sprawl in the middle of a gray winter afternoon. Patches of white from the last snowfall dotted the ground. Once Shannon had confided her fear that someone may be tracking her credit card use, Wolfe had quickly agreed to use his card for both the plane tickets and the rental car.

'I'll pay you back,' she said.

'Count on it.' Still getting used to his quirks, it was hard for her to tell whether he was being humorous or not. At times he seemed dead serious, at other times full of quiet ironies.

To her surprise, he asked her to drive while he navigated. Whatever reserves of energy he had tapped over the last two days – first to head south to find her in San Malo, then to take them both up the coast to San Francisco – were apparently depleted. He looked ashen and drained, and he slumped in the passenger seat as he read off the directions to Katherine Dimitrios's house. She took the Kennedy Expressway east out of the airport, leaving behind the industrial park-like area, its green spaces dotted with high-rise hotels and corporate buildings. Soon they were deep in urban residential surroundings, miles of tightly packed brick apartment buildings interrupted here and there by a busy commercial street.

As she shifted onto the northbound Edens Expressway, she heard his voice. 'This feel like coming home?'

'No,' she said. 'How could it?'

In San Francisco that morning, Wolfe had called Katherine and, at Shannon's request, put the call on the speaker. He spoke in the elliptical code of the underground, but Shannon understood enough to know that he was telling Katherine of Henry's murder and asking to be allowed to come and see her immediately. Katherine, after considerable resistance, finally agreed, her affection for Wolfe coming through clearly in her voice.

'She sounds a little different,' he said after ending the call. 'Older, I guess.'

When she exited the expressway for surface streets, his directions became more frequent. A few miles later they crossed the city line into Evanston, first of the suburbs on Chicago's North Shore. She had once read that the farther one went up the lakeshore, the richer and more exclusive the suburbs became. She took the main road north for a few miles, then turned onto a side street, where they found themselves in a neighborhood of big lawns and old, well-tended houses. Katherine Dimitrios's house was one of these, an imposing place of wood and gray stone.

Not a pretty house, Shannon thought, *almost homely, in fact, solid and unpretentious.*

'I guess she's another one of those revolutionaries with money,' Shannon said as she parked in front.

'She's a lawyer, and so is her husband, Milton. They founded a law firm back in the late seventies, and they've done a lot of public-interest work – sue the big guys, defend the little guys. Like John Paul, except they're out there in the open, not underground. They don't have to live their lives always looking over their shoulders.'

They mounted the front steps to a spacious wooden porch, its roof held up by rough-cut stone columns. Wolfe raised his hand to ring the bell, but before he could touch it the door was opened quickly. A young blond-haired man stood regarding them with a hostile expression on his broad face. He wore an unzipped nylon jacket, and his right hand rested on something on his hip.

Police, Shannon thought wildly. Oh, no. Something's wrong.

'Hello?' the man said.

Wolfe spoke first. 'Uh ... We're here to see Katherine.'

'You mind showing me some identification?'

They both pulled out driver's licenses, and he studied them, making sure the photos matched the faces. He returned the licenses, then stepped out onto the porch. 'I'm going to have to pat you down,' he said, his tone somewhat more polite.

Wolfe's expression showed his bemusement, but he complied, spreading his arms wide and turning his back. He and Shannon had been careful to stow their weapons in his truck at the San Francisco airport.

The man turned to Shannon. 'You too, miss. You can say no, but if you want to go inside, I pat you down first.'

'Pat me down then,' she said, spreading her arms. 'Just watch the hands.'

He did a quick and thorough job, not lingering anywhere. 'Thank you, that's fine,' he said. 'Go on in.'

They stepped into an entryway, then a hallway that held a flight of stairs. The hall furnishings were worn but rich, the moldings dark wood. The house breathed gentility, Shannon thought.

And something else.

Maybe her discovery of the carnage in Henry's apartment had sharpened her olfactory sense. For whatever reason, she picked up on a medicinal odor that belonged more in a hospital than in a home. For an instant she saw her mother's dying face again, and she felt queasy. Through a doorway to the side she noticed a woman sitting in a kind of parlor, looking up from a magazine to regard them with mild curiosity. The woman wore a nurse's uniform.

Shannon and Wolfe exchanged looks of confusion and growing concern.

'This way.' The young man led them upstairs and toward a large bedroom at the front of the house. She noticed that he walked with a slight limp.

'Wolfe? Come in here!' Shannon heard the voice, hoarse and strained but full of enthusiasm, as they entered the room. Her eyes fell on the figure across the room, and Shannon knew instantly that the woman was dying.

Thirty-Two

Katherine Dimitrios sat in a floral-patterned overstuffed chair by a bay window. She wore a bright green robe and furry slippers, and her head was wrapped in a silk scarf of a lighter green.

Her eyes were shadowed and sunk deep in their sockets, her cheekbones sharply prominent. Her robe appeared too big for her.

A huge smile split her pale features, and she held out both hands. 'Oh, my God, look at you,' she almost sang. 'You're not a boy any more.'

Wolfe, trying to hide his shock, went to her, leaning over to take both her hands, then sinking to one knee to embrace her.

'You're a man, my sweet boy,' she crooned, taking his head in her hands. 'My Wolfe.'

They stayed that way for long moments, then he rose, took a deep breath, and said simply, 'Katherine.'

Her eyes went to Shannon. 'And who's this?' she asked, still smiling broadly. 'You have a wife now? A girlfr—' She stopped, and her eyes flew back and forth between them, and amazement took over her face.

'You're Shannon, aren't you?'

'Yes.'

'Well.' Her hands dropped into her lap. '*Well.* This calls for …' She raised her voice. 'Tommy!'

They heard the young man come up the stairs loudly. 'Yes, ma'am.'

'Tommy, would you please bring us a bottle of the Macallan, three glasses, and some ice?'

When he had gone, she had them arrange two comfortable chairs near her and sit down. 'Tommy was on the police force in one of the suburbs,' she confided. 'He tried to break up a fight one night while he was off duty, and he was seriously injured – his spine – almost paralyzed. When he tried to get disability payments, the city fought it because he'd had a couple of drinks with his friends. Milton and I took his case and got him a nice settlement. Now he works for a private security firm.'

Shannon studied her as she spoke and thought she could see the woman Wolfe had described. She had probably never had Diana's beauty, Shannon thought, but when younger she must have been pretty in an elfin kind of way. Her eyes, shadowed as they were by the illness, still had an occasional flash of energy.

'Milton, by the way, is at work. He's taken off so much lately for my benefit; we thought he should spend some time at the office. I didn't tell him you were coming today. I wanted to have you to myself.'

'What's Tommy doing here?' Wolfe asked.

'Well, he's … I guess you'd say he's looking after me.' Seeing their uncomprehending looks, she added, 'I'll tell you all about it. But first things first, and let's start with the most unpleasant.' She tried to straighten up a little in her chair. 'I've got probably less than six months. Cancer. Didn't want you to know, of course. Maybe I would have called you later, toward the end, to say goodbye. But now that you're here …' She smiled briefly. 'I tried on my wig for you about an hour ago, but it looked so phony, I just thought I'd stop with the pretense. When you're dying, it's hard not to look that way.'

Wolfe leaned forward, took one of her hands, and kissed it. His eyes were glistening.

Tommy reappeared with Scotch and glasses with ice.

'Now, young lady,' Katherine said when he had left, 'I want to hear all about you.'

For almost fifteen minutes Shannon talked about herself. As she sipped her drink and her account moved into the events of the past several days, she felt an unaccustomed lightness. This was the first time she had ever told her life story with absolute knowledge, perfect clarity. It was liberating.

'I'm so sorry about Ray and Mora,' Katherine said when she had finished. 'They were soldiers.'

'I've never heard them called that.'

'Oh, they weren't the bomb-throwing kind. The bomb-throwers were stupid, idealistically, tragically stupid. I can say that now, with the benefit of age and the kind of hindsight that impending death gives you.' She laughed, a raspy sound, but genuine.

'No, Mora and Ray were the best kind of people – decent and loyal. They died for friendship. I admire them more than I can say.' Her face took on a more calculating look. 'Now I'll tell you why Tommy's here. Milton and I hired him to look after us because I decided I'd rather die on my own schedule than on someone else's.'

'Quentin?' Wolfe muttered the question.

She nodded. 'I have no doubt he would come after me the way he went for Ray and Mora, and I simply won't wait around. Nor could I stand to see Milton harmed. Tommy has his instructions. I believe he'll guard us with his life.'

'Good,' Wolfe said.

'I spoke with Quentin once. Right after he got out of prison, but before he started killing people again. He called me, and we talked for a long time. It brought back all the feelings I'd had about him years ago. I was afraid of him then, because I knew he was absolutely ruthless. And he knew something about me, something almost no one else knew.' She paused, remembering.

'What?' Shannon prompted.

'He knew that I was one of the bomb-throwers.' Noting their looks of incomprehension, she smiled. 'Let me rephrase that. I was one of them in everything but the deed itself. I had trained for it and committed myself to it. I was so sick of that god damn war I was ready to blow something up just to make the point. The Crowe Institute bombing? It was planned for a team of four, and I was the fourth.'

'You were ...?' Shannon began.

'Ready to go. But at the last minute Diana pulled me aside and told me to stay behind and make the calls to the news media at the hour of the bombing. I begged her to let me go with them, but she was firm. "I'll break your leg if I have to," she said. So I stayed behind. As they left, I heard her arguing with the others. "Katherine's not ready," she told them. It broke my heart. But there was no defying her.'

'Why did she do it?' Shannon asked.

'That's the funny part. I've never talked about it with her. But

Diana had instincts almost like a wild animal. That night, I think her instinct about Quentin told her that something might go wrong, and she wanted to protect me from the fallout, which is exactly what she did. I hated her for the better part of a day, until I realized what had happened. A man and his baby had died a horrible death. None of us had wanted that – except for Quentin. She had sensed it, and saved me from everything she's had to go through since that night. You could say I owe her this wonderful life I've had.'

All three of them were silent for a moment. Then Wolfe spoke up: 'What happened after the bombing?'

'I made the calls to all the media, following our script. I had no idea what had happened until the next morning, when I turned on the radio. Then the phone rang, and I heard Diana say quietly, "It went bad. They have Quentin, and we're going under. Look after yourself." And she hung up.'

'And they've been on the run ever since,' Shannon said bitterly. 'For a bombing they tried to stop.' She looked at Wolfe. 'You must have known about that.'

'I knew about everything except Katherine's role.'

'They tried to take their case to the public later, after they went underground,' Katherine continued. 'And I had no trouble believing that the bombing was Quentin's work, not theirs. But who was going to listen to them? In fact, who was going to listen to me? Even though I was never wanted for any specific crimes, it was no secret that I'd belonged to a group that looked pretty scary to America in the sixties.'

'The Red Fist,' Shannon said.

'You bet; wild-eyed revolutionaries, every one of us. The joke was, although I suppose I believed in the revolution, I was still at heart that uncomplicated little girl from Chicago's Greektown. I joined the Red Fist because of Diana. She was . . .' Katherine paused, remembering. 'She was just a huge presence at that moment in my life. I think I would have joined the Daughters of the American Revolution if she had. The Girl Scouts. Anything.'

'What did Quentin want when he called?' Shannon asked.

'Diana. He wanted to find her. Naturally I told him I had no idea where she was. I don't think he believed me, but that didn't bother me until I heard about what had happened to your parents and I realized how desperate he—'

'How did you find out?' Wolfe interrupted.

'Henry Goines. Good, gentle Henry. He's been one of my few links to the old network. Just hearing his voice could take me back to those days.' Something passed over her face – it might have been pain – and for the first time Shannon saw the full weight of her illness.

Katherine took a deep breath. 'God damn Quentin for what he's doing.'

'What else did he say on the phone?' Shannon asked.

'Well, it was a very disjointed conversation. Quentin was always so high-energy he would blurt out his sentences, and he was still doing that. But … you understand, he didn't really make any threats. He just said it was most important that he find Diana. He said something silly about how he wanted her forgiveness and others' forgiveness. Looking back now, it was an absolute con job. I was polite to him, and after a while he hung up, and that was the last I heard from him.'

'Forgiveness?' Shannon made the word sound like a question.

'Right.' Katherine's sarcasm hung heavy in the room along with the odor of medicine. 'I've been a fighter all my life, and forgiveness is not something that comes naturally to me. I don't forgive our government for all the lives lost in that unjust war – or for what's happening in Iraq right now – and I can't forgive this man for what he's done.'

She looked at their glasses. 'I'm not being a good hostess. Would you like some more Scotch?'

They shook their heads. Wolfe leaned forward. 'Katherine …'

'I know. You want to know where Diana is. What time is it?'

He looked confused, then glanced at his watch. 'Four fifty. Listen. He's going to kill her unless we stop him.'

'How can you stop him?'

'If we find her, I'm sure he'll be somewhere in the vicinity. Shannon is in touch with the FBI. We'll have them scoop him up.' To Shannon, his strategy sounded almost too neat, but she said nothing.

Katherine thought about that for a moment. 'That would expose Diana,' she said finally. 'They want her too. It sounds too risky to me.'

'Would you rather see her dead?' Wolfe's words struck her like barbs. It occurred to Shannon that this was the same strategy he'd used on her, and it was brutally effective.

Katherine looked pained. She shook her head and raised a hand, as if to ward off more words. She started to cough but managed to choke it off. Then a soft smile crept onto her face as another thought took hold.

'I helped deliver you,' she said to Shannon. 'Did this beautiful boy tell you?'

'Yes.'

'What a night that was. John Paul was off in Detroit picking up a donation from a rich member of the network, enough to keep them going for a few more months. Early that morning, we'd heard the FBI was sniffing around my neighborhood, and we were afraid they could bust in at any time, so we decided to move Diana. But just as we got her bag packed, she went into labor, and I called a midwife, an old Greek gal who had helped us out before and would keep quiet.'

She shook her head slowly as the memories returned. 'You were a very tough delivery, you two. Diana, of course, was made of steel, but she wasn't built for child-bearing, and she had a terrible time. I remember a lot of groaning and sweating. She bit her lip until it bled to keep herself from screaming. We just couldn't take the chance on making noise.'

She picked an ice cube out of her glass and held it up, then popped it into her mouth. 'I gave her ice to chew on, everything I had in the fridge. Finally you both arrived, like gifts from God. Oh, I was too much the revolutionary to be religious back then. But over the years I've found that this odd faith I was raised in, with all its incense-burning and funny outfits, has a powerful pull, and I've returned to it. Anyway, there you were, all shiny and bloody. Shannon first, then Wolfe.

'Then Diana slept for ten hours while I took care of our two new arrivals. So you could say I was your first mother, in a sense, at least for a while.'

You probably would have made a better one than she did, Shannon thought. Aloud, she said simply, 'Thank you,' and meant it.

'Katherine, we have to find her,' Wolfe said insistently. 'You know why.'

'She doesn't want to be found – by anyone. I speak to her occasionally, but she calls me. I don't even have her phone number. When John Paul called a few weeks ago, I could tell him quite honestly that I had no idea where she was.'

'Does she know Quentin's after her?'

'Of course she does. And one thing I do know is that she's well protected.'

'Who's protecting her?' Shannon asked.

'Some very capable people.'

'Environmental crazies, just like her,' Wolfe said.

'Maybe.' Katherine looked around. 'I'm sorry to keep asking, but it's gotten uncomfortable for me to wear my watch. Can you tell me the time?'

'A minute to five.' His impatience clearly showed. 'Please—'

'Wait.' She held up a hand, and the room fell silent. Shannon and Wolfe glanced at each other but said nothing.

About thirty seconds went by, and the phone on the table beside Katherine rang loudly. She picked it up immediately and began speaking in a soft and fond voice.

'Hello there ... Aren't you the prompt one? ... Well, I'm actually doing wonderfully right at this moment. I happen to have a couple of visitors: Shannon and Wolfe.' Whatever she heard caused her to grip the phone harder. 'Wait. Wait. Just talk to them for a minute. I haven't told them anything that would help them find you. Hell, I don't *know* anything that would help them find you.' Her voice sank almost to a whisper. 'I don't ask much of you. Just talk to them, won't you?' A long moment went by, then, 'Thank you.'

She laid the phone in her lap and looked at Shannon, who was sitting closest to her. 'You see that thing?' she asked, indicating a speaker box on the table by the phone cradle. 'Push the button on the bottom left.'

Shannon did so, and the box gave off a low hum. It was an eerie sound, because she knew that at any moment the hum could begin transmitting a voice Shannon had not heard since she was an infant. She strained her ears and almost thought she could hear breathing.

Talk, she said silently to the box. *Talk, dammit.*

Thirty-Three

'Well,' a voice said.

They waited, but there was nothing else. So Wolfe stepped in.

'How are you?' he asked, raising his voice a little.

'I'm doing very well. I didn't expect to hear your voice. You really shouldn't be bothering Katherine—'

'Now don't start that.' Katherine interrupted loudly. 'It's a joy for me to see these two children, and you should know that. You just talk to them.'

Silence. Wolfe tried again. 'Diana, we need to see you. Shannon's here because her mother asked her to find you. We're both worried about Quentin, and we know he's looking for you.'

'I'm pretty well hidden, Wolfe.'

'I know. But Quentin has friends, and they're working their way through the network. They've k—' He stopped himself, apparently mindful of the phone line, but then plunged ahead. 'Hell with it. They've killed people, including Henry—'

'Henry?' Her voice dropped almost to a whisper. 'Oh, God.'

'That's right. Henry. And I think it's only a matter of time before they find you.'

'I happen to disagree,' she said quietly, still sounding shaken. 'And even if he did find me, let's just say he would have a hard time getting to me.'

Shannon was listening to the voice so intently she was in danger of missing some of the words. It was somewhere in the lower register of women's voices – an alto, Shannon decided. It sounded intelligent and self-possessed. Shannon desperately wanted to tell herself it was a voice she recognized, but she could not.

'May I speak to Shannon?' For the first time, the voice seemed to hold a tinge of uncertainty.

Shannon took a breath. 'I'm here.'

'Thank you for going to all this trouble. You've clearly found out a lot of things about me. About yourself. Maybe we'll have a real talk someday, but this isn't the time. I'm sorry you got involved. I don't want either of you to be exposed to this. It's already dangerous, and it's going to get worse. I'm mixed up in some things—' The voice stopped, and Shannon heard nothing but measured breathing for a while. Then: 'Some things that could make this even more complicated. What I'm trying to say is, if you were asked to warn me, consider me warned. Just look after yourself.'

'I was asked to find you, not just warn you,' Shannon replied, surprised at the heat in her voice. 'As far as I'm concerned, my job isn't even half done. And you need to know I'm doing this for my mother, who used up her last breath asking me to do it.'

No answer from Diana, and Shannon knew she had failed to convince her. She grew desperate.

She doesn't need any more protection, and everyone knows it, Shannon told herself. *Why don't you just say it? Say the words.*

'I need to see you,' she began tentatively. 'For myself.'

'What does that mean?'

'I need to meet you. Why is that so hard to understand? It's important to me, and if that sounds selfish, too bad. You owe it to me.'

As she spoke, she saw Katherine smiling and nodding her head in approval. For a moment, Shannon thought she might have broken through. But again Diana was silent.

Wolfe spoke up. 'We're going to find you, Diana. Just hope we find you before he does.'

'This sounds absolutely crazy,' Diana said emphatically. 'You're not equipped for this, either one of you.' Then her voice softened. 'Are you taking your medicine?'

'Don't change the subject, okay?'

'The subject is closed. Thank you both for what you're trying to do. Now go home. And please take me off the speaker. I want to talk to Katherine.'

He did so, and the background hum stopped. With a gesture,

Katherine asked them to give her some privacy, so they stepped into the hall.

'You're right,' Shannon said. 'They're still close.'

'Uh-huh.'

'What was that about your medicine?'

'Nothing much. She worries sometimes. At least, she used to.'

'Could've fooled me.'

He studied her. 'Something wrong?'

'Oh, just … There are maybe a hundred things I'd like to talk to her about, and not a single one of them came up.'

'Children!' Katherine's voice summoned them back. They found her looking drained, her face almost gray, but smiling nevertheless.

'Ohhh, was she mad at me. Doesn't like surprises, that girl. But I don't care. You deserved to talk to her, whatever she thinks. The bad news is, she's adamant about not seeing you. And the news about Henry only made her more determined to keep you two out of this. I'm sorry you didn't get what you wanted. Maybe she's right, and you should just leave her to fend for herself.'

'Do you really believe that?' Wolfe asked.

Katherine started to answer, but her face clenched in sudden pain. She bore it, not looking at them, until it had passed. Finally she spoke.

'No, I don't. I think it's lovely, what you're doing. Go on. Find her if you can. Save her, if it's possible.'

She reached up weakly and touched their cheeks as they bent to kiss her. 'Now would you send my nurse up? Her name is Rose. She's a nice Polish Catholic. We love to argue about religion.'

They spoke little on the red-eye flight. Wolfe slept most of the way. It may have been the dim lighting in the cabin, but Shannon thought his face, with its slack features, had taken on some of Katherine's gray cast, as if he had caught something from the air of her sickroom.

It was still dark when they retrieved his truck from the airport garage at San Francisco International. As they sat in it, engine running and the heater on, they tried to plan their next move, but neither was thinking straight. The pace of the last few days had taken its toll, and their brains were fogged in like San Francisco Bay.

At her suggestion, he drove them to the nearest hotel, where they checked in. She could tell how grateful he was for the idea. 'I guess I'm a little rundown,' he said as they rode up in the elevator. 'Just need a few hours to catch up, rest, eat a good meal, and then we'll decide what to do next.'

She started to ask if he had any kind of options left but thought better of it. Katherine, she reflected, had sounded like their last chance.

They had been forced to take a suite, with a bedroom and sitting room. The hotel was hosting a national florists' convention, and their choices had been limited. They found the lobby strewn with floral displays and permeated with the smell of fresh flowers, an odor that Shannon always associated with funeral homes. Her parents' on-campus memorial, although touching, had smelled inescapably funereal.

Wolfe insisted on taking the sofa bed in the sitting room and leaving her the bedroom, and she was too tired to argue. After each had used the bathroom, they quickly said goodnight.

The freshly sheeted bed felt luxurious, and Shannon was asleep almost immediately – then awake again after what could only have been a few minutes. A noise had roused her, a knocking. Someone was knocking on the door, she thought wildly. No matter who it was, this could not be a good thing.

In the next instant, though, she could tell it wasn't knuckles on a door. It was a duller sound, and it seemed to be coming from the wall right behind her head.

Wolfe.

She threw herself out of bed, not knowing what to expect – an intruder? – and, suddenly dizzy, grasped at the frame of the connecting door between bedroom and sitting room to steady herself as she looked into the adjoining room. Through the crack in the curtains, the sky was beginning to lighten, but the room's darkness allowed her to see only the dim outlines of furniture. The knocking was louder, accompanied by a low moaning. Starting to panic, she felt her way to the outer door and threw the main light switch.

Wolfe lay on the floor by the sofa, its bed frame partly unfolded. He wore briefs and a T-shirt, and his body was twisted into a knot, elbows bent and fists balled up under his chin. His mouth was open, and his head was seized in a rhythmic bobbing motion, back and forth. Each time his head was flung back, it struck the wall.

The noises he made were wordless and guttural and frightening.

Thirty-Four

She went to him and knelt down, all sleepiness wiped out by the surge of fear-based adrenalin. His eyes were rolled back in his head, his lips were blue, and spittle drained from his mouth in a steady stream. She smelled urine and saw that his briefs were soaked. The noises that came from him sounded like those of an animal. She winced each time his head struck the wall.

Do something. Standing up, she wrenched the sofa bed open the rest of the way, allowing its legs to thud onto the carpeted floor, and pulled out a pillow. Holding his head with one hand, she forced the pillow between it and the wall. Instantly the banging stopped, although the noises from his throat did not.

What else? Vague memories surfaced, information about seizures, something about the danger of the tongue being swallowed. On her feet again, she dashed into the bathroom, grabbed a washcloth, and returned. As gently as she could, she forced it between his teeth, holding the jaws open a few inches.

Then she sat back on the floor, suddenly dizzy with the effort. *He needs a doctor*, she thought distractedly. The bedside phone was within reach, and she grabbed it, scanning the directory on the dial face, trying to decide which number to …

Wait. The noises were subsiding, the violent movements were diminishing. As she almost held her breath, a full minute went by.

It was over. His body unclenched. His eyes were closed now, and his chest rose and fell deeply as he began to breathe again. Color slowly returned to his lips. She took a deep breath herself, aware that she was sweating, although not as much as he.

Another minute passed, then another. His eyes opened and gained some focus, but on nothing in particular. Carefully, she removed the washcloth. He began to speak, mostly a slurred string of obscenities, words strung together in combinations she'd never heard. In another situation, she would have admired his gutter eloquence.

As he regained control, his language became tamer. '*Wow*,' he said, drawing the word out to an exaggerated length.

'Is that all you can say?'

He turned in her direction. 'Nice tits.' A look of confusion. 'Who the hell are you?'

She was suddenly aware of her nudity but, as with the first time, refused to let modesty dictate her behavior. *He's already seen me*, she told herself. *Why should I care?*

'I'm your—' She stopped, still not ready to use the word in front of him. 'I'm, uh, Shannon.'

'Oh, yeah.' His eyes blinked rapidly. 'How long you been here?'

'I don't know. A few minutes.'

He nodded. 'Big one,' he said almost to himself. 'Big fucker.' He looked around, as if only then aware of where he was. 'Hotel room, right?' One hand swept across his damp groin. 'There I go again. Guess I better …' He tried to get up without much success.

'Here.' She reached for him and slowly got him on his feet. 'Careful.' She steered him into the bathroom, then helped him shakily finish undressing and reached for the bathtub taps.

'I can stand up,' he said almost peevishly, pointing to the shower head. She turned it on and helped steady him as he stood under the spray. After his quick shower, she handed him a towel.

'I guess this makes up for all those years we missed playing doctor, like all the other brothers and sisters,' she said. She could tell his mind wasn't up to processing the joke.

Underneath the humor, she was frightened. This was clearly not his first seizure.

As she helped him back to bed, he murmured, 'Sleepy. Always sleepy. After. Need to sleep. Long time.'

'Right.' She turned down the bed and tucked him in, then returned to the bathroom, turned the shower back on, and stood under the spray for a long time, leaning into it, letting it pound her head, shoulders, and the back of her neck. As the spray cascaded around her downturned face, her eyes burned. Tears? Maybe a few. Tears of helplessness, and of anger.

Just a few days into a seemingly impossible task, she had found that her brother, her partner on an important mission, was afflicted with a terrible condition, one that could conceivably make him useless to her. If he had known about this, and he almost certainly did, he had owed her a warning.

And a more frightening realization: His health was precarious. Coming on the heels of all her recent losses, could she lose him too?

Out of the shower, she rubbed the mist off the mirror and took a quick look at her face.

On one of her house-cleaning gigs, this would have been the time for a Marilyn shimmy or an Arnold pose. Not this time. She did not like what she saw. Bags under her eyes, a grim set to her mouth, and a hopeless look on her face.

She twisted her hair and wrung it like a mop over the sink, then spotted a hair dryer on the wall and finished the job. After toweling off, she started for her own bed, ready to flop down, but paused. *I can't leave him alone*, she thought. Heading for her bag, she pulled out a T-shirt and panties and donned them. *No sense carrying all this family coziness too far*, she told herself. *Don't want things to get downright Freudian.*

In the sitting room, she turned out the overhead light. 'Can you move over?' she asked, but was not surprised to find him already asleep. With a few gasps of effort, she managed to shift his bulk a few inches, allowing herself enough room to slide in beside him.

She lay awake for at least a half-hour, listening to his deep breathing, her heart thudding in her chest, before exhaustion returned. In the minute before she finally slept, she heard Diana's question once again: *Are you taking your medicine?*

Thirty-Five

They sat at the room-service table silently eating – silently, that is, except for the sounds of Wolfe shoveling in a trencherman's breakfast. The curtains were open, the sky was cloudy, and the light was fading fast.

Wolfe had slept for ten hours and awakened looking dazed but not traumatized. With shaky hands, he called room service and ordered three eggs, bacon, toast with butter and jam, a pot of coffee, juice, and three pancakes with syrup.

Shannon was about to tell him that the meal sounded a little carb-heavy and that she doubted she would want any of the pancakes or toast when he turned to her. 'How 'bout you?'

As they ate, she watched him closely, noting his slow and cautious movements, guessing that any experience as wrenching as last night's could not be totally washed away by one night's sleep.

'How are you feeling?'

'Oh … not too bad. Sore, though. From all the clenching. Even my teeth ache.'

After he cleaned his plate, sopping up the remaining syrup with his toast, she poured each of them a second cup of coffee. *It's time*, she thought.

'You want to tell me about it?' she asked.

'I don't remember much,' he said. 'Somebody flashed me while I was on the floor …'

'Very funny.'

'And I vaguely recall taking a shower and getting back into bed. That's about it. But, you know, that's typical. I always forget most of it.'

'Is it epilepsy? Is that what we're talking about?'

'Yep.' He drained about half his coffee cup too quickly, and some of it dribbled down his chin.

'Why didn't you tell me about it?'

'Didn't want to; didn't think you'd need to know. I hoped you'd never see it, so you'd never be bothered by it.'

'Well, thanks for your concern.' She fought to keep her anger under control. 'But when we're headed off on a job that's almost certainly dangerous, don't you think I need to know everything important about my traveling companion? Especially when, if you fall down on the job – and I guess I mean that literally – you could be putting me at risk?'

'Maybe.' He looked uncomfortable.

'This is what Henry was talking about, isn't it? How you and I had to link up because separately we weren't going to be enough.'

She was ready to start in on him, but he looked so beaten down, she found her anger softening.

'Look, I have to ask. How can you handle things, much less emergencies, when you're passing out and smashing into the furniture?'

When he didn't answer, she sighed. 'How long have you had this?'

'All my life, I guess. From the time I was about a year old.'

For some reason, that stunned her.

'And how often?'

'It's been years since the last one.'

'It must have been hard. As a kid, I mean.'

'It was no fun for me. And it gave Diana and John Paul one more thing to worry about. I saw a lot of doctors, I can tell you.'

'It looks scary as hell when it happens.'

'I'm sure it does. A lot scarier for you than for me, since I'm mostly in Never-Never Land while it's going on.'

'Is it dangerous? Could it kill you?'

'It could, but chances are it won't.'

She looked doubtful, not in the mood to believe much of what he said.

'What causes it?'

'It's easier to say what triggers it. Things like stress, exhaustion, doing drugs. I've been careless about the first two just recently. I'll have to watch that.'

'How about drugs?'

'Not lately enough to have an effect on this.'

She didn't like his answer and was about to come up with something caustic when he broke in. 'Would you describe what you saw? Everything?'

'Uh, all right.' She spent the next couple of minutes doing so, omitting nothing.

'And did you do anything?'

She told him about her rudimentary first-aid efforts.

'Thanks,' he said when she had finished. 'You did a couple of things right – putting the pillow next to my head and not trying to hold me down while I was thrashing around. You did one thing wrong – the washcloth. You shouldn't put anything in my mouth.'

'What if you swallowed your tongue?'

'That's an old nurses' tale. I can't swallow my tongue, and if you stuff anything in my mouth, it may do more harm than good. Just lay me on my side. It helps me to breathe. Make sure I'm not hitting any furniture. And let me get through it.'

'You sound like this is going to happen again.'

He didn't answer, just fiddled with his coffee cup.

'There's medicine for this, right? Diana mentioned it.'

He nodded. 'A combination of things. It took years to find the right balance of drugs.'

'Are you taking it?'

'Not right now.'

'Why the hell not?' Her voice rose in volume. She felt like yelling at him, like shaking him.

'Because,' he said, exhaling loudly. 'Because it dulls me. It lowers me a notch. It quiets my brain, and it takes away my edge. I can go through life functioning just fine on the stuff, doing my work, happy as a clam. But I can't do what I need to do right now. With you. Finding Diana and all the other things we need to do. I have to be sharp, my very best. I can't be that way on those drugs.'

'Well, shit, then.' She sat back in her chair and regarded him. He seemed to be putting her into some kind of intolerable position, asking her to endorse behavior that sounded very risky. What choice did she have?

'So you stopped taking your pills. When?'

'Just before I drove down to meet you.'

'Are you going to have another one of these?'

'I don't know. Maybe, maybe not. I hope not. Like I say, we'll try to keep a lid on the stress and exhaustion. But we both need to be ready for whatever happens.'

'Wonderful.'

He looked away. 'I, uh, I may get a warning. If I do, I'll try to—'

'What kind of warning?'

'It's hard to describe. But sometimes I get a taste in my mouth. A little bit like … vinegar. When I get that, I know I have a few seconds before it hits.'

She stared. 'Vinegar.'

'Something else you need to know. These things are usually over in a couple of minutes, and if I haven't fallen onto a table or through a window, I'll come out of it all right. But if I start having them in a series, one after another, or if I have one that lasts as long as five minutes, that could be … Well, I'm saying don't mess around. Get me to a hospital fast. If you can.'

She stared harder. 'You dumb son of a bitch. You're playing with your life.'

He looked down at his plate, at the last two shiny drops of maple syrup he'd missed. He wiped them up with a forefinger and licked them off.

'It's mine, isn't it?'

Thirty-Six

She left him resting in bed and took the elevator down to the flower-scented lobby, then pushed through the revolving door and out to the entryway, where the wintry air chilled her lungs and invigorated her. Off through the Bay Area twilight, other high-rise hotels dotted the horizon, their lights coming on, and she saw planes from the nearby airport making their approaches and lifting into the sky.

She was fuming at Wolfe over his secret illness and because he was, in effect, bullying her into going along with him on his terms. She was angry at herself because, in some hidden part of herself, she probably agreed with him. Wasn't she, in a sense, already risking her own life on this adventure, like a giddy pirate girl waving her toy cutlass? Then why shouldn't he be allowed to risk his?

Three good people are dead. Hey, Diana, you'd better be worth all this. Swear to God, if I find out you're not, I'll turn you over to the Feds myself.

With all the background noise from jets aloft and cars pulling up to the hotel entrance, she almost didn't hear her cell phone ringing. She pulled it out of the pocket of her jeans and flipped it open. *Unknown caller*, the screen said.

'Hello.'

'It's Special Agent Tim Dodd.'

'Yes?'

'I've been trying to reach you. Leaving messages on your home phone.'

She started to ask him how he had gotten her cell number but realized how silly the question would sound to the FBI. 'I've been away.'

'Where are you?'

Careful. 'Oh, just visiting some friends. Personal stuff.'

'Do you mind if I ask if your friends are in the Bay Area?'

What the hell? She quickly decided that she did not want to be caught in a lie. 'Well, they just might be.' She made her tone light, almost playful. 'Why are you asking?'

'I won't waste your time. You were seen entering and leaving an apartment building in the Lower Haight district early yesterday, around the time a man named Henry Goines was killed in one of the apartments there.'

She backed up to the wall of the entryway by the valet parking station and leaned against it. Her knees were rubbery. She wondered if Myron had talked to the FBI, and she felt disappointed in him. She tried to think of something to say, something to dissuade Dodd, to exonerate herself. The best she could come up with was, 'Who says I was there?'

'A neighbor. Someone who lives across the street and spends a lot of time watching the area, the buildings. Some people would call her a snoop. But she has good eyesight and a good memory. When we showed her a photo of you, she recognized you. She says you were with a young man with dark hair.'

Three quick thoughts struck her. One, good old Myron had stuck to his story, and there was no reason for him to be implicated. Two, the FBI was after her, but for the wrong reason. Three, no one had identified Wolfe. She had time to warn him, to make sure—

'We don't think you're a murderer, Miss Fairchild.'

'What?'

'Think about it. If I thought you'd killed anyone, would I call you up to tell you?'

She laughed in relief, so loudly one of the valets turned around. 'No, I guess not.'

'We know about your parents' connection to Henry Goines, from a long time ago. Harold Birdsong has been very helpful with that – the history. He says the two of you had a good talk, and you understand that whatever this man Quentin Latta is up to, it goes way back. Here's the thing …' He paused, as if choosing his words carefully. 'I suspect you're looking into your parents' murders, and that's why you're doing all this traveling. I'm sure you feel strongly, but believe me, it's not something you want to do on your own.' A lecturing tone crept into his voice. 'Latta is a very irrational and dangerous man. We think he's now killed three people, and he's just getting started. Harold, I believe, told you who the real targets are.'

'Yes, he did.'

'Well, we need to stop him now. I want to meet with you. I'm here in San Francisco.'

'Oh, right.' Uneasily, she looked around at cars in the vicinity. Could he know exactly where she was?

'I want you to tell me everything you've learned in your travels. And then I want you to promise me you'll go home and wait there until things are wrapped up one way or another.'

'I don't know if I can do that.'

'Now listen, Miss Fairchild.' She heard a new edge in his voice. He sounded much more buttoned-down and much less likable. 'I sympathize with your loss, but you have no business being involved in this.'

'No business?' She couldn't keep the edge out of her own voice.

'Nothing you've ever done qualifies you to be playing detective right now. You've got a quick temper and not the best judgment, and it's gotten you in trouble in the past. This is the time when you need to step back and let law enforcement do its job. This man could be on your trail right now.'

'I don't think that's—'

'I shouldn't even have to be explaining this to you. But think for a minute. He's killed three people – killed them in the worst, most sadistic manner – just because he thought they could point the way to his old enemies. Two of these people were your parents. Why hasn't he gone after you in the same way? Or your sister? Could be he thinks they might have passed on some information to both of you before they died.'

'Well, that's crazy. My sister and I don't know anything.'

'Maybe. But now we've got you playing detective, dashing all over, looking up old friends of your parents. For all I know, you've picked up a few things here and there. Maybe you're even developing an idea of where Quentin Latta can find Diana Burke and John Paul West.'

He's too smart, she thought. *Way too smart.*

'Let's assume for a minute you have learned some things,' he went on. 'You know what I'd do if I were Quentin Latta? I suppose I could scoop you up and cut off your fingers with those pruning shears he's been using.'

Her stomach turned at the image. Pruning shears. So that's what—

'But I wouldn't do that.'

'All right. What would you do?'

'I'd just follow you. That's all I'd have to do. Follow you, and see where you go.'

She was silent. His words made sense, although they presented a convoluted image. Shannon and Wolfe had been seeking Diana and John Paul on the theory that Latta was ahead of them. But now it could be equally plausible that they might be ahead of him – might, in fact, be leading him to his target. Which version was true? The riddle made her head hurt.

'I suppose you and your boyfriend would take care not to be followed. But this man Latta's not alone. He could be on your tail right now, and you wouldn't know it. Here's something you may not know. Quentin Latta, or someone who looks an awful lot like him, has been spotted in the San Francisco area within the last two days.'

The news chilled her.

'So?'

'So there's nothing I'd like better than dangling you out there until he shows up. But the agency has ethical problems with using civilians that way. So here's what we'll do: You're going to see me first thing tomorrow, tell me what you know, and then head back to San Malo. Or I'm going to have you picked up, along with your boyfriend, as a material witness.'

'You just said I'm not a suspect.'

'You're not, but that wouldn't keep us from holding you for a while. You wouldn't like the federal detention facility here. I've seen it, and it's not a comfortable place.'

She felt hemmed in, with no good choices. If she saw him, if she promised to be careful, maybe she could talk him into leaving her on her own for a while longer.

‘All right,’ she said finally.

‘Give me your location and I’ll come there in the morning.’

‘No.’ She knew it was best to keep the FBI away from Wolfe. ‘I’ll come to you.’

‘Fine. The field office opens at nine.’

‘Can we do it earlier? I just want to get this over with.’

‘All right.’ Exaggerated politeness. ‘Where, then?’

‘Uh . . .’ She thought furiously. ‘A park.’

‘Golden Gate?’

‘No, that’s too big; someplace smaller. Wait.’ More thinking, then a memory of a place she had visited once with an old boyfriend. ‘Do you have a map?’

‘Yes.’ She heard paper crackling.

‘There’s a corner of the Presidio down by the Marina where there’s a little park with a lagoon,’ she began, ‘and something that looks like ancient ruins.’

More crackling. ‘The Palace of Fine Arts,’ he said.

‘That’s it. Let’s meet there on the inland side of the park. There’s a bench or two. We’ll find each other. You can bring Mr Birdsong if you want to.’

‘I’m afraid I can’t. Right about now he should be on his way east to interview an old fellow inmate of Quentin Latta at the federal penitentiary. And the warden too, I believe.’

‘Too bad.’ She felt almost comfortable with Harold Birdsong, if it was possible to say that about a man who had chased Diana and John Paul for decades. Birdsong and Thomas Orlando, the San Malo police detective, she decided, were both policemen who showed touches of humanity. Tim Dodd, less so.

‘Will you bring your boyfriend?’ he asked.

‘Do you want me to?’

‘We don’t need him for anything right now.’

Shannon reflected on that. The FBI may have asked around her neighborhood in Ben’s Beach and concluded that she was now traveling with TeeJay. *Let them go on thinking that*, she told herself.

‘How about six thirty?’ she asked Dodd. On her only other visit to the park, she had walked there at sun-up and found a surprising array of early risers, mostly joggers and dog walkers, so she knew it would not feel isolated or dangerous. Especially with an FBI agent there.

'When you say early, you mean early.'

'I want to get this over with fast.'

Thirty-Seven

Looming up out of the early-morning bay-side fog, the Palace of Fine Arts could have emerged from a fairy tale or from the pages of one of Shannon's childhood picture books. Her memory had been faulty on one count: The structure didn't resemble ruins but a complete work, an ornate creation dominated by a towering dome well over a hundred feet high. Flanking the dome were massive colonnades that curved around a lagoon.

Shannon sat in Wolfe's truck. Minutes earlier, she had eased into a curbside space at the edge of the park that enclosed the palace and lagoon. Wolfe, she hoped, was still asleep. He had appeared to need another full night of catching up, and she was glad to leave him behind with a terse note in case he should wake up before she returned. It gave no details, said only that she would be out for a while. No sense giving him reason to worry. Later in the morning, she could explain it all, and they could return to the subject of their long-delayed plans. She felt intense pressure to be gone. Time was running away from them, whether Quentin Latta was on their trail or already had Diana in his sights.

Her watch read a few minutes shy of six thirty. No sign of Dodd. Down in the park – it lay somewhat below street level – figures moved in the mist. A man in a parka walked a tiny dog on a leash along a curved concrete path that ran by the lagoon. On the grass, a woman slowly went through what looked like tai chi moves. A man in a tattered raincoat hunched over a trash barrel, fishing for anything he could use. As a backdrop to these modern figures, the sprawling neoclassical structure, an enormous anachronism, loomed across the lagoon like the setting for a dream.

She was getting impatient. It was now precisely six thirty, and still no sign of Dodd. *You wouldn't expect the* FBI *to show up late for a date*, she thought. She decided to head for one of the park benches, advertise her presence, and wait for him there.

As she opened the door, she glimpsed a figure standing just inside the beginning of the colonnade near the lagoon, where the pale morning light ended and the columns and trees darkened the dirt path. Because of the angle, she had no clear view, but the figure appeared to be waving. An instant later it disappeared, but before Shannon could reflect on that, she spotted Dodd. The agent was about fifty feet away, leaving a car at the curb and striding hurriedly into the park, headed for the nearest columns of the colonnade – and, apparently, the spot where the figure had stood.

Dodd was going after that person, whoever it was. A few seconds later, he too disappeared behind the nearest column.

She thought of calling out to him but quickly discarded the idea. Instead, she simply pursued him. Maybe he had misunderstood the precise meeting place and mistaken someone else for her, she thought. She could catch up with him in less than a minute, and—

A quick, muffled sound from within the maze of columns, almost like an amplified cough, clearly noticeable in the morning quiet. Her steps faltered, then resumed. Soon she had left the grass and was making her way along the dim-lit path, the columns forming a dense forest that towered above her.

She came to a bend in the path, where it turned left and curved around the edge of the lagoon on its way to the dome, now a huge presence almost overhead. To the right, one leg of the path dead-ended in a tangle of trees and water's-edge shrubbery.

It was there she saw him.

At first all she could make out were the legs, almost comically splayed where they emerged from the water. Approaching, she saw the rest of him barely submerged in the lagoon, resting face up in the shallows.

Then she stood over him, barely breathing. She heard Wolfe's voice in her head: *Don't touch anything*. No need. It was all clear. Special Agent Tim Dodd's face looked skyward through a few inches of murky water still troubled by the splash of his body. Twin jets of bubbles left his nose and mouth on their way to the surface, where they broke silently. Joining them there was a thin, wavering stream of crimson emerging from a small hole in his forehead.

He appeared even younger in death.

She gulped air and looked around. From her near-hidden location, the slow-motion life of the park on the other side of the lagoon looked normal. No one had seen her. Yet.

But who . . . ?

Then she saw the distant figure, running full-tilt through the far colonnade and out of the park. Shannon faintly remembered something that lay in that direction, a kind of children's museum with a big parking lot. Seconds went by, then she heard an engine roar to life and tires squeal.

Get out of here, you idiot. Head down, she willed herself to look small and inconsequential as she moved at a fast walk back along the path and out the way she had come. A minute later, she sat behind the wheel of the truck. One more quick look across the park, where all was still peaceful. But it would not last, and she needed to be far away from there.

Just before twisting the ignition key, she replayed a few quick seconds in her mind. The running figure had worn a hooded sweatshirt and had been relatively slight. Not much to go on.

But Shannon had no doubt as to who it was. She had looked into that face, known that insincere smile, felt the grip of those cable-strong hands, and smelled the breath as it mingled with the musty scents of her parents' garage.

Thirty-Eight

She only made it two blocks before she had to pull over. The muscles in her right leg were beginning to twitch, she was having trouble catching her breath, and she felt a noise building in her head. Her brother, it seemed, was not the only one with storms in the brain.

Although she had never before had a panic attack, she thought she could discern the symptoms. *Slow down, dammit.* She took a few deep breaths and tried to assess what she knew. Dodd was dead, almost certainly at the hand of the woman who called herself Lonnie, and soon the FBI would be on the hunt. Whoever got swept up in the dragnet, guilty or innocent, would not be treated gently.

Shannon could not discount any of the things Dodd had told her. If Lonnie had been stalking the FBI agent, it was not hard to believe that Shannon and Wolfe themselves were either being followed or being sought. The agent's death might mean that she and her brother could be the targets of both law enforcement and a band of killers.

Of all the options available to them, none looked attractive. If they tried to take cover, sooner or later they would almost certainly be found. If they resumed their search for Diana, they would be even more exposed. With no leads on Diana and a federal agent now dead, Shannon could see only hopelessness.

She felt like a traveler in an unexplored land far from home and the remnants of her family. She had chosen this journey, but with every step she grew more and more uprooted and cut off. *I can't go back*, she told herself. *I can only go forward, to wherever that takes me.*

In her panicky state, one thing seemed clear: She needed help. If only her mother and father could be just a phone call away. Once, before her feelings of alienation began to take over, she had found it simple to talk to both of them. But they were gone. So was Henry. She would have to seek help elsewhere.

Her thoughts turned first to Harold Birdsong. She didn't totally trust him, any more than she trusted any policeman. For one thing, he had suggested to her that Lonnie was not a threat, was little more than a twisted groupie. On that subject, she was convinced, either he was clueless or he had misled her.

Still, he had shared a mass of information on Burke, West, Latta, and her parents. He knew things. And she desperately needed a friend in the FBI.

Reaching for her phone and wallet, she pulled out the card he had given her and dialed his number. Almost instantly a voice told her the phone was out of service.

Out of service? That only added to her queasiness. A call to the information operator elicited the number of the Los Angeles field office of the FBI, where a male voice answered the phone.

'Can you put me in touch with Harold Birdsong? He's a retired agent who's been consulting with your office.'

'Just a moment.' Muffled voices in the background, and the man was quickly back. 'I'm told he's, uh, unreachable at present. If you'll give me your name—'

'Never mind.' She broke the connection.

She wanted one of her rare cigarettes and, even more fiercely, a drink. Could Lonnie or her friends have caught up with both agents at once? Could Birdsong be dead too?

She realized that her mantra *Don't tell police* was losing currency, and she didn't care.

Consulting the stack of cards in her wallet, she dialed the number for Detective Thomas Orlando at San Malo PD. A recording this time, but at least it was in his voice.

'This is Shannon Fairchild, and I need to talk to you.' She didn't leave her cell phone number, knowing he had it. She had watched enough television to know that it was possible to track someone's location through cell phone use, but she took comfort in the fact that as far as she knew, the San Malo police had no immediate interest in finding her. That could change quickly, though.

When she got back to the hotel the room was empty. Wolfe had left his own note, as terse as hers. *Out for a while.*

It was barely eight in the morning, and already she felt beaten down, almost breathless in her anxiety. Her insides felt like the Gordian Knot. She and Wolfe needed to decide their next moves. Until he returned, she was at a standstill.

In the sitting room, she opened the mini-bar and found an array of miniature booze bottles. She scooped up several and took them into the bathroom, where she undressed and began running hot water in the bathtub. She eased herself into the tub, gasping at the heat and the immediate sense of release, and dumped in some of the hotel's bath gel for a feeling of luxury.

She eyed the tempting little bottles lined up on the edge of the tub, reached for one and twisted off the cap. It was a Napa Valley chardonnay, and it went down smoothly, hitting her empty stomach like a soft, warm explosion. Next came a bottle of Vat 69, then some Johnny Walker Red . . .

She lost count, but the only thing that mattered was the new and wonderful feeling of lassitude that swept over her. The Gordian Knot eased open. She began humming to herself, and the humming almost drowned out the sound of her phone ringing. Reaching over the edge of the tub, she worked it out of her pants pocket.

'Hey, Shan?'

It was TeeJay, and she gave a great sigh at the sound of his voice. They hadn't spoken in a while, and he was calling to find out how she was doing. He sounded worried. She began talking in a low and affectionate voice, almost a whisper. At this time of stress, having him on the other end of the line was as soothing as a warm bath. The time passed quickly, and she only realized the conversation was over when the dial tone told her he'd hung up.

Careful, she told her sleepy self. *Nobody wants a drunk for a girlfriend.* Then she eased herself back down in the scented water.

She awoke to find her chin submerged and Wolfe shaking her. He was not gentle.

'What the hell?' he said almost under his breath, then said it again.

She raised a hand to ward him off, splashing him in the process. 'I'm awake,' she said without much conviction.

'What are you doing?'

'Just having a …' She looked around, as if to verify that she was indeed in a bathtub. 'A bath.'

'You're drunk.'

'Oh, yeah.' She struggled to sit up, trying to cover her strategic zones with both hands. 'Girl get a little privacy here?'

He picked up one of the empty mini-bottles, dropped it on the bath mat. 'Want to tell me why you're drunk at nine thirty in the morning?' He stood up, grabbed a towel, and tossed it at her. She arranged it clumsily, and it became immediately soaked, but it did the job.

'Good reason. Best reason. Everything turned to shit, that's what.'

He waited.

'We'll never find Diana. And you know it.' Every word took an effort. 'Now I find out there's a good chance that Quentin Latta's looking for us. And Tim Dodd's dead.'

'Who's Tim Dodd?'

'Oh. Forgot. You don't know him. FBI guy.'

'What?' He stared at her, mouth open. Then he bolted from the room and was back in seconds with something in his hand. A small white pill. He placed it between his teeth and cracked it down the middle, handing her half. 'Take this.' He filled a glass at the sink and thrust it at her. 'Go on.'

'What is it?'

'God dammit, Shannon, just take it. I'm going to call room service and get us some coffee. You want breakfast too?'

'Uh … sure. I guess. Toast and cereal and, uh, juice.'

'I want you to take a cold shower and get dressed. You've got to tell me everything, and I need you to be sharp.'

Even in her blurry condition, she could tell that the old Wolfe was back, vigorous and focused. 'Well. Okay, then.'

Thirty-Nine

She sat fully dressed on the side of the bed and ate breakfast. Wolfe had ordered two pots of coffee, and he kept her cup filled. Slowly she felt herself emerge from the haze of alcohol, and a faint buzz in her ears told her that the change wasn't due simply to cold water and hot coffee.

'What was the pill?' she asked.

'Speed,' he answered. 'Prescription stuff. Pretty big dose, so I cut it in half. If you need more, I've got it.'

'Aren't you the little pharmacist?'

'So you want to tell me now?'

Haltingly, she took him through the most recent events, starting with the FBI agent's phone call the previous evening and ending with her grisly early-morning rendezvous at the park. He looked grim throughout. She went on to tell him about her attempts to reach Birdsong and Orlando, and the grim look turned angry.

'What are you doing calling them?'

'We can talk to cops without giving away everything,' she said with a heavy sigh. 'They want Quentin Latta caught as much as we do. And with an FBI man falling down dead almost under my nose, we're going to need somebody on our side, somebody who believes we didn't do it.'

He relaxed just a bit. 'You mean *you* didn't do it, *kemo sabe*.'

'That's hilarious.'

He pulled out his cell phone, flipped it open, and fingered the screen for a few seconds. 'This came in while you were out and I was asleep.' He held up the phone so she could hear. A robotic voice announced the presence of a message, then Katherine Dimitrios's voice emerged:

'Wolfe, call me. It's important.' A soft laugh. 'But then isn't everything in our world these days?' The robotic voice started up again, but Wolfe cut it off with a click.

She stared at the phone. 'What do you think … ?'

'Who knows? But I didn't want to call her until you were back on this planet.'

'All right. I'm back. Call her. Speaker, please.'

The buzz of the dial tone, the beep of the numbers, the ringing. Then Katherine's voice, sounding tired, and Shannon felt a twinge of sadness, knowing the tiredness was just a prelude to something final and terrible. She leaned forward as Wolfe spoke.

'Katherine, it's Wolfe. And Shannon's here.'

'Oh, wonderful. Now listen—' They heard a male voice in the background, talking urgently, and Katherine's voice grew fainter as she answered him. 'Now you stop. Just stop. This is my business, and if it's one of the last things I get a chance to do, I'm taking care of it.'

Silence on the other end for long seconds, and her voice came back to them. 'It's Milton,' she said, drawing an uneven breath. 'He wants me to stay out of this. Of course he does. But he doesn't understand everything that's involved. You children do, I'm sure.'

Another breath, even more ragged, and Shannon thought she could hear the rattle of phlegm in her throat. 'I'm wasting time. Do you have something to write with?'

'Yes,' Wolfe said loudly, pulling out a pen as Shannon grabbed one of the hotel's notepads from the bedside table and handed it to him.

'Write down *Maple Valley, Washington.*'

'All right.'

'And this address.' She spelled out the street name and then repeated it. 'You need to be there by nine tomorrow morning. If anyone asks, tell them you're there for a piano lesson.'

'A what?' Shannon exclaimed.

'I've got that,' Wolfe said quickly. 'Is there a phone number?'

'Surely you jest. In all these years, I've never had a number for her.'

They heard Milton's voice in the background again, and Katherine spoke forcefully. 'Now go, children. And promise me you'll be very, very careful. I've lost too many friends. I couldn't stand the thought of losing both of you.' Her voice caught again, and this time Shannon knew the cause wasn't physical.

Shannon spoke up. 'How did you—'

Katherine's laugh was free and unforced, and she suddenly sounded years younger, healthy again, a girl of the revolution. 'I called in all my debts. They have a term here in Chicago. It's called *clout*, and it's usually about politics. Well, I used the clout of a dying woman, and that's a powerful thing. Nothing can stand up to it. Not even Diana Burke. She always had the stubbornness of a mule but, bless her, she knew when she was beaten. Although I have to say –' her voice turned wry '– that Diana seems to have her own reasons for saying yes. So maybe we're doing her will after all. Sounds familiar, doesn't it?'

She was seized with a series of coughs that made Shannon wince. When she regained her breath, they could hear the effort behind her words.

'From my talks with her over the last few days, I have a feeling …' Katherine's words trailed off.

'What is it?' Wolfe asked.

'Something's on her mind, something that makes it hard for her to focus on anything else. It's made her more talkative than she's ever been with me. She mentioned a name once – the name Adam – as if she were about to tell me a story, then changed her mind.

'It sounds as if she's involved in something important that's about to happen. I'm not sure what, but it reminds me of the old days, when she and John Paul would be planning an operation, and you could feel it in the air.'

Wolfe chose his words carefully. 'Is this what I think it means?'

'Yes. It's what we all think it means. You shouldn't waste any time.'

'Will we find her there?' Shannon asked, unable to shake the doubt from her voice.

'Hmm. You know, her world is full of shadows and uncertainty. But I don't think she would lie to me now. Go to her, children.' She forced a lighter tone into her voice. 'And let me know how this adventure turns out, won't you? I'll be right here.'

'I love you, Katherine,' Wolfe said. As he ended the call, Shannon found herself saying silently, *So do I.*

Wolfe was already in motion. 'Let's get packed and hit the road.'

Forty

They were out of the hotel by eleven. After stopping at a gas station for maps of Oregon and Washington state, Wolfe found the town of Maple Valley outside Seattle. He did some quick measurements and estimated that the drive would take them around thirteen hours plus the necessary pauses. That gave them more than enough time, but they had no reason to linger in the Bay Area and every reason to get out. They quickly decided to make it to Seattle late that night, sleep for a few hours, and drive to the rendezvous in the morning.

'If we eat on the road and make our rest stops quick, we should be able to get there by one a.m.,' he said, with what sounded like enthusiasm. Shannon realized that he liked these marathon driving trips, and she recalled that TeeJay did too. One of those guy things, she decided.

She groaned to herself. Although by no means a delicate flower, she nevertheless liked the occasional comforts of the road. A long lunch break helped; and, at the end of the day, a firm mattress, a good meal, and unwinding with a couple of glasses of wine were all part of her traveler's creed. A driving trip with her brother, though, was more like being on the road with Jack Kerouac. Then she reminded herself what lay at the end of this road.

Aloud she said, 'Let's do it.'

Swapping off behind the wheel as she and Henry had done, they headed north to the end of the Sacramento Valley, where agricultural country gave way to hills and the temperature began to drop.

When Shannon slid behind the wheel at their first changeover, she found her brain beginning to cloud up, so she asked him for the second half of the little white pill, washed it down, and took them back on the road. Wolfe made himself comfortable beside her and, with only a little urging, began to talk about his life growing up with Diana and John Paul. It was a life lived on the edge, he told her, where at any moment it might be necessary to run.

'Both of them kept a bag packed with clothes, money, fresh IDs, whatever we'd need if we ever had to drop everything and hit the road suddenly. When I got old enough, I had my own little bag too. You can bet *that* made me feel grown-up.'

'Did you ever have to do it? Drop everything?'

'Once. I was about ten, and we were living in a little town in North Carolina, near the coast. John Paul came home one day and said, "Pack up. Everything in the car. Ten minutes." He'd spotted someone in town, a stranger, and got a bad vibe off of him.'

'You mean he uprooted his whole family just because of that?'

'Uh-huh. And you know what? He was right. It took a while for us to get the story straight, but eventually we heard it all. Less than an hour after we left, our little rented house was surrounded by cops, Feds, and the media. They would have had us, except for his instinct and our training.'

She shook her head. 'What a life. What a God-awful way to grow up.'

'You're right. But exciting too. When I was small, it was like a game to me. Hide-and-seek. Cowboys and Indians. John Paul would take me in the woods, and we'd split up and communicate by walkie-talkie. "Just remember, go to Channel Eight," he'd say. "You'll always find me there." And sure enough, there he was. It was great fun, but after a while I realized it was more than that. He was training me for the day when I'd need those skills.

'Then, when I was sixteen or seventeen, I knew I didn't want to spend my whole life playing fugitive games and being on the run. And why should I? They'd chosen it; I didn't have to. As soon as I could, I left.'

'What did you do?'

'Oh, I knocked around; tried a few jobs. Took some college classes at the University of Arizona. I was married once for about five minutes. Eventually wound up in the woods in Northern California, where I found a lifestyle I liked and a little community of misfits like me. I've been happy enough.'

'What do you do?'

'I'm a small businessman.'

The answer did nothing to satisfy her curiosity. She was about to press him when he said:

'I wondered about you. I pictured you as an ex-cheerleader-type, married with kids, very white-bread.'

'Actually, you've just described my sister, Beth.'

'You surprised me, though. You're more like me than I ever would've thought. Like them, too.'

'You think so?' She was oddly pleased. Her feelings for Diana and John Paul had not warmed appreciably, but she had no doubts as to their strength and magnetism. To be compared with people like that ...

'I've got no gripes about my upbringing,' he went on. 'I owe them for pretty much everything I am. They home-schooled me a lot, exposed me to music – rock, folk, classical, pretty much everything. I was reading *Soul on Ice* when kids my age were reading the Oz books. Maybe they wanted me to be a junior revolutionary – that's why they gave me this name – but I don't think they were unhappy when I left to make my own way. They'd trained me to do just that.'

'What's revolutionary about your name?' she asked. Before he could reply, the historian in her came up with the answer: 'Wolfe Tone. Is that it? They named you after—'

'Theobald Wolfe Tone – one of the first of the Irish revolutionaries, way back in the seventeen hundreds. The English sentenced him to death, but he slit his own throat before they could hang him. Diana and John Paul thought he'd be a good role model.'

Shannon laughed and shook her head in near disbelief. 'To give a kid a name like that ... But I suppose I shouldn't be surprised.'

'Hey, I always kind of liked the name. It made me stand out in the crowd. And it's no worse than yours.'

'What do you mean? Shannon's just a name.'

'I'm talking about your middle name. Patrice.'

'Oh, my God, you're not telling me they named me after ...' She couldn't finish the thought.

'Patrice Lumumba.' He seemed amused. 'I looked him up again before I came to see you, just to refresh my memory. He was an anti-colonialist and the first prime minister of Congo when they kicked the Belgians out back in the early sixties. But he was too far left to make people comfortable, so the CIA stirred up a military coup against him, and before long he was dead.'

'They named me after a *man*?'

'It's a good name. Malcolm X called him the greatest African who ever lived. If I were you, though, I'd be more worried that they named us after a couple of *dead* men. Martyrs. Just like Nadja and Ernesto. Think they were trying to tell us something?'

While he was speaking, she had noticed that he had occasionally turned around to look out the back window. Now he leaned against his window, giving the side-view mirror a long look.

'You must love her a lot,' she commented, 'to be going to these lengths to help her.'

'Maybe I do,' he said. 'There are plenty of folks who'd tell you she's not very lovable, and I probably wouldn't argue with them. But she's a lot of other things. Including my mother. I'm helping her because ...' He shrugged. 'I don't really have any choice. How about you?'

She didn't answer, but possible answers came to her silently. *It's not because I love her*, she told herself. *How can you love someone you've never known?*

Maybe it's because if I do this thing, if I take on this responsibility, if I even try to save her life ... then she'll notice me and acknowledge me. And that would make it all worthwhile.

She heard the rush of wind. Wolfe was lowering his window to fiddle with the side-view mirror. His eyes were on it for a long time.

'What is it?'

'Car back there. I first noticed it an hour ago, before we stopped for gas. Then, when we pulled up at the pumps, he found one way over on the other side, as if he didn't want to be noticed. At that distance, I couldn't see who it was. When I finished topping us off – you were in the restroom – I got a sidearm from my bag and started over to say hello. But he pulled away from the pump before I could get close.'

'Was it a van?'

'No. Just a regular sedan. Blue four-door. Toyota, maybe.'

'A man?'

'There was a man at the pump. That's all I could tell you. Big guy, wearing a knit cap. Could have been others in the car. Anyway, I've been watching for him ever since we got back on the road, and there he is. He's smart enough to keep six or eight cars between us, but every time we change lanes, he does too.'

He rolled up his window. 'You want to try something?'

'Uh, sure.'

He peered ahead. 'Exit ramp coming up, with an overpass. Take it.'

She had a lane to cross, and the exit was coming up fast. Too fast. 'I can't,' she shouted. The shadow of the overpass went like the blink of an eye.

'God dammit,' Wolfe yelled back at her. 'All right, get in the fast lane, quick as you can.'

There were cars in the way. As she wheeled toward the lane, one of them, in the center lane, hit the brakes, then blasted her with the horn. The fast lane was full, and the lead car, a big Cadillac Escalade, would not slow to let her in. When Shannon pulled abreast, the driver, a young man, looked at her through slitted eyes and stepped on the gas.

'Get around him!' Wolfe yelled. 'You can do it!'

She floored the accelerator and felt the big engine propel the truck ahead with a roar, caught a glimpse of shock on the other driver's face. The SUV began to drift behind.

'Now hit the brakes, hard left, and take us over the median.'

'*What?*'

'Do it! He'll get out of your way.'

'Oh, shit.' She followed his command, jamming on the brakes and wrenching the wheel over. As they crossed the fast lane and flew off the pavement, she heard the squeal of brakes behind her, and her whole body tensed for the impact.

But there was none. The SUV fish-tailed wildly on and off the concrete, throwing gravel, then found its way back onto the freeway, horn blaring furiously.

They dove into a grassy gully, full of rocks and ruts that rattled their teeth. The gully bottomed out, and she powered the truck up the other side, bumping all the way. She had to pause for critical seconds in the face of oncoming traffic, all of it honking, then floored the accelerator and twisted the wheel hard left again. They hit the concrete with tires screeching and started back the way they had come.

'Whoa!' she yelled. 'That was—'

'Now the off ramp. Quick!'

She crossed three lanes, accompanied by another symphony of horns, and sped up the ramp to the overpass, where she stopped. Wolfe jumped out and peered out over the freeway for long minutes, both ahead and behind, then got back in.

'Well?' Her heart was pumping double-time.

He looked grim. 'No sign of him.'

'What does that mean?'

'It means he did something. While we were making our demolition derby moves. He could've done his own U-turn across the median and headed back the other way, so we couldn't get a look at him.'

'So we're being followed.'

'Yep. And he'll be a lot more careful now. All we can do is get back on the freeway and step on it.' He opened his door. 'I'll drive.'

'Damn. Just when I was starting to love off-roading.'

Forty-One

Wolfe drove faster than she had, asking her to keep an eye out for black-and-whites.

They clearly needed to lengthen the distance between themselves and their pursuer. Once they had settled into Wolfe's road rhythm, she relaxed to a small degree.

As they drove, Wolfe provided their soundtrack, and she was pleased to find that his musical tastes seemed as broad as hers. A collection of operatic arias, followed by some Dave Brubeck, and then a little Muddy Waters.

The hours went by, along with the changing scenery. 'Oregon's up ahead,' Wolfe said under his breath as they crossed the Klamath River.

To Shannon their surroundings looked greener and felt cooler than California; she remembered the biting chill of Montana and was glad she had packed some warm clothes.

With each mile, she felt herself drawing nearer to Diana. Somewhere up ahead lay the most momentous encounter of her life, but the feeling brought her no comfort. Her stomach began to ache, and she knew it had nothing to do with food. The prospect of finally meeting Diana played havoc with her system. Her appetite had begun to fade hours ago. Each time they stopped for food, she could bring herself to eat only a few bites.

She imagined herself as a high-wheeling hawk looking down on the world of roads and travelers. From up there she saw the two of them racing northward to meet Diana even as she made out other pursuers – some behind them, some closing in on their destination from another angle. Who would get there first? Would she and Wolfe be too late?

Daylight ended early at that latitude, so it was past dark when they reached Portland at about eight thirty. They barely paused, though, to replenish food and gas and were soon on their way again. She was getting tired and knew that he was, too, but neither wanted to let it show.

This brother of mine's as proud and stubborn as I am, she thought. *And why should I be surprised?*

It was well past midnight when they pulled into a truck stop just short of Seattle. Wolfe parked in a far corner of the lot. They had agreed that, late as it was, getting a hotel room was too much trouble and that they might as well sleep in the truck.

She stretched out across the back seat, using her bag as a pillow. Wolfe reached over the seat and hauled his duffel bag up front, unzipped it, and extracted something from it.

'Back in a minute,' he said. It was more like ten minutes, but when he returned, he seemed more relaxed. 'Been all over this lot,' he said, 'and I don't see anything unusual. No Lonnies, no Quentins, no strange cars.'

He lay down in the front, resting the calf of one long leg over the steering column.

Her exhaustion reached down to her bones, but the truck stop was noisy with air brakes, grinding gears, and occasional horn blasts. Her mind was even noisier. While waiting for sleep, she decided to give voice to a question – in a way, the most important one of all.

'Would you tell me about her?'

She heard a theatrical groan from the front seat, followed by a long pause.

'So you want a bedtime story?' he said finally. 'All right, but just until I get sleepy. Where do I start? She was probably a terrible mother. She couldn't boil water – John Paul would do a lot of the cooking. If I came home crying over a skinned knee or something like that, she wasn't the place to go for consolation. That's why I learned to look after myself.

'All of her energy and brains got poured into the bigger things of life – ideas, the movement, how to influence the largest number of people; people in the abstract, I mean. When it came to people up close, it was harder to get her to focus. She was all about the big picture.'

'Stopping the war, you mean.'

'Right, but after a while that wasn't relevant any more. By the mid-seventies the war was over, and Diana and John Paul were talking about how to deal with racism and hand more power to the working class. Not to mention making sure the FBI wasn't following us home. When you've got all that on the brain, you don't spend much time thinking about what's for dinner.'

She laughed. 'I'm sorry, but that sounds almost funny.'

'It is. My mother the revolutionary.' She heard him grunt and shift position. 'And the talking they'd do – hours of wrangling over doctrine. Which revolution is more pure, North Vietnam's or Cuba's? Is it better for draft evaders to stay in Canada or return home and go to prison as a political gesture?'

'I get the picture.'

'Pretty boring for a little boy. But there were compensations. We had Timothy Leary at our dinner table one night, Eldridge Cleaver another time. Even I knew who they were. Very cloak-and-dagger, those dinners, because we were deep underground.'

'I'd like to have been there.'

'Looking back, I think Diana and John Paul lost themselves in talk because they weren't taking action any more. Trying to live quietly underground, with me in tow, turned them away from practicing revolution and more toward just theorizing about it. The Vietnam War eventually ended, but it wasn't really because of them.'

His words came more slowly now. 'They couldn't end racism, and I'm not sure they made a better world. On top of that, they wound up fugitives. They must have been unhappy with the way things turned out. Unfinished business, you know? So they headed off in different directions – one of them deciding to work within the system, the other still trying to monkeywrench it.'

'My mother the revolutionary.' This time it was Shannon who spoke the words.

'When the environment came along as a left-wing cause, Diana must have felt she was being handed a gift, something new to get excited about – a reason to hold secret meetings, to make speeches, to take direct action. I swear, I think she must love the sound of bombs going off.

'In a way, it's too bad the left isn't getting more stirred up over this war in Iraq,' he said. 'With Diana around, we'd see a lot of broken glass in the street.'

'So tell me more about her.'

A sigh. 'Okay. Let's see …' He was quiet for a moment. 'Smart. Usually the smartest one in the room – along with John Paul. Charismatic, and she knew the effect she had on people, although she didn't wave it around like some big personalities do. She hardly ever raised her voice, but people listened to her.'

'But a terrible mother,' Shannon murmured.

'Yep. But I remember something else. I had the flu, was really sick for a long time. One evening, John Paul had just fixed me some soup. I was in bed coughing and feeling generally rotten, and I noticed her in the doorway watching me. "I haven't been much good to you, have I?" she said.

'I couldn't think of any answer to that, but I probably agreed with her. "What can I do?" she asked me. For some reason, I said, "Read to me." So she sat down on the edge of the bed and starting reading me one of the books they had just gotten published, the one about the pirate girl—'

'*The Corsair's Daughter.*'

'Right. She read me a chapter, and after a while I was asleep. The next night she came in and picked up right where we'd left off. She'd never read to me before, so I began looking forward to it every evening. And damned if she didn't read me the whole book.'

'That's—'

'Then I started feeling better, and things were back to normal. She never read to me again. But for a while there, it was pretty good. You know, I try not to hold anything against her. She's who she is. Sure, every now and then I wish I'd had a mother who fed me chicken soup and snuggled with me in bed. But then I remember Diana at her best, the woman who inspired people, and I'm glad that I'm her son.'

'People have died because of her.'

'That's right, they have. But she's always been ready to die for what she believed in. And so has he.'

He exhaled a long breath. 'End of bedtime story. Goodnight.'

*

Wolfe's internal clock got them up at eight. They paid a small fee to shower in the truck stop, had breakfast in the restaurant, gassed up, and were back on the freeway just before nine. With Shannon navigating, they drove to Maple Valley, a town with a rural flavor southeast of Seattle. They found the street in a residential neighborhood of middle-class homes. Wolfe slowed as they approached the address they sought.

He stopped and looked around. 'Check that number she gave us.' Shannon did. It was 2709. They had just passed 2707, and up ahead was 2711.

What should have been 2709 was a vacant lot. From the looks of it, the lot had been vacant for a long time.

'All right,' Shannon said, 'what's going on?'

'God dammit, Diana,' Wolfe muttered. 'Playing tricks on us?'

'Why would she do that?'

'All kinds of reasons.' He sighed. 'But mainly to make it harder to—' He stopped at the sound of an engine behind them. Shannon turned around to see an old VW bus pull up close. A van.

Wolfe's eyes were on the rear-view. 'Is that the kind that followed you in Montana?'

She was about to answer when the van's doors opened on both sides and two people emerged.

'Get down!' Wolfe grabbed for his duffel bag, hauled it onto his lap, unzipped it, and plunged his hand inside.

Forty-Two

Two figures, one male, the other female, advanced unhurriedly toward the truck.

'You know them?' Wolfe's voice was tense.

The man, who had almost reached Wolfe's window, was outsized, hulking in a heavy parka. She could see his breath on the air.

'No.'

Wolfe relaxed a little but kept his hand out of sight in the bag. The man leaned over and rapped lightly on the window. 'You lost?'

Shannon eyed the woman, who now stood beside her door. She was young and slight, with a mop of black hair and a fur-lined denim jacket.

Talking through the glass, Wolfe spoke up. 'Maybe we are. We're, uh, looking for a piano lesson.'

The man appeared to be in his thirties, with a military-style brush cut that reminded Shannon of Detective Orlando's. He made a circular motion with his forefinger, and Wolfe, after some hesitation, rolled down his window.

'Names?'

'Wolfe. This is Shannon.'

Unexpectedly, the man eased his expression into a light grin. 'I'm Stack,' he said. 'This is Judith. You want to follow us?'

As the pair returned to their van, Wolfe and Shannon both let out audible breaths. 'What the hell . . . ?' she began.

'Diana's people,' he said. 'She's jerking us around, like I guessed. Nobody gets to her right away. You've got to go through layers. It was like this in the movement.'

'What fun.'

The VW pulled around them. Wolfe put the truck in gear and followed.

Keeping off freeways, the van led them along a circuitous route through a succession of large and small communities east of Seattle. After about forty minutes they passed two small towns, then came to a third. Turning off at one of the few downtown traffic lights, they went along a series of residential blocks until they came to a street of small, neat houses set on good-size yards. The van stopped in front of one, and Wolfe pulled up behind it.

Neither of their guides made a move to get out. Shannon rolled down her window, feeling the cold air, to get a better look at the house. It was single-story and small enough to qualify as a cottage, with a tiny front porch partly hidden by a trellis that in warmer weather might be covered with a flowering vine. A new sedan sat in the driveway in front of the garage.

'You know something?' Shannon said abruptly. 'I'm really tired of riding. My legs are stiff, and I'm going to stretch them. I'd also like to know why we're here.'

She got out and walked over to the passenger side of the van, where Judith rolled down her window. 'Some reason we picked this spot to park?'

Judith gave her an impassive look as Stack answered. 'Yeah,' he said, glancing at his watch. 'Can you just wait a few minutes?'

'I've been waiting for days. Is she in there?'

'What if she is?'

'Well, then I'm going in.'

'You don't want to interrupt the piano lesson, do you?'

'The what?'

And then she heard it – the faint sound of a piano. She strained to hear. The melody was familiar. After a few notes, she had it: Beethoven's playful *Für Elise.* But played haltingly, somewhat mechanically, with little feeling. Errors crept in, then more. Finally it stopped abruptly. An awkward silence lasting a few seconds, then the piece began again. This time the pianist was in full control, especially in the lyrical sweep of the treble notes.

As she stood leaning against the van listening, Wolfe joined her. He too heard it, and the music made him smile.

'Diana?' she asked.

He nodded.

'You didn't tell me she played the piano.'

He shrugged.

Her eyes strayed to the mailbox and the name on it. *North. She's still using the author's name*, Shannon thought with some surprise, and the expression *Hidden in plain sight* came to mind.

The piece ended softly. A few minutes later the front door opened, and a woman came out with a little girl of ten or so, who was carrying sheet music. Following them onto the porch was a tall, white-haired woman wearing a long-sleeve, long-skirted print dress. She leaned over the girl, said something, and rumpled her hair. Grinning, the girl clutched her sheet music to her chest, ran down the steps, and got into the car. Her mother followed her, and seconds later they backed out of the driveway and left.

Shannon stared at the woman on the porch, who by now was looking at her. Was it Diana? It had to be. Yet her dress was almost dowdy, and her hair, once long and dark, was now casually short and shockingly white. The effect was very much that of a small-town piano teacher.

'Amazing,' she said quietly.

Instead of coming over, the white-haired woman simply waved and went back inside. 'What's going on?' she asked the two in the van.

'Be patient,' Stack said.

Ten minutes went by, then fifteen. The door opened, and a very different woman came out. She wore a heavy jacket, khaki pants, and boots, with a baseball cap on her head. A big duffel bag hung from one shoulder. Turning, she double-locked the front door, checked the front windows, came down the front steps, taking them two at a time, and crossed the yard to the street.

'Well,' she said, dropping the bag to the ground. 'Hello, Wolfe.' She put a hand to his cheek, then hugged him quickly and hard. 'Look at you.'

He turned to Shannon. 'And this—'

'Is Shannon. I know.'

Shannon knew that the longest and most important journey of her life – to find the woman who had given birth to her – had come to an end. It was still only a beginning, and she did not know what lay ahead. But this much she had accomplished, and as she stood face to face with Diana, she felt slightly breathless. She tried not to stare and failed. *Say something* to *her, idiot*, she told herself.

'It's good to . . .' she began haltingly.

'We shouldn't stand around in this neighborhood.'

That was Stack, and at his words Diana's face became focused and businesslike. 'Right,' she said briskly, heaving the bag up to her shoulder. 'Let's get out of here.' To Shannon and Wolfe she said: 'We'll talk later. I need to ride with these two characters and get caught up on a few things. You can follow us. It's not far.'

With that she wrenched open the back door of the van, flung her duffel bag onto the floor, and followed it inside. As she swung the door closed, she slapped the back of the seat. 'Let's go.'

Shannon and Wolfe barely had time to get the truck going before they saw the van turn a corner at the next block. He gunned the engine, and they were off. When they had the van comfortably in sight, he looked over at her.

'And I thought we were all finished driving. Silly me. How're you doing?'

'Just great.'

'Not really, huh?'

'No. It wasn't exactly the reunion I had in mind.'

'I know. You wanted her to show a little more emotion. Well, she doesn't like to lose control. Don't let her intimidate you.'

'Do I look intimidated?'

'Just a little. That's the effect she has on people. She's human, though.'

'Sure. My mother the revolutionary.'

Forty-Three

Before long they were again on the 90, westbound this time, headed back toward Seattle. At the interchange with the 5 they turned south, retracing their earlier route. The giant Boeing aircraft plant swept by on their right.

'Oh, man,' Shannon sighed, putting her feet up on the dashboard, 'I'm sick of all these roads.'

Wolfe said nothing. She glanced over at him and noticed that he was looking tired again. *We should have swapped off miles back*, she berated herself; *I wasn't paying attention. Too late now.*

'Turn signal.' The van was in the right-hand lane, about to exit. They followed. Minutes later they were following Diana and the others through an industrial area of warehouses and hangars, concrete and high fences. The van crossed a set of railroad tracks and turned a corner onto a road that led between tall, anonymous, aluminum-sided buildings. It stopped in front of one, a structure about a hundred feet wide and twice as deep. The building was freestanding and unfenced, with double doors large enough to admit the biggest vehicle. Shannon looked up and down the road. It was quiet, suggesting that these buildings were used mostly for storage.

Diana got out and went to a human-size door on the right, where she used a key on two locks and opened it. Stack and Judith went inside, and a minute later the double doors slowly drew apart, accompanied by a grinding noise. Diana drove the VW bus inside, and the truck followed.

Wolfe pulled up behind the halted van just as the double doors began to close. They got out of the truck. At first Shannon could see little, since the interior light came only from a series of skylights high up in the peaked roof. Then someone began throwing switches, and the cavernous interior was gradually illuminated by row after row of fluorescent lights.

Shannon mouthed a silent *wow*. The interior was one giant space, a huge metal shed with a concrete floor and a vaulted ceiling dozens of feet high. Tiers of shelves lined both side walls, some of them stacked with crates of various sizes. The near end where they stood was a large patch of concrete, clearly used for parking. Halfway back on the left a space of about thirty by thirty feet had been loosely marked off with cots and other pieces of furniture. Against the wall was what looked like a rudimentary kitchen.

The other three were in motion, pulling their bags out of the van and carrying them over to the living area. Diana was on a cell phone.

'Where are you?' She sounded like a woman in charge, Shannon thought, someone used to getting answers to her questions.

'We'll look for you tonight,' she went on. 'You've got the directions?' After a pause, she added, 'I know you don't want to miss the fun. See you soon.'

She snapped the phone shut and turned to the newcomers. 'I bet you're hungry. Let me fix you something to eat, and we can talk.' She led them to the living area, where Shannon noticed that most of the cots had sleeping bags laid out on them. Diana pointed out two bags that were still rolled up. 'Those are yours. You'll find the bathroom in the back.'

At the kitchen counter she opened a cabinet. 'We've got beef stew, beef stew, and beef stew.'

'Sounds good to me,' Shannon said, and Wolfe agreed.

'Diana, let me,' Judith said. She began pulling cans off the shelf and put a big pot on the stove. 'Go spend time with your friends. I'll bring it over.'

'You've got things to do—' Diana began.

'Please.'

'All right. Thanks.' She turned to the two of them. 'Come on, then.' She led them to a rear corner of the warehouse. Shannon noticed a room had been partitioned off here, with a door and two windows, opposite a smaller room that Shannon guessed was the bathroom. Diana led them inside.

'Home sweet home. For the next few days, anyway.' About the

size of the average bedroom, the space held a cot with sleeping bag, a cheap table with reading light, a few chairs, and a bookshelf with a handful of books on it.

Motioning for them to take chairs, Diana sat down, swept the cap off her head, and raked her fingers through her short hair. She crossed her legs, resting an ankle atop a knee, and looked at Wolfe fondly.

'I can't help staring a little,' she said. 'You look very good.' Then she turned to Shannon.

The face Shannon looked into was clearly older than the face in the photos. The eyes appeared less open, more hidden, than those of the young woman who had stood at countless microphones and whipped crowds into a frenzy. The short white hair was something of a shock. But she was still slender – even more so now, almost sinewy-thin, with the tendons in her neck standing out prominently. And as Shannon studied her, the face before her dissolved and the face in the photos slowly materialized, like a camera trick in one of those old romantic movies.

For her part, Diana looked at Shannon for a small eternity, with an expression of such intensity Shannon felt as if the woman were trying to look inside her. Diana's gaze went to Wolfe, then back to Shannon. She was clearly comparing them. Finally her features relaxed into the faintest of smiles.

'You've come a long way.'

Shannon nodded.

'I know it wasn't easy; dangerous, even. And I appreciate what you're trying to do. It was Henry who brought you together, wasn't it?'

Wolfe nodded. 'He said you needed our help. He also said …' He glanced sideways at Shannon.

'What?'

'He said he thought Shannon was in danger, because she was poking around, asking questions. But he told me not to mention that to her, because she wouldn't admit she needed protection. So I didn't.'

'Smart of you,' Shannon said wryly.

Wolfe gestured toward the windows that looked out on the vast space outside the room. 'Stack and Judith,' he said. 'Do they know who we are?'

Diana shook her head. 'All they know is that you're not part of this operation but that you can be trusted.'

'Are they part of Free Earth?'

'Yes, they are.' Her smile was proud. 'We're what you might call the invisible part of the organization. A small number now, but more are on their way. It's an amazing group of people, and you'll get a chance to know some of them.'

'Now,' she said to Shannon, 'I want to hear whatever you have to say.'

Shannon stared at her lap for a few seconds, thinking. Then she raised her eyes. 'You know about Ray and Mora and Henry.'

'Yes.' Diana spoke the word softly but her expression did not change. 'I heard everything from Katherine. I'm very sorry about all of them, and especially about your parents. Whatever I do from now on, I'll be doing it for them.'

Shannon felt a stirring of anger, fought to keep it down. *Whatever you do*, she felt like saying, *I doubt if it would make up for all the loss.*

'My mother said some things just before she died,' she went on. 'Part of it was a warning to you and John Paul, which you don't really need any more—'

'You went to see him. Katherine told me. How is he?'

'He looked fine.'

Wolfe broke in. 'When Henry was killed, I called him to warn him. There was no feedback. I can only guess that he's deep under by now. I hope he's all right.'

'So do I.' Diana turned back to Shannon. 'Go on.'

'This is what she said.' Shannon hesitated, then spoke her mother's words one more time, the way she had repeated them to John Paul. '*They killed Ray. Bastards. I saw it. We didn't tell them anything. I was so proud of him. Don't tell police. You have to find them and warn them. God, he's so full of hate. We should have guessed.*

'And then the last thing she said was, *We're giving back the treasure.* And not long after that, she was dead.'

Diana's mouth was partly open, and for the first time she looked shaken. 'Thank you for bringing that to me.'

'John Paul knew what she meant by the treasure, but he didn't say what it—'

'It's her, isn't it?' Wolfe broke in, speaking to Diana. 'It's Shannon, right? The treasure is code. That's the word you used when I overheard you and John Paul talking about Shannon, and I wouldn't leave you alone until you told me the truth.'

Diana didn't respond.

Wolfe turned to his sister. 'You're the treasure. It's the word they used for you whenever they talked with Ray and Mora, both before and after you were born. Mora knew she was dying, and she was giving you back to your birth parents.'

He addressed Diana again. 'But you can't take her back, can you?'

Diana looked somber. 'No. I can't take her back. For reasons that should be all too clear.'

'You don't have to explain,' Shannon said.

'Maybe I do. I owe you that, at least. I've picked a life for myself that most people would call insane. There's no room in it for a man or for children. There's barely room for friends, and then only a very special kind. I wasn't much of a mother to Wolfe, and the fact that he turned out as well as he did is no credit to me. He's his own good self.'

'I'm a grown woman,' Shannon said defensively. 'I'm past needing a mother, and I don't need you.' The words came with more of an edge than she had intended. Or did they?

'Fair enough,' Diana said, and the air of an uneasy truce hung in the room. 'Could we go back to your mother's words? There's something else there. The man who's full of hate.'

'That's Quentin, obviously,' Wolfe said.

'If it's obvious,' Diana went on, almost to herself, 'then why did she say, "We should have guessed?"'

'Because we should have guessed?' Wolfe said with a laugh.

'Maybe.' She did not look convinced.

A knock on the door, and Judith entered, balancing a tray with three bowls of stew. Shannon's stomach was still uneasy with tension, but her hunger was beginning to overwhelm her, and the stew smelled delicious. They pulled up their chairs around the table and ate, the two travelers ravenously, Diana as if she simply needed fuel.

When he had finished, Wolfe wiped his mouth with his hand, hitched his chair back, and said, 'I'm curious. You didn't want us to find you, and Katherine said you were very stubborn about it. Why did you change your mind?'

'Oh ... A couple of reasons. Katherine's my oldest and best friend, and I'm about to lose her. When she put it on that basis – the last favor I could do for her – I couldn't say no.'

'And the other reason?'

'I finally decided that with Quentin and his murderous friends out there, it was too dangerous to let both of you go wandering around in harm's way. I thought I'd pull you in where I could keep an eye on you.'

'Very motherly of you.'

'No, just practical. He's probably the most dangerous person I've ever known, and I hear that prison has sent him over the edge. He's already taken three good people from us. I didn't want him getting his hands on either of you.'

She appeared to be searching for words. 'There are things in motion right now. Important things. The next few days will be ... memorable. I'm going to be totally caught up in this, and it will make things a lot simpler if I know where you are.'

'All right,' Wolfe said without much conviction. 'Aren't you afraid Quentin might find you?'

She took a moment to answer. 'I'm concerned. He knows just about everyone in the movement, and there may be a few of them who have no love for me. But I think I'm pretty well hidden. And even if he found me, he'd have to get past the people around me.'

'And now you've got us.'

'Right.' Diana didn't look reassured by that. 'What do you see yourself doing?'

'Keeping an eye out for Quentin. You may have people protecting you, but I'm guessing none of them have laid eyes on him lately. Shannon has. And he's changed.'

Diana looked surprised. 'You saw him?' she asked Shannon. 'Did he know who you are?'

'I'm not sure, but I think he probably did.'

'And he didn't try to hurt you?'

'No. I can only guess that he's been hoping I'd lead him to you.'

'And did you?'

'No. We were careful.'

'Would you describe him? To all of us?'

'She can,' Wolfe broke in. 'But we can keep a lookout for him, along with this woman who apparently hangs out with him. Shannon had a run-in with her too. If we spot them anywhere around you, we can bring the police down on them in a way that won't have to involve you.'

Diana gave Shannon a curious look. 'What do you think of this plan?'

'Not much. I can't speak for Wolfe, but I'm no bodyguard. I don't have any illusions that I can protect you from anybody, especially someone as scary as Quentin.'

'Then what brought you here?'

Shannon paused. These words were hard to speak. But they had to be uttered. 'I had to meet you,' she said slowly. 'Ever since I learned about you from John Paul, I've felt that I had to find you and talk to you. That was the real reason Mora sent me to find you. The warning was the least important part of it. What counted to her was bringing the two of us together.'

Diana nodded, her expression softening slightly. 'That sounds like her,' she said quietly. If Shannon had expected her to say something affectionate or emotional, she was disappointed.

'There's another thing,' Shannon continued. 'I won't lie about this. I came here because Quentin's on your trail, and we don't know when he might find you.'

She watched as both Diana and Wolfe absorbed the meaning of her words. They waited for her to go on.

'Ever since Henry was killed, I've had the feeling that we – that you – were running out of time. I've already lost one mother. If I'm about to lose another, I'd at least like to get to know her first.'

An awkward silence hung over them until Diana pushed her bowl aside and spoke. 'That's pretty blunt,' she said in a neutral tone. 'As I told you, I'm glad you came. But your needs and mine are very different. You may have an image of me that's not … not who I am. And that could mean that you've come here for the wrong reasons—'

'I get it,' Shannon said quickly. 'You're not the motherly type. The last thing you need is some lost, needy daughter showing up, looking for …' She reached for the right words, then remembered something Wolfe had said. 'Looking for hugs and chicken soup. Well, that's not me. I can take care of myself. I'm here for one reason. To see you before Quentin does, because when he finds you …'

Her words where shot through with pent-up anger. Through it all, Diana never changed expression. It was Wolfe's loud throat-clearing that told Shannon she might have gone too far.

'Anyway,' she finished in a quieter voice, 'I won't get in anyone's way. Now that I'm here, I'll do whatever I can to help Wolfe. If he believes we can protect you, I'm willing to try.'

'Good,' Diana said emphatically. 'I'm satisfied with that.'

'What's the job you're here to do?' Wolfe asked.

'Let's just say I've got something even more important than Quentin Latta on my mind right now.'

Shannon spoke up. 'You want to tell us what this thing is?'

'No. The less you know the better.'

'It's a night crawl, isn't it?' Wolfe seemed almost amused.

Shannon looked puzzled. 'A what?'

'A night crawl is an operation against a target, and it's usually violent.'

They both turned to Diana. 'The less you know the better,' she repeated calmly. 'I will tell you this, though.' Her expression took on a new intensity. 'We're going to make a move against people who are killing this planet. It's going to be remembered for a long time.'

Forty-Four

A knock on the door, and Judith looked in, holding what appeared to be an armload of blueprints. Stack stood behind her. 'Busy?'

'Meeting time,' Diana said, her tone businesslike. 'We'll talk more later.'

At the door, Wolfe momentarily blocked their way as he appeared confused as to whether to pass them on the left or right. He ducked his head, muttered 'Sorry,' and let them go by.

The door closed behind them, and Shannon and Wolfe looked at each other. 'You looking for a dance partner?' she asked.

'No, I wanted to slow them down. I saw some lettering in the corner of that blueprint, and I needed a chance to read it.'

'Uh-huh?'

'It was kind of spidery, the way architects write. All I could see were two initials, because they were enlarged. Looked like an *S* and a *C*.'

'Snooping?'

'Yeah.' He wore an almost wistful grin. 'I want to know what she's up to – this thing that's going to be remembered until the mountains crumble and the redwoods fall. Call me curious.'

They walked over to the living area and began unrolling their sleeping bags. Shannon laid hers out noisily, slapping the dust out of it.

'You mad at the poor sleeping bag or at something else?' he asked.

'I wanted to know what she was like, and now I know,' she muttered in between slaps. 'Mora wanted me to meet her, and I did. Mission accomplished.'

More pummeling. 'She's cold, isn't she? Tough and cold. But I should've known what to expect. You already described her pretty well, didn't you?'

He reached over and touched her arm lightly. 'Nobody ever called her the Mother of the Year, you know?'

'Right. She's special. Henry told me. She rallies troops at the barricades, that kind of thing.'

'Yep. Well, she is what she is. And she didn't seem to think much of my little security plan. But I don't care. We're here to look out for her, so let's just focus on that. Here's my idea.' He gestured toward the cots, and they sat down.

'Every few hours, one of us could take the truck out and just cruise this area, in and out of the warehouse streets, over as far as the freeway and back, looking for vehicles that don't seem to belong, out-of-state plates, people who don't look like they work here, that sort of thing. What do you think?'

'Fine,' she said without enthusiasm. 'The more we stay out of her hair, the more we'll be tolerated around here.'

'I'll go first, soon as I can get somebody to show me how to work that big door.'

'While you're gone, I think I'll make a call.' In answer to his questioning look, she explained.

He nodded reluctantly. 'I guess one of us should,' he said. 'But keep it brief.'

By early afternoon the meeting had broken up, and Wolfe and Shannon had learned how to operate the giant double doors. It was arranged that if one or both of them were outside and needed the doors opened, they would rap a signal – two knocks, followed by three, then two more. In such an atmosphere, it was easy for Shannon to imagine that she was part of a creaky old detective thriller or Gothic novel. Then she remembered that none of this was pretense. It was real, and somewhere down the line the consequences would be just as real.

When Wolfe had gone, she found a quiet corner of the warehouse, unlimbered her cell phone, and searched her phone's memory for the number Henry had punched in as they stood on the rooftop – was it really less than two weeks ago? She found it, selected it, and heard it ring. John Paul's matter-of-fact voice came on with a recorded message, and – given the acrimony with which they had parted in

Montana – she felt surprised at the good feeling it gave her.

'It's Shannon,' she said quietly and urgently. 'We found her. She's well. But she's planning what you used to call a night crawl, and it's going to be something important and, I'm sure, risky. There's no sign of, uh, the one who's looking for her. But we're watching for him.'

She took a breath. 'That's our situation. I wanted you to know we're worried about you and hope you're in a safe place. Contact us if you're able to, but don't take any chances.' She had a second thought. 'You can also use our Chicago friend to be in touch with us.'

Ending the call, she had no doubt that Diana would throw a fit if she knew that Shannon had called John Paul, even though she had not given away their location. There was no point in telling him where Diana was. He was protecting himself now. The job of protecting Diana, if such a thing were possible, had fallen to her children.

She punched in another number and was soon talking to Beth. The family had settled into their vacation cabin at Big Bear Lake. She could hear the boys at play, a sound that made her feel a touch of sadness. It was not the first time Shannon had ever considered what her lifestyle choices had cost her.

'Try not to worry,' she told Beth. 'Things will get back to normal someday.'

'Promise?' Beth asked wryly. 'How are you? *Where* are you?'

'Got to go. Give everybody my love.'

She walked over to the living area, where she took a seat on her cot, near where Stack and Judith were resting. *I'm getting to be an old hand at this*, she thought, *a natural at cloak-and-dagger. If I'd been born a couple of decades earlier, would I have wound up in the movement? Would I have marched, followed Diana or another Joan of Arc like her, maybe even accompanied her on a night crawl or two? Would I have been good at it? Would I have wound up being … her?*

She tried to imagine where Quentin Latta might be at that moment. Was he on their trail? Was he close? Two immense events were converging: Diana's 'night crawl,' whatever it was, and the moment when Quentin would find her, as he must. To Shannon, they felt like planets colliding, things over which she had absolutely no control. What was she doing here?

She glanced over at her companions. Judith's eyes were closed, but her posture looked rigid, as if relaxation were impossible.

Stack was reading. Shannon took a peek and made out the title. It was one she had heard of, a popular history of the Battle of Thermopylae.

'I know how that turns out,' she said to him.

'Me too.' He grinned, eyes still on the page. 'Bad for the Spartans.'

'But only in the short term.'

'Right.' He tilted the book on his chest to get a better look at her. 'They fought smart. They didn't have the numbers, so they made up for it in strategy. And courage. And they made a difference.'

'I know.' *Just like our little band of eco-warriors, I suppose.*

She stretched out on her cot, testing the softness of the sleeping bag. It felt good. *Maybe a little rest*, she thought. She closed her eyes …

Then opened them a minute later as she realized Diana was standing over her, wearing warm-up pants and a heavy turtleneck sweater. 'Those just for show?' Diana asked, indicating the extra pair of shoes Shannon had brought, now sitting under her cot. 'Or do you run?'

She sat up. 'I run.'

'Good, let's go,' Diana said, their recent acrimony apparently forgotten. 'I suggest gloves and a cap. It's brisk out.'

Forty-Five

Minutes later they were jogging at an easy pace along the industrial road, with Stack following them about thirty yards behind.

Shannon glanced back. 'I'm guessing he's carrying something.'

'Good guess. I don't go many places without company – Stack or someone else. I imagine it's a little like being a high-profile celebrity. Except that I don't want people to recognize me. And I never sign autographs.'

Shannon was getting a feel for Diana's brand of humor. It was wry, usually deadpan, sometimes sarcastic, and often very funny. It had echoes of the way Wolfe talked. Matter of fact, Shannon thought she could even hear a little of herself.

'He's not the only one carrying,' Diana went on. 'Where did you get the neat little snub-nose?'

'Hmm? At a gun shop not far from …' The significance of the question sunk in. 'Did you look through my bag?'

'Sure. At least Stack did. He's in charge of security. Don't take offense. Everyone who comes to see us for the first time gets the privilege of a bag search. He put it back right where he found it, along with Wolfe's. That boy has a real arsenal. I don't know where he got his attachment to guns. It wasn't from me.'

'Right. You prefer bombs.'

'The same goes for your cell phones,' Diana continued, ignoring the gibe. 'He didn't touch them. I'm going to assume both of you can be trusted not to give out the wrong information to anyone.'

Shannon immediately felt a stab of guilt over the call to John Paul but wiped away the thought. Surrounded by doubt, she had decided to trust her instincts.

The two were in sync now, in running rhythm, their feet striking the pavement at exactly the same instant. Diana, she could tell, was fit.

They noticed some movement about a hundred yards ahead, where a truck had backed up to a loading dock and workers were unloading cartons. The pace of Stack's footsteps picked up, and he passed the women at a good clip.

'He's taking point,' Diana said. 'A little army lingo I've learned from him.'

Stack scrutinized the scene, both men and truck, nodding to the workers as he passed, then slowed his pace and dropped behind the joggers again.

'All clear,' Diana said. 'There's usually not much activity around these buildings, but whenever we see anybody, Stack checks them out.'

'Is there anything you can tell me about him? Without breaking your rule, I mean.'

'Sure. He's an ex-Army Ranger who fought in Afghanistan, saw some things he wished he hadn't, felt responsible for some of them, and left the army wanting to fight a different kind of battle. For a bigger and better cause than nationalism. He discovered the biggest cause of all – fighting for the survival of the whole planet – and not long after that, he found us. He's been like a right arm to me.'

'And Judith?'

'She's a Ph.D. in environmental science who taught for a few years before getting the itch to do more. She flirted with Greenpeace for a while, then decided they weren't radical enough. Her moment of truth came when her brother was crushed to death by an earth mover while he was trying to stop logging in the Olympic Peninsula. She saw it happen, and on that day she decided she wanted to be not just a resister but a fighter. She changed her name—'

'That's not her real name?'

'She picked a name from Jewish folklore. Judith was a woman who saved the Hebrew army by cozying up to the enemy general. Once she was in his tent, she got him drunk and cut off his head. Early feminist, you might call her.'

'I'll say.'

'Judith – our Judith – had a lot of unfocused anger. When she joined up with us, we gave her targets for it.'

Shannon thought back to John Paul's story about Free Earth's attack on the ski lodge. He had mentioned the builder's name. What was it? Then it came to her.

'Targets like the Swann Group? I hear they have a reputation for not being very kind to the Earth.'

Diana didn't respond right away. Glancing sideways, Shannon saw her looking straight ahead, little puffs of visible air exhaled with each breath. Diana pointed down a road to their right, and they turned onto it, the slapping sounds of their shoes on concrete echoing between the tall buildings on both sides.

'Oh, they're not alone,' she said finally. 'We have a long list.' It sounded almost too casual, Shannon thought.

'Besides Stack and Judith, you have more coming?'

'Several more. We'll total eleven, not counting you and Wolfe, and we'll need every one. The first two – Linc and Kyle – will show up tonight. Kyle is one of the young firebrands, but Linc and I go all the way back to Chicago in sixty-eight. He's really the only one left from the old movement, and he's still out there on the front lines. You heard about the World Trade Organization riots here in Seattle a few years ago? Linc was right in the middle of them.'

Linc. The name sounded ... And then she remembered. John Paul had mentioned a Linc, said he had disappeared, but added: *There's a good chance he's with her.*

'Speaking of the movement, I've been reading about you,' Shannon said. 'You've come a long way since the old anti-war days.'

'I haven't changed, even though the world has. I still want to make a difference. Back then, the enemy was our own government. Now, it's anyone who tries to exploit this planet and the life on it – both individuals and corporations. They're easier to hit than governments.'

'Individuals?' The meaning of the question was obvious.

Diana looked at her briefly. She was breathing more heavily, and Shannon, too, could feel the effects of their second mile. The cold air felt sharp in her lungs.

'Individuals sometimes get roughed up. But that's all. Free Earth bombs things, not people.'

'Then the Crowe Institute—'

'Was a terrible mistake. It was Quentin's doing, not ours. He knew there was a watchman in the building, we didn't. When we saw it was too late to stop it, we got out. I'm sorry it happened.'

'John Paul told me he accepts responsibility for it.'

'I don't.'

They ran in silence for a long way, turning here and there. Finally they reached the warehouse and stopped, hands on knees, panting. Wolfe, back from his patrol, sat in his truck.

'You're in good shape,' Diana told her. 'I'm feeling those twenty years you've got on me.'

'It's more like twenty-five, isn't it?'

'Let's not count.'

Shannon asked Wolfe to fill Diana in on their plan to set up a rough security perimeter around the location and patrol it regularly.

'Sounds workable,' Diana said tersely when he had finished. 'I recommend you don't keep it going after dark, though. You're going to need your sleep, just like all of us.'

Before replacing Wolfe in the truck, she followed Diana inside. They walked over to the coffee pot, where Diana poured herself a cup.

Raising it for a sip, she looked at Shannon through the vapor. 'Quentin or no Quentin, I'm glad you're here. Wolfe Boy too.'

'You call him Wolfe Boy?'

'Uh-huh.' Her eyes crinkled at the memory. 'It's a family joke. We used to say he was raised wild. It's almost true.'

She stirred her coffee. 'Do you know if he's taking his medicine?' she asked casually.

'I think he is,' Shannon answered without thinking. *I hope that's the last lie I have to tell for you, Wolfe Boy.*

She climbed into the cab of the truck and fired up the big engine. Before she could put it in gear, her phone alerted her to a text message.

It was from TeeJay, and it was short and sweet: CALL ME

She dialed his number immediately. When he answered, she said, 'You rang?'

'I did.' He sounded tense. 'I hadn't heard from you for a while, and I been a little worried. Ever since I heard about the FBI guy, and somebody tryin' to grab your sister's little boy—'

'What? How did you hear about that?'

'You told me. Yesterday mornin'.'

Oh no. 'I told you all that?'

He laughed softly. 'And more. Somethin' about a brother too. I didn't even know you had one. You almost talked my ear off. Hate to say this, but you sounded stewed to the gills. A little early in the day for you.'

'Oh, Lord. TeeJay, I didn't mean to tell you all that.'

'It's okay, I don't blame you, after everything that happened to you. But when I didn't hear from you for a while, I got to worryin' about you runnin' around Frisco gettin' in more trouble. Are you okay?'

'I'm, uh, fine.' She thought quickly. Enough people had been put in danger. She didn't want to add TeeJay to the list. He was one of the few people she had left. 'I don't want you to worry about me. Or my sister either. She's safe.'

'Good. But it's you I'm most worried about. I'm in Bakersfield wrappin' up some business and got a taste for a free meal at your place. Are you back from Frisco?'

'No. I'm in Seattle, of all places. But I hope to be back soon. When I am, will you set aside some time for me?'

'Okay, wanderin' girl.'

Forty-Six

She patrolled slowly around the area, crisscrossing the streets, occasionally bumping over railroad tracks. She saw normal industrial activity – trucks loading and unloading, men rolling hand carts. Nothing that looked suspicious. No gray van, no hulking, mustached man in a shapeless coat, no skinny, spooky-looking blonde.

After two hours she returned. It was growing dark, and more beef stew was bubbling on the stove, so Wolfe invited her to bring the truck inside for the night. Meals, it appeared, were purely functional, not social. Stack ate standing up at the counter, Judith sitting on her cot, Diana at the table in her room. This time she did not invite anyone in for company.

Shannon and Wolfe filled their bowls and found a place to sit on the floor, leaning against some shelving. Midway through the meal, her phone rang, and she pulled it out of her pocket. It was Thomas Orlando, the San Malo police detective.

'You called me a while back,' he said. 'I'm sorry, I, uh …' He sounded tentative and tired. 'I was away for a few days. Personal business. I just got back to my desk, and I apologize …' He appeared to lose his train of thought. She wondered if he'd been drinking, even though that seemed uncharacteristic of him.

'I did want to talk to you.' Wolfe was looking at her curiously, but she wagged a finger at him, indicating she was not going to put this call on the speaker phone. Not in this place, where others might overhear.

She lowered her voice. 'Look, I, uh … Things have been happening.'

'Are you all right?'

'I guess so.'

'Where are you?'

When she didn't respond, he said, 'The patrol that goes by your house says you haven't been home for a while, even though your car's still there.'

'That's right.'

'Where are you?'

She felt hemmed in already and could not bring herself to answer.

'By the way,' he said, sounding amused, 'if you're worried about someone tracing your cell phone, don't be. The Feds are still tapping phones, but these days they're concerned mostly with terrorists. You haven't gotten involved with any of that crowd, have you?'

You might be surprised, she thought.

'Want to tell me where you are? Strictly voluntarily?'

'Not right now. Let me just say a few things. Something happened in San Francisco the other day. I imagine you heard about the FBI man, Tim Dodd.'

'Uh-huh. He was killed.'

'Well, I was there when it happened. Right after it happened, I mean. I didn't have anything to do with it, and I wanted to make that clear.'

'What were you doing there? What did you see?'

Briefly, she told him about Dodd's request for a meeting and how she found him newly dead. After hesitating briefly, she described the figure who ran from the scene.

'A woman?'

'It looked like a woman. I'm thinking Lonnie, the one who's been complicating our lives lately.'

He processed that silently for a moment. 'All right. I'll get the word to the FBI. She's turning into a one-woman crime wave, and we need to find her.'

'I tried to call the other FBI man – Harold Birdsong, the one who's retired – but his phone doesn't work, and the people at the office in LA—'

'There may be some bad news about him,' Orlando broke in. 'He's disappeared. They found his things in the hotel room he shared with Dodd, but not his gun or ID. His phone was smashed. And there were signs of a struggle.'

'So …'

'It's just conjecture, but the people looking for Burke and West may have dragged him along to help them. He's been chasing them longer than anyone in the Bureau, and he'd be invaluable to people who want them dead. But back to you: What were you doing at a murder scene?'

'I was—'

'You're chasing after Quentin Latta, aren't you?'

'I suppose you could say I am.'

He let out an exasperated breath. 'The FBI and San Francisco PD are looking into another murder from a few days ago. I don't have the name in front of me here, but the scene was very similar to the one at your parents' house. Fingers cut off. You know anything about that?'

She thought it best not to answer. He could guess anyway.

Another audible breath sent static over the phone. 'I warned you about this. You're going to get yourself killed, just like your mother and father.'

'I want to be as honest as I can with you. Yes, I am looking for Quentin Latta. But it's not as irresponsible or dangerous as it sounds. If I find him, I'll call the nearest police or FBI office. How's that?'

'You're taking insane risks.' He spoke in a softer tone. Then he added: 'If it's any comfort, no one's looking for you in connection with Tim Dodd. Or the other thing either, as far as I know.' She heard the crinkle of paper. 'Henry Goines.'

'Can't tell you how glad I am to hear that. If you know what the FBI's up to, you must still be digging around in this thing yourself.'

'Strictly on my own time. I have an interest in it.'

'And have you turned up anything new?'

'I think I'm the one who's supposed to be asking the questions. Still don't want to tell me where you are?'

'No, at least not yet. I'm sorry. I promise I will when I can.'

'All right.' His tone was gruff. 'Be mysterious. Just don't be stupid.'

'I'll do my best. Have you learned anything new about Quentin Latta?'

She could feel his resistance. Policemen, she thought, must be a lot more comfortable asking questions than answering them.

'Oh, not much,' he said finally. 'Mostly background about his friends and enemies in stir.'

'Harold Birdsong was supposed to go interview the warden and some of the inmates. Tim Dodd mentioned it to me on the phone the day before he was killed.'

'Really? I made some calls to the prison myself, and I didn't hear about that. Could be he never made it there. Anyway, I mentioned to you that Quentin was high up in the Aryan Tribe, the prison gang. One of the guards I talked to said a few of the members of the Tribe – Quentin's protégés, you might call them – finished their stretches and were released before he was. They may hook up with him on the outside. Their thing is white supremacy, of course, but they might want to join in anything else Quentin has in mind, as long as it's good and bloody. There was one guy in particular, named Mobius, who apparently worshiped Quentin. He's out on the streets now, and anyone dumb-headed enough to be looking for Quentin should keep an eye out for this guy too.'

'So what's he look like, this Mobius?'

'I'm getting the particulars on him in the next day or so. I'll let you know. Now answer one of mine: Do you have any clue about Quentin's whereabouts?'

'No. That's the truth.'

'If you find him, will you do the smart thing and call the cops? Both FBI and local? Let them take care of him?'

'Yes. I already said so.'

'I wish I could believe you. I hope you have the sense to stay out of trouble. But that's probably asking too much, isn't it?'

She was touched by his words. 'Thank you for being concerned. I mean it. What was the personal business that took you away?'

'Hmm? Oh, it was my daughter. I may have mentioned her to you.'

'Our very first conversation. You said she had some problems. You also said I reminded you of her.'

'I suppose that's true, but if you met her, you wouldn't take that as a compliment.'

'So what happened with her?'

'Your life is plenty complicated right now. I don't want to lay my problems on you.'

'Please tell me.'

A quiet sigh. 'All right. I haven't said much about her for years, and that got me nowhere. Now I'm trying to look at her as an object lesson, something people can learn from.'

He paused, then went on, 'She's a druggie. Has been since her teens, and she's now thirty-three. So you might say it's her life's calling. My wife died six years ago, and I think Corinne's problems contributed to her death. Corinne's been in and out of hospitals and clinics forever. I took some time off three days ago when I heard she'd tried to kill herself. It turned out to be more of a gesture than the real thing, but the place where she was staying didn't want any suicides on the premises. So I moved her to another clinic – one of the few we haven't tried – and crossed my fingers.'

'I'm sorry to hear that.'

'She looks a little like you. Or did when she was younger and less messed up. The night your parents were killed, I looked at you and thought, *If Corinne had gotten better breaks, she might have turned out like this one. Might have gone to graduate school, owned her own business. Who knows?*'

'I'm not sure I'd be the best role model,' she said as gently as she could. 'I have my own ways of messing up, as you know.'

'Yeah. Well, try to hold that down to a minimum. And be careful.'

'I will.'

'I'll send you the stuff on Mobius soon as I get it. G'bye.'

She sat with the phone in her hand, saddened by the call.

'Anything I should know?' Wolfe asked.

'Oh, yeah. A possible new player in the game.' As she began telling him about Mobius, they heard a banging on the warehouse door and a loud voice: 'Anybody home? It's raining out here.'

Both tensed until they saw Judith run to open it, smiling broadly. 'It's Linc!'

Forty-Seven

He stood just inside the door, his rain parka dripping on the concrete. When he shed it, Shannon saw a strongly built man with shoulder-length hair, black with faint streaks of gray. His skin was dark, his face broad with sharply defined cheekbones. His ethnicity was hard to place.

'What the hell,' he said, looking around at them expressionlessly. 'This the wild bunch I'm gonna rock 'n' roll with? You guys don't look very dangerous to me.'

'We're just the first wave,' Stack said, stepping up to give him a soul handshake and a one-armed hug. 'Good to have you with us, Linc.' Judith followed with a bigger hug and a kiss on the cheek.

By now his eyes were on Shannon, and they widened in mock surprise. 'You made it, huh?'

As the sound of his voice sank in – deep and rough around the edges – she knew him: Front Porch Man.

'You're probably not too happy to see me,' she said. 'The way I remember, you wanted me to stay at home, all safe and warm.'

'Maybe I did, and maybe I didn't,' he said, smiling faintly, stepping closer. 'Maybe I just stopped by to check you out, see what you were made of. Maybe there were people interested in what I found out.'

'People like Diana?'

Instead of replying, he looked at her brother. 'You're Wolfe,' he said with obvious pleasure. 'You probably don't remember me. You were four or five, and I was the guy who crashed at your house in Denver late one night, smoked a little dope, talked a little politics, and then moved on.'

Wolfe could only nod in surprise.

Linc's expression turned sober. 'Where's—'

'Right here,' Diana called out as she approached the group. She wore a smile of welcome, but it faded when she saw his look.

No one spoke for a moment. Then Diana said, 'You've got some news?'

He nodded, his expression still grave.

'You'd better come on back.' She led him to her room and closed the door.

Shannon didn't try to contain her curiosity. 'All right, who wants to tell me about this guy?'

'Linc? Definitely one of the main men in this operation,' Stack said. 'He's the only one of us who knew Diana in the old days.'

'The anti-war days,' Wolfe said.

'Right. He's kind of a counselor to her, you know? He was a teenage grunt in Vietnam, got wounded by shrapnel and poisoned by Agent Orange, came home sick and spent time in hospitals. Soon as he got his discharge, he went looking to join up with others who were against the war. Diana and her people were the baddest ones out there, so they were a natural fit.'

'Tell them about the statue,' Judith prompted him.

'Hmm? Oh, yeah. In sixty-eight, during the fighting in Chicago, there was this dude who climbed a statue in Grant Park and raised a Viet Cong flag. Police hauled him down and kicked his ass real serious. Pictures ran all over the world. That was Linc.'

'He looks almost Indian,' Shannon said.

'He's a mixture, what I heard; Black father, Indian mother. He was raised on a Mohawk reservation somewhere in New York state—'

He stopped at the sound of a raised voice coming from the room. Diana, shouting in anger.

'Motherfuckers! Spineless little shits!'

There was more, a barrage of expletives. Shannon understood how Wolfe had acquired his profane vocabulary.

The door flew open, and Diana emerged with Linc, who was stone-faced. She stabbed numbers into a cell phone, put it to her ear. After a moment, she spoke into it.

'You call me and explain,' she said, her voice lower now, chillingly precise. 'Explain this fucking betrayal. And tell all the others on the committee to call, too – every one of those dickless cowards.'

She snapped the phone shut, jammed it into her pocket, and faced the others.

'No one else is coming,' she said bitterly. 'Grace, Kyle, Redwood, Boone … They've all bailed out. The committee had a secret meeting this morning and voted to withdraw all support from us. We're a renegade group, they said. They contacted Grace and the others and made them choose: Either quit this operation or get booted out of Free Earth. They told them we were going to fail and would wind up dead or in prison. All except Linc fell into line. Nobody's answering their phones.'

Linc touched her arm. 'I talked to Kimo. He's still doing his part. He'll be at the work site every night until we go in.'

'Maybe we can give him a bigger role—'

'I don't think so. This is as far as he's willing to go. Soon as we make our move, he heads back to his family in LA. Way I see it, we're lucky to have him just opening doors for us.'

'All right.' Diana took a big breath, and Shannon saw a new expression cross her face. It was doubt.

'We're alone in this,' she said quietly. She thought hard for a moment. Then: 'I honestly don't know if we can go ahead with only four of us. Take a minute to consider. If you decide we should fold it, there's no shame in that. I'll follow your wishes.'

She turned, walked back to her room, and closed the door.

Forty-Eight

The group stood quietly, then Link motioned for them to sit on the concrete floor. They formed a cross-legged ring, looking at each other.

'You two – your votes don't count,' Linc said to Shannon and Wolfe. 'But you should hear it. The rest of us need to decide.'

Stack looked grim. 'Didn't anybody see this coming?'

'She did, I think. We talked a few days ago, and she said the committee was getting mushy on the idea. For some time now, she's been saying they wanted to move into the mainstream, tap into more donations. Every time "Free Earth" and "eco-terrorism" crop up in the same news story, it scares away support. We've become an embarrassment, a threat. They're cutting us loose.'

'How do you stand?' Stack asked him.

'Hell,' Linc responded, 'I'm riding all the way to the end of the line. Where she goes, I go. When the war ended, the thought of having to get myself a straight job scared the shit out of me. Diana offered me a chance to keep blowing things up.' His face twisted into a nasty grin. 'Don't want to sound like a groupie or anything, but I'd follow this lady to the gates of Hell.'

'I'm not quitting,' Stack said.

'I can't quit,' Judith said. 'This is for Adam.'

Shannon stared at her quizzically, remembering Katherine's mention of the name. Then she made the connection. 'Your brother? The one who was killed?'

Judith nodded.

'I'm sorry.'

'We're all sorry,' Linc said brusquely. 'And we're going to do something about it.' He looked at Stack. 'You still Mr Security around here?'

'That's right.'

'So are we,' Wolfe said.

'No offense, but he's security,' Linc said. 'You're extra.'

He turned to Judith. 'You're—'

'I'm transportation. I pick up the truck tomorrow.'

'And I'm Mr Demolition Man,' Linc said with obvious satisfaction. 'Where's the stuff?'

'Everything's back there.' Stack inclined his head toward the rear of the warehouse.

'Good. Those weenies who dropped out were mostly back-up anyway. If we eliminate some jobs and double up on others, we might be able to pull this off.'

Stack looked at Judith. 'You and I need to pitch in and help Linc load the truck.'

Reluctantly, Judith nodded.

'It's only dangerous if you don't know what you're doing. He's an old hand at this.'

'All the way back to the Pentagon bombing in 'seventy-two,' Linc said, grinning broadly. 'And wasn't that a fun time?'

He unfolded his legs and got up. 'Whoa,' he said with a grimace. 'Suddenly I'm not twenty any more.'

He clapped his hands. 'All right. We can put on this show, boys and girls.' He started for the back of the warehouse but hesitated, then turned to Shannon, his expression easing into something more gentle. 'Why don't you go tell her how we voted?'

Nervous, she opened the door without thinking to knock. Diana was seated at the table, her head in her hands. At the sound of the door opening, she looked up, and her face was a map of despair. *Almost defeat*, Shannon thought, but not *quite*.

Age was there too, now that Shannon could see her plainly. The years of conflict, hiding, living on the run had left their mark on her. Shannon felt the smallest stirring of what might be pity.

Diana sat up straight, ran her fingers through her hair. She didn't speak, but her eyebrows went up, questioning.

'They, uh … they all voted to go on,' Shannon said haltingly.

'Why did they send you?'

'Linc thought I should tell you. I don't know why.'

A tiny smile with no humor in it. 'Good for him. He thinks he's looking out for me.'

'I thought you'd be happy to hear.'

'I am. But I'm really not surprised. They're comrades. We've been through a lot together. It's just that …'

'What?'

'I don't know that it's enough. We've never run an operation with odds as long as this.'

Without being asked, Shannon seated herself in one of the chairs. 'But they're with you. They almost worship you. They're ready to follow you.'

'I know.' There was no satisfaction in her expression. She rubbed her eyes hard. 'I'm just wondering if I should still be leading them.'

'I can't believe that.' It came out almost a whisper. 'Not after everything I've heard and read about you. If you won't lead them, there's …' Her voice trailed off.

'I know. There's no one else. I'm really an endangered species, you know? The last of a breed. Fighting the good fight. Leading my little band of eco-guerrillas against Goliath. The only trouble is, no one's cheering on the sidelines any more. As I said, we're alone.'

She slapped the tabletop with her palms. 'What the hell,' she said abruptly. 'I love long odds.'

Her expression changed, and there was pain in the look she gave Shannon. 'You and Wolfe will have to go.'

'Why? You said—'

'I know what I said. That was then, when I thought this thing had even a snowball's chance in Hell of success. Now it has even less. I won't see the two of you killed.'

'I don't—'

'You came here to see me, to meet me. You've done that. And I'm glad. Now it's time for you to leave. You're not deeply involved. No one's told you details about the operation, when or where—'

'We're staying. I'm speaking for Wolfe too.'

'You don't understand,' Diana said wearily.

'I think I do. This thing is dangerous. But you've made it clear that Wolfe and I are not a part of it anyway. We'll just follow his plan while you follow yours.'

'You can't separate these functions neatly,' Diana said. 'We've got a major attack on a target coming up. If anything goes wrong, people die. We've got Quentin and his killers looking for me. If they find anyone in my circle, they will kill them. And we've got the Feds circling out there, a part of my life for almost as long as I can remember. They're getting closer to me, and they will use deadly force. People around me could lose their lives. You—'

Shannon stood. She felt the muscles in her legs quivering. 'I'm staying.'

'*Why?*'

'If you don't understand by now, you never will.'

She closed the door and leaned against it, breathless to the point of dizziness. She had not planned what she would say to Diana. The words had just come out. Now it was too late to take them back. But she did not want to.

Rejoining the group, she looked meaningfully at Wolfe. 'I told her we're staying,' she said. 'All of us.'

Forty-Nine

By ten the overhead lights had been turned off and, one by one, the group had settled onto the cots. Outside, a light rain pattered on the metal roof and glass skylights. Shannon found the sound soothing, one of the few comforting things she could recall in recent days.

She had stripped down to her underwear and stashed her clothes underneath the cot. There appeared little need for modesty in this group. The warehouse interior felt like a tomb, cold and damp, but the sleeping area had been made more habitable by two electric space heaters, their coils glowing, that created a reasonably warm cocoon within a ten-foot radius.

Linc, Stack, and Judith seemed to be asleep already, their cots near each other on the other side of the living area from where Shannon lay. She and Wolfe had arranged their cots end to end, and they lay down head to head, so they could converse in low tones if necessary. For an instant she had an image of the two of them head to head in the womb, but it was crowded out of her mind by all the day's events. She heard Wolfe roll over. 'Awake?' she whispered.

'Uh-huh.'

'I'm still curious. What do you do for a living? Exactly, I mean.'

'I'm a gentleman farmer.'

She thought about that for a while. 'Let me guess. You grow marijuana.'

'Bingo.'

'Is this the guy who told me drugs are bad for his seizures?'

'Yeah, but that wasn't the whole story. Most of them can make it worse, but weed is actually good for it. I discovered that by accident. While the doctors were fine-tuning my drug cocktails to keep the seizures under control, I found that an occasional smoke works almost as well. There's a difference, though: If I smoke, I won't have as many seizures. If I take the drugs, I won't have any at all, but I will have the side effects I told you about.'

'Are you smoking now?'

'Haven't found the right time or place lately. I don't smoke while I'm driving or with other people, unless they're kindred spirits.'

'I'm pretty kindred.'

'So you are. If we ever get out of this Puccini opera we're in, you should stop by my place in the woods.'

'You have guard dogs and alarms and people trying to rip you off?'

'I've got good security and friends nearby. But you need to understand: I'm legal, or as legal as it's possible to be in California today.'

'How so?'

'I grow medical marijuana for dispensaries. They sell to people who have doctors' prescriptions. A lot of them are cancer patients; some even use it for epilepsy. Ever since 'ninety-six it's been legal in California to grow and use medical marijuana – at least at the state and local level. The dispensaries and the growers get busted every now and then by the Feds, who don't pay attention to local laws, but if you keep a low profile, you're generally okay.'

'How long have you been growing?'

'For years, off and on. Before the law was changed, I was one of those colorful outlaw pot growers. Now I'm just a quasi-legal gentleman farmer.'

'How boring.'

She had been lying face up and eyes open, staring into the vast dark space and lulled close to sleep by the rain and the whispered talk, when she became aware of a light. Turning her head, she saw that it came from Diana's room. The shade over one of the two windows had just been raised to reveal a low light inside, possibly a reading lamp.

Seconds later she heard a quiet stirring. Linc had rolled out of his sleeping bag and was heading toward the room. Without knocking, he opened the door, went in, and silently closed it behind him. Almost immediately the shade was lowered.

'How about that?' The whisper was from Wolfe.

When she didn't answer, he asked, 'Bother you?'

'Hell, no,' she whispered back with a little more vehemence than planned.

'Whatever the general needs before the battle, right?'

'I suppose. Stonewall Jackson used to pray to God and suck on lemons, and that seemed to work pretty well for him.'

'My mother. Still a babe,' he said with a chuckle. 'I love it.'

She dreamed about an insistent telephone that would not stop ringing, even after she picked it up. Abruptly awakening, she realized it was her cell phone, deep in the sleeping bag. She dug for it, flipped it open, mumbled, 'Hello. Wait a minute,' then swung out of her cot, the concrete floor icy underfoot. Dragging the sleeping bag with her, she managed to work it around her shoulders as she walked, careful to avoid bumping into anything. The only light came from the dim glow of the space heaters.

She made her way to the far wall, where giant shelves loomed overhead almost to the ceiling.

'Hello?'

'Don't say my name.' It was John Paul. Once again, despite all their differences, she felt irrationally pleased at the sound of his voice.

'Are you okay?'

'Yes. Sorry to call you so late, but I've been on the move a lot lately, and just came to rest. More important, though, are you and your traveling companion all right?'

She tried to keep her voice upbeat. 'Yes. Do you want to talk to him?'

'After we finish. We should keep this short. Has he been getting enough rest? I know what can happen when he gets tired.'

'I think he has.' She made an instant decision not to tell him about the seizure. *He has plenty to worry about*, she thought.

'I've talked with our friend in Chicago. It sounds as if there are signs of an operation shaping up. Do you know anything about it?'

'Very little, and that's the way she wants it.'

'You're not a part of it, I hope.'

'Don't worry about that.'

'Can you tell me where you are?'

'No.' Her defiance surprised her. 'She wouldn't want me to, and I agree. You should keep your distance from us.'

'All right,' he said briskly. 'Just try to look after yourself, since I suspect no one else will. I want to tell you something: Even though she may want to keep you in the dark, I think the more you know, the better you're able to protect yourself. I heard a name from our friend, the name Adam—'

'I've heard it too.'

'I did a little research. Do you know about the anniversary?'

'What? No.'

'He died three years ago. His friends have talked about revenge, but nothing has happened yet. The anniversary of his death is the day after tomorrow. If there's to be an action, I'd bet that would be the date.'

As soon as he said the words, she knew he was right. They needed to hold off Quentin and his band of killers for another day or more. And then survive the operation, whatever it was.

As Diana had said, long odds.

She realized he was speaking to her. 'Hmm?'

'Do you remember the things I said to you just before you left?'

'Yes.'

'I meant every one of them.'

'Thank you. I—'

'Don't fall under her spell. She has her life to live, you have yours.'

'I won't.' *But haven't I already?* she asked herself. *A little?*

'Now you'd better go get the other one I need to talk to. Please give him my apologies for waking him up.'

A minute later Wolfe was talking quietly into her phone, and she was snuggled back inside the sleeping bag.

Those words I said? Unfortunately, I meant them too. But I don't mean them any more.

Fifty

Morning came abruptly, with noise. Shannon rolled over. It was cold and still dark, although she could see the gray outline of the skylight windows far above her. Someone was talking. Not screaming like before, but talking loudly and insistently.

Again, the voice was Diana's, from behind her closed door, and the lights were on in her room. The volume of the voice rose and fell, but clearly another crisis was brewing.

Then the door flew open, and Diana came out, barefoot and wearing the cotton warm-up pants and pullover she apparently slept in. She threw on the lights in the living area.

'Everybody up!'

They rolled out of their sleeping bags and began putting on clothes. Shannon looked at her watch. It was not yet six.

'Preston called.' Her breath showed in the air. 'Somebody hit the Free Earth HQ in Portland.'

Stack stood up, pulling a sweater over his head. 'They take anything?'

'He thinks they did. The place was ransacked, the safe cracked. Then they set fire to the offices, to cover their tracks. Everything pretty much burned, but the fire department could tell the safe had been emptied.'

Shannon leaned over toward Judith, who was nearby. 'Who's Preston?' she whispered.

'Director of Free Earth. The little shit who cut us loose, with some help from his friends on the committee.'

Judith turned to Diana. 'There's not supposed to be anything—'

'I know.' Diana sounded grim. 'Anything that would tie the office to our night crawling. Preston swears there was nothing there. Mostly just the books showing the above ground organization, the names of donors, the kind of thing he needs to hang on to our nonprofit status. And donations, of course, which makes it look to the cops like a simple robbery. But— ' She broke off, looked around. 'I need to get some shoes on. Can anybody make some coffee?'

In a minute she was back. Shannon and Wolfe had moved to the kitchen counter and were busy with the coffee pot.

'You said *but*,' Judith prompted Diana.

'Right. Preston says he kept my phone number in the safe.'

'God dammit,' Linc said under his breath.

'Just the number?' Shannon asked.

'Just the number. No name. He says that's the only thing that might have done them any good, and then only if they figured out what it was. I think I believe the asshole. He may want us out of the organization, but he doesn't want us dead. No, I smell Quentin in this.' She began pacing back and forth, thinking. 'I'm not too worried. This little group of ours is mostly in my head anyway. If the phone number leads them to my house, all they've got is my house, and I don't need to live there any more.'

Shannon was amazed at her coolness, her readiness to cut herself off from the place she had once called home. *But isn't that what it means to be underground?* she asked herself. *You have no real home.*

'So.' Diana looked in control again. 'We'll be on alert, but we won't change anything. Where are we on the truck?'

'It's parked a half-mile from here,' Judith said. 'I'll pick it up this morning and bring it over—'

'And we'll get started on it,' Stack finished.

'Good.' Diana turned to head back to her room. 'Excitement's over, troops. Now it's back to the drudgery of trying to save the world.'

Linc shot Shannon a look and a nod that said, *See? She's back.*

The rest of the morning seemed to move in quick-time, like an old silent film run at the wrong speed. Stack and Judith took off with the van, and before long they were back with an additional vehicle. The new one was a big rented Strider truck, painted orange and plastered all over with the Strider logo. It measured more than 20 feet long, with a noisy engine indicating a lot of mileage. They opened the big warehouse doors, and Judith carefully maneuvered it inside, parking it along the right-hand wall.

Wolfe offered to take the first patrol. As he left, Diana and her aides, under Linc's supervision, busied themselves in the rear of the warehouse. After about ten minutes, they began moving large containers up front using a hand cart. Each container was a drum – Shannon guessed the 50-gallon size – with its top sealed with a metal strap. Taking turns, Linc and Stack rolled each one over to the rear of the truck and onto a hydraulic lift platform that allowed them to transfer the drums into the interior. Shannon noted a new, sharp smell in the air. It reminded her of a laundry room.

Early in the process, Diana came over to where Shannon sat on her cot. 'Anything else you need to be doing right now?' When Shannon hesitated, she added, 'You can use my room if you want.'

Shannon got it. The less she knew the better. She moved into Diana's austerely furnished room, closed the door, and took a seat behind the table. Through the grimy windows, she watched the activity at a distance. A small feeling of unease began to take shape inside her, shifting around, looking for room to grow.

I know what they're doing. They're putting together a device, the way you'd assemble a kit that came in the mail, with screws and panels and a badly translated instruction sheet. Only this thing isn't a bookshelf or a stereo cabinet. It's destruction: Destruction in the back of a truck. It was a truck bomb that tore apart the Federal Building in Oklahoma City and the underground garage in the World Trade Center, back before people learned to use airplanes as killing machines. People died in the Federal Building and in the garage too. But this is supposed to be different. Diana said so. If the plan succeeds, no one gets hurt. Free Earth bombs things, not people.

Then why am I so scared?

To focus on something else, she pulled out her phone. It was a smart phone – much smarter than its owner, she liked to say – and one of its many features was Internet access. She had barely used it, since e-mailing and surfing the Net were much easier on her home computer. But she was far from home, and she needed help from the World Wide Web.

So, after a few tentative finger motions, she began trying to find out if anyone had ever died as a result of Free Earth's guerrilla actions.

For twenty minutes she searched, all the while trying to ignore the muffled clanks and thumps from the front of the warehouse. Some of the results were familiar to her, some not. People threatened, occasionally roughed up. Vehicles sabotaged and run off the road. Tractors and skip loaders firebombed, structures burned down, including a partly constructed ski resort deep in the Colorado wilderness. One logger was maimed, losing part of a hand, when his chainsaw struck a spike thought to have been planted by Free Earth.

Blood had been drawn, no question. But, as best she could tell, the only death had been one of Free Earth's own – Adam Miller, 22, crushed by an earth mover on a scenic wooded hillside in Washington state. Among the horrified onlookers was his sister, Rachel Miller, who one day would change her name to Judith.

She was about to break the Internet connection when she thought of another avenue she wanted to explore in more depth – the Swann Group.

After a minute's keystrokes, she found herself surveying a business conglomerate breathtaking in its reach. Logging, mining, oil exploration equipment, wilderness surveying, resort development, lobbying.

The chairman of Swann, it appeared, was a big game hunter who counted the Vice President of the United States among his friends and hunting companions. Pending legislation to curb some of Swann's activities had dissolved under the onslaught of an army of lobbyists aided by friendly congressmen. A major class action suit against Swann had fallen apart when the lead plaintiff, a retired New Mexico schoolteacher, was invited to the White House during National Teachers Week and soon thereafter was hired as a consultant to the New Mexico Board of Education at a generous salary.

And so on. Shannon found it amazing and almost amusing, the power of this corporate giant. It was untouchable. *When all else has failed*, she wondered, *how do you deal with this kind of arrogance?*

She was about to power down the phone when her eyes lit on one last search result, some kind of announcement. She scrolled down to it.

The item was from *Business Week.* The Swann Group, long based in Wilmington, Delaware, was consolidating all its continental US operations in a single place. The new base would be located in an imposing office tower already under construction.

In … She blinked, cursing the small print on the small screen.

In Seattle.

The fingers of her left hand twitched, and the phone slid out of her hand, landing on the table with a noise that startled her. She picked it up quickly. The screen was still lit.

She clicked on the item to call up the rest of the article. It was dated three months earlier. Groundbreaking was last spring, she read. The foundation and the first few floors had been laid down. Completion was expected late next year.

Twenty stories tall, clad in reflective glass, it would tower over the heart of downtown Seattle. Flanked by landmark hotels and businesses, it would look down on the famous harbor and the storied old market.

This was it. She laid the phone down carefully. No proof, of course. But some very convincing circumstantial evidence.

The initials on the blueprint were not *S* and *C*, they were *S* and *G*. The Swann Group.

The target.

Tomorrow, Diana and her friends were going to blow a hole in the center of the biggest city in the Northwest.

And Shannon and Wolfe, who had come there as rescuers, were beginning to take on some of the appearance of collaborators.

The door opened, and Diana leaned in. Fatigue showed on her face. Her tone was friendly yet businesslike.

'Wolfe's back.'

Shannon got up just as her phone emitted its distinctive sound indicating an incoming text message.

U THERE? It was TeeJay.

She tapped her answer. YES. A LITTLE RUSHED.

He came back right away. IM AT WAYFARERS MOTEL JUST OFF 5 NEAR SEATAC. WORRIED BOUT U. CAN U COME OVER?

Her mouth fell open. Making sure that Diana had closed the door before leaving, she sat back down, eyes on the glowing screen.

Sea-Tac, she knew, was the main airport for Seattle and Tacoma. TeeJay, although he didn't know it, was just a few miles south of them.

What was he doing here? And why would he come all this way without letting her know?

She tapped four letters: WAIT.

Fifty-One

She met Wolfe at the door. He looked inside, noted the activity around the rented truck, then wrinkled his nose. 'Uh—'

She motioned him outside, and they clambered into his pickup. 'What's going on in there?' he asked.

'After you left, they started loading that big truck with steel drums from the back of the warehouse. There are a lot of them; it's still going on. I think it's some kind of bomb.'

'I think you're right,' he said, staring at the looming blank doors of the warehouse. 'I got a whiff of ammonia when I stepped in the door.'

'What's that mean?'

'Ammonium nitrate's a type of fertilizer. When you stir in fuel oil, usually diesel fuel, the mixture's explosive. Use enough of it, along with the right trigger, and you can purely blow something to Hell.'

'There's more,' she said. 'I think I know the target. And the timing.'

'Tell me.'

He sat patiently through her explanation. At the end, he nodded, his gaze on something far off. 'It's too much of a coincidence, isn't it? Them putting up a big-ass high rise in downtown Seattle, and her settling into a quaint cottage right outside town. Wouldn't surprise me if she moved into the place right after they announced plans for the building, just so she could start reconnoitering. It'd be just like her.'

He muttered something under his breath.

'What?'

'I said she's pushing it. Whether she plans to actually take down a skyscraper, even one still under construction, I don't know. But setting off a truck bomb in downtown Seattle – that sounds dangerous as all get-out. Even if the other buildings nearby are shut down after hours, there are still people walking around—'

'I know. But what can we do?'

'Well, we can't stop her, short of blowing the whistle on her, and I'm not prepared to do that. Are you?'

She hesitated.

'Well?'

'Well, goddam her anyway,' she burst out. 'I came up here to try to save her life. That's all.'

'Right. It's gotten a lot more complicated, hasn't it?'

They sat in silence for a while, the windshield beginning to steam up from the heat of their bodies.

'There's, uh, more.'

He looked at her, waiting.

'You remember my boyfriend TeeJay? I told you a little about him.'

'Yeah?'

She began telling him everything, speaking slowly at first, then more rapidly as it all spilled out. The time she had told TeeJay about Diana and John Paul, even while vowing to keep him out of it for his own safety. Then her drunken phone conversation with him at the airport hotel, when she had told him much more than she had ever intended – about Wolfe, about the death of the FBI agent, about the attempted kidnapping of Beth's little boy. Finally, her last talk with him when she had told him she was in Seattle.

Throughout, she felt Wolfe's eyes on her and found it hard to look at him.

'So he knows everything,' he said, his voice hard. 'This fucking stranger, a guy I've never met. Your *boyfriend.*' His sarcasm lay heavy on the word. 'He knows pretty much all your family secrets.'

'He knows a lot of them. But I was careful not to tell him where John Paul lived.'

'Because you were sober that time? What about the time you were shit-faced?'

'Not even that time.' *God, I hope I didn't.*

'Do you know how incredibly stupid and dangerous it was to tell him anything, Shannon?'

'I know it was stupid. Even though I know I can trust him, I shouldn't have involved him in any way. But there's one more thing.'

He exhaled loudly.

She told him about the exchange of text messages.

'He's in Seattle? No.'

'Yes.'

'That's crazy. What's he doing here?'

'I don't know. Maybe he's determined to help me. He offered to before, and I turned him down. He's persistent. Actually, it might be good to have someone like him on our side. He's not afraid of anything.'

'What if I don't want this guy on my side? This is for the two of us to do, Shannon. We can't trust anybody else on this. It's too dangerous. Imagine what Diana would do if …' He stopped. 'How do you know the text message came from him?'

She hesitated. 'All I know is it came from his phone.'

'Exactly. How do we know Quentin's not using this guy's phone? How do we know he's not already killed him?'

She had no answer to that, but her expression said everything.

'Call him. Right now.'

She did and got the flirty female voice again, so she clicked off without leaving a message. 'Either he's not there or he's not picking up.'

'Then we need to go over to this motel and try to find him. If he's not there, that could tell us something too.'

He got out. 'I'll let Diana know we'll both be gone for a while.'

She sat in the truck, berating herself. Wolfe was right. Even if TeeJay's motives were good ones, she should never have let him in on her secrets. It made him vulnerable. If he had become one of Quentin's victims, she would never be able to forgive—

The ring of her phone jolted her. Hoping it was TeeJay, she answered just as Wolfe opened the door and swung himself up behind the wheel.

It was Detective Orlando. She quickly put him on the speaker to show Wolfe she wasn't hiding anything.

'Are you all right?' Orlando sounded genuinely concerned.

'Yeah, I guess. I'm being careful, like you said.' *How to express everything that's happened?* she thought. *Even if I could tell him, I wonder if he'd believe it.*

'Good. I've learned a few more things about Quentin. The deputy warden has finally gotten a little more forthcoming. Harold Birdsong, it should come as no surprise, visited Quentin several times over the years, all the while trying to pick his brain about where his former friends might be holed up. To no avail, I'm told.

'But the main thing is … well, a couple of things. First, Quentin had a wife, something that didn't turn up at first. He married her young, and she stayed quietly in the background through his activist days and his years in the joint. She died, uh, nine years ago.'

'Yeah?' She felt Wolfe lean over as he listened.

'The wife had a daughter, born after he was imprisoned. They lived in Atlanta. Over the years, starting when she was in her teens, the daughter visited him more than the mother.'

'Really.' A daughter. Shannon began to wonder …

'She absorbed all of it, the deputy warden told me – all his hatred, all his desire for revenge. It came through in their correspondence, at least as much as they could allude to without getting censored.'

'Uh-huh?'

'Daughter's name is Dixie. Dixie Latta. I got a copy of the photo from her Georgia driver's license, and I'm sending it to you. Let me know if … Well, just take a look at the photo. You should have it now.'

'Call you back.' Shannon went to her e-mail, saw it, called it up, and there she was.

Lonnie.

A few years younger, wearing a friendly smile and looking fairly attractive, her dirty-blonde hair brushed out so that it framed her skinny face. The only thing that set this photo apart from a thousand others was that unnatural, too-eager light in her eyes, the light that said there were things she wanted very badly.

'Damn.' It came out like a sigh.

'Quentin's daughter?' Wolfe asked, craning his neck to get a look at the screen.

'Uh-huh. It's also Lonnie, the one who's been tracking us, the one I think killed Tim Dodd.'

'Oh, man.' He pondered that, then nodded. 'Maybe we should've guessed. Like your mother said about the man full of hate. We should've guessed.'

'Maybe.' She rang Orlando back. 'It's her. It's Lonnie.'

'I thought so.'

'You know, Harold Birdsong told me Lonnie was some kind of crazy groupie who followed Quentin around—'

'He might not have been far off. She sounds crazy for sure. But instead of groupie, how about adoring daughter who adopts her father's enemies as her own? Now listen.' He spoke carefully, and his voice rose a notch in volume. 'They're both bad news, Dixie and her father, and you should watch out for them. Based on what they've done, they're among the most dangerous people I've ever had cross my desk.'

'Believe me, I know.'

'And this guy Mobius? He's not just a disciple of Quentin. He began cozying up to Quentin's daughter while he was still in stir, the warden tells me, and it's a good bet they've hooked up now that he's on the outside. The FBI is looking for all three of them. Just your average cozy family, with the menfolk wearing the same little white-supremacist tattoo—'

'What's that?'

'It's the way the Aryan Tribe mark themselves. They're a little secretive about it, so they hide the tattoo on the underside of their right arm so that it's visible only when they raise the arm.'

'Raise the arm. And, uh, what is it, exactly?'

'It's . . .' She heard the crinkling of paper. 'Here it is. Two parallel thunderbolts – sound familiar? It's the symbol of Hitler's SS. Two parallel thunderbolts overlaid with—'

'A cross?'

'Yeah. How did you know?'

'Just a guess.' Her stomach began to churn. A tiny idea, almost invisible, was taking shape, like a worm just poking through the last layer of earth before it reaches sunlight.

'But you don't need the tattoo to identify him. He's got a nasty scar on the left side of his neck where one of the Mexican Mafia *cholos* tried to cut his throat in the chow line.'

Scar on the neck. The worm wriggled again.

'He likes to use a blade himself. You might call it his weapon of choice. We think he was very likely the one who used the shears on your parents and on Henry Goines.'

All she could do was breathe heavily into the phone and try to repress the mental images that, like a whole nest of worms, waited to swarm her brain.

'Are you there?'

'Yes. And you're going to send me his picture.'

'I did already.'

'Hmm?'

'There are two photos in that file, including the charming Mr Del Mobius.' He spelled the name for her. 'Take a look, and promise yourself you'll do whatever it takes to avoid him. He may be the worst of the lot. I'm on my way to work.' He sounded rushed. 'We can talk later. Remember what I said about being careful.'

He hung up, and she went back to her e-mail. With fingers feeling thick and meaty, she found the second photo, clicked on it, and his face filled the screen.

A small sigh, almost a moan, escaped her. The face – shown full-front and right profile – was younger by several years than the one she knew, but there was no mistaking it. There at the Adam's apple was the beginning of the scar, the one that had touched her heart – left by a knife, she now knew, not the blade of a plow.

The subject regarded the camera with no expression, no hostility, no apprehension. He looked almost at ease, this young man with the face she had often thought of as beautiful. Even knowing what she knew, she could detect in it no hint of the savagery behind it. With a sadness that ached, she looked at the face and found herself, against all reason, wanting to stroke it.

Fifty-Two

The thought was gone in an instant, replaced with shame and hatred. He had helped slaughter first her parents, then Henry. He would probably have no trouble doing the same to her.

Which meant that she might have to kill him.

Wolfe was staring at her uneasily. 'Something's wrong. Is that Mobius?'

'Yes.' She handed him the phone. 'It's also TeeJay.'

'No! What?' He stared at the face on the screen. 'This is the guy you told everything to? Jesus, Shannon!'

'I know. I told him. Now we have to go find him.'

'Goddam right.' Wolfe was breathing deeply, and he looked more pale than usual. He seemed to be making a supreme effort not to take out all his anger and frustration on her, although she couldn't have blamed him if he had.

His hands gripped the wheel hard as he tried for control. The words *I'm sorry* were about to form on her lips when he began speaking.

'Okay, here's what we need to do. We've got no reason to think he knows our exact location. Not a word to Diana yet. We'll let the FBI know where he is. We can give them his cell-phone number too, but we should find him first. If Quentin and Lonnie are with him, the cops can sweep up all of them. If not, at least he's been neutralized.'

'Right.' She looked doubtful.

'What?'

'It's just that …' She gestured vaguely. 'I don't know. It's amazing, how well he fooled me. He's very, very smart. He's so smart, I wonder if he's even at that motel.'

He thought about that. 'Didn't give you a room number, did he?'

'No. I suppose we could call the desk and ask for him.'

'Unless he didn't register under his own name. His own phony name, I mean.'

'Let's try.' Her face felt warm, and she knew it was shame. *I've got to make this right.*

She flipped open her phone, called information, and got the motel's number. Ringing it, she spoke for a moment as he listened in. No one was registered under the name TeeJay Goss or any variation that occurred to her.

'If we can't find him, the FBI could have trouble too,' Wolfe said. 'His cell number won't help much if he keeps his calls short. We're going to have to call him and get his exact location. Try him again. If he still doesn't pick up, leave a message saying you've got to talk to him right away.'

'All right.'

He heard the hesitancy in her voice and held out his hand. 'Dial it,' he said. 'I'll do the talking.'

She did so, and the number rang. Incredibly, TeeJay answered.

'Shan?' The familiar drawl drew out her name into a long syllable, and the eagerness in his voice almost broke her heart.

'No, this is Wolfe. I'm her brother.'

'Yeah! She told me about you. Where is she?'

'She's not here right now. Listen, TeeJay, things are happening, and we need to meet.'

'Well, I'm ready. Been followin' you two for days, like a hound dog on a scent, wonderin' when I was gonna get a chance to help out.'

'Right away. Starting now. Just tell us your room number, and we'll be right over.'

'Sure 'nuff. And you just put her on the phone.'

'I told you—'

'I know, I know.' He sounded as if he had all the time in the world. 'I'm sure y'all are just bein' careful. But what if you're not who you say you are? I got to be careful too. C'mon, put her on. And you guys can be havin' a beer with me soon as you get over here.'

Wolfe, his brow pinched in worry, let out an exasperated sigh. Shannon reached for the phone, even as he mouthed the words *Be careful.*

'It's me.'

'Well, it sure is. Takin' a long time for us to hook up, ain't it?'

'Yes. TeeJay ...' She felt the faint sting of tears that would not flow.

'Uh-huh?'

'I'll, uh, keep this short.' Her voice, she knew was about to betray her. She could feel her throat beginning to tighten with emotion – love, hate, and everything in between – and she knew she must hang up soon or he would hear something amiss. 'What's your room number?'

Nothing from him for a moment. Then: 'I got a better idea. Meet me in the lobby. There's places to sit, and the bar's right next door. How's that?'

She looked questioningly at Wolfe, and she knew he was thinking the same thing. No room number, no way to pinpoint his location for the FBI. If they insisted, he would only get suspicious. Still, she thought, seeing him face to face, then reporting that to the Feds, was better than nothing. Let them take it from there.

Wolfe nodded reluctantly.

'That's ...' Unbidden, the sight of her father's scorched face rose up before her. She gasped, tried to turn the sound into a cough.

'You all right?'

'Sure. Sure.' A deep breath. 'I was about to say that's fine. How does twenty minutes sound?'

As they drove south on the freeway, the slick, steel-gray surface of Puget Sound was faintly visible off to their right and the Seattle skyline behind them was almost lost in the mist. Shannon chewed over the latest revelations, none of them encouraging.

'Some things are starting to make sense,' she said, trying to stay analytical. 'I met him about two months before my parents were killed. According to what the FBI told me, that was right around the time Quentin got out of prison. This whole thing was rigged. Quentin sent him to get close to me, to find out if I knew any of my parents' secrets. I didn't, of course, but I followed their little script anyway. I got interested, I began digging, and pretty soon I had carved out my own special mission – to find Diana and John Paul. They were all keeping an eye on me, just to see if I might lead them anywhere. And like a fool, I did.'

'Well, you may have been a fool, I won't argue that.'

'Thanks.'

'But he sounds like a smart one, all right.'

'Quentin looked me up, maybe just out of curiosity, that day I saw him out on the harbor. Lonnie did too, but she was clearly the bad cop of the bunch. She tried to beat it out of me. Her timing was terrible, though, because at that point I knew exactly nothing. TeeJay was the smartest. He just charmed me, stayed close, never asked too many questions. I even volunteered information about Diana and John Paul. I actually told him I was their daughter. That must have been the moment things began to pay off for him, and he knew that I might lead him somewhere, if he could just be patient.

'And then I just kept feeding him information. Drunk or sober, it didn't seem to matter. The blue sedan that followed us out of San Francisco – that was probably Quentin, using information I'd let slip to TeeJay. We shook him off, but I couldn't keep my big mouth shut, and before long I was giving away the fact that we were in Seattle, and that let him narrow down his search.

'God, I was dumb. A brainless bitch. I can't believe—' She stopped with a sharp intake of breath.

'What?'

'The voice on his phone.'

'What voice?'

'There's a female voice that takes his messages. I never liked that voice. It sounds a little smug, and I always figured it was an ex-girlfriend.'

'Let me guess.'

'No need to guess. It must be Lonnie.'

She sank back into her seat, silent with self-disgust.

The Wayfarers Motel looked like a favorite with truckers and others who needed a bed and a hot meal but could forgo some of the other frills of travel. By the time Wolfe turned into the big parking lot in back, they had agreed on a story. They would make one more attempt to elicit TeeJay's room number, then, with or without it, tell him they would be back in an hour with Diana. The reason: She wanted to meet this new protector, this close friend of her daughter, and take his measure. That should keep him waiting long enough.

'We've got company.' Wolfe sounded disgusted.

'Where?'

'Don't turn around. It's the VW bus, just pulled into the lot. Diana must have sent one of our friends from the warehouse to keep an eye on us.' He muttered an obscenity. 'They still don't trust us to take care of ourselves. And you know something?' He shot her a look. 'Maybe they shouldn't.'

She kept quiet.

Wolfe parked the truck, keeping an eye on the VW in a side mirror. 'Let him sit there,' he said finally. 'We still have a job to do.'

Getting out, Shannon scanned the parking lot and was encouraged when she recognized TeeJay's truck, with its unmistakable bright red color and its Ole Miss decal on the rear window.

'You have your .38 on you?' Wolfe asked as they approached the building, patting his own pocket for reassurance. 'Just in case something goes wrong.'

'I do.'

They walked through a back entrance and along a corridor lined with vending machines selling candy, caffeine pills, even truckers' caps. The small front lobby was outfitted with some comfortable chairs, a coffee station, and a TV tuned to a sports channel. A café sat off to one side and an invitingly low-lit bar off to the other. There was no sign of TeeJay.

Wolfe settled into one of the chairs with a view out the front windows while Shannon went to the registration desk to ask again if TeeJay – she could not yet bring herself to think of him by his real name – was registered. He was not, nor was anyone under the name Mobius.

She shook her head as she rejoined him, and they sat gazing out the windows for a while. Even through the plate glass they could hear the whine of traffic out on the 5. At the moment everything seemed painted in shades of gray, with a sheen of moisture on the pavement from a light overnight rain. Far to the northwest, over the Pacific, a bank of thunderclouds was gathering.

'We know he's here somewhere,' Wolfe said abruptly. 'Let's give him fifteen minutes.'

They gave him thirty, during which time Wolfe went to the bar and came back with a glass of tomato juice with an enormous celery stick jutting out of it.

'Anything in that?' she asked, trying not to sound judgmental.

'Maybe.' He took a big swig and eased back in his chair.

At the thirty-minute mark they left. Out in the lot, the red Ford F-150 was nowhere to be seen.

'He knows what we're up to,' Wolfe said wearily. 'He heard it in your voice. I heard it myself.'

She didn't bother to argue. It was true. She had fallen for his scam, his refreshingly plain down-home talk, his lovemaking, everything about him. How could he have read her and her needs so well? And now, if that were not enough, she had warned him. He had heard the emotion fill up her throat and known that the game was up.

The VW bus was still parked one row away from them.

'Might as well let him know his babysitting duties are over, whoever it is,' Wolfe said, heading toward the bus.

Shannon got in the truck but was out again in a second at the sight of Wolfe waving frantically to her. She raced over to find him standing by the driver's door. His face said it all.

She looked in through the open window. Stack lay on his side, a small, bloody hole in his left temple, more blood soaked through his shirt on the right shoulder. The console and steering wheel were lightly flecked with red. The engine was still running.

TeeJay, she screamed silently, *did you do this?*

And the silent answer came, leaving no room for doubt.

Fifty-Three

'Shot twice,' Wolfe said, his voice a monotone. 'You see his knuckles?' He pointed to the raw skin across the tops of both hands. 'He didn't have time to reach his gun, but he fought.'

I hope he hurt you, she told her new and worst enemy. *Oh, I hope he hurt you.*

They scanned the rows of parked cars. Everything appeared normal. For now.

'We've got to get moving before someone notices what happened,' he said. 'And we can't leave Stack here.'

She thought hard. 'We may have to.' Moving away from the van, they talked intensely for a few minutes, aware of time passing too swiftly.

Finally Wolfe agreed. 'You're right,' he said, his shoulders slumped. 'Diana wouldn't want a body in the warehouse, not when we're all getting ready to pack up and move out. Knowing her, she won't leave a trace of us behind. So …'

'So we have to leave him here. Should we take his ID?'

'No need. It won't be his anyway. Same thing with the van. It'll be registered under a phony name.'

'Just like yours and mine.'

He pulled out his phone, hit numbers, and in a moment was talking to Diana in a low, strained voice, using the oblique language of the underground. 'She wants us back now,' he said as he closed the phone.

They took surface streets back to the warehouse, stopping half a dozen times to check for pursuit, even doubling back twice. They were not being followed.

At the warehouse, they found the little group in shock, all momentarily robbed of words. Linc was the first to speak.

'The son of a bitch is getting close, isn't he?'

'We'll honor Stack later, when we can,' Diana said. 'For now, the best way is to finish what we started.'

Linc and Judith nodded.

Diana looked hard at Shannon and Wolfe. 'I need to know everything you can tell me.'

'I'm the one to tell you,' Shannon said.

'Then follow me.'

It was one of the worst moments of her life. Never had she felt such a sense of failure, such a certainty that she had betrayed others who trusted her.

They were in the small, starkly furnished room with the door closed. Diana sat in one of the chairs, and they stood in front of her, ignoring her suggestion that they sit down. Speaking haltingly, Shannon told the story. She did not embroider or try to justify herself. Diana's eyes never left her, her expression never changed.

At the end, Diana asked a few questions. She asked to see the photos of Del Mobius and Dixie Latta on Shannon's phone. She asked for a few more details about Mobius's background, especially while in prison, and she asked them to confirm that they were not followed from the motel. She closed her eyes briefly, thinking.

Then she stood up quickly, running her hand through her short-cropped hair and tugging down the tail of her pullover. 'Let's go talk to the others.'

Linc and Judith, hands smudged with dirt, were taking a break from their work on the truck, half-sitting, half-lying on cots with coffee cups in hand.

'Wolfe and Shannon went out to follow up a lead on Quentin, and I sent Stack to keep an eye on them,' she began. 'I should have known better than to assume anyone could outsmart Quentin and his people. Now Stack's dead, and I bear some responsibility. He was a good soldier.'

She cleared her throat. 'Stack was killed at a motel just a few miles from here, which proves that Quentin's closer than we thought.' The other two listened, their faces painfully intent.

'There's no reason to think they know exactly what we're up to, but that doesn't matter. They're too close. We have to assume the worst, that they could locate us anytime. Because of some information Shannon's turned up, we know a lot more about them. They number three. Shannon has some photos to show you, and she'll describe the way Quentin looks now. All three are very dangerous, and they're clearly after me, not you. Anyone who stays with me could become a target.'

'Excuse me for butting in,' Linc said, 'but I believe we've already had the dramatic scene where you ask the ones who are ready to march into the valley of death to step over the line.'

'We're having it one more time,' Diana said.

'And I'm stepping over the line.'

'Me too,' Judith said, gnawing on what was left of a fingernail.

'We usually go on night crawls unarmed,' Diana went on, 'but this time I'm making an exception, for obvious reasons. Anyone who wants to take a weapon can do so.'

Catching Wolfe's smile, she added, 'You two will probably go armed to the teeth.'

'Count on it,' he said casually.

'Of course, you have the same choice they have.'

'I've already given you our answer,' Shannon said.

Diana looked at her for an extra moment, then addressed all four of them. 'So we're agreed, and it's on for tonight.'

Shannon tried to hide her surprise. *I thought it was tomorrow*. Then she realized: *Of course. If we move late tonight, the attack will fall during the early hours of the anniversary.*

'How much more work on the truck?' Diana asked Linc.

'Uh … about two man-hours. Then the final hookup at the site, say twenty minutes.'

'The two of you will have to finish up, and soon as you can,' Diana said. 'We need to stay on schedule. Every hour that goes by increases the chance of their finding us.'

'The weather—'

'I know. It'll just add to our troubles. There's a storm coming tonight. If I could postpone, I would, but it has to be tonight. What did you decide on the fuse?'

'Powder,' Linc said. 'It's more old-fashioned than electrical, but it's also simpler, and it fits our needs. Timothy McVeigh used it in Oklahoma City, and it worked fine for him.'

She looked around, waiting for more objections. When none came, she said briskly, 'All right, then. H-Hour, as Stack would call it, is two a.m. Judith will take the truck out at eleven thirty, and the rest of us leave this place right at midnight.' She pointed to a tall steel cabinet to the left of the kitchen counter. 'For those of you who don't have them, you'll find rain parkas in there.'

She headed back to her room. Shannon stood staring after her, almost gaping.

'You're wondering why she didn't rip you a new one in front of everybody,' Wolfe said quietly.

She nodded.

'That's not the way a leader behaves.'

Fifty-Four

Shannon and Wolfe huddled for ten minutes with Linc and Judith, talking quietly about their three known adversaries. Shannon called up the photos on her cell-phone screen and passed them around. Then she told them everything she could recall about Quentin – his looks, clothing, even the sound of his voice.

The pair returned to the job on the truck, and Shannon thought she could almost feel electricity in the air. *This really is going to happen*, she thought. A catastrophic event was being planned, assembled in front of her. Everything seemed almost too calm. She half-expected to hear raised voices, shouts, an ominous soundtrack underscoring the gravity of it. But there was no drama. The truck might have been sitting in a garage with workmen puttering around in the well-lit interior, conversing in low tones, making occasional small sounds with their tools.

She took Wolfe's pickup out, slowly cruising the industrial streets, looking for anything. But the coming storm seemed to have sent most people indoors, and she saw little activity through the rain-speckled windshield. She made herself drive for two hours, playing first the radio and then some of Wolfe's CDs for distraction, but the music gave her little comfort. She saw TeeJay's face between the soft slaps of the windshield wipers, then Quentin Latta's, and she watched them merge into one menacing visage. Hatred ached inside her. The .38 rode on the passenger seat, and she reached over occasionally to feel its walnut grip.

She didn't know if she had murder in her, but she knew that, given the right provocation, she was ready to try.

When she returned, the work on the truck appeared to be finished. Judith sat on her cot, immersed in a book, and Wolfe lay with arms crossed under his head, staring up at the peaked roof high overhead. Linc emerged from the bathroom wrapped in a towel, his head wet. He began laying out clothes – anonymous military-surplus fatigues, high-top boots, a floppy hat. He was unusually quiet.

Linc's body, the color of coffee with a splash of cream, was marked by several pale scars, the traces of old battles against various foes. He noticed Shannon's look.

'Punji stake, Mekong Delta, 'sixty-six,' he said, pointing to an ankle that bore an ugly gash. He fingered a smaller scar over his left eyebrow. 'Nightstick, Chicago, 'sixty-eight.' And what looked like seared flesh on his right shoulder: 'Tear gas canister, Seattle, 'ninety-nine.'

'Sorry if I stared.'

'Hell, I'm proud of my campaign ribbons. A pretty girl looks at me, I'm not complaining.'

Earlier, Linc had rolled up Stack's sleeping bag and placed on the bare cot the book he had been reading about the small band of warriors who fought a gallant but losing battle against the Persian army. Next to the book sat a pair of highly polished combat boots, which Stack had apparently planned to wear on the operation.

The rear doors of the rented truck stood open. Shannon walked over and looked inside the cargo area.

The interior was a mass of tightly packed steel drums. The floor of the truck had disappeared under them, leaving no space to walk or crawl. Atop them stood two more drums, identical to the rest except for a girdle of duct tape holding fast a book-size slab of what looked like modeling clay.

She held her breath. She knew she was looking at a massive bomb, but oddly that was not the first thing that entered her mind. Instead, the sight of the steel containers made her think of an old and grainy newsreel image showing an array of cans that held poison gas, a grisly cache uncovered at one of the many liberated Nazi death camps.

Both scenes, past and present, suggested things ordinary and industrial. Inside the containers, one material was gas, the other explosive. And yet both brought death on a grand scale.

Free Earth bombs things, not people, she felt like chanting to herself, over and over. *Not people.*

She walked over to the kitchen counter, where Diana was replenishing the coffee pot. 'How's the weather out there?'

'Starting to rain a little, and getting colder,' Shannon told her. 'Visibility's not so great. The radio says this storm's coming down from Alaska.'

'All that way? Aren't we lucky?'

Dinner was early and subdued. Everyone, Diana included, sat around on the cots spooning up beef stew. It was barely six o'clock by the time they had finished. As she washed her bowl and spoon, Diana said, 'It's going to be a long night. All of you should try to get some rest in the next few hours.' She went to her room and closed the door.

Shannon tried to comply. She lay down and closed her eyes, willing all the hobgoblins in her mind to go away for a while. The next few hours – days, even – were so full of uncertainty and danger, all she could do was try to blot it out for now. She called on what she knew about meditation techniques, and little by little her breathing and heart rate began to slow. The rain on the skylight was heavier but remained a calming sound. She decided to let it act as a lullaby, to see if—

'Asleep?'

She turned her head. It was Judith, crouching by her cot, speaking low.

'Nope.'

'I don't want to bother you.' Her words came out rapidly, her normal mode of speech. 'I just … I wanted to ask you something. You don't have to answer.' Her brow was furrowed in thought, or worry, as if she'd been wrestling with the question. Shannon thought she knew what it was.

'Are you her daughter?' It came out in a whispered rush. When Shannon didn't reply, she went on hurriedly. 'You don't have to tell me if you don't want to. I just—'

Oh, what the hell. I've broken enough rules. What difference does one more make? 'Yes,' Shannon said. 'I am.'

'I knew it. You look so much like her. I had no idea she had a child. None of us did. But now that I see you with her, you look so natural together. It explains why you're here. I think I resented you at first, showing up in the middle of things. But you deserve to be part of this.'

Shannon couldn't think of a reply. Underneath the woman's high-strung demeanor and obvious intelligence, she could see a layer of decency, and Shannon began to appreciate what it must have taken for her to leave the ivory tower for a life of discomfort and dangerous commitment. *Another one of those failed academics like me*, she thought. *An angry woman. A soul sister.*

'I've never met anyone like her,' Judith went on. 'I can only imagine what it must have been like growing up with her for a mother, and I envy you. The things she must have taught you.'

Shannon laughed to herself. The words sounded like Lonnie's. The difference was, Judith clearly meant them.

'Oh, yeah. It was very ... different.'

'And Wolfe ... I have to ask about him, too. He's so much like—'

'Somebody talking about me?' Wolfe hadn't moved, but he had clearly heard.

'Oh. Sorry.' Judith sat down on the floor, flustered. With her shag of hair and her fleecy pajamas and wool socks, she suddenly looked much younger.

'That's all right,' he said. 'It's true. We're the lost children of the fairy queen, come to claim our inheritance. We wish you no harm.'

Judith laughed softly, eyeing him. It occurred to Shannon that she had seen Judith eye him several times over the course of the last couple of days, but she hadn't thought much of it. Now it dawned on her: She likes him. The disenchanted Ph.D. with the unfocused anger likes the rumpled gentleman pot-grower from the north woods.

'So the family secret's out.' That was a deeper voice, and Shannon saw Linc roll out of his bunk in T-shirt and skivvies and pad over to join them.

'You knew,' Judith said in a chiding tone.

'But you didn't need to know.' He sat down beside Judith and crossed his legs Indian-style. 'The scuttlebutt won't get outside this group,' he said to the other two. 'We're not gossips.'

'What are you, then?' Shannon asked.

'Wild-eyed, tree-hugging, bomb-throwing, militant motherfuckers,' he said casually.

'How nice.' She liked him, with his swaggering competence, his history with Diana. Matter of fact, she liked both of them. *It must be easy making friends at the barricades*, she thought.

'We owe you,' Linc said to her, 'for that intel about Quentin. We'd heard a little about him but not the other two. Thanks for bringing us up to speed.'

'You're welcome.'

'I need to know what we're up against. How good are they?'

She thought for a moment. 'I guess you could call Quentin the mastermind. They say he ordered people killed in prison. His daughter has inherited all of his hate for Diana. She came at me once, and I can tell you she's physically strong and pretty damn vicious. The other one, Mobius, may be the worst of all. He likes to use a knife. We know he's tortured three people.' She paused, trying to stay focused. 'I guess we can assume all of them will have guns.'

'Fine,' Linc said. 'So will I.'

'I'm curious,' she said. 'What happens to this warehouse when we're through with it? Does Free Earth own it?'

'Oh, no,' Judith spoke up. 'We're renting it. We've had it for months, under the name of a company that doesn't exist. When we leave tonight, we pack out all our gear and activate the sprinkler system. Everything should get washed down pretty well, including fingerprints. Sooner or later, people will probably figure out that we were here, but they won't find anything useful.'

'Something bothers me,' Wolfe said.

'Yeah?'

'Shannon and I, we're not supposed to ask too many questions. Our job is just to watch Diana's back. But I'm wondering about the timing of this … this thing. In a few hours, that truck is pulling out of here, and we think we know where it's going.'

The other two looked at him expressionlessly.

'You don't have to tell us anything now, but we'll know soon. We think the target is the new headquarters building for the Swann Group, downtown. And that's what bothers me. Let's just say, hypothetically, that Free Earth wanted to hit the Swann Group really hard, and they saw their chance with this new building. Well, if you want to do maximum damage, why not wait until the building's finished, or almost finished, instead of going after something that's only half-done?'

Linc and Judith exchanged glances. 'We've wondered the same thing,' he said slowly. 'Forget hypothetical. That *is* the target. It's been the target for well over a year, when we first heard about the plans for the building. We figured we'd wait until they'd finished it. But a few weeks ago Diana told us that she'd picked the anniversary of Adam's death as D-Day. There was some argument, but when she's set her mind on something, that's it.'

He looked over his shoulder. 'Hmm.' Then he got up and headed toward the back of the warehouse. Watching him go, Shannon saw that Diana's shade was up again, the same dim light showing inside the room.

In seconds, though, he was back. 'She wants to see you,' he said to Shannon.

Fifty-Five

As she approached the open door, Shannon could hear faint music. It was the sound of voices singing a melody she'd never heard before. Diana, resting on her cot, beckoned to her and pointed to a chair.

'What are you playing?' Shannon asked as she sat. On a table next to the cot, along with a lamp and a few books, sat a music player, connected to a small speaker.

'Oh, that? It's the prayer from *Hansel and Gretel*, the opera. Have you heard it?'

'No.'

Diana reached over and turned up the volume slightly. The voices, accompanied by minimal orchestration, sounded pure and clear. 'These are children singing. I like to play this when I'm about to take on a challenge. It clears my head, helps me to get centered.'

'What's it about? The song, I mean.'

'Well, the opera's a fairy tale,' Diana said, 'so you know how much relevance it has to the real world—'

'Wolfe told me once that you and John Paul filled the house with music. One day songs of revolution, he said, and the next day something classical.'

Diana laughed. Shannon thought it may have been the first time she had heard her laugh out loud.

'He's got a good memory. Anyway, Hansel and Gretel are separated from their parents, lost in the forest. It's nighttime, and they're afraid. To help themselves go to sleep, they sing their bedtime song, which is really a prayer. It starts off, *When at night I go to sleep, fourteen angels watch do keep* ... And after a while, they drift off. And while they're asleep, angels actually do come and watch over them.'

She caught Shannon's look. 'And no, this doesn't mean I necessarily believe in angels.'

'What do you believe in?'

She shrugged. 'Whatever battle I'm fighting at the moment.'

'Isn't there a witch in the story?'

'Uh-huh. The witch entices them into her house and almost has them for dinner.'

Shannon couldn't remember the rest. 'But their parents save them?'

The children's voices climbed to a sweet high note on the word *Heaven*, then descended into quiet. The song was over.

'No,' Diana said. 'They have to save themselves.'

'Oh. You wanted to see me?'

'Just for a second.' She reached over and switched off the player, then shifted into a more comfortable position on the cot. Atop one of the books sat a pair of reading glasses.

'Just my idle curiosity,' she began. 'I was wondering about you and that degree you've been chasing.'

'You know about that?'

'I know a lot about you.'

'Do you? Well, I chased it for a while, and then I stopped running.'

'Any particular reason?'

'Hmm? I don't know.' She was starting to feel the old defensiveness. 'I guess I lost interest in the whole academic thing.' She made a vague gesture. 'I'd lined up a dissertation on the French Revolution, and one day I asked myself, who cares whether I write it or not?'

Diana nodded. 'Sometimes you wonder if history really has any bearing on what we do today. But I think it's the job of the historians to push our faces in it, make us see all the mistakes we've made. Take Vietnam and the anti-war movement.'

'Are you saying you made mistakes?'

'We all did. I think the biggest was our failure to enlist more of the country – blacks and working-class whites. With those numbers, we'd have had enormous strength. We almost could have stopped the war at the ballot box, without even going to the streets.'

'So what happened?'

'We got impatient. And, I suppose, arrogant. When the blacks and the blue-collar whites didn't climb on board right away, we didn't try to woo them. We just went our own way. After a while, the movement was a bunch of over-privileged white kids talking to each other. We split into radicals and moderates, and the radicals – John Paul and I, Bernardine Dohrn and Bill Ayers – hijacked the movement. And the next thing we knew, bombs were going off, and we were the bombers. We didn't attract anyone with our violence. We alienated them.'

'You sound amazingly like John Paul.'

'Well, hindsight's a wonderful thing. Knowing what I know, I would've handled things differently, and maybe we could have ended the war earlier. We'll never know.'

'I'm confused,' Shannon said, exasperation in her voice. 'Why would—'

'You're wondering: If violence was a mistake back then, why am I carrying on with it today?' She pursed her lips, thinking, and in the low light Shannon could see deep shadows under her eyes.

'Because it's not a mistake today, it's all we have left. There's no coalition to be formed, no one to march with us. The old, moderate anti-war movement drew in millions, because everyone had a stake in the outcome. Today, those who care enough about the environment to take direct action are a tiny group, and most of us are – let's face it – white and privileged. The rest of the world is too busy trying to stay alive, to put food on the table, to be concerned about whether farmers burn another million acres of Amazon rainforest or the Japanese kill another thousand whales this year.'

This sounds more like a speech than a conversation, Shannon thought. *But it's a powerful one. I can see why people used to listen to her.*

'Somebody has to stand up for the Earth. Those on the other side are too powerful for us to win by lobbying or leafleting or picketing. They think they can just ignore us.'

She sat up on the cot and leaned forward, holding Shannon with her gaze. 'Free Earth is not here to make friends or alliances. We're here to kick some ass, and to keep doing it until it hurts them.'

The room fell quiet. Shannon waited.

Diana smiled at her. 'Sorry for the lecture. Damn, I do miss those times, you know? An auditorium full of people, and me with a microphone in my hand, squawking my head off.'

She shook her head fiercely, as if to clear it. 'We were talking about you. No more lectures, all right? It's your life. I don't have the right to tell you how to live it. All I'm saying is: It's now time for some serious study of the politics of the sixties and seventies, one of the most messed-up periods this country's seen in a long time. You could do it. You're smart, you have an incisive mind – yes, I know that about you, too. You could take a clear-eyed look back at all of it, and – who knows? – maybe give people a new perspective on it.

'Look around you. This country's just blundered into a brand new war, and how long will it take to get out of it? Will we make the same mistakes all over again? The historians could help keep that from happening.'

'I don't know ...'

'I might even help out with a few interviews. You could ask me anything. Wouldn't surprise me if John Paul agreed, too.'

'Really?'

'Really. Imagine publishing a paper with fresh quotes from two of America's most wanted fugitives.' She grinned. 'What a thrill, huh?'

'Historians are impartial. Don't expect me to do you any favors.'

'Hey, take your best shot.' Diana rubbed her eyes. 'You can think about it. Now I've taken up too much of your time. We should all be getting some rest.'

At the door, Diana stopped her.

'Watching you and the way you turned out, sometimes I wonder what my life would have been like if I'd gone into teaching, the way you started to do. I could have made a damn good teacher.'

'You would have.' Shannon looked at her across the distance that now separated them.

'What about me?'

'Hmm?'

'If I'd come up during your time, could I have done what you did?'

Diana's smile showed delight at the question. 'I'd have marched anywhere with you.'

Shannon was still in a daze when she crawled back into her sleeping bag. Who was Diana to step back into her life after all these years and start prescribing a career path for her? *You can tell she's used to managing people's lives.*

On the other hand, the possibilities were fascinating. A new direction of study. Radical politics of the past hundred years. It might be too narrow to confine her field to the Vietnam era, so why not expand it to include earlier decades? The socialism of the thirties? The Red Scare of the fifties?

Soon, though, another thought took over, a much more troubling one, and it had nothing to do with Diana's words. Shannon's mind strayed back to Linc's comment about the timing of the attack. Once, he said, they had intended to target the completed building, but something happened to make Diana change her plans.

Shannon thought she knew what it was: Quentin. When he emerged from prison, Diana knew she must make her move now, because later she might not be alive.

As troubled as her thoughts were, exhaustion finally took over, and she was able to sleep. It seemed as if only minutes had passed when she felt a gentle touch on her shoulder. She opened her eyes to see Linc looking down at her, a tight smile on his face.

'It's time.'

Fifty-Six

The city looked deep in a winter sleep. At a few minutes after midnight they sped north on the 5, the freeway that had brought them there and now was leading them to one final place, where a new drama would be played out before the next day dawned.

Shannon rode with Wolfe in the Dodge Ram, rain thrumming on the roof of the truck, her insides one giant knotted fist. He looked no more relaxed than she; his deep-set eyes locked on the road, his fingertips playing paradiddles on the inside of the steering wheel.

This time they were trailing Linc's vehicle, a Ford Explorer that had logged many miles. Linc and Diana were on board. According to plan, Judith had eased the rented Strider truck out the big doors of the warehouse just before eleven thirty and slowly driven it away. Her job was to avoid the freeway with her sensitive cargo, carefully take surface streets all the way to their destination, and meet them there. At precisely midnight, the two-vehicle caravan had departed, taking the faster route.

'Good luck,' Diana had said quietly to the little group just before Judith's departure. 'We won't meet here again. When the job's finished, we'll scatter, stay low, and let a lot of time go by before any contact. Wait to hear from me. Everyone straight?'

Nods all around. They had formed a tight circle, each putting out a hand. Then they had spoken the words, *For Adam, for Stack, and for the planet.* Shannon and Wolfe joined in.

Now, with Wolfe at her side in the cab of the truck, she squinted through the windshield to keep the van in sight. The wipers, cranked up to maximum, were not doing a very good job.

'Uh-oh,' Wolfe said just as she realized the problem. 'This stuff's turning to sleet.'

It was true. The rain had thickened, taken on more weight. It hit the glass with a crystalline slap, then instantly melted into mush. The road surface began to glisten, and the sparse freeway traffic slowed down. Up ahead, Linc touched the brakes once, twice, making his red lights glow, and Wolfe backed off the gas a little.

Driving carefully, eyes straining, they proceeded seven miles up the freeway before the Explorer's turn signal alerted them to prepare to exit. As Wolfe maneuvered into the exit lane, Shannon's eyes took in the sweep of the downtown skyline to their left. The thick cluster of high-rise hotels and office buildings were partly cloaked in the driving sleet, their upper stories mostly dark; only an occasional neon sign identified a particular building.

Then, just behind the SUV, they descended a steep and lonely downtown canyon toward the harbor, everything shiny-wet. With much commercial lighting darkened, the brightest things were the stop lights, which glared at them in startling green or red, each wearing a corona of mist.

Another turn, deep in tall buildings now, and Shannon saw something up ahead on the right, something vacant, a hole where a building should be. Nearing it, she saw that the site was sheathed in wood, a twelve-foot-high fence all around it. A dark, angular mass loomed behind the fence, hard to make out. The Explorer pulled into a temporary dirt alley separating the construction site from the building next to it and quickly stopped. The rented truck was there, its orange showing bright just before the van's lights were cut. Judith stood beside it, a small figure in a hooded parka.

Wolfe stopped at the curb across the street from the alley, and he and Shannon watched the trio gather at a twenty-foot-wide chain-link gate. As expected, it was already unlocked. Kimo, their comrade who had managed to wangle a security job with Swann months earlier, had left the gate unlocked and walked off the site, leaving behind only his phony identity.

As they watched, the two halves of the gate swung aside on rollers, and within a minute the rented truck was backing into the opening. It disappeared, and they saw Linc and Diana follow it on foot. Quickly the gate was rolled shut, but under the plan it was not to be re-locked. When it came time to leave, every second would count.

Wolfe let out a big and ragged breath of air. 'All *right*,' he said. 'Now it's you and me, out here looking for evildoers. Let's go over it one more time.'

They did, quickly. Each had a cell phone with the number of the local FBI office programmed in it. Wolfe had run a test earlier in the evening and confirmed that the number, if rung, was answered. The voice on the other end might be a security guard in the building or a sleepy intern or a real FBI agent. All that mattered was that if they needed to call the Bureau, someone would pick up.

They also had gadgets dug out of a locker in the rear of Wolfe's truck – a pair of walkie-talkies to stay in contact with each other if they got separated and a pair of small, almost palm-size, crank-powered flashlights that put out enough light to penetrate the dark but not enough to be seen at a distance.

And, of course, they had weapons. Wolfe, she knew, carried at least two guns. He didn't volunteer any information on their caliber or performance, and she didn't ask. Shannon carried the .38 in the deep right pocket of her parka, with six extra shells. When he saw her pocket it, back in the warehouse, he said, almost jokingly, 'Is that all?'

'Yes.' She was in no mood for levity.

'If you want anything else, I've got some choices for you.'

Their plan was simple: They would make the rounds of the streets around the site. If they spotted any of the enemy, they would immediately call the FBI, along with 911 for the Seattle PD, and announce their discovery. Diana would be alerted and left to decide if she wanted to be in the neighborhood when the law arrived. As to how she would feel about being handed such a choice, they dared not even conjecture.

It sounded simple, but it raised a host of questions. What if Quentin's people spotted them at the same time? What if things turned violent? What if Diana refused to leave?

On a more practical level, how could they expect to spot anyone in this weather? The sleet was coming down steadily, with occasional gusts of wind behind it. Recognizing a face at twenty paces could be a challenge, which meant that identifying anyone would require walking up to them. The danger was obvious.

Wolfe started to put the truck in gear but stopped. 'I don't like it,' he said.

'Well, I don't either, but—'

'No. This is something else.' He turned to her. 'Why did he invite us over to the motel? If he never planned to meet us, I mean. Why the wild-goose chase?'

'TeeJay?' She thought for a moment, sampled a few explanations, but wound up discarding them all. 'I don't know. It doesn't make much sense, does it? Maybe he just wanted to get a look at us without our seeing him.'

'He didn't need to get a look at you, and what does it matter what I look like?' His fingertips were tapping the wheel again. 'He wasn't planning to kill anybody, at least not at first, because he didn't know Stack would be following us. It only makes sense,' he said slowly, 'if he needed us there for some reason.'

'I don't—'

'If he needed us … or the truck.'

They stared at each other. A thought began to take shape in her mind, but he was ahead of her. He found the small flashlight, opened the door, and sprang out. 'Wait here.'

He disappeared from sight, but she heard him working his way around the truck, making little knocking and scraping sounds. It went on for a long time. Finally he returned, a devastated look on his face and something in his hand. Closing the door, he showed it to her.

It was made of black plastic, about the size of a cigarette pack, with a simple magnet mounted on one side and a two-inch aerial protruding from one end.

'Oh, shit. Don't tell me.'

He nodded. 'This was stuck to the rear axle. I thought only cops used them. I'm not enough of a techie to know for sure, but I'd still bet money this is a transmitter.'

'So they know where we are?' She looked up and down the street. Few cars and no pedestrians. It was one of the loneliest city streets she had ever seen.

'Not necessarily. At least not yet. But this can sure as hell help them find us. We've got to do something.'

'Break the damn thing.'

'No. Something better.' He fired up the engine, did a tight U-turn, and sped down the steep hill to the next cross street, where he made a right turn and pulled into the first space he found by the curb. This street was busier than the other, with a few cars going by every minute. When a taxi passed them, he pulled out and trailed it, telling her in rapid-fire bursts of words what she needed to do. By the time the cab stopped at a red light, they were ready.

She jumped out and ran up to the driver's side. 'Sir! Excuse me!' she exclaimed, making faces and jumping up and down with the cold.

The cabbie rolled the window halfway down. 'Ma'am?'

'Listen, I'm sorry, but I just cannot find my way back to the freeway. I'm about to run outta gas, and my mom's expecting me, and ...'

'The Five?' He gave her an odd look. 'Two blocks down, take a right, go up the hill all the way to the top, look for the freeway sign.'

She glanced toward the rear of the cab, saw Wolfe give her a thumbs-up as he sneaked, bent over, back to the truck.

'Thank you so much!'

She was barely seated when he did another U and raced back the way they had come, passing the fenced-in site on their left, they turned up the steep street and parked at the same spot.

He killed the engine. 'Stuck it behind his rear bumper,' he said. 'With luck, he'll leave the neighborhood.' His face had not relaxed. 'But this may buy us only a little time. They're smart, and they know Diana. They may have already figured out what she's up to.'

'Should we tell her about this?'

'No. If I know her, she's on automatic pilot by now anyway. This information wouldn't stop her, it would just give her more to worry about. We see the bad guys, we tell her. Anything less than that, we stick to the plan.'

Unhappily, she agreed.

'But I think cruising the streets is starting to look less effective,' he went on. 'We need to do what the sentries call tightening our perimeter.' He waited until she understood his meaning.

She nodded. 'We need to get onto the site.'

'In my opinion.'

'All right, let's go. What time do you have?'

'Uh, twelve twenty-seven.'

'Me too. Remember, no matter what happens, we need to be far away from this place at two.'

Moments later they were at the chain-link gate. Wolfe rolled one of the two halves aside far enough to allow them entry, then pulled it shut behind them.

Fifty-Seven

Turning, Shannon caught her breath. She was looking down into an enormous pit, thirty or forty feet deep, its length and breadth almost one-third of a city block. At its bottom was a jumble of machinery, materials, and piles of earth. Small lights glowed here and there, illuminating their immediate areas, probably functioning as security lights to prevent pilferage.

Looming overhead, glistening with sleet and blotting out part of the charcoal-gray sky, was a gigantic skeleton of steel. The unfinished structure stood about fifteen stories high, she estimated, with more to come. It consisted of concrete flooring, steel pillars, and girders, with messy piles of building materials collected on every floor. Shannon guessed that the building's ground floor would ultimately stand at street level, and the three or four levels that descended below ground were intended for parking.

A tower crane, taller than the height of the building, rose on the near side of the structure, and climbed skyward, looking down on everything.

There was no sign of the others or the truck. Peering into the ominously lit, cavernous space, she thought briefly of Dante's *Inferno* – then chided herself for the thought. *You need to focus,* she said silently, *and you need to work on not being afraid.*

Her eyes turned upward. She knew that the destruction of this building, even the crippling of it, would be an earth-shaking event. And that she might witness it.

They found one of several earthen ramps, wide enough for vehicles, which led down into the pit, and they descended carefully to the bottom, where they conferred quickly and decided to split up. If they stayed in motion, they reasoned, they should be able to spot any intruders and alert the other by walkie-talkie. It was a rough-edged plan, made on the fly, but it was the best they had.

He went left, she went right. She had cranked a full charge into her little flashlight, and she thumbed the button occasionally to light up her path. It was rough going, but oddly the shiny layer of sleet on the ground and on the surfaces of objects made it easier to discern things in the near dark. She walked slowly, moving into and out of lighted areas, threading her way around skip loaders, a concrete mixer, and other pieces of equipment.

Everything was quiet. She had lost sight of Wolfe within seconds. The raised hood of her parka kept her head mostly dry, but sleet stung her nose, and she had to wipe her face every now and then.

She circled around the edge of the pit nearest the main street, headed for the edge that abutted the side street. Up ahead, in the corner of the excavation, stood a small structure with windows – probably the now-abandoned guard shack.

She walked cautiously around it to find the door, two steps up. It was closed. She tried the knob, and it opened. Illuminated by the soft light in her hand, the inside was only about seven by seven feet and contained two chairs, a wall calendar, a table with some coffee mugs, and in the corner what looked like a crumpled tarpaulin.

The interior smelled rank. She shined her light at the tarpaulin.

It moved.

She jumped back, almost toppling off the step. She dug frantically for her pistol – why didn't she already have it out? – and pointed it at the shape in the corner.

'Don't move!' Instantly she countermanded herself. 'Stand up. Very slowly. I've got a gun.'

'Oh ... *shit.*' The tangled mass moved, heaved upward, separated itself into two halves. The light picked out two filthy faces, framed by matted hair under heavy caps. She recognized neither of them.

'What the hell are you doing here?'

'Uh, how 'bout keepin' outta the weather?' The voice was tired and sarcastic. She realized with a shock that the other one, the one who had not spoken, was a woman.

'Well, you can't stay here.'

'Who're you?'

An instant's hesitation, then: 'Police. I need you out of here right now. It's, uh, an emergency. We're doing a search, and we need to clear out this place.'

More hopeless cursing, but they began to move. It struck her that they were used to being rousted. By cops, security guards, store owners. She felt a stab of pity but quelled it. *Better to be cold*, she told herself, *than to die in a fireball.*

Outside the shack, they huddled together for a moment, then started for another of the steep dirt ramps, this one almost opposite the location of the gate. 'How did you get in here?' she asked them.

'Coupla loose boards, up top there,' the man said wearily.

'All right,' she said in her official voice. 'Be careful. Goodnight.'

''Djou get Little Man out already?'

'What?'

'Little Man. We kicked him outta the shack, 'cause he was mean drunk on T-Bird.'

'Well, where did he go?'

'I don't know, lady. Someplace outta the wind, I guess.' They had reached the top, where, almost magically, they parted two boards and passed through.

It's not time to panic, she thought, *not yet. But someone else is sleeping around here, and he'll surely die tonight if I don't find him.* She pushed back her sleeve and flicked the light at her watch. It was almost one. *A little over an hour to go.*

Quentin and his crew were a mortal threat but not yet a certainty. What was certain was that someone named Little Man was sleeping off a bottle of fortified wine in a sheltered spot nearby, and he would not survive the night where he was. She doubted that she had time to search through the entire construction site. He might even have taken refuge on one of the upper levels of the building, where, although windy, it would at least be dry.

Wolfe could help in the search, she thought. But someone needed to watch for intruders.

Only one thing to do. She cut across the center of the pit and began trudging directly toward the gigantic steel structure. Somewhere in there was Diana.

Two minutes later, breathing heavily, she stood at the base and peered into the darkness. Nothing. *Where would they put the truck? Think.*

There was no likely way to get it above ground level without using the crane, which still stood silently. The lower levels, on the other hand, could have parking ramps already in place. If so, the truck could simply have been driven up to any level of the garage.

A temporary workman's ladder was secured to the side of the building, stretching up as many floors as they had built. She had seen one on another side too. It looked like a good way to get up and down, but she didn't need it right now.

Thumbing the light, she stepped off the dirt and onto the concrete slab that stood at the building's lowest level, then advanced into the interior, careful to avoid the countless piles of material strewn in the way. Somewhere in the center of the building, just beyond a concrete shell that she surmised would one day hold a bank of elevators, she found the ramp and walked up it to the next garage level. She saw nothing there, or on the next level.

When she reached the fourth level, which she guessed would ultimately lie just beneath the ground floor, she noticed that it was not entirely dark there. High up on a building across the street, a hot-pink neon sign burned through the falling sleet. The building apparently housed the headquarters of a mattress manufacturer. *Sleepy Rest*, it read, and it cast its pale color over the whole scene like the hand-tinted frames of a silent movie.

Then she saw a moving, hand-held light illuminate something bright orange. The truck.

In the gloom, she saw Diana holding the light, and more light filtering out from the open rear of the truck.

Diana saw her approach. 'You're not supposed to be here. What happened?'

'Nothing. I mean no sign of them. But …' She thought quickly and decided Wolfe had been wrong to keep this from Diana. 'But we found something under the truck. Wolfe thinks it's a kind of transmitter. We got rid of it, planted it on a taxi. But still, there's a good chance—'

'They know roughly where we are,' Diana finished. 'Smart of

them. And smart of you to get rid of it. Well, we'd just better hurry up then.' She turned back to the truck.

'Wait. There's one more thing. I found two people sleeping in a shack down at the bottom of the excavation and moved them out of there.' She found herself talking fast, breathlessly. 'The thing is, there's somebody else around here too. They told me. He's been drinking, and he holed up someplace. I don't know where ...' She trailed off.

Diana nodded. 'And?'

'Well, I'm going to try to find him. But if I can't, then you need to call this off.'

Diana's face was more visible now in the light from the truck. Her expression had not changed. 'I thought you were watching for Quentin.'

'I was. I am. But there's a man out there—'

'I'm not calling anything off. Each of us will do what we have to do.'

Shannon was stunned at her words. Then she understood. Diana, as Wolfe had said, was on automatic pilot, absolutely committed. Nothing would stop her, not the approach of Quentin and his killers, not even the chance that someone – a sleeping drunk, a bystander, a noncombatant – might die.

'I thought Free Earth bombed things, not people.'

Diana made a small gesture. 'Never deliberately. But this is my war, and you and I know that people die in war.'

'The way they died at the Crowe Institute? I thought you were better than this.'

A noise from within the truck, and Linc hopped out. 'Everything okay?'

'Fine.' To Shannon she said, 'You'd better get to work. Time's short.'

'Yeah.' She heard the bitterness in her own voice. Looking around, she said, 'Where's Judith?'

'She's gone. I sent her away.'

'You what?'

'I took another look at her tonight, and I told her she wasn't right for this. I told her she should go back to Colgate and teach students and live her life.'

'You thought she might die, didn't you?'

'That's right. All of us might. I just wanted to make sure that the ones who remain are all right with that. She wasn't.'

Linc was looking on wordlessly.

'Am I?'

'I think you're braver than you know. But this isn't your war, and I still don't intend for anything to happen to you or Wolfe tonight. So get back to what you were doing, and keep away from me. Most important, remember to be far away from here at two.'

Shannon began to turn away when she heard a noise behind her. Diana's form grew rigid, and Linc had a handgun out in a fraction of a second.

'Well, here you are.'

She had heard the voice only once, but she recognized it immediately. She turned to see a large man swaddled in a shapeless coat coming toward them. As he drew near, she saw that he wore no hat and that his forehead was broad and high, just as she remembered.

Fifty-Eight

He stood about six feet from them, clearly visible now in the faint light that leaked from the rear of the truck. The sign atop the distant high-rise gave his face an unearthly pinkish cast. His expression appeared to hold no menace, only something resembling curiosity.

At the edge of her view she saw the heavy pistol in Linc's hand, barrel steady.

Kill him. The unexpressed thought filled her head. *Kill him because of what he did to my parents. Kill him before he kills us.* Her hand started for the pocket of her parka.

Quentin's hands were empty. He raised them in a palms-out gesture, then let them drop. 'I'm not—'

'Search him,' Diana said to Linc.

He did so quickly, with one hand. 'Nothing,' he said.

'I came to talk,' Quentin said to Diana. 'I've been looking for you the longest time—'

'And killing all the way,' Shannon broke in. 'Isn't that right, you sick piece of shit?'

'You're the daughter,' he said, turning to her. His smile looked almost affectionate. 'We talked out by the water once.'

'Yeah. You told me your own daughter was a banker. Kind of an exaggeration, wasn't it? I'd say she falls more into the category of white trash. Takes after her old man.'

'That's unkind. But I don't blame you for hating. You've lost a lot. I pity you. I just hope you won't hold me responsible for it.'

Shannon was struck dumb for a moment. Then she found the words.

'Who tortured my mother and father, Quentin? Were you the one, or did you just stand there and give the orders?'

'I know what happened,' he said evenly. 'But I wasn't there, and I didn't give the orders. I'm very sorry about your parents.'

'Bullshit. You're a liar—'

'What the hell do you want, Quentin?' Diana broke in. 'Talk fast, because we don't have much time. And I could still decide to let Linc kill you.'

Quentin focused on the truck. 'This is going to be a big one, isn't it? I know about your new cause, and I admire you for it. No one's going to get hurt tonight, right?'

'That's none of your business. What do you want?'

'Just a few minutes with you. A conversation.'

Diana appeared indecisive, a rare look for her. Finally, at a gesture from her, Linc handed her his gun, and she walked with Quentin to the edge of the concrete floor overlooking the pit. While Shannon fidgeted and watched, they talked, standing close together, the falling sleet a silvery backdrop to the scene. Quentin now appeared agitated, waving his arms. At one point, he walked away a short distance, then came back to talk and gesture more.

'Don't worry,' Linc said. 'She can handle this.'

'I'm glad you think so.' She gave him a hard look. 'She said you're ready to die. Are you?'

'I am.'

'And Judith wasn't.'

'No. Judith … well, I liked her, and she worked hard, and she cared a lot. But she was afraid, from the very first day. She threw up at the warehouse, back in the bathroom. She might have let us down tonight, without wanting to. Diana did the right thing.'

'I'm curious. How can you tell when you're ready to die?'

He laughed lightly. 'Tough question. All I know is, I've been ready ever since Nam. Difference is, I've got a better reason now. But I don't plan to die. I plan to live. I'd better get back to this.' He disappeared into the truck, where his work noises resumed.

As she kept her eyes on the two figures, her mind returned to the missing Little Man. She needed to get back to her search, but not until the issue of Quentin was resolved in some way. 'How much time do we have after you light the fuse?'

'I'll light two of them, in case one fails. The answer is twenty-five minutes. Plenty of time for us to get away.'

'Just don't jiggle anything, okay?'

He laughed again, louder. 'Don't worry. This stuff is very stable. Everything in here could take a bullet. Except the detonators.'

'I'm so relieved.'

It seemed an eternity, but the conversation out at the edge of the building was over in five minutes. The two figures separated, and Shannon was astonished to see Quentin walk away, back into the darkness toward the ramp, as Diana returned.

'You let him go?'

'It was either that or kill him,' Diana said grimly. 'And I'm not about to kill a man whose mind is slipping.'

'He was gaming you.'

'Maybe. But I'm a pretty good judge of people. Toward the end, he melted down in prison. He's a sad case. He's gone ... *soft*. Found religion, and all he's interested in now is forgiveness for what happened at the Crowe Institute. It's eating him up. He says he's on his way now to talk to the widow of the young man killed at Crowe, the night watchman. The mother of the baby girl. He wants her to forgive him, too, but he's not hopeful.'

'He killed Ray and Mora and Henry.'

'I don't think so. Apparently that was the work of his lovely daughter and her boyfriend. And speaking of the boyfriend, you should have had more sense.'

'Don't lecture me. Quentin's been chasing you—'

'To find me and ask my forgiveness for involving me in those killings. Just as he told Katherine when he called her.'

'This is crazy,' Shannon almost shouted. 'We've been hearing that TeeJay and Lonnie were just working for Quentin, doing what he wanted. Now you tell me it wasn't even his idea?'

'They've been traveling with him, using him to track down members of the network – to track me down. They would move in and do their work, try to extract information from those people ...' She sighed. 'From Ray and Mora and Henry. For a while, Quentin didn't realize what they were doing. He truly seems to be off on a planet of his own. But then he saw something on television that mentioned Henry's murder, and he put it together.'

'And he's still with them?'

'He can't stop them. When they figured out where we'd be tonight, he demanded that they let him speak to me first.'

'A couple of murdering lowlifes? Why would they let him do that?'

'Because he's her father,' Diana said patiently, 'and she loves him.' She thought for a moment. 'This doesn't make him a nice guy. He won't interfere with what they're doing. He's interested only in his own salvation, not theirs.'

'It still makes no sense. Once Quentin wanted you dead; now he doesn't. But his daughter is still trying to get at you? Why in the world . . . ?'

'That's the part I don't understand, and he wasn't helpful. It's pretty clear that something else is driving them. Something or someone.' Another sigh, and she appeared to snap back to life. 'We've got work to finish, and we don't have a lot of time.'

Something in Diana's words chilled Shannon, and she waited for the rest.

'Now that Quentin's had his talk with me, I'd bet they're coming.'

Fifty-Nine

She had to make herself leave the shelter of overhanging concrete to return to the wind and the stinging sleet and the dangers of the pit. Two murderers were out there somewhere. Maybe they were still on the street, hearing Quentin's report. Maybe they had already entered the site. She had to believe that there was still time to do what she had to do. She told herself, over and over, that it was in her power to save at least one life tonight – a man she didn't know – and she had to try. And she took what comfort she could in the .38 with the walnut grip that sat heavy in the pocket of her parka.

This time she descended the shorter way, easing herself three levels down the precarious ladder to the dirt. She was thankful that visibility was getting even worse. Intruders would need lights to make it around all the obstacles on the site, while she was getting a little more familiar with the terrain and should not have to use her flashlight as much.

At the bottom, she pulled out the walkie-talkie and thumbed the transmit button, sending a short burst of static out on Channel 8, the one Wolfe had selected. A moment later she got an answering burst. In a few seconds of conversation she got his location and arranged to meet him at the concrete mixer, near the center of the excavation. She pulled the .38 out of her pocket.

It took her a minute to get there, and she saw him huddling next to the mixer, shivering. 'Are you all right?'

'Fine.' He leaned against the motor, apparently resting, holding his gun at his side, his walkie-talkie still in his other hand.

She moved up, putting her mouth close to his ear, and quickly told him everything, stressing the urgency of finding the man who had taken shelter somewhere in this nightmarish place and then the sobering news about their pursuers. The details of Quentin's role she would save for another time.

Wolfe straightened up wearily. 'I'm not sure we have time to find this guy now.'

'Why not?'

'Need to show you something.'

He led her around the mixer to the other side, where the large bin was used to mix concrete. Looking down, she saw something between the two mixing shafts. She shone her light on it.

Judith.

She lay like a doll thrown down by a spiteful owner, limbs splayed in different directions. Her head was covered loosely by the hood of her parka, but Shannon recognized the boots she had worn, as well as the sadly chewed-down nails of the one hand that was visible.

'No.'

Wolfe reached into the bin and lifted the hood a little, leaving the face covered but showing the gash that disfigured her throat from one side of the neck to the other. Shannon shifted her light to the bottom of the bin, where it reflected on an obscene red-black pool of still fresh blood, just beginning to be diluted by the falling sleet.

He cursed softly. 'So they're already here somewhere, probably looking for Diana. They're our first priority now. We need to give the others time to light the fuse and split. Calling the FBI won't do the job any more. We need to just find these fuckers and deal with them before they find her. Are you with me?'

Certain that her fear was written all over her face, she nevertheless nodded.

'We'd better start with the area nearest the building and work our way out. That way we might intercept them. Ready?'

Another nod. She waited, but he didn't move. An odd look came over him, as if he'd sensed something. He seemed to be sniffing the wind.

'What's that smell?'

'I don't …'

A new look seized his face, one of panic. He appeared about to speak, but something stopped him.

Shannon knew instantly what was coming. She could do nothing.

His eyes lost focus, and he emitted a deep, prolonged groan. She stepped back, terrified, dropping the light, then went to him, grasping one of his arms. It felt like wood. His entire body stiffened, the groan trailed off, and then his legs abruptly gave way, dropping him to the sodden ground. An instant later, he began to twitch.

She looked around wildly. There was no time to tend to him. She could only hope that he survived the seizure and the long minutes on the freezing ground until she could return for him. What she did in the next few minutes could determine who lived and who died. She would not want Wolfe to stay for her either.

Still, it was the hardest decision she had ever had to make.

Picking up the flashlight, she plunged through the sleet – was it her imagination, or was the stuff changing to snow? – and over the uneven ground. Each plan they had devised, she thought, had wound up broken into pieces. Now, with Wolfe out of action, there was no question of her hunting two killers on her own. All she could do was return to Diana and Linc and try to help defend against the coming threat.

After stumbling and falling too many times, she was sore, out of breath, and on the verge of losing what self-control she had left. But she had reached the towering structure. Pocketing the flashlight, she shifted the .38 to her left hand, grasped the railing with her right and began to pull herself up just as the walkie-talkie in her pocket emitted several bursts of static.

She pulled it out. The static was loud and irregular, but she heard no voice. It tore at her, because she knew that somehow Wolfe, in his involuntary movements, was triggering it. *Soon*, she told him silently. *I'll be back for you soon.* She turned the volume switch off, replaced the device in her pocket, and took hold of the ladder again.

'Damn, you're makin' a lot of noise.'

She turned, and there he was, just a few feet away, thin shoulders hunched against the cold. TeeJay had vanished, to be replaced by Del Mobius. Next to him stood Dixie Latta, the woman once known as Lonnie. Both were hooded and wild-eyed and holding pistols, and she just had time for the fear to register when Mobius stepped in close, swung his hand holding the gun, and smashed her in the face.

Sixty

Shannon both felt and heard bone buckle in her nose as fire swept through her eyes and into her brain.

She yelled, falling back against the ladder, then dropped to her knees. The pain was so extreme, it blinded her and stole her breath. She felt a hand take the pistol from her. She dropped the light and cradled her head with both hands. They came away bloodied.

Slowly her eyes began to focus in time to see Mobius pocket her gun. He waited, observing her as if she were a laboratory animal, then said, 'Surprised to see me?'

'No.' The word came out coated in blood. She realized her lips and chin were sticky with it and that she could not breathe through her nose. 'I heard all about what a lying shithead you are.'

'That's good. Well, you can take us to Mama now.'

'Fuck you.'

Dixie advanced on her, grabbed her by a bunch of material at her throat, and yanked her to her feet. Shannon saw the woman draw back her arm, the one with the gun, and was able to duck most of the blow. Still, it struck the side of her head hard enough to send her back to her knees.

'You do like he says,' Dixie said, clearly enjoying the moment. 'Didn't I tell you I'd see you again, girly-girl?'

She pulled her upright again and leaned forward, pinning Shannon against the ladder, preparing for another blow. Shannon tried to raise her arm, but the pain was making her dizzy.

'She'll just keep on hittin' you,' Mobius said with what sounded like concern. 'Might as well take us to see Mama.'

Shannon spat blood. 'All right,' she muttered.

'Good girl. Where is she?'

'Up there.' A vague gesture.

'How 'bout your hotshot brother?'

'Him too.'

'He the one making all the static?'

She nodded.

'Well, you better go first. Dixie'll be right behind you.'

'Can I shoot her? You know, after?' the woman asked in a matter-of-fact tone.

'Now you hush. You know we said we'd turn her loose. The brother too. Remember?'

Shannon knew he was talking for her benefit, that they'd kill her along with the rest. She might have only a minute to live. The dizziness grew, the snow swirled, and she thought she heard voices.

'Let's go.' Mobius's words were flat, almost lost in the wind. There was no more time. She turned to the ladder and put one foot on the lowest rung.

Then the voices returned, and she recognized them. She heard herself and Wolfe, back in the warehouse, talking about weapons as they readied their gear.

If you want anything else, I've got some choices for you.

Such as?

Well, there's this little beauty. Light, almost no recoil, fits snug in this ankle holster, you'll hardly know it's there. It's locked and loaded. To use it, just flick off this safety.

I don't know ...

Here, give me your leg. See?

'After you, girly.' Dixie gestured with the gun, ready to hit her again.

Shannon raised her foot to a higher rung. She stood with her left side toward them. They couldn't see her right hand as it hiked up her pants leg and lifted the small automatic out of its black nylon holster.

She took a ragged breath through her mouth, filling her lungs with icicles. Her head was on fire. She prayed she had enough strength for this.

'Move!'

She held out her left hand, as if pleading with them, found the safety with her thumb and flicked it, just the way he had said.

Then, her hand shaking with cold and fear, she swung the gun around toward Mobius. No time to steady her grip with the other hand, no time to take aim. When she thought she had it centered on his chest, she pulled the trigger just as he let loose a yell of rage. The small gun cracked fire and bucked lightly in her hand. He threw up both arms and went over backward.

Dixie next. Her gun arm was coming up. Even less time to aim. Shannon jerked off a shot. Too fast. Her grip had loosened, and the recoil made the barrel jump. Dixie screamed, grabbed her head, and crumpled to her knees.

Shannon stepped forward. She saw Mobius's pistol lying on the ground, shiny with slush. Dixie had lost hers too, and she was pawing at the ground with one hand, the other holding her head wound, and screaming all the while.

Dixie's gun lay nearest, so Shannon bent over to reach for it. Aware that the screaming had suddenly stopped, she turned in time to see the other woman rise to her feet, yank a big-bladed knife from her coat, and advance on Shannon with a howl.

The blade was poised to sweep toward Shannon's face when she jammed the barrel of the gun into Dixie's chest and pulled the trigger twice. The woman's face froze with the shock of the impact, and she collapsed like a puppet with severed strings.

Then back to Mobius. He lay face up, his features already partly obscured by snow. He groaned, saw Shannon's face over him, focused his eyes on her, and said, 'You're somethin'.'

She tried to spit blood at him, but it was yanked away by the wind.

'Just die,' she whispered.

And he was still.

It was over.

Shannon limped to the ladder and grabbed it with her free hand. Adrenalin drained from her body, leaving her weak and empty. Overhead, the steel structure seemed to swoop in great circles, and she knew she was in danger of passing out. One minute, two minutes passed as she clung to the ladder. Then her vision cleared a little, and she came back.

She carefully put away the small gun that had saved her life. Then, gritting her teeth, she went through Mobius's pockets until she found her .38. Even in her fuzzy-headed state, she knew it was vital not to leave this particular gun behind. Pockets weighed down with pistols, she began trudging through the gathering snow back toward Wolfe. When she found him, he was lying on his side, breathing heavily but no longer twitching. He seemed to be coming out of it. She could not carry him, and she could not afford to wait, so she left him again, this time easier in her mind.

It seemed to take forever to pull herself up the ladder to the fourth level. Finally she was there.

She made out the figure of Linc just as he slammed the rear doors of the truck. Diana, beside him, saw her and tensed, then recognized her as Shannon approached.

'What happened?' They both stepped forward and caught her. 'You're hurt.' Linc took most of her weight and lowered her to a sitting position by the side of the truck.

Shannon took the deepest breath of her life and let it out. It stung. She realized that, weakened as she was, the cold was making it hard to breathe. She found herself panting.

'It's finished,' she said between breaths. 'I found them down there. Mobius and Quentin's daughter. I had to sh-shoot them. They're dead.'

Diana leaned over her, looked her in the eyes, and put a hand on her shoulder. 'Good.' The touch felt like an accolade. 'Where's Wolfe?'

'He had a seizure, but I think he's all right. We have to g-go get him.'

'All right.' She straightened up. 'We're all going. Linc just lit the fuse.'

'What?'

'We heard shooting. We knew we couldn't wait any longer. The fuse is lit. We have less than twenty-five minutes.' She reached down for Shannon's arm, and Linc took the other. They lifted her to her feet.

'No. I told you there's a man sleeping out there—'

'He'll have to take his chances.'

'No!' Shannon pulled away from them. 'You're going to kill him.'

'You don't know that for sure.'

'I thought you were all through killing people.'

'Diana …' Linc began hesitantly. 'If there's a civilian out there, this doesn't feel right.'

'Tonight's our night to make a statement, and it's been a long time coming,' Diana said to him, her voice rising a little. 'You've been with me every step of the way on this. Are you going to quit now?'

The three of them grew silent. A wave of dizziness struck Shannon, and she sank back down to the concrete, her back against the truck, just as hell exploded around her.

She was aware of several things at once – the racketing boom of an automatic weapon, its noise magnified by the concrete floor and ceiling, the slap of bullets against the metal side of the truck, the light spray of wet fragments on her hair and face as Linc's head split open, and Diana's explosive gasp as another slug took her full in the chest.

Sixty-One

The echo of the shots died away, leaving nothing but the wind. Shannon sat huddled against the truck, covering her head, muscles clenched so hard they hurt. To her right, Linc was bent over in a kind of crouch facing the rear wheels. Slowly unfolding her arms, she leaned over and touched his side, his shoulder, then the soggy horror of his head. She drew her hand back as if burned.

To her left, Diana lay face up, breathing noisily. Shannon reached out, touched her face.

'*Oh.*' Just that, followed by another loud, labored breath.

Shannon heard something. About fifty feet away, a barely visible figure emerged from behind a concrete pillar and advanced toward them. It was a man, an oversize man, and he walked with shuffling steps. *Quentin*, she thought. As he drew near, she saw that he held a large weapon in front of him. And then, even before she could make out his face, she knew him.

He stood looking down at the three of them, two living, one dead. Pointing the weapon at Linc, he nudged him twice with his foot. To Shannon he said, 'Don't move.' Then he turned to Diana.

'Oh, Lord,' he said with a reedy chuckle, looking down at her. 'Finally.' He leaned closer. 'It's you, isn't it? You look different. But it's you.'

Diana's eyes were open, and she spoke.

'What?' he said.

'*You're … so … full of … hate. We … should have … guessed.*'

'You should have. But you were too busy looking over your shoulder for Quentin. All the time, I was still hunting you. I felt like a failure, and everyone at the Bureau knew it. Until today. Today I have you. And someday I'll have John Paul West. And then I'll really retire.'

He looked around briefly. 'Where are the others?'

Shannon was about to respond, but Diana's breathy rasp intervened. 'We … killed them.'

'You did? I'm impressed. I really thought they'd get to you, but … I was ready to step in and clean things up.'

He almost giggled, a fat man's upper-register laugh. 'I want this to go on and on, so I can enjoy it. But I have to hurry. Gunshots won't carry far in this weather, but somebody may have heard them. I'm not exactly here officially. So …'

He carefully laid his weapon on the ground, and when he laboriously arose, he was holding a handgun. 'Better for close in,' he said. 'More precise.' And to Shannon: 'I'm sorry about you.' His meaning was clear.

'Wait,' Shannon blurted out, knowing how comical the word must sound from one about to die. Her mind raced. How to keep him talking instead of killing?

'Quentin changed his mind about Diana,' she said hurriedly. 'But his daughter kept going. Why?'

'Money,' he answered, delight and self-satisfaction in his voice. 'A big chunk of my pension, actually. I worked on Quentin all the years he was in stir, preparing him to help me find Burke and West. Then, when he got out, I found he'd gone through a changeover. Full of love and remorse.' Disgust crept into his voice.

'So I went to work on the daughter and her boyfriend. She still had a lot of hate for Burke and West, which helped. And Mobius, well … Together, they were two psychos looking for a good, bloody job. They went to work for me, and we just strung Quentin along, telling him we'd take him to Diana if only he'd use his contacts to help us find her. And so he did. It cost me a lot, but you know what? Worth every penny.'

He jacked a round into the chamber of the automatic, and the noise sounded to Shannon like execution day. With the pain still throbbing in her head, she began to hallucinate, imagining she saw figures moving in the background, by the pillar.

She began to claw her way into the pocket of her jacket, knowing he would see the movement, knowing she had no time.

'You first,' he said, leveling the gun at her head. 'She can watch you—'

One of the figures took shape, then the other. She heard a shot, surprisingly muted. The big man stiffened, sucked in his breath. Another shot, and he fell forward onto Shannon. She felt buried, unable to breathe, and she sank into the dark.

Dark. And cold. When she opened her eyes, a man loomed over her, a faint light behind him, and for an instant she felt terror, knowing her nightmare had returned. Then the light shifted to the side, and she made out a bearded face, brow furrowed in worry. And she knew him too.

The face moved away. 'I think she's got a broken nose,' she heard John Paul West say to someone. 'Otherwise …'

She turned her head to the right. Linc's sad form was crouched as before. A few feet away lay the large, rounded shape of Harold Birdsong, like something washed up on a beach.

Noises to her left, where she now saw John Paul and Wolfe leaning over Diana, who continued to emit ghastly wheezing sounds with each breath. John Paul had his ear to her mouth, trying to catch the words she was trying to say.

Wolfe came to Shannon's side. He looked half asleep but determined. 'You all right?' he asked in a slurred voice.

She nodded.

'You kill those two down there?'

Another nod.

He squeezed her shoulder. 'Good girl.'

'Diana?'

A shake of the head, and he lowered his voice. 'Bullet through the lung. She's not going to make it.'

Bullet through the lung. For an instant she was back at Mora's bedside, breathing in the hospital odors and seeing the pain twist her face. *Please,* she thought. *Not again.*

She saw John Paul straighten up from Diana's side and look helplessly toward them. 'I can't make it out,' he said. 'Something about a sleeping man—'

'Oh, my God!' Shannon scrambled to her feet. 'They lit the fuse. The bomb's ready to …'

John Paul went quickly to the rear of the truck and flung open the double doors, lighting up the interior. Inside, the steel drums reflected the overhead light and two other points of light high up in opposite corners of the cargo area that winked and sputtered like children's sparklers.

John Paul scrambled atop the drums of explosives. They all saw that Linc had duct-taped the two fuses to run the length of the space, then converge on the two drums, which had what Shannon now knew must be plastic explosive attached to their outsides. Linc had added one last touch. Protruding from each slab of explosive was a brass rod to which the fuse was attached.

The two fuses, burning steadily and at the same pace, had advanced to within two feet of the drums.

Moving as delicately as he could, John Paul pulled first one, then the other detonator from its brick of explosive.

'Knife!' he yelled.

Shannon ducked around the side of the truck to Linc's body. Breathing an apology, she moved his right leg enough to allow her to withdraw his combat knife from its sheath.

'Here.'

Holding one of the fuses by its unburned length and ducking his head to avoid sparks, he sawed through it just short of the brass-clad detonator. His knife slipped once, and he cursed. The fuse parted, and he repeated the action on the second one, breathing so loudly they could hear him outside.

Then it was done. He gently laid the two detonators atop one of the drums, exhaled loudly, and tossed the remaining few inches of burning fuses to the concrete outside, where they sputtered out like snakes with nothing to bite.

Shannon knelt by Diana and put a hand on her forehead. Her breathing was worse now, ragged and frightening.

'Anything I can do?'

A small head shake. 'You've … done … enough. More than—' A soft, bloody cough stopped her.

She made a sound, and Shannon leaned in close, waiting. It came again, and it sounded like the word *Sorry*, but she couldn't be sure.

Then another sound, this one clearer. 'Cold.'

'Yes.' Shannon lay down beside her and wrapped her arms around her. It was awkward, but she tried her best. She lay that way for a while, eyes closed, her breath warming Diana's cheek.

Distant voices, coming closer. John Paul stooped down, placed a hand on Diana's throat and kept it there for long seconds. Then he said, 'Shannon.'

'She's cold.'

'I know. She's gone. We have to leave.'

Dazed, they stepped onto the street. Shannon looked back at the high grid of steel and felt like a traveler who had just returned from another dimension. But instead of coming back to reality, she stood in the midst of an eerily quiet downtown, muffled by winter, a place with an unreality of its own.

The air had less bite to it, she noticed, and the snow had reverted to rain. She hoped it would wash away every trace of them, but she knew the dead would remain. And, of course, the bomb.

The three of them talked briefly about where to go, then made their decision. 'I think I'll leave my car right here on the street and let the rental company try to grapple with it,' John Paul said. 'Mind if I hitch a ride with you?'

'You rented a car to go to the truck bombing?' Shannon asked. She felt so lightheaded, the idea struck her as hilarious.

'No. I believe a Mr Gabriel Pettigrew rented the car. I have no idea what happened to him.'

As they made their way south out of Seattle on the familiar freeway in the rain, Wolfe, still coming down from his seizure, slept in the back. John Paul drove, and he and Shannon rode in silence for a while.

Then he said, 'I don't understand what she meant about the sleeping man.'

She explained.

'Ah.' He nodded several times, eyes on the road. 'Then it makes sense now. What she said was, "Let's not disturb his sleep."'

Sixty-Two

The world outside was deep green and the color of rose. Shannon sat beside Wolfe on an overstuffed and sagging sofa, John Paul not far away in a soft, enveloping easy chair of the same faded design. In the fireplace, a wood fire held its own against the damp chill outside. A row of three picture windows looked out on an old-growth evergreen forest and the beginnings of a spectacular Northern California sunset.

Once again, she was a mess. Her eyes, their undersides bruised black and purple, resembled those of a raccoon. Over her broken and reset nose she wore a plastic splint held in place by surgical tape. Stitches had been taken in the bridge of the nose to repair the gash left by the gun butt. Her nostrils were packed with gauze, and she breathed audibly through her mouth. Her throat was dry. Her head hurt.

They had come to Wolfe's house, located on a forested hillside at the end of a dirt road miles from the nearest town, around noon that day after eight hours traveling and two hours spent in a local medical clinic for Shannon's treatment. All three had promptly fallen into beds and slept for a few hours, then awakened and spent the rest of the afternoon somewhat adrift. Shannon had wandered into a bathroom, where she stood and gaped at the face in the mirror. 'A disaster area,' she said to her reflection and wondered how long before she would have her old face back. It wasn't perfect, but she had grown to like it. A few others had, too.

As she stood there, Wolfe came in. 'Sorry,' he muttered. 'Door was open.' He fumbled through the medicine cabinet, shook a pill out of a bottle, and swallowed it.

'Is that … ?'

'Yep. Back on the old meds. My usual dull self again.'

She felt a rush of relief. One less thing to worry about.

Now, after a dinner of steaks thawed from his freezer and grilled by Wolfe, they sat with glasses of wine in front of them, talking in soft tones. In the background, Mozart's majestic *Requiem*.

Beginning with the drive down and continuing during the day, Shannon had learned fragments of things: John Paul, after talking to Katherine in Chicago and Shannon at her secret location, began putting together what he knew. A big operation was being planned, a night crawl, and it was coming on the anniversary of Adam Miller's death. From the Internet he learned that the logging site in Washington state where Adam had died was owned by a subsidiary of the Swann Group – and that the giant corporation's headquarters were rising in Seattle. It was not conclusive, but it was enough to bring him out of hiding and put him on a plane.

He arrived at the construction site too late that night to see anyone arrive. But he heard Wolfe's inadvertent distress call on the walkie-talkie, because he was carrying one himself.

Here Shannon interrupted. 'And you knew where to listen?'

'Not for sure. But we'd done a lot of training when he was younger, and we always used—'

'Channel Eight,' Wolfe finished. 'Force of habit. Lucky for me we both remembered.'

John Paul searched the site until he found Wolfe in the snow and helped revive him. They found the bodies of Mobius and his girlfriend and made their way carefully up the interior ramps, arriving on the fourth level just in time to hear a burst of automatic weapon fire and see that someone – they knew not who – had just brought down Diana and one of her men. John Paul, firing a weapon in anger for the first time, barely had time to save his daughter's life, but not Diana's.

There were many details in the story, but for Shannon what stood out was this: He had come because they were in danger and he cared about all of them.

Several hours into their drive they had stopped for food at a gas station convenience store. As Shannon stood waiting to pay, she glanced at the small TV screen over the clerk's station. It was tuned to CNN, the sound muted, and the image made her draw in her breath sharply. It was a cordoned-off crime scene, swarmed by police, and in the center stood the orange truck. At the bottom of the screen were the words *Notorious 1960s Fugitive, Ex-FBI Agent, 4 Others Found Slain in Failed Seattle Truck Bombing.*

She looked away. It was too soon.

Sometime before Wolfe put the steaks on the grill, she had forced herself to make a call. When Detective Orlando answered, she could tell from his tone that he had been waiting nervously to hear from her. She felt bad about the lies she would have to tell him, but she knew the truth would lead to too many other questions, all of them dangerous to herself and people she had come to love.

Speaking carefully to disguise her vocal problems, she told him her story: She had never left San Francisco because she had failed to pick up any decent leads on Quentin Latta's whereabouts. Further, she had heard about the killings in Seattle, including Harold Birdsong and the well-known fugitive Diana Burke. Not to mention Del Mobius and Dixie Latta, Quentin's sidekicks.

'Who do they think …?'

'Too early to tell. The crime scene is a major can of worms, I hear. Quentin Latta would be on anybody's list of suspects. But Birdsong is also looking dirty. The FBI wants everyone to know he wasn't acting for them. They seem to be working on a theory that his sometime partner, Tim Dodd, found out that Birdsong was going way off the reservation, with an agenda of his own, and Birdsong killed him, or had it done, in San Francisco. You were lucky you didn't show up on the scene just a few minutes earlier.'

'I keep telling myself that.'

'You sound funny. Got a cold?'

'Oh, yeah. A big one. It's these San Francisco winters.'

She went on to tell him that she was exhausted from her travels and that she was coming home before long, after stopping off to see a friend for a while.

'Well, look me up when you get back. When do you think that'll be?'

'Oh, a few weeks.' *However long it takes for my latest injuries to fade.*

She ended the call just as Wolfe was finishing his own. Katherine's health, he told her, had suddenly worsened, and she had been unable to talk to him. Her brief message was passed on by her husband: *I'm sad she's gone but glad you're alive. I love you both.*

Leaning back into the sofa cushions, sipping her wine, Shannon studied the two men. Wolfe looked as if he had just survived Napoleon's retreat from Moscow. John Paul, although less ravaged, appeared moody, and she had no doubt that he was grieving over Diana even as he was regretting the need to kill a man. By now, she knew him well enough to know that he was not the killing sort.

There was a time when she would have said the same about herself. Not any more.

She had felt many emotions when she faced Del Mobius and Dixie Latta in the wind and cold less than a day ago – fear and panic among them – but not for a second did she doubt that they needed killing.

She turned to Wolfe again. 'It's time somebody said it.'

They both looked at her.

'We failed. We couldn't—'

John Paul raised a silencing hand. 'No. It was Diana's failure, not yours. She was beyond saving. She'd simply gone too far. Back when we were in our twenties, she told me she didn't expect to make it to thirty. It'll be a cop's gun, she said, or maybe even one of our own bombs, like the one that killed three of the Weatherman troops in that townhouse.'

Wolfe spoke quietly. 'Her time was back then, when she led an army in the streets to end a war. By the time we found her, her army was down to a handful, and all she had left was her passion for fighting. I wish I had known her …' His voice trailed off.

'Back then?' Shannon said. 'Me too.'

'I'm glad you didn't,' John Paul said forcefully.

In answer to their questioning looks, he went on, 'You're both a lot like her. If you had known her then, you might have followed her all the way to the bitter end, the way Linc did. When she chose a life of violence, she knew she was on borrowed time. I'm just glad she got to spend her last days with both of you.'

He raised his head, listening. Mozart's choral voices were clashing, blending, soaring. 'She always loved that,' he said. 'But right now …

I've got enough death on my mind already. Do you mind ...?'

'No.' Wolfe jumped up. 'You name it.'

'Well ...' He grinned. 'She always liked Lead Belly too.'

'Say no more. My name's Wolfe, and I'll be your DJ tonight.' In a minute Huddie Ledbetter's distinctive baritone poured out of the speakers, singing goodnight to a hot mama named Irene and yearning for the time when the train known as the Midnight Special would shine its light on the wall of his lonely prison cell, signaling his freedom.

That song made Shannon think of John Paul and his long exile. 'When are you leaving?' she asked him.

'Early tomorrow, I think.'

'Where are you going?'

'Back to Billings, to see if I can ease into my old life without too much noise. If I'm reading the tea leaves right, the only one still out there is Quentin, and he's ...'

'No longer a threat.'

'Well, let's hope so.' He leaned forward and tapped on the wood of the coffee table.

'You know,' Wolfe said slowly, 'he may be in a position to help you now.'

'By changing his story? I wouldn't count on it. Even if he did, he doesn't sound like the most reliable witness, does he?'

He stretched his arms overhead and yawned. 'I've always been the hopeful sort. Believe it or not, I think this world of ours is slowly improving, inch by inch. But I don't hold out much hope for myself personally. No, I'll just go on.'

'You won't get away without saying goodbye?' Shannon asked.

'I promise.'

She could not stop asking questions. 'Do you think this is the last time we'll see each other?'

He waited a long time before answering. *Always on the run*, she thought despairingly. *His whole life*.

Finally he said, 'I'll bet that oddball Uncle Don – the one in New York? – just might get off his duff and find his way out to California every now and then.'

'I thought he was ... you know, *dead*.'

'Reports of his demise have been greatly exaggerated.'

Wolfe offered them more wine, which both declined. He offered them a smoke, which stirred more interest, since they knew they were somewhere near ground zero of the North American pot-growing industry.

'I'm a boomer, last time I looked,' John Paul said, 'and you're talking about my generation's drug of choice.'

Wolfe took the lid off an upright glass and wood tobacco humidor, stirred the contents with his finger, and pulled out a pinch of the fragrant contents. In a minute or two he had rolled a generous spliff and began passing it around.

'Part of my crop,' he said. 'It's called Mendocino Rush, grown right up the hill, and – what's that old line? – I think you'll be amused by its presumption.'

Shannon took the joint and sucked up a lungful.

'Easy,' he said. 'This is designer quality. If you're used to street stuff, you'll find this stronger.'

She did, almost immediately. She sank back into the cushions and watched the sunset deepen and the room darken. The joint came back, she took one more long toke, and decided to go for a walk.

'Don't go far,' Wolfe called out to her. 'The chapel looks nice at sunset.'

Taking a jacket, she went out the side door and through the yard. Just this side of the trees stood a long growing shed made of plastic sheeting stretched over a steel frame, where Wolfe nurtured his seedlings before planting them in the ground. A few hundred yards farther was the farm, which Wolfe had shown her earlier in the day, its arms laid out in a V-shape up a hillside. The area was bare, since he had harvested his plants in the fall and would not plant the seedlings until the spring.

Her breath making little steam-engine puffs ahead of her, she followed a path through dense growths of fir and other evergreens to what Wolfe called 'the chapel,' a clearing ringed by tall trees and carpeted by moss and moist earth. With an audible sigh, she sank down onto her haunches, her back against a rough-barked, westward-facing tree.

The lowering sun was framed by thick trunks and greenery. It had rained sometime before they arrived, and the clouds that remained were washed with color.

Her head was a balloon full of helium, and she realized that it no longer hurt. The home-grown marijuana also seemed to have sharpened her senses. Except smell, she reminded herself, trying and failing to dilate her damaged nostrils.

As she watched, the sky caught fire, and she began to see unexpected things. *Just one of those little stoned visions*, she told herself.

Suspended somewhere between her and the fire in the sky, a wheel began to turn slowly. It resembled the yin-yang she had on the back of her neck, and she watched it with interest. One by one, faces appeared on the slowly turning wheel until it was dotted with them. Around and around they went, like painted ponies on the carousel she had ridden once as a child on the Santa Monica Pier. Faces. Not frozen, but moving, changing expressions. Some appeared to be talking to her.

Without warning, her bruised eyes were awash in tears, stung by the salt in them. She heard gasping, racking sobs and knew they were her own.

The faces were those of the dead.

Linc, Stack and Judith. Whatever their flaws, they *had* sought a better world.

Tim Dodd, who went by the book and died doing his job.

Harold Birdsong, who wanted something so much he gave up everything to get it.

Dixie Latta, who intermingled love with hate. Del Mobius, a soulless man who had followed first her father and then money. Both had died by Shannon's hand, a burden she bore lightly at the moment but one she suspected would grow heavier with the years.

Henry. Sweet, burned-out Henry, forever a child of the '60s, who should have had a better life and a gentler death.

Diana, who gave birth to her but was more suited to be a mother to ... what? Revolution? Whatever else might be said about her, she chose her path.

And in the center of the turning wheel, the last two, side by side, smiling. The two who had taken her in, raised her, taught her, done their best for her, and perhaps deserved a better daughter. This quest of hers had brought her here, where she could at last acknowledge her parents. Was it too late to thank them? she wondered. In this magical place at sundown, her mind elevated to another level, she could try.

So she whispered the words *thank you* to her mother and father.

A footstep on the soft ground. 'Hey.'

Wolfe bent down, touched her shoulder. 'Are you all right?'

'Sure.' She dabbed her eyes and would have sniffled if the gauze had allowed. 'Just letting something out.'

'I know. Come on. It's almost dark.'

She got up, staggered a little, looked around in the dimming light. 'You could get lost out here this time of day. I bet some people have to leave a trail of breadcrumbs.'

'I'll show you the way back.'

And he did. Just before they reached the house, she could hear, faint but clear, the sound of children's voices praying for an untroubled sleep.